Praise for

A GOLDEN LIFE

"In this captivating novel, a young woman becomes the confidante to both the powerful and powerless of Old Hollywood—all while trying to outrun her own painful past. Ginny Kubitz Moyer beautifully renders an entire cast of complex and tender characters who remind us just how precarious and precious life can be. You'll love it."
—KATHERINE A. SHERBROOKE,
author of *The Hidden Life of Aster Kelly*

"Once I started Ginny Kubitz Moyer's *A Golden Life*, I couldn't put it down. A story about confronting the past and owning one's story, this novel is filled with enchanting period details, memorable characters, and an ending you won't see coming. Five gold stars for this truly entertaining read!"
—SUSIE ORMAN SCHNALL, author of *Anna Bright Is Hiding Something* and *We Came Here to Shine*

"Step into the lavish world of 1930s Hollywood in Ginny Kubitz Moyer's *A Golden Life*. A vibrant, captivating, and entertaining read!"
—ASHLEY E. SWEENEY, author of *Eliza Waite*

"*A Golden Life* is a story of human connection that spans generations; a love story; a story of family, secrets, and facing our truths. Like me, you'll fall in love with the characters that populate the pages of this exceptional novel."
—SUSEN EDWARDS, author of *What a Trip: A Novel*

"Ginny Kubitz Moyer weaves a tapestry of fascinating characters destiny appears to have brought together. Though they lived close to a century ago—which Moyer captures in minute and believable detail—their concerns and challenges will speak to contemporary readers. A well-written, lively, and engaging read!"

—JUDE BERMAN, author of *The Die* and *The Vow*

"*A Golden Life* masterfully captures the Golden Age of Hollywood. The prose glimmers with tension and mystery, revealing the raw ambition and resilience that define a young, headstrong woman's journey through early adulthood. It's a luminous tale that lingers, like the echo of applause after the final curtain falls."

—JOANNE HOWARD, author of *Sleeping in the Sun*

"Step into the late 1930s epicenter of Hollywood's Golden Age. . . . Moyer touches on larger life issues, including women's limited choices and stereotypes and how society came to expect relationships to emulate the glittery romance Hollywood cinema created. Unputdownable!"

—FRANCINE FALK-ALLEN, author of *A Wolff in the Family* and *Not a Poster Child*

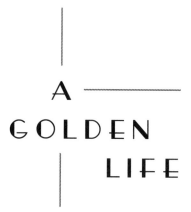

A

GOLDEN
LIFE

A
GOLDEN
LIFE

A Novel

GINNY KUBITZ MOYER

SHE WRITES PRESS

Published 2024
Printed in the United States of America
Print ISBN: 978-1-64742-722-1
E-ISBN: 978-1-64742-723-8
Library of Congress Control Number: 2024909905

For information, address:
She Writes Press
1569 Solano Ave #546
Berkeley, CA 94707

Interior design by Stacey Aaronson

She Writes Press is a division of SparkPoint Studio, LLC.

For Amy, my sister, my first and best friend
And for Dad, who dreams big dreams and cherishes small joys

PART ONE

CHAPTER ONE

1938

F rances Healey was not in the habit of buying movie magazines. *National Geographic* or *Life* magazine, yes; *Modern Screen* or *Motion Picture*, no. But that morning in March, when she saw a glossy issue of *MovieFone* at the newsagent in the train station, she didn't think twice before passing a dime across the counter. And twenty minutes later, as the train began its steady southward progress through Santa Barbara County, she took the magazine out of her pocketbook, pausing briefly to study the blonde starlet on the cover. Like a college girl settling down with a textbook, she turned deliberately to the first article, recrossed her legs into a more comfortable position, and began to read.

BELINDA VAIL: THE GOLDEN GIRL NEXT DOOR
MY INTERVIEW WITH A STAR ON THE RISE!

BY LOIS MONTGOMERY

I'm sitting in the palm-fringed atrium of an exclusive Hollywood restaurant on a late Tuesday morning. Sadly, the service is lackluster at best. It takes ten minutes for a waiter to come to my table; when he does, he is so distracted by something in the distance that he nearly clips my ear while handing me the menu.

I'm about to say something caustic when I realize what has caught his eye: a vision in a powder-blue suit and hat, just coming into the restaurant. It's Belinda Vail, here for our interview.

"I'm so sorry to be late!" she effuses. "I overslept. So many late nights filming *Mississippi Spring!*"

She's smaller than she seems on the screen, no more than five foot three. Her hair is a rich blonde, and her eyes are frankly and appealingly blue. She has the sort of beauty you don't often see here in Hollywood, fresh and artless; no sophisticated airs for Miss Vail! She orders a coffee, and it appears at the table promptly, served with a courtly flourish.

"So you've had a busy schedule," I say. *Mississippi Spring*, co-starring John Garfield, is one of the most highly anticipated pictures of the coming season.

"Oh, so busy!" she exclaims. "We're working like mad on this film. When it's all done, I want to go somewhere and sleep for a week!"

I ask where she'd like to go. Palm Springs, I expect her to say, or a dude ranch in the San Fernando Hills . . .

"I'd love to go back home to Plover, Nebraska," she says wistfully, folding her hands on the table. "If only I had the time."

I look surprised, and she smiles. "It's a far cry from Hollywood, I know. But it's different there, in a small town, where people are real and kind. Not that they aren't here," she says, with an apologetic wave in my direction. "It's just— it's the Midwest, and it made me who I am."

I nod with sudden understanding. Of course! Her two biggest roles so far—the childhood friend who blossoms before Dick Powell's eyes in *Glory Street,* and the shy English maiden who charms cavalier Errol Flynn in *Heaven for the King*—well, they have something in common.

"You've had great success as the ingenue," I say. "As the girl next door."

"Even when the girl lives in a castle," she laughs.

"Do those parts have their roots in your childhood? In small-town America, where people are real and kind?"

She pauses, her lips pursed. Deep in thought, she's a charming picture, and I am glad my husband did not accompany me to this interview (he did ask, as any red-blooded man would do!).

"You know," she says, "I believe you're right. That's what I know best, the life of a small town. I've only been in Hollywood for a few years. Perhaps the glamour hasn't quite changed me."

"What's the hardest thing you've had to do in the pictures?"

"Speak in an English accent," she says, "for *Heaven for the King*. I felt like such a dunce! It was so hard to learn."

"But you did it beautifully," I say, and she thanks me.

As we eat I mention the rumors about her and Tyrone Power. Is it true there's a little flame burning between them?

"Oh, no, not at all," she says candidly. "He's a dear friend. But he's not where my heart lies."

It's an opening that a journalist can't pass up. "Where does your heart lie?"

She looks down, fiddles with the fork. "With someone else," she says almost reluctantly. "Someone who is not in front of the cameras."

"But someone in Hollywood?"

A pause. "Yes."

Well! A mystery! And who could it be? A director, producer, screenwriter? Whoever it is, he is one lucky man.

I say so, and she shakes her head. "No, I'm the lucky one. To get to make these pictures: it's everything I ever wanted. I don't know what I did to deserve it."

A look at her wristwatch; she is apologetic. It's time for her to return to the studio, to be transformed into the southern maiden who captures a Union officer's heart. "You should see me trying to walk in those crinolines!" she laughs.

"Thank goodness fashions have changed since the Civil War."

I have one last question for her. "So if you could play any part," I ask, "any part at all, what would it be?"

She surprises me by answering immediately. "Lady Macbeth," she says, her eyes lighting up. "I've always longed to play her. Which actress wouldn't?"

As she hurries out with a smile and a final wave, I ponder her answer. I can't think of anyone less fitting to play the Scottish termagant than this Midwestern girl, the very picture of sugar and spice and all that is nice. But inspired by the immortal bard, a question rises to my mind: "Is this Hollywood's next big star I see before me?"

Most emphatically: Yes.

Frances closed the magazine, putting it on the seat beside her. She turned to look out the train window, watching the treeless hills roll past under an overcast sky.

That last question, about the role Belinda Vail would most like to play: that was when the interview really began to get interesting. Right at the very end. She took off her glasses, polished them, settled them back on her nose. In her limited experience with movie magazines, she'd found that the interviewers rarely asked the stars about anything of substance. Maybe they thought their readers only wanted breezy, predictable interviews about inconsequential things. Or maybe the stars themselves balked at any question that was too revealing, that might jeopardize the careful image they presented to the world.

That, she thought with wry recognition as she watched a hawk circling in the sky, was something she could understand.

"Excuse me," said a voice. "Could you tell me if my hat's on straight?"

Frances turned to the woman in the seat facing her. She had a round face, a cheap traveling dress of turquoise wool (how warm for today, Frances thought with sympathy), and a small hat, which, in spite of numerous hairpins, was listing to one side.

"Not quite," said Frances. "Shall I fix it?"

"Please," said the woman.

Frances leaned over and gently repinned the hat. It was several years out of fashion and smelled faintly of mothballs.

"Thank you," said the woman. "You're a peach. I was sleeping, and anytime I do that my hat slides all to heck." She surveyed Frances in a friendly way. "Did you get on at Santa Barbara?"

"I did, yes."

The woman reached into her pocketbook and took out a small paper bag. "Ginger drops. I always have them on the train." She held the bag out to Frances. "Do you want one?"

Frances didn't, but the woman was so obviously eager to repay her for the millinery favor that she smiled and took one. It had been years since she'd had a ginger drop. Its spicy bite was instantly, aggressively familiar; for a moment it took her breath away.

The woman sighed, flexing her small feet inside highly polished shoes. "I always think I'm going to like taking the train, and then I don't. I guess I'm so used to having my children around I get bored on my own."

"Where are you headed?"

"To Oxnard, to help out my sister. She's just had a baby, her first. Do you have children?"

"No."

"Married?"

"No."

The woman nodded. "You look like you aren't. I mean," she said, indicating Frances's stylish navy suit and hat, "you look like a working girl. A career girl. That's a good thing to be," she added, as if afraid she had caused offense.

Frances laughed. "I think so too. Most of the time, anyhow." The ginger drop was now small enough that she could swallow it, so she did. "So how is your sister doing? My name is Frances, by the way."

"Enid," said the woman. "Enid Sturbridge. Nice to meet you. It's her first baby, and it was a real rough birth. Her husband is—well, let's just say he's not used to being told no. In a certain room of the house, that is." She raised an eyebrow significantly. "But the doctor told her to wait three months. Her husband's being a real stinker about it, pouting and complaining. And the baby's colicky, so she's worried sick, and it's causing problems with her milk."

"Sorry," she said after a moment. "I shouldn't be so frank. I guess I'm used to being around my married friends."

"It's quite all right," said Frances. "I'm sorry she's having such a hard time."

"Me too. Anyway, when I'm there I can cook and clean and let her rest. She's a sweetheart, Gloria, a real sweetheart. She deserves a break."

"She's lucky to have you," said Frances earnestly.

Enid looked surprised, then pleased. "It's the least I can do. Sorry, I'm talking your ear off. I should let you read in peace."

"No, not at all," said Frances. "I'd always rather talk than read a magazine."

Enid reached for another ginger drop. She offered the bag to Frances, who lifted her hand in refusal. "Well, you're easy to talk to somehow." She looked at Frances speculatively, taking in the brown hair, the glasses, the subtle makeup. "Are you a teacher, or something?"

"No. I'm a secretary."

"Who for?"

"No one at the moment. I'm on my way to interview for a new job. In Hollywood."

Enid's eyes widened. "In the movies?"

"Yes." Frances's innate discretion would normally keep her from saying more, but since Enid would be bowing out of her life once the train reached Oxnard, likely never to return, she added, "I have an interview tomorrow morning. For secretary to a producer at VistaGlen Studios."

"Gosh, that's exciting." Enid indicated the magazine on the seat. "You'll see all those stars in real life."

Frances felt a little thrill shoot along her veins: the thrill of the fresh start, of the possible. "It'll be different, that's for sure."

"How do you get a job like that?"

"Well, you have to give a good interview." She pressed the nail of her index finger gently against the base of her thumb, then did the same with the other three fingers in turn, an old habit of hers. "Hopefully, I will. But it's mainly because of my last employer, in Santa Barbara. He used to be a costume designer for the studio, and he gave me a recommendation."

"You must be good at what you do."

"I've always liked things to be organized. That's important for a secretary."

"Sure," said Enid thoughtfully. "But you're also good with people. Believe it or not, I wouldn't run on like this with just anyone. There's something about you that makes me feel . . ."—she wiggled one foot, looking for the word—"well, that makes me feel safe. I'm probably not making any sense."

Frances looked at her frank and open face and felt a tightening in her chest. "Thank you, Enid," she said. "That's nice to hear."

"It's the truth." Her gaze fell on the magazine by Frances's side. "You know what you should do in Hollywood?" she said thoughtfully. "Work for the magazines. Interview the movie stars. I bet they'd tell you things they wouldn't tell anyone else. Better than that Lois what's-her-name that writes the columns."

Frances smiled and gestured toward the crown of Enid's head. "Your hat is slipping again, I'm afraid."

"Darn the thing," said Enid. She held still as Frances repinned it.

"That's what I get for trying to be fashionable. Anyhow," she said as Frances sat back down, "that's my two cents' worth. I bet you'll meet lots of interesting people at the studio."

"I hope so," said Frances. "Although I think almost everyone is interesting, if you get to know them."

"Well, you've certainly made me feel interesting," said Enid. "It's a nice change."

Time passed quickly until Oxnard. "I'm sorry, Frances," said Enid as she gathered her things. "We talked so much about me, I hardly asked about you. Mother would ask where my manners were."

"Don't apologize. I enjoyed our conversation. And I hope things go well for your sister."

She watched Enid cross the platform, then greet a lanky man with a sullen expression who kissed her cheek reluctantly. The brother-in-law, she thought with interest, watching him take Enid's suitcase. Enid turned back to the train, made a cartoonish grimace behind his back for Frances's benefit, then lifted her hand in a wave.

Frances grinned and waved back, sorry to see her go. She'd enjoyed Enid's stories of domestic life, especially the one about trying to find homes for the puppies that the family dog had inconveniently produced. ("That's what we get for letting her out of the yard when she was in heat. We must have rocks for brains.") Enid had a ready sense of humor and the ability to laugh at herself: two qualities that Frances herself possessed, and that she recognized and valued in others.

Seven years before, when Frances had been preparing to leave for college, her prospective roommate had written to ask what she liked to do. Frances had written back a list of her favorite things— dancing, eating lemon meringue pie, walking on rainy days, laughing—but hadn't known how to explain what she *really* enjoyed doing.

She'd thought of writing, "I love watching people," but that sounded like something one would do with binoculars; "studying people" wasn't right, either, for it sounded too detached and academic. In the end, she'd finally written, "I love getting to know people and learning who they really are." Even that, she decided as she sealed the envelope, didn't quite capture it.

For her interest wasn't one-sided, nor did she regard others merely as subjects for study. Innately compassionate, she might chuckle at a ridiculous character in a book, but she would never laugh at a person confiding in her. Enid hadn't been the first to say she felt safe with Frances.

Her gaze rested on the magazine cover featuring Belinda Vail's lovely face. What would she have asked the starlet, given the chance? For a moment she imagined herself with a steno pad and pencil, not taking dictation as a secretary but listening, asking questions, and understanding, truly understanding, another person. She opened her pocketbook, took out a small pad and pencil, and wrote three questions in her neat script.

What do you hope people will remember about you, fifty years from now?

Tell me something you loved to do when you were a child.

Five years ago, would you have been able to imagine your life as it is today?

She pressed her fingernails into her thumb again mechanically as she stared out the window. A memory had risen out of the past, a memory of the first steno pad she'd ever owned. She was nine, and she and her father had just seen an accident on El Camino Real, two cars colliding near the Episcopal church. No one was hurt, but a crowd gathered and a newspaper man had asked her father for what he'd seen, scribbling his answers with lightning-fast speed in a notebook. "I'd like to do that," Frances had said as they walked home. "I'd like to have a notebook and ask people questions."

He looked down at her and smiled. "You'd be good at that, kitten." And the very next day, she found a small notebook and perfectly sharpened pencil on her dresser. She picked it up, smelled the fresh paper, and tested the needle-sharp point of the pencil against the pad of her thumb. He could not have given her anything that would have delighted her more.

That was who her father had been: quiet, encouraging, and kind. Perhaps he still was.

Frances closed her eyes, resisting the pull of memory. With effort she focused on the implacable *chug-chug* of the train. It was taking her farther from home than she had been at any time in the past five years. *They have no idea where I am,* she thought; *they won't know until I write to give them my address. They won't know unless I write to give them my address.*

Opening her eyes, she watched houses and backyards flash past, laundry fluttering on clotheslines behind low fences. Yes, she would write to tell them where she was. Even with all that had happened, she would write. But she would do it later rather than sooner.

She sat up straight, closing the steno pad with the brisk efficiency that kept the past at bay. She stowed the pad and pencil in her handbag and snapped the clasp shut. Then she picked up the magazine, opened it to the next article—"Handsome, Strong, and Able: The Many Charms of Clark Gable!"—and read until the conductor announced her stop.

CHAPTER TWO

As the taxi drove through downtown Hollywood the next morning, Frances looked around with interest. At first glance she saw storefronts, offices, restaurants, and people walking down the street as they would in any other town. There were women with smart pocketbooks and elegant hats and women in less elegant hats with shopping baskets over their arms; there were men in suits scanning newspaper headlines as they walked, two burly deliverymen unloading crates by the curb, a policeman directing traffic briskly through an intersection. Then as they drove up Vine Street, she caught sight of the hat-shaped sign for the Brown Derby restaurant perched high against the sky, and it was suddenly no longer any other town, but Hollywood.

The trees she saw were mostly palms and citrus, as she'd expected, but occasionally she spied a eucalyptus or a pepper tree with its long, feathery leaves. They drove down a residential street lined with Mediterranean-style stucco houses, small and trim, with the occasional mock Tudor or older shingled Craftsman with a deep porch. The browning hills in the distance were a reminder of the region's dry climate, but the houses all had lush lawns, neat rectangles of green not only in front of the house but even in the strip between sidewalk and street. Magenta bougainvillea grew in luxurious abundance along fences and walls, and when the taxi paused at an intersection, Frances caught the sweetly irresistible smell of lemon blossoms from a nearby tree. She breathed deeply, as much to savor the fragrance as to calm her slight nervousness.

She had expected VistaGlen Studios to be far on the outskirts of town, but in fact it was just a few minutes away from Hollywood Boulevard, its white walls and ornate entrance gate seeming to rise straight out of the sidewalk. "Here we are," said the taxi driver, tilting back his cap. "Whatever you're here for, miss, I hope it goes well."

The uniformed guard at the gatehouse was similarly friendly. "Interviewing with Mr. Merrill, are you?" he said when Frances identified her errand. He verified her name on a typed list, then pointed to the two-story Colonial-style building sprawling behind a wide green lawn bordered with dark pink oleanders. "Check in with the first-floor receptionist." He smiled encouragingly. "Best of luck to you, Miss Healey."

Just before the front entrance, Frances paused to survey herself in the mirror of her compact. Her dark hair, with its natural wave, was tidy; her lipstick was neat and unsmudged; and thanks to the iron at the YWCA, her blouse was crisp and neat. She checked on the angle of her navy-blue hat and grinned, remembering Enid. It was impossible to check the seams of her stockings; she'd have to trust they were straight.

Here we go, she thought to herself, fighting a sudden wave of nervousness. She took a deep breath and remembered Cyril Flike's white hair and fine-boned face, last seen in the shade of the oak trees of Santa Barbara. "You'll be perfect for Lawrence Merrill," he had said as he got slowly into the back of the big car that was taking him to the train station. "He'll be lucky to have you."

Was he right? She was about to find out.

M r. Merrill's office was on the far end of the second floor, down a lushly carpeted hallway. In the bright anteroom, his secretary rose from her desk, holding out her hand. "Miss Healey? I'm Dina Ramos. Nice to meet you." She indicated the closed door. "Mr. Merrill is finishing a phone call. Have a seat, why don't you. He'll just be a few minutes."

"Thank you." Frances sat down on the small sofa facing the desk as Dina resumed her work. She was a petite brunette in a red dress with, Frances noticed, a round collar similar to the one she herself was wearing; that little detail felt obscurely comforting. She was opening mail with graceful efficiency as a diamond winked on her left hand.

"You've just come from Santa Barbara, haven't you?" Dina asked.

"Yes, I arrived here yesterday."

Dina smiled. "We're changing places, you and I. My fiancé is from Santa Barbara. We're getting married there in two weeks."

"Oh, congratulations. How exciting."

"It is. I'll miss working, though." She looked toward the door, which was still closed. "He's fairly particular about who he hires," she said in an undertone. "Mr. Flike's recommendation went a long way." She unfolded a paper, scanned it, placed it in a pile to her left.

"How long have you worked here, Miss Ramos?"

"Call me Dina, please. In this job, a year and a half. I was at another studio for two years before that." She froze suddenly, an envelope held in the air, tilting her head toward the office, then turned back to Frances. "He's off the phone," she said in a low voice.

Frances sat as straight as possible, beating back another quick flutter of nerves. The door to the inner office opened, revealing a man in a dark gray suit and navy tie. He gave a brief, impersonal smile.

"Miss Healey? I'm Lawrence Merrill."

She stood up and shook his outstretched hand. He held open the door. "Please, come in."

I t was a large office, with windows on both sides. He indicated a seat in front of the huge desk and then seated himself in the leather swivel chair behind it. His hair was brown, lighter than her own, with a hint of gray at the temples. He was tall, over six feet, and had a rather narrow face with brown eyes. He was younger than she had expected: late thirties, perhaps.

"It's nice to meet you," he said. "You had a good trip from Santa Barbara? No problems with the train, I hope."

"No," she said. "It was an easy trip, thank you."

Even sitting, he appeared tall. He sat like a successful man, his shoulders straight. "A man who slouches looks like a man who doesn't care," she heard Mother Florence say.

He tapped a paper on his desk. "I don't normally hire secretaries who are new to Hollywood. But you got a glowing recommendation from Cyril. And he's a difficult man to impress."

"He was very good to work for. I learned a great deal."

"You didn't want to go to Paris with him?"

"I'd have liked that, but he didn't take a secretary."

"Probably hiring one there." He picked the paper up, smiling briefly at it as if picturing Cyril's face. "I haven't seen him in years. I'll have to visit him when he's back in the States."

She waited, her hands folded in her lap. He put the paper back on the desk, opened a carved wooden box, took out a cigarette, and lit it. He looked at her as he settled back in his chair.

"So why did you decide to become a secretary, Miss Healey? Instead of"—he waved a half circle with his cigarette—"a nurse, say?"

The question surprised her, but she respected it, and him for asking it. It reached beyond the tidy outline of her professional experiences to something more essential and revealing.

"I like working with people," she said. "Working closely, that is. I like getting to know one person well instead of many people superficially." His eyes were fixed on her, his expression unreadable. "I've always been organized too. I don't care for loose ends. I make sure things are wrapped up neatly.

"Also," she added after a moment, "I tend to faint at the sight of blood."

He laughed, which made him look years younger. She smiled too, relieved that her bit of levity had been appreciated. "Well," he said, "this office has seen a lot, but we haven't had bloodshed. Yet." He tapped some ash into the ashtray. "You worked in a law office, too, before working for Cyril."

"Yes. Bennett, Ingram and Bennett, in San Luis Obispo. I was there for about three years."

He scanned a paper on his desk. "They also gave you an excellent reference. What made you leave?"

There was a pause, long enough that he glanced up at her. She said, "I was ready for something new. Something different."

She expected him to inquire further and was glad when he merely nodded. "Well," he said, "I've no doubt that Cyril provided that." He leaned back in his chair. "I'm willing to give it a go, Miss Healey. You should know that occasionally I'll need you to work evenings or weekends, sometimes with no advance notice."

"That's quite all right."

"You have a place to stay?"

"I'm at the YWCA at the moment."

"Ask Miss Ramos. She might know of a girl looking for a room-mate." He leaned forward, bringing his hands together on the desk, the right one still holding the cigarette. His tone became serious. "Another thing, and it's critical. Cyril made a point of praising your discretion. You're new to Hollywood, Miss Healey, but gossip is the lifeblood of this town. You'll be privy to some information that will need to be kept confidential. About projects in the works, or the personal lives of our actors and actresses. I need to have absolute faith in my secretary."

"I'm not one to gossip, Mr. Merrill. I never have been."

"Good." As he stubbed out the cigarette, she took the opportunity to study him. His face was more handsome in profile than it was head-on; he was no matinee idol, but there was a line to his cheek and a downward curve to his mouth that was somehow appealing. It was disconcerting to discover this. She would much rather work for an ugly man.

He looked up and she looked down, embarrassed by her thoughts. He seemed not to notice.

"Let's do a two-week trial then, Miss Healey," he said. "If it's satisfactory to both of us, we'll make it permanent. All right?"

She was elated but hid it behind a professional smile. "Yes, thank you, Mr. Merrill."

"Good." He stood up, and so did she. "Miss Ramos will show you the ropes. She'll stay on a few more days, just to get you acquainted with the office. So I'll see you here tomorrow morning, eight o'clock. Be ready for some dictation."

"I will, Mr. Merrill. Thank you."

He nodded, giving the same impersonal smile. "Goodbye, Miss Healey." He had already turned to the pile of papers on his desk, absorbed in the next task.

In the outer room, Dina glanced up from her typing as Frances closed the door behind her. She smiled. "Two-week trial starting tomorrow?"

"Yes."

"Good. With those references, I'm not surprised. Something tells me you'll fit in just fine." She typed quickly, clearly finishing her letter, then cranked the paper out of the machine. "In fact, we can go over some of the basics right now, if you'd like. Or would you rather enjoy your last day of freedom before the job begins?"

"No, I'd love to get started."

Dina grinned. "Like I said: You'll fit in just fine." The phone rang and she picked it up, her voice brisk. "Mr. Merrill's office." A pause. "Yes, Mr. Hirschberg." She sat looking at Frances for a moment as a male voice droned faintly on the end of the line, then she held the phone in place with her shoulder as she reached for a notepad, scribbled something, turned the pad around and pushed it across the desk. *Take a walk and come back in ten*, it said in shorthand.

Frances smiled and left.

S he went downstairs to the reception hall, but this time she took the doors that led into the studio. Soon she was walking across a large grassy quadrangle bisected by a cement path, beyond which were paved streets and huge buildings in all directions. The quadrangle reminded her somewhat of a school campus, even to the flagpole at its center, but there the resemblance stopped.

She took one of the streets and walked slowly, passing a small charming bungalow with a white picket fence, then a Spanish-style office building with a red tiled roof, then a huge rectangular building with *SOUNDSTAGE ELEVEN* printed above the door. And moving in every direction, like busy ants, were fascinating people: an executive in a blue suit; two young women who looked like secretaries; a gray-haired woman with a tape measure around her neck, carrying a hatbox in each hand; a man in a chef's hat and apron pushing a trolley of cakes and a silver coffee urn; and what must have been extras for a period movie, three men in Renaissance hose and doublets and large hats with feathers, walking toward her and talking about baseball. She laughed aloud at the incongruity of it, and one of them looked at her, startled, then appeared to realize the reason for her amusement. "Those Yankees are errant knaves," he said with a grin, and she smiled back, delighted with him and the vibrant new world around her.

It would be a challenge, working in the pressure-filled environment of a studio instead of Cyril's peaceful home, but she was hungry for it. She wondered if he had known even before she did that she was ready to move to a larger, more active stage. It would be like him, she thought with sudden affection, to have intuited that.

As she turned back toward the administration building, she caught sight of a young man by the soundstage. He was in shirtsleeves and suspenders and he was walking by himself, his hands in his pockets, smiling broadly off into the distance. Frances had always loved it when a person was walking alone and smiling with no visible reason to do so, and she paused on the sidewalk to watch him. He continued along, grinning to himself as if some secret delight powered him from within, as if he had just heard some news so good he could not possibly keep it inside.

Normally, she would enjoy speculating about what was making him smile, but she had an appointment to keep. So she quickened her pace, her heels clicking on the sidewalk, as she made her way briskly back to Mr. Merrill's office.

CHAPTER THREE

A

s predicted, Dina was helpful in the search for lodgings. Within twenty-four hours, she had connected Frances with Audrey Gifford, a secretary at Warner Brothers who was looking for a roommate for a two-bedroom flat. Like many buildings in Hollywood, the apartment house was a modern architect's fantasy of old Spain, with decorative iron balconies and colorful tiles on the front steps and foyer floor. Honeysuckle bloomed by the entrance, and the flat had its own telephone line. "No more talking to a fellow in the boardinghouse hall, where anyone can hear," said Audrey. "Once you've had your own line, there's no going back."

Audrey was from upstate New York and had been in Hollywood for three years. She was the secretary for Harold Dersh, a unit producer at Warner Brothers, the parallel to Frances's job. Tall and curvy, she had auburn hair and eyes so blue they were almost startling. "Back home, nearly all the girls I went to school with are married," she said, sitting on the edge of the twin bed as Frances unpacked her trunk. "Raising their second or third baby. That's fine someday. But I'm going to live while I'm young." She was a mix of small-town frankness and sophisticated cynicism, friendly and unpretentious.

"So where are you from, Frances?" she asked.

"Near San Francisco." Frances unwrapped a framed print of the Italian countryside and set it carefully on the bureau. "South of the city."

"That's a pretty picture."

"It's somewhere outside Tuscany, I think," said Frances. "It was a gift. Someday I'd love to go there in person."

"I'm just dying to go to Europe. My friend Mitzi and I used to talk about visiting her cousins in Vienna, but we never did." She grimaced. "She must be worried about them, these days. Her uncle is a rabbi, see. I hope they're okay."

"Gosh, I hope so," said Frances soberly. Since the annexation of Austria by Germany just weeks before, newspapers had been reporting stories of harassment and violence against the Viennese Jewish community. It was horrifying to read the stories, to imagine how quickly one's world could become unrecognizable and unsafe. "Has she had any news from them?"

"I haven't written to her in a while. I'll ask next time I do." Audrey walked over to a box of books. "Want me to unpack those?"

"Sure. I was going to put them on the desk."

Audrey studied the first book. "*Pride and Prejudice.* Can you believe I've never read it?"

"Oh, you can borrow it anytime. It's wonderful."

"*Walden.* We were supposed to read it in school, but I never did. *Little Women*: that's a good one."

"My favorite. I always wanted to be Jo."

"I liked Amy, at least until she married Laurie." She picked up the next book and grinned. "*Sons and Lovers.* That's NOT one we read in school. Oh, and *The Book of Common Prayer.*" She raised an eyebrow at Frances. "Promise not to preach at me if I come home late."

"Don't worry," promised Frances, shaking out a green dress and putting it on a hanger. "Preaching isn't my style."

"That's a relief. And of course, *Standard Handbook for Secretaries.*" She set it down with a flourish as Frances closed the closet door. "There. Library is now open."

"Thanks for your help."

"Sure." Audrey nodded at the bureau, where the framed print of

Tuscany sat alone. "So that's it? No family photos, or handsome young men for me to covet?"

Frances laughed. She liked Audrey's easy nature and unapologetic prying.

"No, there's no man in my life," she said. "And . . ."—she paused, threading the delicate balance between honesty and privacy—"my family isn't in my life either." She buckled the trunk. "It's a long story."

"I'm sorry."

"No, it's fine. Just don't be surprised if you don't hear me talk about them."

Audrey looked at Frances speculatively but not unkindly. It was clear that she was curious, but she would respect the boundaries her roommate had set; that made Frances want to say more. "I'm not a fugitive from the law, or anything," she explained. "Just ready for a fresh start."

"Well, Hollywood is full of girls who want to get away from something," said Audrey kindly. "A small town, a bad marriage, whatever." She adjusted the bureau scarf, pulling it clear of the drawers. "You'll fit right in."

"That's good to hear," said Frances, grateful for the support. She glanced out the open window at the soft blue of the evening sky, against which a tall palm tree stood like an exclamation point. "I just need to get through the two-week trial period."

"Oh, it's a piece of cake. Get to work five minutes early, stay late without complaining, keep your steno pad handy, don't share studio secrets. That's basically it."

"I can do that."

"And make your boss think he's brilliant, no matter how ridiculous he is." Audrey grinned. "It's not just the movie stars who act in this town, Frances. Everyone does."

―☀―

F rances settled into the studio almost as easily as she settled into her apartment. It was part of her nature to adapt readily to new surroundings, and it helped that Dina was there for the first few days to explain the intricacies of the job.

She quickly grew to love the ritual of arriving each day, unlocking the office, which was always refreshingly cool no matter how warm it was outside, opening the blinds, and watching the morning sunlight flood in through the window. It was a pleasure to use the expensive typewriter, which was so new that the smooth keys offered no resistance to her touch. There was a large mahogany desk and file cabinet and a potted plant with leaves so shiny she sometimes wondered if they were polished by the cleaning lady who came in every evening.

Mr. Merrill's office, naturally, was more impressively furnished than her own. He had a fireplace—it appeared never to have been used—and there was a large couch with an end table, as well as chairs that could be pulled closer to his desk for meetings. A closet held a small bar, well stocked with bottles (he rarely drank, though many of his visitors did). The teakettle was kept in her office, and if any visitor requested coffee, a quick ring to the commissary would produce it within minutes. There was one small framed photo far back on his desk, showing a girl about five years old sitting on a pony while Mr. Merrill held the reins. "He's a widower," said Dina when Frances asked if he was married. She paused in her filing, as if about to say more, then Mr. Merrill buzzed and the conversation was never resumed.

Frances soon learned that the administration building housed the offices of all the unit producers and other executives, including Irving Glennon, the head of the studio and the only one to outrank Mr. Merrill. It was the building where decisions were made, projects approved or axed, and budgets signed: the governing body of the studio, Dina explained. But it was only one piece of a fascinating world, and Frances was eager to see the rest. On her lunch breaks she ate quickly, then used the remaining time to wander the studio, absorbing the sights and sounds of a place unlike any she'd ever seen.

There was the commissary, where Romans in togas and Victorian ladies in crinolines ate lunch with cameramen in shirtsleeves. There were the small white bungalow dressing rooms for the studio's largest stars, charming houses with picket fences that looked like they had been accidentally dropped in among the massive soundstages. The studio had a research department, and a long, low office building for the screenwriters, as well as a gymnasium and an infirmary and even a barbershop. There was a schoolroom for the studio's child stars and stand-ins; once Frances had to run an errand there, and it had been a jolt to see the curly head of Jimmy Buttons, the young boy who played a precocious street urchin in a popular series of pictures, bent over a page of sums like any other ten-year-old in America. And it was fascinating to wander through the back lots. The turn-of-the-century New York street used in Jimmy Buttons's pictures ran for a long block, then abruptly became a quaint English village with half-timbered buildings and thatched roofs. There was a Western town, a Paris boulevard, and a colonial village, used to great effect in *Drums of Revolution*. And it all happened under the Hollywood sky, which was invariably blue and beautiful. Frances had heard that some Broadway actors scorned the movies, insisting that the only real acting happened on the stage, but even they could not deny that it took a great deal of imagination to stand under a 75-degree sky and pretend to shiver in a New England winter.

As expected, the job was far more complex than working for Cyril. As the studio's top unit producer, Mr. Merrill was involved in the creation of what seemed to be a staggering number of films, so the office was visited by a constant parade of contract stars, directors, studio publicists, and screenwriters who came in clutching bulky folders of typescript. Frances attended many of these meetings, sitting to the side in a leather-covered chair with metal studs, scribbling notes in shorthand. Other meetings happened in secret behind the closed door, meetings for which she was asked to procure coffee or, for the urbane director Neville Stevenson, black tea steeped for precisely four minutes, with two lumps of sugar. He requested it that way her second day on the job, and she noted his preference in her personal steno pad. The following week, when he came for another meeting, she had the tea ready and waiting. He accepted the cup absently and took a sip, then paused, delighted. "Exactly the way I like it," he said. He nodded to Mr. Merrill. "This girl is a prize, Lawrence."

Mr. Merrill looked directly at Frances, which was a change; when he gave dictation, he usually stared off in the middle distance or leaned back in his chair and gazed at the ceiling. But now he regarded her with a faint smile, though his comment was directed to Neville. "Don't you dare try to poach her," he said. "She's just started."

And after the meeting was over, he paused by her desk. "It's not been the full two weeks, Miss Healey, but I don't see any need to prolong the trial period. The job is officially yours."

Her heart soared; she'd been confident in the work she was doing, but nothing was certain until it was certain. "Thank you so much, Mr. Merrill." Then she added impulsively, "Was it the tea?"

He looked surprised, then his face relaxed into a smile.

"Neville's a temperamental fellow," he said, "and he's been unhappy with the casting of this picture. Everything helps. Even a cup of tea."

Audrey, who was painting her nails at the table when Frances returned home, squealed upon hearing the news. "Congratulations! I'd jump up and hug you if I could."

"Thanks. It was a nice surprise."

"Too bad we don't have any champagne," said Audrey. She moved the nail polish so Frances could sit down. "Sorry, I know this smells awful. But I've got a date tonight. He's a screenwriter at the studio."

"Someone you like?"

"Well enough to get dinner out of it." She glanced up. "Want to come? I'm sure Sid has a friend he could call. We could celebrate your good news."

"No, thanks. I'll have a quiet night in with a book."

"*The Book of Common Prayer*?"

"Sure," Frances deadpanned. "I'll pray for the success of your date."

"Don't pray too much. I don't want to get married yet." Audrey applied some polish carefully to her left index finger. "Sure I can't tempt you?"

"I'm sure. My dates will be a novel and a cup of tea." Frances surveyed the living room, with its wing chair and walnut rocker and braided rug. "If only we had a sofa," she said. "That would be cozy, wouldn't it? Maybe right under the window."

"Mmm." Audrey frowned at her nails.

"Mr. Merrill is getting a new one for his office. I wonder what's happening to the old one. If I weren't so new there, maybe I'd ask discreetly."

Audrey laughed. "I wouldn't want any producer's couch in my house, thank you very much."

"Why not?"

Audrey looked up, surprised. "Casting couch, of course. How do you think most of these new starlets get their roles?"

"Oh." Frances, not expecting that, blinked. "Oh. I see."

"Sorry. I feel like I just destroyed your innocence."

"No," said Frances. "It's—no, you didn't. That just hadn't occurred to me."

"Well, that's how the executives are. And they don't just go after actresses. I had a terrible time with Mr. Dersh the first few weeks I worked for him." Audrey regarded her fingernails critically. "He did his damnedest to back me into every corner he could find."

"What did you do?"

"I'm quicker than he is. I always managed to slip away. Finally, I said, 'You remind me so much of my grandfather, Mr. Dersh.' That put an end to it." She grinned. "I also invented a boyfriend who was a boxer. So remember that, if you ever need it."

Frances took a tangerine from the fruit bowl and began to peel it, the sharply sweet fragrance masking the smell of the nail polish. It was fascinating and, on another level, disturbing that Audrey could speak so lightly of such an unpleasant experience. Perhaps working in Hollywood caused a girl to develop a certain kind of armor. "Mr. Merrill hasn't tried anything with me," she said. "I don't think he's likely to either. That's the good part about being a plain Jane with glasses."

"Plain nothing," said Audrey. "I'd kill for your legs. And your cheekbones." She waved her hand back and forth. "No, if he's left you alone, it's because he's otherwise engaged."

"Engaged? Dina didn't mention that."

"Not that kind of engaged. Not marriage. I mean I'm pretty sure he's seeing someone." She pressed her lips together as she looked at Frances. "I'd say more, except once I start it it's going to be hard to stop. And there are certain things I can't talk about publicly yet."

"That's intriguing."

"Studio secrets. Don't tempt me."

"I won't. I don't want you to get in trouble with your boss."

"Thanks," said Audrey. "He's a randy old goat, but it's still a job I want to keep. But you'll find out about it soon." Her eyes were alight with intrigue. "And I hope I'm the one to tell you."

CHAPTER FOUR

W hen she had taken the job, Frances knew that she would be working with some of Hollywood's biggest stars. Even so, it was always a shock when the office door opened and an actor she had seen only in black and white walked into the room, in person and in color.

She concealed her awe and found that even the most glamorous stars responded well to her friendly efficiency. Occasionally, the interactions were negative; Evelyn Deane, the studio's most popular screwball comedy actress, proved to be surprisingly cold and aloof, and once Frances had to call studio security to help with Sampson Oliver, a rugged leading man with a notorious noontime drinking habit who stumbled into the hat rack and knocked over a lamp. But most of the time the stars were amiable and refreshingly real.

"So how are you finding Hollywood?" asked Loretta DeWitt, a raven-haired stunner known for her role in *The Three Musketeers*. She sat in glamorous state on the sofa, waiting for a meeting with Mr. Merrill, the spicy scent of Tabu perfume discernible even several feet away.

"It's fascinating, Miss DeWitt," said Frances. "It's like a world of its own."

"You bet it is," said Loretta. She spoke with a Texas twang, one never heard on the screen. "Nothing prepares you for this place." She pulled out a compact. "I came here when I was nineteen, and I couldn't believe I was in Hollywood. Still can't, some days." She held the compact out at eye level, moved it an inch to the left while turning her head in the opposite direction, then snapped it shut. "That makeup man is worth his weight in gold," she said with satisfaction.

"Is it strange," Frances asked, "to see yourself in a movie?"

"Oh, the first time was awful. You think you look one way, and then you see the movie and you look totally different. It's . . ."—she gestured with the hand holding the compact, looking for the right word—"bizarre. Just bizarre."

"It must be."

"Especially," said Loretta, raising a penciled eyebrow, "the first time you see yourself in a love scene. Oh Lord, I blushed and blushed. But then I got used to it. Mama never has, though. There are some films of mine she still won't see." She grinned, putting away the compact. "It's funny, you know? I learned how to kiss from the movies. In that theater in Plano, Texas. Fifteen-year-old me, never had a beau, learning what to do."

"I learned how to kiss from the movies too," said Frances. She had never consciously realized that before; it was an almost startling discovery. She had a vivid memory of Jerry Kelleher, her first high school boyfriend, leaning toward her on the darkened front porch, his face intent and eager just before she closed her eyes.

"We all did, I bet."

"Goodness," said Frances. "What on earth did people do before Hollywood?"

"Fumble around like idiots, I guess," said Loretta. "And now I'm the one doing the teaching." She laughed. "Sweet Jesus, the responsibility. I'd better do a damn good job."

Occasionally, as Frances leaned over the sofa in Mr. Merrill's office to open or close the window, she remembered the conversation about the casting couch. It was an uncomfortable thing to recall. She was not naive, but the thought that sex could be used in so coldly transactional a way, and that the practice was apparently so common in Hollywood, was disconcerting.

As the weeks passed, however, she saw no evidence that Mr. Merrill cast his films that way. Beautiful women often came to his office, but he usually kept the door open. If it had to be closed, it never stayed so for long, and the women always departed calmly, their hairstyles and makeup still intact.

In general, Frances found that he was courteous but driven. When she left the office at five o'clock, he was usually still there, on the telephone or reading a script. Some nights he asked her to stay behind, but usually his evenings were dedicated to watching the dailies, the raw, unedited film that had been shot that day. He had a personal car and a driver, a young man named Sherwin, who ferried him from home to the studio. "Mr. Merrill will stay until nine tonight," Frances would phone his housekeeper, Mrs. Daley, who always responded, "Thank you, Miss Healey. Sherwin will be there on time." Frances wondered if the chauffeur, who lived with his wife in a flat above the garage of Mr. Merrill's home, ever found it difficult to be constantly on call. But Mr. Merrill always thanked her any time she stayed late at the office, and she assumed he did the same to his driver. It was proof, she mused, that a little politeness could build a great deal of good will.

In fact, as time passed, she became aware of Mr. Merrill's impressive skill in dealing with people. The job of producer required both diplomacy and a backbone of steel, for on any given day, there was at least one person with complaints or concerns. A director who was dissatisfied with the leading lady, a leading lady feuding with her costar, a screenwriter who wanted a tragic ending as opposed to a happy one: Mr. Merrill listened quietly but noncommittally, paying respectful attention while revealing nothing. When the person in question grew agitated or angry, Mr. Merrill would nod to Frances, signaling her to pour a glass of water and offer it quietly. It was a gesture that managed to communicate two things: *I can see that you are upset*, and *I know what you need before you are aware you need it.* It was a subtle reminder that Mr. Merrill was the one in control. She almost never saw him angry. His gravitas was one of his strengths.

But one day she was taking notes on a meeting when a disagreement erupted between Sal Hirschberg, head of the finance division, and Neville Stevenson. Neville wanted more funding for some extra scenes, but Sal was unwilling to give it, citing the studio's underperformance on the last few films. The conversation grew increasingly heated, artistic vision versus financial pragmatism, and in the end the accountant stormed out of the office while Neville sat back in his chair and rolled his eyes. "Let him take a walk and blow off steam, Neville," said Mr. Merrill. "He'll be back."

"We need to go over budget if we're going to shoot those scenes. And the film doesn't work without them."

"I know. And Sal knows. Give him time to get used to the idea."

Neville reached for his tea. "These Jews," he said under his breath. "It's like getting blood out of a stone." His voice was quiet, but Mr. Merrill heard. He stood up abruptly, so abruptly that his chair slid out from underneath him and hit the wall.

"If that's what you think," he said, "then you can leave. My office. And the picture." He was gripping the edge of the desk, his jaw set. Neville looked up from his cup, his eyes wide in a rare expression of surprise.

No one moved or spoke; the moment seemed balanced on a knife point. Then Neville, apparently realizing that urbane charm would go further than defensiveness, put down his cup and made a slight bow. "My apologies," he said. "That was unbecoming of me." He nodded to Frances as if asking her pardon as well, and then they both looked at Mr. Merrill, who was still standing behind the desk.

"Perhaps I'll take a walk myself," said Neville, getting up from his chair. "Smoke a cigarette. Maybe Sal will be back by then."

Mr. Merrill gave a curt nod, and Neville left, closing the door behind him.

In the silence, Frances turned to her employer. He was staring at the door, then met her eyes.

"To say that now," he said. "Especially now, with everything in the headlines." He pulled the chair back into place and sat down.

"I'm glad you said what you did," she ventured.

He leaned back wearily. "I don't usually lose my temper, Miss Healey. Only for things I feel strongly about."

"If I may say so," she said after a moment, "I think that's a good thing to feel strongly about."

He looked at her speculatively. She read the dawning question in his eyes.

"No," she said. "I'm not Jewish. And I've never suffered like they are. But I think . . ."—she paused, looking for the right words—"I think I know a little of what it's like to be powerless. To be at the mercy of other people's . . . narrow-mindedness."

He was looking at her as if he'd never seen her before. She grew hot with shame. To think that she, who prided herself on her professional demeanor, was saying this to her employer.

"Excuse me," she said, standing up quickly. "I'll bring in your mail now, if you'd like."

"Yes," he said after a moment. "Yes, thank you, Miss Healey."

CHAPTER FIVE

A udrey came home at five thirty the following evening with a carton of Chinese food. "We're eating an early dinner," she said to Frances, "then we're going to a nightclub. I will brook no argument. It's about time we celebrated your job."

"Without dates?"

"Someone will ask us to dance, guaranteed. Especially if you wear the green dress. The clingy one."

Frances took two plates out of the cupboard. "What, the jersey dress? I'd hardly call it 'clingy.'"

"Well, it does accentuate your figure. Men have been known to like that." Audrey opened the carton and deftly extricated a noodle. "And my coral lipstick is the perfect shade for it." As she chewed, she studied Frances thoughtfully. "Do you have to wear your glasses?"

"If I want to see the man I'm dancing with, yes."

"I guess some men go for girls with glasses. And they do suit your face." She took the milk bottle from the icebox. "I predict you'll make a conquest tonight."

"I don't care about that," Frances said, and meant it. "I'll just be happy to dance again."

T he club was a lively place, vaguely Byzantine in style, with high ceilings inlaid with colorful mosaics. Audrey and Frances had barely sat down at the table when two men materialized, approaching from different directions. "Just as I predicted," said Audrey under her breath.

The men noticed each other, and each immediately accelerated his gait. One man, a dashing fellow with the look of a Latin band-leader, reached the table first. He greeted them both but swiftly took the seat next to Audrey, leaving the other fellow, a square-jawed man with blond hair, for Frances. He sat down next to her, introducing himself, gallantly hiding his disappointment. Frances wasn't in the least offended; she'd found their display of male competition rather amusing. His name was Gene—"Gene Valentine," he said, "like the holiday"—and they chatted for a few minutes before he invited her on the dance floor. She accepted eagerly, and they moved out into the swirl of couples.

She'd last danced at the El Paseo in Santa Barbara, nearly two months before. It had been far too long, she thought as she moved lightly in Gene's arms. A verse into the song, he looked at her with admiration. "You're a terrific dancer," he said with surprise.

Dancing always made her more daring and playful than usual. "If you're so surprised by that, why did you ask me to dance in the first place?"

He started to answer, then stopped. "Never mind," he said. "There's no way to answer without sounding like a heel, or an idiot. Let's just say I've learned you can't judge a book by its cover."

"That's still rather insulting, you know."

"Forgive me. I'm just a simple fellow who can't put words to-gether." He gave her a spin, and she moved neatly back into his arms as the song ended. "I'll put it this way: you look like a librarian, and I have now learned that librarians can dance like Ginger Rogers."

She laughed. "I'm a secretary, not a librarian. But since you com-pared me to Ginger Rogers, I forgive you."

He grinned boyishly. "Good." As the band stood up for a break, he offered her his arm and they went back to the table. Audrey waved from across the room, where her date was introducing her to the others in his party.

He pulled out her chair and she sat down. "So what kind of work do you do, Gene?"

"I'm a teller," he said, sinking into his chair and unbuttoning his jacket. "At a bank."

"Do you enjoy it?"

He looked at her with a glimmer of interest and respect. "I'm not sure anyone has ever asked me that. Most people don't think it matters." He raised his hand for the waiter, then turned to her. "What will you have?"

"A sidecar, please."

"Make it two," he said, then turned back to Frances. He had an appealing face, blue eyes under a thatch of crinkly blond hair. The boy next door, thought Frances, but with—she glanced at his breadth of shoulder—more musculature.

"I do enjoy my work," he said. "It's steady, and it pays the bills. It pays them well," he added, grinning as if to show that he knew bragging was unseemly.

They chatted for a while about their respective jobs as his fingers moved on the tablecloth, tracing the weave of the fabric. He had solid hands, with blond hair glinting on the knuckles in the light from the shaded lamp on the table.

"You probably deal with a lot of people, in the course of a day's work," she said.

"I sure do. It's interesting, seeing people's lives. The checks they deposit, what they withdraw. You can tell pretty quickly whether a person is happy or not."

"How?"

"By their manner, I guess. Some of the wealthiest people have long faces, as if there's nothing to look forward to. And then you can see a fellow cashing a paycheck each month, not that much money really, but he looks so happy, like he's thinking about getting a good dinner or going to the pictures with a girl. That's nice."

She liked that, and him for saying it. He took one of the glasses the waiter set down and raised it while she lifted the other. His eyes were merry. "To dancing. And to the charming lady who is teaching me to revise my first impressions."

"I'm happy to do so," she said. She took a sip, savoring the cool tartness of the cocktail on her tongue. When she put down the glass, he was looking at her appreciatively. He wasn't the sort of man she usually found attractive—a little too hearty, a little too practiced—but she felt herself glow inside, a glow that was partly the dancing but also the attention of a man who was pleasant and engaging and with whom the stakes were low, just as she liked them to be.

"See? You did make a conquest," said Audrey. Frances twitched open the blinds and watched Gene's Ford pull away from the curb. "It was good of him to give us a ride home."

"A fellow doesn't do that unless he wants to." Audrey kicked off her shoes. "He'll be calling you soon."

"Maybe." Frances sat down in the wing chair and rubbed her feet, which were pleasantly sore from the dancing. "I wouldn't mind seeing him again. What about your fellow?"

"Vincent? I like him. He asked me out for Friday, but I said I have plans."

"Do you?"

"No. But it won't hurt him to wait a few days. Absence makes the heart grow fonder, et cetera."

"You'd better be careful. It might make your heart grow fonder too."

"I'll take the risk," said Audrey. "Speaking of hearts, did Gene say his last name is Valentine?"

Frances nodded as she rubbed her right instep. "Easy to remember."

"Maybe love will be in the air."

"I hope not," said Frances reflexively. "I've just started this job. I don't need any distractions."

"Fair enough." Audrey stood up. "Want some Ovaltine?"

"Sure."

"By the way," said Audrey as she took the milk bottle out of the icebox, "I think I can tell you now. About Mr. Merrill and his secret *amour.*"

"Oh." Frances stopped massaging her feet and sat up. Her first reaction was wariness. "I hope this isn't something I shouldn't know."

"I'm actually surprised you don't know already," said Audrey. "They're really keeping it under wraps, I guess." She found the pan and poured in some milk. "His lady love is—are you ready?—Belinda Vail."

"Belinda Vail? Really?"

"Really."

"Gosh." Frances resumed rubbing her feet. The magazine she'd read on the train came to mind. *Someone in Hollywood, but behind the cameras,* Belinda had said.

"She's under contract with us, but Irving Glennon is negotiating her release for a picture at VistaGlen. And that," Audrey said, dropping her voice, "is completely confidential. I'm only telling you because you're going to find out soon anyhow. Don't mention it to anyone."

"Of course not," said Frances. She absently pressed her fingernails to the base of her thumb, one at a time, thinking. "Belinda Vail. It's hard to believe."

"Why?"

"I don't know. Maybe it's just hard to imagine her . . . in modern clothes. Going out to a nightclub with someone. Someone I actually know."

"Well," said Audrey, "it'll cost VistaGlen a pretty penny to get her for this picture, I can tell you that."

"I wonder how long they've been together."

Audrey lit the gas burner under the milk. "Who knows. It could have been going on for a while."

"I wonder what role they want her for," said Frances. "Some costume drama, probably. Another sweet ingenue."

"Maybe," said Audrey mysteriously. "And I won't say anything more."

CHAPTER SIX

F rances's curiosity was satisfied the following Monday, when a
courier from the screenplay department delivered a bound
draft. *KITTY RIDLEY*, it said on the cover. She stared at it, her
typing forgotten, then turned the first few pages gingerly, as if they
were the leaves of a rare and fragile book.

"It's finally here," said Mr. Merrill, and she started and almost
dropped the screenplay.

"Don't look so guilty," he said. "Anything you couldn't read
would be sealed and marked. You'd know not to open it."

"Kitty Ridley," she said. "The child performer from the Gold
Rush?"

"The very one. Have you read the book?"

"I certainly have." *A Golden Life: The Story of Kitty Ridley* had
been published when Frances was in high school. "I remember staying up all night to finish it."

Like thousands of readers, she'd been enthralled by the story of
Miss Ridley, one of the most colorful legends of Gold Rush history.
As a small child in the 1850s, the precocious Kitty had been launched
by her mother on a tour through the California mountains, performing
song and dance routines in the mining camps. Kitty's blonde curls
and nimble dancing feet and lark-like voice made her wildly popular
among the prospectors, many of whom tossed gold pieces to the stage
in appreciation. "The Darling of the Sierras," as she was known, later
parlayed that fame into a successful career as a stage actress in San

Francisco. Men dueled for her, and the mayor's son attempted suicide when she would not return his love. In the 1870s, her national tour led to stampedes for tickets, and her Juliet was said to be one of the most iconic American theater performances of all time. Perennially youthful, she'd played the role into her forties, when a fire in a theater where she was performing had led to her dramatic rescue by a French aristocrat, who was one of her many admirers. The fire had been a turning point for her, author Myrtle Dobson explained, and in 1895 she had married him and moved to his chateau in Provence.

There was even a grainy, flickering film clip of Kitty Ridley, less than thirty seconds long, made the year of her marriage. She was strolling through the Luxembourg Gardens in Paris in a stylish dress and dramatic hat, and as she passed the statue of Marie de Medicis, she paused and gave it a look before resuming her walk toward the camera. "From one queen to another," said the confident tilt of her head. But just as notable was the reaction of the men in the background, men who were smoking or reading the newspaper, for every one of them visibly turned to watch her, as if compelled by the sheer force of her beauty and vitality. After the publication of *A Golden Life*, the clip had been found and shown in newsreels across America, leading countless high school girls, Frances among them, to try to imitate the "Kitty Ridley strut."

After her marriage, however, Kitty had disappeared from the public eye. Her husband had gone missing three years later on an expedition to Egypt, presumably killed by brigands, and she was believed to have died with him (though there were those who maintained that she had been captured and sold into a harem where she had lived on for decades, aging but still beautiful). *A Golden Life* read like a novel, so much so that at times Frances had wondered what Myrtle Dobson's sources were. But it was impossible not to be captivated by the story, or by the cover photo of the stunning twenty-two-year-old Kitty with her abundant blonde hair and vivid black eyes.

"She had quite a life," said Mr. Merrill. "Practically made for the screen."

"It has romance and action and dancing," said Frances. "Something to please everyone."

He grinned. "Now you're thinking like an executive."

"And a wonderful female role. Who will play Kitty?"

The moment the question was out of her mouth, she knew what the answer would be.

"We're arranging with Warner Brothers to borrow Belinda Vail," he said. "It's not yet public, but it soon will be. So don't be surprised when she shows up in the office."

"Of course." She tried not to reveal that she already knew. "Should I keep that to myself?"

"For now, yes. Irving will go public with it soon. In fact . . . Miss Vail and I have been seeing a fair amount of each other. Unrelated to this movie."

She wondered at his need to justify it to her but smiled neutrally. "I understand, Mr. Merrill."

"Let's see this script." He held out a hand, and she gave it to him. He stood for a moment, looking down at it, his face intent.

"I hope it will be a success," said Frances.

"I hope so too," he said. "We're putting a hell of a lot into this picture." His word choice, and the urgency in his voice, surprised her.

Mr. Merrill gave Frances permission to read the script, so she took her lunch break in the office, eating carefully so as not to sully the pages. It was a radical departure from Miss Vail's usual roles. The Kitty Ridley of the film, like the Kitty Ridley of the book, was no blushing ingenue. She may have looked angelic, but she could shoot a pistol, wore bloomers out in the streets of San Francisco, and loved nothing more than riding her black horse Diablo on the beach near the Cliff House, so fast that even her most ardent suitors could hardly keep up. She had enjoyed the company of multiple lovers—the screenplay certainly emphasized this fact—but she had boldly eschewed marriage, at least until the dashing Frenchman carried her away from the burning theater and her values were forever altered.

The book had been adapted by Grayson Greene, one of the studio screenwriters, a large, untidy man of forty who always seemed to have slept in his suit. He had the nicotine-stained fingers and cynical one-liners of the once-successful novelist who had been wooed by Hollywood and, out of financial necessity, had answered the call. Frances liked his unabashed slovenliness and dry wit. "What did you think of the script?" he asked as he waited for Mr. Merrill.

"It's very engaging. I haven't read many scripts, though."

"Doesn't matter. I trust your judgment. You look intelligent."

"It's the glasses."

"No, it's not. Any fool can wear glasses." He filled his cheeks with air, then let it out slowly, making her think of a drawing of the wind in the corner of an old map. "Favorite scene?"

Frances thought. "Probably the one where Diablo throws her into the ocean and she breaks her wrist, and all she does is laugh. I remember that from the book. It's so effective, the way you wrote it."

"Good to hear. Any scenes you didn't like?"

Frances hesitated, but Grayson, with his rough candor, was a man who would want the truth. "The final scene," she said slowly. "When the count rescues her and carries her out into the street."

Grayson nodded. "Where she says, 'You've saved my life. Now I'm giving it to you. I'll be yours forever.' And they kiss, with the glow of the burning theater behind them."

"I'm not sure it would really happen like that." Frances paused, but Grayson was looking at her steadily, waiting for her to elaborate. "This is a woman who guarded her independence for decades. Even in a big moment like that, I'm not sure she'd . . . say it quite that way."

"You're absolutely right," said Grayson. "That scene is pure unmitigated bullshit. And I knew it was bullshit when I wrote it." He leaned toward her, lowering his voice as if sharing a secret. "But you see, Miss Healey: people *want* bullshit. They want the happy ending. And that means a woman choosing life with a man over life on her own. You see?"

"I think so."

"Because," he said as he straightened, his voice heavy with sarcasm, "we all know that's the only way for a woman to be happy."

The apartment phone rang that evening. "Ginger Rogers? It's Gene Valentine."

Frances felt a surprising rush of pleasure. "And how are you?"

"Just fine. Glad to hear your voice."

He invited her out dancing the following evening, and she accepted, thinking afterward that Audrey would surely have invented an excuse to put him off for a week. But dissembling was not in her nature, and she was eager to dance again.

They went to the Trocadero this time, a famous watering hole for the stars. In the crowd Frances saw Cary Grant, Joan Bennett, and Loretta DeWitt, who recognized her across the room and waved. "Look at you," said Gene. "Friend to the stars. I'm flattered you're here with a regular guy like me."

"You should be," said Frances. "If Cary Grant asks me to dance, you're on your own."

He laughed, and she did too. There was something undemanding about Gene. Their interactions were easy, playful, making her feel as if she were in high school once again.

His arms were tighter as they danced this time. When he dropped her off at her apartment, he did not kiss her goodnight, though there had been a brief moment where she had thought he might. She could not quite decide, as she stood under the archway of the foyer and waved goodbye, how she would feel if he had.

F rances had grown accustomed to seeing movie stars in real life, but the first time Belinda Vail walked into the office, Frances was momentarily speechless. The actress was even more beautiful in person than on the screen. Black-and-white film did not capture the gold of her hair, the deep blue of her eyes, or the rose-tinged flawlessness of her complexion. This was an actress, Frances thought, whose career would absolutely flourish in the new Technicolor. She wore a stylish short-sleeved suit with pink and green stripes and a large pink hat, both of which set off her girlish beauty to great effect.

Belinda paused by the desk and smiled, the same artless smile Frances had seen dozens of times on the screen. "You're his secretary? How nice to meet you. Is Lawrence in?"

"Yes, Miss Vail." Frances stood up. "I'll announce you."

"No, don't trouble yourself." Belinda moved to the door and opened it, which revealed Mr. Merrill sitting at his desk on the telephone. At the movement of the door, he looked up swiftly. "Oh, he's on a call." She turned back to Frances, still standing in the open doorway, her back visible to the inner office.

"If you would like to have a seat," said Frances delicately, "I don't think he'll be long." Mr. Merrill, she knew, disliked having the door open while he was on the telephone.

"No, thank you. I've been sitting all day. Sometimes you just need to stand." She gave a pretty, apologetic smile. "Are you new to Hollywood?"

"Yes. I recently moved here from Santa Barbara."

"That's such a nice town." Belinda held out her right hand, examined her nails, and looked satisfied with what she saw. Then she turned her head over her shoulder to look back into the office. It was a consciously graceful turn, the sort an actress would make when the cameras were on her. When she turned back she was smiling, and Frances could see the look she'd just given Mr. Merrill, one of intimacy and shared secrets.

"Can I get you something to drink?" Frances asked. "Some coffee, or tea?"

"Thank you, no."

Frances went back to filing invoices. She could hear Mr. Merrill's voice, sounding impatient, and then a pause; then there was another impatient murmur, as if he were trying to end the phone call.

"I'm sorry. What's your name?" Belinda suddenly asked.

"Frances. Frances Healey."

"Frances. Are my seams straight?" Belinda turned her back, and Frances moved out from behind her desk to check. They were silk stockings, far more expensive than any Frances owned.

"Yes, Miss Vail. They're perfect."

But Belinda seemed not to hear. She had rested both hands lightly on the doorframe, her back straight and her chest lifted, as if posing for a magazine. She had turned not because of her stockings, Frances realized, but to remind Mr. Merrill of the full glory of her presence, to show him her face and figure and smile, any one of which would make a man immediately wrap up his business and hurry to her side.

And sure enough, Mr. Merrill set down the phone with a definitive click and came quickly out from behind his desk. Belinda lingered a moment in the doorframe before saying, "I couldn't wait any longer, darling," and moving toward him.

Without being asked, Frances discreetly closed the door.

CHAPTER SEVEN

The next week was a busy one for the studio. *Meet Me in Moonlight*, the comedy directed by Neville, had its premiere, and two days later, *A Golden Life* was formally announced to the world. Belinda's expensive release from Warner Brothers was widely discussed in the Hollywood papers and taken as proof that her star was on the rise. Casting decisions were announced to the eager public: Theodore Grant, VistaGlen's most popular romantic lead, would play her husband the French aristocrat, and child star Bonnie Benson would play the young Kitty. The film's director was Simon Kerr, a dark-haired, slender young man with a surprisingly modest demeanor. He and Grayson were often in the office making final revisions to the script, and there were preliminary meetings with costume designers and studio composers and the publicity department. And Belinda Vail was a regular visitor, too, always coming in on a cloud of lily-of-the-valley perfume.

It was fascinating, Frances thought: Hollywood was full of beautiful women, but they were beautiful in different ways. There was the sculptural perfection of Greta Garbo, the patrician elegance of Katharine Hepburn, and the graceful warmth of Jeanette Mac-Donald, and each had ardent male fans. But there was something in Belinda's girlish blonde beauty that set her apart, that seemed to evoke a particularly strong reaction in men. "Some women make a fellow feel protective," Audrey had said once, and Belinda was a perfect example of that. Her beauty was stunning but accessible, with a tinge of vulnerability and sweetness that seemed to bring out the courtly side of every man, including Mr. Merrill.

Their relationship, no longer secret, added a new flavor to life at the office. Frances regularly ordered flowers on Mr. Merrill's behalf, to be delivered to the star's home ("Pink roses, please; she doesn't care for red ones"). The couple frequently took lunch in the canteen, Belinda holding his arm as they left the office. When Mr. Merrill and Belinda went to a premiere together, Frances ordered a corsage ("White orchids are her favorite, Miss Healey"). There was a photograph of them in the newspaper the next day: Belinda in a long satin gown with the orchids pinned to her shoulder, and Mr. Merrill in an evening suit, his face half-turned as if he were not aware of the photograph being taken. Belinda was facing the camera, her mouth curved in a radiant smile.

Judith Kerr, Simon's elegant wife, remarked on the photo when she came by the studio. "My husband didn't even tell me they were a couple," she told Frances. "Men don't notice these things, I suppose." She was holding her son, Rory, a wriggling toddler. "But I think Belinda will make a good Kitty Ridley, don't you? It's no stretch to imagine every man staring as she walks by."

"Yes, I think it's a good choice."

Shifting her son in her arms, Judith glanced toward the closed door to the office, where Simon and Belinda were meeting with Mr. Merrill. "Any idea how much longer they'll be? Simon and I were supposed to go to lunch at one."

"I'm sorry, Mrs. Kerr, I don't know."

Judith angled her head awkwardly to discourage Rory from grabbing her hat. "Well, I'll give it another five minutes. That's about how long this fellow will last." Rory let out a wail. "All right, you can get down." Freed from her arms, he toddled over to the sofa and smacked both hands on the cushions several times, looking back at his mother with a beaming smile.

"It's such a hard age," said Judith, pulling down the jacket of her suit. "His nanny has a migraine, or I'd have left him at home."

"How old is he?"

"Fourteen months. Walking now, and so proud of it." As if taking a cue from her words, Rory set off at a toddling run, straight for the open bottom drawer of the file cabinet. "Rory. No."

Frances awkwardly intercepted the boy before he could grab a file. She squatted down, holding his tiny shoulders as he wailed at being thwarted from his goal.

At knee level he smelled of talcum and warm hair. Leftover tears starred the lashes of his blue eyes. His open mouth gave a view of tiny white teeth. She could not remember the last time she had been close to a child so young.

He stopped wailing suddenly and stared back at her as if transfixed. His eyes moved as he studied the contours of her face.

"My goodness," said Judith, impressed. "He's besotted with you."

Frances let go of him and stood up. Rory tilted his head back to continue looking at her, an action that made him sit back on his seat with a thump, but he did not cry. He stared at her and babbled something.

"It must be my glasses," said Frances. "Maybe he's not used to them."

"I don't think so," said Judith. "I wear reading glasses at home."

The door to the inner office opened with a rush of conversation and laughter. "Judith!" said Simon, breaking from the group and coming over to kiss his wife. "Have you been waiting long?"

"Long enough." She smiled at Mr. Merrill. "Hello, Lawrence."

"Judith, good to see you. I'm sorry to keep you waiting. You've met Miss Vail, of course?"

"Once, I think. At the Brown Derby." Judith smoothed her dark hair unnecessarily, a movement that made her look almost self-conscious. "It's nice to see you again."

"And you, Mrs. Kerr." Belinda's smile was wide and admiring. "Your husband is a genius. But you already knew that, of course."

"Of course," said Judith. She glanced at Frances and her eyes widened slightly, in a mute, discreet commentary.

"Ready for lunch, Judith?" asked Simon. He had scooped up his son, who immediately began playing with his father's lapel.

"Yes, I'm famished."

"We'll walk out with you," said Mr. Merrill. And they left: Simon with his son, Mr. Merrill and Belinda, and then Judith, who paused for a moment to look after the star. She turned to Frances, leaning slightly across the desk.

"I'm not a jealous woman," she said in a low voice. "And Simon's never given me any reason to doubt him. But I'm very glad to know Miss Vail is taken."

With her natural interest in other people, Frances enjoyed going out on dates. She nearly always said yes when a man invited her to dinner or dancing, although she was adept at extricating herself if a man came on too strong or showed an interest in exclusivity. The ideal evening, for her, was light, pleasant, and casual.

So in the first weeks of her acquaintance with Gene, she knew she wasn't the only girl he was seeing, and she was glad; there was no danger of any romantic entanglement. But after their fourth date, a movie at Grauman's Egyptian Theatre, he stopped the car by the curb of her apartment and slipped his hand behind her neck and kissed her. She kissed him back, enjoying it. A small voice inside her urged caution but was overruled.

Several moments later, he pulled back and exhaled softly. "I've wanted to do that for a while," he said. His eyes traveled over her fondly, from the top of her head to the point of her chin. "And I want you to know I'm not going out with other girls anymore, Frances."

"Aren't you?"

"Not as of tonight. I like you so much more than I thought I would at first," he said, with the candor that she found disarming. He grinned. "See? Another woman might have slapped me for saying that."

"I haven't ruled it out," she teased him. He drew her back to him.

"This could be something, you know," he said, his mouth brushing the hair at her temple. "It really could."

Yes, it could; and it was that awareness that made her pull away, on the pretense of adjusting her coat.

"Or it might not be," he said, noting her reticence, "but it can't hurt to find out." He took her left hand, tracing the back of it lightly with his thumb. "What do you say, Frances? Should we make this exclusive?"

She pressed the nail of her right index finger against her thumb, thinking. Normally she would refuse, but she liked Gene's easygoing nature and sense of humor; she liked the playfulness between them, which would surely be a guardrail against anything becoming uncomfortably serious. And her heart, through her own choice, had been a locked room for years. Perhaps it was time to crack open a window and let in some light.

"All right," she said at last. As he moved in for another embrace, she held up her hand like a policeman and added, in a tone of half-joking warning, "As long as there is an exception for Fred Astaire."

He laughed. "Those are terms I can agree to," he said, leaning in to kiss her again.

One day at noon, Mr. Merrill came out of his office just as Frances was putting on her hat. "Miss Healey, I'm going to the canteen for lunch. I'd like you to join me, if you would."

"Of course," she said, hiding her surprise. She thought of the chicken salad sandwich she'd packed to eat. It wouldn't keep, but she could hardly say no.

As they walked across the quadrangle, she could tell there was something on his mind. He looked serious, but in a different way from the way he looked when there was a problem with a film.

The canteen had window tables reserved for executives, so they threaded their way through a knot of cameramen, cowboys, and chorus girls wearing short robes over their skimpy costumes. A waiter appeared and handed them menus; producers did not have to wait in line with everyone else.

Once the order had been taken, he picked up the salt cellar, moving it around in his fingers. Sitting across from one another at the small table, they were closer than they were in the office. He had large, well-shaped hands; they were like the ones you would see in an advertisement for a watch, she thought.

"Miss Healey," he said. "I need your help with my daughter. Sally. She's thirteen."

"Oh," said Frances in an involuntary expression of surprise. She thought of the photograph on his desk, the small child on the pony. "I didn't realize she was that old."

"She goes to school in upstate New York, has for the last year. The school hasn't worked out—they never do—so she's coming out here." He paused as a waiter put two coffee cups on the table. "She'll be here a week from tomorrow."

"That will be nice for you."

"She's not the easiest child, Miss Healey. Understatement of the year. Anyhow, she'll be here for the summer, then she'll be going up to Hillsborough. It's about fifteen miles south of San Francisco."

"I see." Under the table Frances pressed the fingers of her right hand against her thumb, one at a time.

"My sister Rosemary has found a school for her there. Catholic, a convent school. Maybe the nuns will succeed where others have failed." He took a sip, grimaced slightly, then put the coffee down. "This is weaker than usual."

"I can order you something else."

He shook his head briefly, as if not wanting to be diverted from what he'd come to say. "Sally doesn't have much to do here, and I don't want her just rattling around the house. My sister Rosemary, saint that she is, will entertain her some of the time, but I don't want to tax her generosity. That's where you come in, Miss Healey. I'm prepared to go without you in the office for a time, if it will get Sally off my hands."

His tone was neutral, but his choice of words took Frances aback; it was shocking to hear him speak so impersonally about his own child. She hid her reaction behind the accommodating smile of the secretary. "Of course, Mr. Merrill. For how long?"

"Let's start with a day, part of a day, just to break up the week. Do whatever you want. Sherwin can drive you to the beach, or downtown, shopping. Or take her to the movies."

"What do you think she would like to do?"

"I've no idea. I'll leave that to you. Spend whatever you need." He glanced up from his coffee cup. "I trust you to recognize the natural limits of that offer."

"Of course, Mr. Merrill. I'll be happy to help."

"Excellent," he said. "Thank you, Miss Healey." And he leaned back and took out a cigarette, clearly more relaxed than he had been when they entered the canteen, and she was left to wonder what would make a father regard his only child as an inconvenience, a problem to be solved.

"Well, that's a new one," said Audrey that evening as they walked to the Pantages Theatre to see a film. "Babysitting the boss's daughter."

"She's not a baby. She's thirteen."

"Even worse. It's a terrible age."

"Have you ever had to do anything like this?"

"For my boss? No." They paused at a traffic light on the corner. Up ahead the neon marquee of the theater, with its garish primary colors, dominated the evening sky. "Though I've had to do other things not in the job description. Once I had to call the mental hospital for an actress who was having a nervous breakdown. She was throwing things and scratching Mr. Dersh's face, totally out of control. Don't ask who it was. I can't tell you."

The traffic signal changed and they crossed the street. A man in a convertible whistled at them. "But honestly," said Audrey, ignoring him, "I think I'd rather deal with a mental case than with a thirteen-year-old."

CHAPTER EIGHT

Gene called to invite Frances to a Sunday afternoon at the beach. "It'll be fun," he said. "We'll do a picnic there. You pack the lunch, and I'll do the eating."

"That's a terrible deal. What do I get out of it?"

"How about I kiss you on the sand? Over and over, like Valentino?"

She laughed, her face growing warm. "I'll think about it."

On the drive there, they talked about the Kitty Ridley film, Frances being careful to share only what she was authorized to discuss. "It sounds like a good picture," said Gene. "Kind of a different role for Belinda Vail, though."

"I know. It'll be strange seeing her as something other than an innocent maiden."

"I bet she'll pull it off. She's a real stunner, just like Kitty Ridley was. I don't normally go for nineteenth-century women, but that photo on the book cover—" He whistled.

"You're trying to make me jealous, aren't you?" Frances teased him, and he laughed.

"Don't worry," he said. "I'd much rather have a flesh-and-blood brunette. Especially an intelligent one."

It was a beautiful day, mild and bright, and the beach was crowded. "Not bad," said Gene as they traipsed over the sand. "Ten degrees hotter, and it would be perfect."

"You like hot weather?"

"Absolutely. I'm a summer kind of guy. July is my favorite month."

"I don't like July," she said involuntarily.

"What? No fireworks, no parades?"

"I like the Fourth of July," she said, "just—not the rest of the month." She could feel his gaze on her, intent and curious, so she stopped and said brightly, "This is a good spot, don't you think?"

They staked their claim with a blanket, then went to the dressing rooms to change into their swimsuits. Gene's muscular body was lightly tanned, the color of toast. "I'm so white, aren't I?" said Frances, indicating the flesh exposed by her blue polka-dot suit. "You can tell I'm not from Hollywood."

"I believe they call that alabaster skin," said Gene. He smiled as if to himself, looking at her as she stood on the sand.

"What?"

"Your legs," he said. "They just go on forever, don't they?"

He saw her expression, and his own changed. "Sorry. Did I say something wrong?"

"No," she said. "I'll race you to the water." And she took off at a run and he followed, laughing, unable to catch her before she splashed into the waves.

They were in the water for twenty minutes until the arrival of three determined children with inner tubes drove them back to the sand for lunch. Frances opened the hamper and pulled out meatloaf sandwiches, left over from what Audrey had made the night before. "I've got two apples in here also," she said, "and sugar cookies."

"I'm touched that you baked for me."

"I didn't," she said. "My roommate made them. I'm terrible in the kitchen."

"Well, it's a good thing you aren't perfect. It would be far too intimidating." He leaned in for a kiss.

"You aren't hungry?"

"Sure," he said, in a low voice. "But I owe you something for the picnic, don't I?"

His lips were salty and warm. The kiss could have gone on much longer, but she pulled away, regretfully indicating the nearby blanket with a tilt of her chin. "We don't want to scandalize the children, Gene."

"Right." He reached for the closest sandwich, studied it appreciatively, and took a bite. She took another and nibbled the edge, brushing sand off her legs.

"So you don't cook much," he said. "Your mother didn't teach you?"

"She died when I was two."

"I'm sorry."

There was nothing to say in response, so she nodded. Again, he bit into his sandwich heartily. He did everything with gusto, she thought.

"Your father never remarried?"

"He did," she said slowly. "When I was twelve."

"What was she like?"

Frances thought of Mother Florence: her black marcelled hair, her aggressively plucked eyebrows, her trim suits. "Difficult," she said.

"Cinderella's stepmother kind of thing?"

"Sort of. Not quite." She reached for the hamper and began rearranging the things in it, moving the dewy soda bottles to one side and the apples to another.

She looked up to find Gene studying her. "What?"

"I gather you don't want to talk about her."

"No. I mean, not here. Not on this beautiful day."

"All right," he said. "We can do it another time."

"Do we have to?" she asked, making her tone deliberately light.

He reached for her hand, covering it with his.

"If you're going to be my girl," he said simply, "I want to know more about you. That's not surprising, is it?"

"But I don't—" she said, then stopped. She had been going to say, "But I don't want to be your girl," but that wasn't strictly true. She wanted to go out with Gene, to laugh with him and kiss him, but she felt again a little prickling of caution that the future he was envisioning was not the one she wanted.

His gaze was quizzical, on the edge of being hurt. She didn't want to say it, to ruin the sunlit day.

"Let's not dwell on the past," she said. She gestured to the blanket, the sand, the sea. "Isn't this enough? Today, right now?"

His face relaxed into a smile. He slid a hand lightly up her leg, ankle to knee, then back down again.

"Sure, it's enough for now. But," he said with a boyish grin, "I'll want to know more about you later, Miss Healey. Count on it."

Frances had no memories of her mother, who had died of pneumonia when Frances was only two. Photographs showed a slender woman with dark hair and lively eyes who had apparently loved music, dancing, and Paris, a place she'd visited twice. It was her mother who had chosen the large framed etching of Chartres Cathedral that hung in the entry hall, an image that Frances unconsciously associated with coming home.

The Healeys lived on Chapin Lane in Burlingame, California, a well-heeled suburb south of San Francisco. Frances was six when they moved into the large white Colonial with green shutters and a square portico, a house shared by Rita, the widowed live-in housekeeper who had been part of the family for as long as Frances could remember. She had gray hair that she wore in a low knot and small gold earrings and a memory full of recipes learned from her Italian mother. Even in the lean years of the Depression, the Healeys ate well; Frances's grandfather had been a shrewd investor, and the family money gave them a financial security that many lacked. Grandpa Healey had also founded a large department store in town, now run by Frances's father, which was able to stay open and relatively successful. "It's a good thing, too," Rita had said. "Think of all those people losing jobs if he closed."

It was a happy childhood. Although her father was busy with the store and Rotary, he was nearly always ready to spend an evening playing checkers or listening to their favorite radio programs. Some evenings he sat by the fireplace, wearing his favorite dark green cardigan and the slippers he put on in the evenings, nodding intently while he listened to Frances read the compositions she'd written for school. "You're a good writer," he said. "You catch little things. Much like your mother did."

There was wistfulness in his voice when he said those things, and it was not until much later that Frances realized he was missing not just her mother but female companionship in general. "It's not right for a man to be alone," eleven-year-old Frances overheard their neighbor, Mrs. Gould, say to her grown-up daughter. "And it would be a good marriage for any woman." She added, "Even with the child," which Frances found insulting; she was always polite to Mrs. Gould, but the woman had harbored a grudge against her ever since she had spotted nine-year-old Frances up in the privet tree with her notebook, looking over the fences into the neighboring yards. "I'm just taking notes, Mrs. Gould," Frances had said when the woman demanded to know what she was doing. "Like a journalist. I want to know what is going on in our city."

"You come down from there, young lady," said Mrs. Gould, her face red with indignation. "People have a right to privacy." After that Frances was careful only to scale the tree when Mrs. Gould was out.

In time, she realized with shame that the woman was right; people deserved their privacy. The tree-scaling came to an end, and curiosity about the doings in the neighborhood became curiosity about people in general: who they were, what they wanted, and what made them act as they did. At twelve she started using her notebook to describe people she knew, attempting to capture their essence in words. Mrs. Gould was a woman whose wealth left her aimless and who would gossip less, wrote Frances, if she actually had to cook her own dinner. Rita was a woman motivated by love and loyalty: to the Healeys, and to the memory of her dead husband. Frances's father was a mild-mannered man who was successful because he cared about his community, and others saw and respected that. He liked routine and liked things to be tidy, at home and at work. His pride was the flower bed back behind the detached garage, a small patch where he grew beds of primroses in winter and begonias in summer. It was always the same flowers and the same layout, but he anticipated each new season with delight. Frances would offer to help, but he always thanked her and directed her to the other parts of the yard, where roses grew and where Rita tended vegetable beds. "It's your father's thing," said Rita once. "Everyone needs a little corner that's just their own."

The Healeys were so comfortable and content that, to Frances, it was a surprise when he announced his intention of marrying again. For a man who loved routine, it seemed enormously out of character. "I'm very happy," he told her, "and I hope you'll be happy, too, having a new mother in your life."

Florence Kendrick—"Call me Mother Florence"—was a widow of forty, childless, whom her father had met through mutual friends in Redwood City. In her notebook Frances described her as a handsome woman, a phrase she had often seen in books. Mother Florence had perfectly marcelled hair, perfectly manicured eyebrows, and was fond of well-tailored suits with narrow belts. Although she was smiling and courteous at their first meeting, Frances could sense that Mother Florence would have preferred that the man she was marrying did not have a daughter.

Frances tried to like her. She went with her new stepmother to the flower show at the country club, which had her yawning; she attempted to shop with her, but Mother Florence was irritated when Frances wanted to read magazines at the newsstand. "Come along, Frances," she would say in her genteel but pointed voice. It was impossible to relax around her. It seemed that she and Frances were running parallel to each other, two different planes that never intersected.

But her father was content, and Frances could see that having a wife made certain things in his life run more smoothly than they had before. There were now dinner parties at the Healeys' home, with people from the country club or business associates of her father's, and there were Christmas cards sent for the first time in years. Sometimes she heard her father whistling in the early morning. She realized that there had been gaps in his life that he had never complained of, but which nothing but a wife could fill. And for that, she was willing to put up with Mother Florence and all of the changes she caused in their lives: lunches of Waldorf salad instead of the comforting ravioli ("Your menus are too Italian," Mother Florence had complained to Rita); the fact that Frances could no longer put her stocking feet up on the divan as she read; Mother Florence's silent but unmistakable disapproval of Frances's friend Betty Wykoff, whose mother ran a boardinghouse near the station; the fact that the etching of Chartres Cathedral in the entry hall had been taken down and replaced with a huge gilt-edged mirror. Frances hated the mirror. It meant that as soon as you came into the house you were confronted with your own reflection, with the state of your hair and your hat, instantly aware of how others saw you.

But marriage made her father happy, impossible though that seemed, so Frances learned to answer politely and to vent her frustration to Rita. "You just stay strong, lovey," Rita said one day, pinning clothes on the line at the side of the house. "You're doing a good job. Keeping her happy but still being you."

"It's so hard, though."

"Don't I know it. But it won't be forever. You'll go to college someday."

"She never yells, you know," said Frances. "When she's unhappy it's a very . . . *controlled* unhappiness."

"Not like my mother," said Rita. "The whole block knew when my mother was unhappy."

"It kind of—"

"What?"

"It makes me wonder what would make her yell. What would make her really angry?"

"You're trying to find out? That's crazy."

"I'm not. I'm just curious."

"Always curious, you," said Rita. "You need to be one of those— what are they called, those head doctors?"

"An analyst."

"An analyst, sure. You'd be a good one."

"I'd rather be a writer or a journalist." She took a nightgown out of the bin, Mother Florence's new one. She held it up to her body, and the hem trailed on the ground.

"Give that here," said Rita, taking it from her. "You'll get it dirty. Maybe that will make her yell, since you seem so set on knowing."

"Don't worry, Rita," said Frances, giving her a quick kiss on the cheek. "It was just a thought. I don't plan to make her that angry, now or ever."

And, at the time, she meant it.

CHAPTER NINE

The following Wednesday, Mr. Merrill came into the office at eight forty-five as Frances was watering the plant. She straightened, putting her hand under the spout to catch the drip. "Good morning, Mr. Merrill."

"Miss Healey." He paused by her desk, still in his hat and coat, briefcase in hand. "Sally is here. She got in last night."

"Oh. How nice."

"Miss Vail is coming over to the house for dinner tonight. She wants to meet Sally." There was a tension in his voice and manner that she'd never seen before. "I suspect it won't be the most comfortable evening, so I'm going home early, we'll eat early, and then I'll take Miss Vail dancing. I think it'll help to have a reason to leave."

"Of course. Shall I make reservations?"

"Yes, a table for two at La Conga. Let's say eight o'clock. And you'll need to reschedule my four o'clock appointment with Johnny Kemp. See if he's free tomorrow afternoon." He moved toward his office, then stopped and turned back.

"One more thing," he said. "I'd like you to take Sally out on Friday. Sherwin will pick you up at your home and bring you to my house to get her. Be ready at nine o'clock. Take her out for the morning, give her lunch, whatever. I want you back here in the office by one."

His tone was different than it usually was: more imperious, less polite. The introduction of Sally into his world had clearly unsettled him. "I will, Mr. Merrill."

"I'll give you money to spend. If you need more, I'll reimburse you." He reached for the doorknob, then paused. His eyes met hers. "And thank you, Miss Healey."

"I'm looking forward to meeting her."

He raised an eyebrow as if suspecting insincerity; then, seeing she was being honest, he gave a grim smile. "We'll see how you feel on Friday," he said.

A t exactly nine o'clock on Friday, Mr. Merrill's car drove up to the apartment. "Good morning, Miss Healey," said Sherwin, holding open the door to the back seat. He was a man of about twenty-seven or twenty-eight, with black hair and a cleft in his chin and a pleasant, neutral demeanor.

As they drove, she looked at the back of his head under his blue uniform cap. For all the times she'd arranged for him to pick up Mr. Merrill at the office, she had never actually spoken to him. It must be odd, she mused, to be a driver. You knew your employer's daily routine, you were privy to some of his most personal moments, yet there was always a distance between you. Much like being a secretary, perhaps.

"It's a beautiful morning," she said. "Of course, I've rarely seen bad weather here."

"That's true," he said. "It's a very mild climate."

"Are you from California?"

"No, Miss Healey. I'm from Minnesota. I've been here two years."

"That must have been a big change. Such different weather."

"I haven't worn my coat once since moving out here. My wife loves it. She says it's good for raising kids." They were at a stop sign, and he waved to let a pedestrian go ahead.

"How many children do you have?"

"None yet. My wife is expecting our first in September."

"Oh," she said. "How exciting."

"It is." She could hear the pride in his voice. "We're very happy about it, Janice and me."

"I'm so glad," she said, and rolled down the window to get some air.

Mr. Merrill's house was a large one on a small rise, sitting behind a sweep of immaculate green lawn and treelike camellias. It was light yellow stucco with high windows and white plaster medallions above the doors, reminding Frances of the villas she had once seen in a book about Lake Como. She was greeted by Mrs. Daley, the matronly housekeeper with whom she'd spoken many times—"How nice to meet you in person at last, Miss Healey"—and a moment later, Sally appeared in the entrance hall.

She was taller than Frances had expected, with a gangly, awkward figure. She wore a blue print dress with a white collar and a red cardigan, ankle socks, and saddle shoes. Her light-brown hair was tied in two pigtails low at the back, and she already wore her round-brimmed hat, as if she had been waiting for Frances to arrive. She looked, Frances thought, like any other unremarkable thirteen-year-old: much as she herself must have looked, in fact.

"Sally?" She extended her hand and smiled. "I'm Frances Healey. It's nice to meet you."

The girl shook her hand primly. "It's so lovely to meet you too," she said, in a crisp, perfect English accent. "I always enjoy meeting Father's acquaintances." It was like hearing royalty speak; Frances could not conceal her surprise.

At the confusion on Frances's face, Sally looked satisfied, even triumphant. *Ah*, thought Frances, *this is what Mr. Merrill meant.*

"Where would you like to go?" she asked the girl. "We can go downtown, or to the movies. We have until one o'clock."

"Downtown would be lovely," said Sally. She picked up a satchel draped over a chair near the door. "I've some money to spend. I'd quite like to see the shops here." She peeked out the window. "Ah, there's Sherwin waiting. He's such a good chap."

Frances bit back a smile. "He certainly is." She indicated the door. "Shall we?"

She was curious to see how the conversation would continue, but for the first few blocks of the drive the girl sat with her face turned to the side window, deliberately and ostentatiously silent. For all her queenly posture and posh accent, she had the pigtails and the bitten fingernails of a young child. The satchel on the seat beside her was a juvenile one, embroidered with the face of a white cat. Thirteen was such an awkward age, Frances thought with a pang. She remembered how disorienting it had been to have the body of a woman and a mind that scrambled to catch up, and she felt a wave of sympathy for the girl sitting beside her.

"I'm surprised to hear your accent," she said gently. "I didn't know you had grown up in England."

Sally turned to her quickly, suspicion in her eyes, but at the openness of Frances's face she seemed to relax. "I didn't," she said, still with the accent. "I spent a few years at my grandparents' home when I was small."

"They're English?"

"From Shropshire. They have a house that's three hundred years old. Almost a castle." She gestured to a mock Tudor they were passing. "Not fake, like these."

"I'd love to go to England sometime."

Sally studied her, her eyes narrowed. "Would you really?"

"Yes, very much."

Sally shrugged. "That's the kind of thing people say just to be polite. Even when they don't mean it." She moved her satchel to the floor. "Like when I met you just now, you said it was nice to meet me, but I know you didn't mean it. It's just one of those things people say."

Frances thought about the best way to respond and finally said, with an attempt at playful humor, "You said it was nice to meet me too."

Sally gave her a look of supreme disdain. "I know. It's one of those things people have to say. I just told you that." She turned back toward the window.

Frances glanced into the rearview mirror just as Sherwin did the same. Their eyes met for a brief moment, long enough for him to communicate a look of unmistakable sympathy.

"Tell me about England," she said to Sally. "And I really want to know."

Sally used a ragged fingernail to pick at the upholstery of the car. "It's lovely. Green, all year round. There are sheep all over the hills. And everything is old."

"What's the oldest thing you've ever seen there?"

"Probably Stonehenge. You know it?"

"I do, yes. From pictures, that is."

The car turned onto Hollywood Boulevard, which bustled with the usual morning activity. "Where shall I drop you off, Miss Healey?" asked Sherwin.

Frances turned to Sally. "Is there a store you'd like to visit?"

"The bookstore. I don't have anything to read."

"Pickwick Books, then, please," said Frances to Sherwin. As he parked the large sedan along the curb, she felt hopeful. If Sally liked to read, perhaps there was the chance to forge a connection after all.

As Sally and Frances entered the store, a woman with blonde curls was moving books from the register to a table. "Good morning," she said with a friendly smile. Nodding to Sally, she added, "The children's section is in the back."

"Thank you," said Sally, her posture queenly, "but I am not a child. We English look younger than we really are."

"Oh," said the woman, dropping a book. "I'm terribly sorry." She looked so flustered that for a moment Frances thought she might drop a curtsy.

Sally inclined her head with a benevolent gesture. "It's an easy mistake," she said. "You're not the first to make it. Please don't let it trouble you." Moving to the fiction section, she began scanning the shelves as if looking for something.

Frances smiled kindly at the woman, who had recovered her wits enough to pick up the fallen book. Perhaps Sally would be happy to linger in the store and read; it would certainly be an easy way to occupy the hours before lunch. She looked over at the girl, who had picked up a book and was reading avidly. Her neck was bent, and once again, Frances felt a stab of sympathy for her. What was it about the back of the neck that always made a person look so vulnerable? Perhaps in Sally's case it was the pigtails with the crooked part, a reminder that the girl had no mother to help her.

Frances studied the titles on display at the nearby table. Just as she picked up a novel by Edna Ferber, Sally closed the book she was holding and walked quickly to the register. The shopgirl hurried behind the counter to take the book from Sally, reading the cover aloud.

"*Sons and Lovers*, by D. H. Lawrence. I haven't read it yet."

"I hear it's excellent," said Sally in her posh voice.

Frances's first instinct was to speak up in protest. "You're very young to be reading a book like that," she wanted to say. "I don't think your father would approve." But before she could do so, Sally caught her eye, with a kind of mute appeal. *Don't blow my cover*, her eyes pleaded, and all at once Frances remembered how it felt to be thirteen years old, wanting to do what she was not allowed to do, her fate in the hands of adults who professed to know best but who in fact rarely did, so she was silent as the shopkeeper rang up the purchase.

Outside on the street, Sally put the book into her satchel. She looked sidelong at Frances, as if waiting for a delayed reprimand, but Frances merely checked her watch. "What shall we do next?"

Sally indicated the newsstand a few feet away. "I'd like to buy some chewing gum."

While Sally made her purchase, Frances studied the magazines on display. Hanging at eye level were multiple copies of *Photoplay*, with Belinda Vail on the cover. She was smiling beatifically from underneath a wide-brimmed straw hat tied with a huge bow under the chin. Her hands were together, fingers laced, and her chin was resting on them at a coquettish angle. It was the kind of pose a woman would never make in real life, for any reason, thought Frances with mild amusement.

Sally paid the cashier and put the gum in her satchel. She gestured toward the magazine display. "Have you met her?" she asked Frances.

"Who, Miss Vail? Yes, she's often at the studio."

"I met her the other night." Sally studied the magazine with a sullen expression, almost a scowl. She was no longer speaking with an accent, Frances noted. "Let's go to the pet store," she said abruptly.

"Do you have a pet?"

"No, but I like looking at the puppies."

"That's fine," said Frances, hoping that Sally would not want to buy one; it was hard to imagine Mr. Merrill being pleased with the sudden acquisition of a dog.

They walked in silence to the corner where Sherwin was waiting with the car. As he got out and came around to open the door for them, Sally asked, "Did you see Belinda Vail in *Heaven for the King*? The picture about the Cavaliers and Roundheads?" She once again sounded like British royalty.

"No, I didn't."

"You should," said Sally. She smiled with obvious satisfaction. "Her accent was atrocious."

᠅

To Frances's relief, they left the pet store without making any purchases. Sally's whole demeanor had changed in the presence of the puppies on display; she smiled and laughed and squealed with delight when one licked her chin. Next came lunch at the restaurant of a nearby hotel, where Frances ordered iced tea and an omelet and braced herself for what Sally would choose. She would not put it past the girl to request champagne, at which point she, Frances, would be forced to intervene.

But Sally, to her surprise, ordered a simple Coca-Cola and roast beef sandwich. The high spirits of the pet store had abandoned her, and she seemed flat and subdued. For a long while she was silent, barely responding to Frances's various conversational openers, staring out the window at the people passing by.

When the drinks arrived, she took a single sip, then swirled the straw slowly in one hand while resting her head in the other. On the sidewalk outside a dachshund wearing a tartan coat was being walked by a woman in a matching cape. "That's cute," she said listlessly.

"You'd like a dog someday, wouldn't you?" said Frances.

"I'd like one now. But it's not fair to the dog if I'm just leaving for school anyhow. That's what Father said." She scowled as if she disliked having to acknowledge the soundness of her father's logic.

"So you've spent time in New York and in California," said Frances. "Which one do you prefer?"

Sally shrugged. "If it's not England, it doesn't really matter." She twirled the straw again. "I guess I liked New York. Not the school, really, or the other girls. But I liked the buildings. They were pretty. I liked when the leaves changed in the fall. And I liked Mrs. Wolf."

"Who is Mrs. Wolf?"

"The housemother of our dormitory." Sally's expression softened. "She was old, with children of her own all grown up. But she was always happy to see me when I knocked on her door. She would make fudge for the girls, and she taught me to play Hearts. She was the only person I cried about leaving."

Frances couldn't think of anything to say that did not sound like a platitude, and she was glad when the waiter arrived with their plates. For all Sally's listlessness the moment before, she started in on her sandwich eagerly. They ate in silence for a few minutes before Frances spoke.

"How is the sandwich?"

Sally shrugged. "It's all right."

"I hear you're going to a new school."

"A convent. The Sisters of the Holy Blood or something gruesome."

"I hope you'll like it there."

"I'll either like it or I won't. There's no other option."

"Well," said Frances, "you might find it boring, or challenging. Or inspiring."

"But in the end, I'll like it or not like it. Like I do with anything." Sally took another bite of her sandwich.

"So what do you like?" asked Frances, seizing the chance to steer the conversation in a more positive channel. "What are some of your favorite things?"

"England," said Sally. "I like history, and Shakespeare. And Mrs. Wolf. I like Leslie Howard"—she smiled—"he's dreamy. I wanted to go to a premiere to meet him, but Father said I was too young. Errol Flynn is handsome too. And I like rain." She glanced at the sky. "Not that it ever rains here."

"What don't you like?"

Sally looked suspicious. "Why are you asking?"

"I just like to understand people."

A waiter came by to refill their water glasses. He was young and lanky, with prominent ears. Sally regarded him fixedly, and when he finished, she gave him a smile and said, "Thank you very much, my good man." She sounded like a squire at a coaching inn.

The waiter started and looked helplessly at Frances, who smiled back kindly. "We'll take the bill, too, when you have a moment," she said, and he turned aside, almost bumping into a waiter shouldering a tray.

"Maybe you can guess," said Sally.

"Sorry. Guess what?"

"What I don't like."

Frances gave a neutral, secretary's smile. "I don't think I know you well enough for that."

"Just try," said Sally, leaning forward, her shirt front almost in her plate. She had dropped the accent. "Just try, and I promise to say whether you're right or wrong."

Frances toyed with the last of her omelet, not wanting to commit to a course of action. But Sally was watching her eagerly, with no hint of sullenness; she looked like an eager child and sounded like one, so after a moment Frances set down her fork and said, "You don't like sunny days."

"I already said that."

"You don't like baseball. Or any sports."

"Cricket is okay. The others are boring."

"You don't like being told what to do."

"Nobody does."

Frances thought of Leslie Howard and Errol Flynn. "You don't like boys your own age."

Sally nodded, a new respect coming into her eyes. "That's true. Most of them are pimply and stupid."

"You don't like arithmetic."

Sally looked disappointed. "You're wrong. I actually do, if it's taught properly."

The waiter brought the check, and Frances opened her purse to take out the bills Mr. Merrill had given her. She looked at her watch. "We'd better leave, if we want to be back at the studio on time."

Sally took a leisurely sip of her drink. "I don't want to leave yet."

"Your father told me to be back at one, you see."

Sally shrugged elaborately and twirled the straw in her glass.

"Sally," Frances said gently, "your father is my employer. I need to be there on time."

The girl looked up, considering. "I'll give you one more chance to say something I don't like," she said at last. "If you are correct, we'll leave. If not, we stay until I want to go. All right?" Her eyes, fixed on Frances, were bright with triumph.

The riddle of the Sphinx, Frances thought with grim amusement, wondering how on earth she'd managed to find herself entirely at the mercy of a thirteen-year-old. But she had to admire the girl sitting opposite and stirring her Coke, a young girl who was taking control of her own life in the only ways she could. "All right," she said.

Sally smiled. "I'll give you a minute to think," she said, taking another long sip.

An idea flashed into Frances's mind, one that could not be ignored. Underneath the table she pressed each finger against her thumb, weighing the risk of saying it.

"So," said Sally, "what else don't I like?" She pushed the glass aside and folded her hands.

Two women walked by the table, talking brightly, their voices high and loud. As Frances waited for them to pass, she studied her young charge. The girl's eyes were the same color as her father's, fixed on Frances, waiting.

When the women were gone, Frances leaned forward. "You don't like Belinda Vail," she said quietly.

There was a pause in which Sally regarded her steadily, not blinking, just long enough for Frances to wonder if she'd gone too far. Then the girl stood up, picked up her satchel, and pushed her chair under the table.

"We can go now," she said.

CHAPTER TEN

"Well," said Mr. Merrill when Frances came into his office with her steno pad, "you survived your morning with my daughter."

"I did. She's a most unusual girl."

"You're very diplomatic. Did she speak with an accent?"

"Nearly the whole morning."

"It's a new thing with her. I wish she wouldn't. It just confuses people."

"I think . . ." Frances paused, striving to explain her thoughts delicately. "I think that's probably why she does it. There's not much in her life she is in charge of. No one is, at that age," she added quickly. "The accent is something she can control."

Mr. Merrill took so long to respond that she feared she had been too frank. He surprised her by saying, "You should be an analyst, Miss Healey. You're probably right."

"I like trying to understand people," she said by way of explanation. "I always have."

The phone in her office rang and she stood up, but he waved it away. "Let it ring." He gazed out the window at the sky. "If I give her control over some things—buy her a dog, say, or introduce her to Leslie Howard—will she stop with the accent?"

"I'm not sure it's quite that simple. I think it's something she'll have to decide she doesn't want to do anymore."

"Her mother was English," said Mr. Merrill. "Sally was very

young when she died. Perhaps it's her way of feeling close to her again." The train of thought seemed not to be pleasing to him; he looked almost grim, staring out the window. Then he opened the wooden box on his desk and took out a cigarette. "At least she was civil to Belinda last night." He glanced up. "Did she say whether she . . . likes Belinda?"

"She didn't say." It surprised Frances, this instinctive desire to protect Sally. And it wasn't exactly a lie, she rationalized to herself. Sally had not actually *said* how she felt about the starlet.

He nodded, disappointment flickering briefly across his face. Then he smiled wryly. "It was probably good for Belinda to meet her," he said. "She could learn a lot from Sally's accent."

The following Tuesday, just before noon, Frances was covering the typewriter when Mr. Merrill emerged from the inner office. "Miss Healey," he said, "are you free for lunch?"

"Not today, I'm afraid. I have an appointment with the optometrist."

He looked unhappy. "Sally is coming here. She wanted us to have lunch at the canteen, and I told her we could, for half an hour. I was hoping you could take her instead."

"I'm sorry, Mr. Merrill. I would if I were free."

"No, that's fine." He ran a hand over his hair. "But Belinda is on her way here, and—" He paused as the door opened and the actress herself entered, wearing a suit and hat of deep rose. "Belinda."

"Lawrence." She moved toward him, in a cloud of urgency and lily-of-the-valley perfume. "We need to talk."

"Not now, Belinda."

"You have to meet with the publicity department. That photographer, the tall one. He doesn't understand. Hasn't he read the script?"

"We'll talk later."

"He keeps shooting me as if I'm still an ingenue. That's not what this role is, Lawrence."

"I know, Belinda. We'll talk about it later today, I promise."

"But why not now?" She grasped his arms, looking up into his face entreatingly.

The door opened and Sally entered. At the sight of her father and Belinda, she stopped short. She wore the same round-brimmed hat Frances had seen before, this time with a blue skirt and a yellow blouse, a color that did little to enhance her complexion.

"You're early, Sally," said her father. He put his hands on Belinda's elbows stiffly, moving her body away from his.

"No," said Sally. "I'm right on time." As if to underscore her point, the clock in her father's office began to chime.

"Hello, Sally," said Belinda. "How nice to see you again. And what a charming bag you have."

Sally held the cat satchel closer to her body. "Hello, Miss Vail. I wasn't expecting to see you here." The accent was back, more crisp than ever.

Belinda smiled brightly. "Have you come for lunch? You can join your father and me." She turned back to Mr. Merrill. "Shall we all go to the canteen, darling?" Her fingers traced the lapel of his suit, picking up an invisible piece of lint and flicking it away.

Mr. Merrill looked from Belinda's face to his daughter's sullen one, then turned to Frances. Instinctively, she gave him a brief, sympathetic smile. He did not react, and it occurred to her that sympathy was probably something he rarely had occasion to see on the faces of his employees.

"All right," he said, turning back to Belinda. "We'll go."

"Miss Healey," said Sally. "Can you come too?"

"No," said Mr. Merrill before Frances could answer. "Miss Healey has an appointment to keep."

Frances was touched by the sudden disappointment on the girl's face. "Perhaps another time, Sally."

Sally lifted her chin. "We'd better hurry, then," she said like a princess bestowing a favor. "I don't have much time. There's only forty-five minutes before Sherwin comes back for me."

She left the room quickly, followed by Mr. Merrill and Belinda, who was holding his arm. The tension lingered in the air even as Frances put on her hat and closed the door behind her.

That evening, Frances sat down at the kitchen table and wrote a brief letter home. She mentioned that she had a job in Hollywood and included her address. It wasn't a long letter; she was due to meet Audrey and another secretary from Warner Brothers at the Brass Rail Restaurant and had no time to say much more.

As she put the letter into the envelope and addressed it, she realized that an outside observer might wonder why, after weeks in Hollywood, she had chosen to write the letter when she had less than five minutes to do so. The most benign explanation was that she was disorganized, but that, of course, was not true. She had known she would do it eventually but had been waiting for the right moment, and she was honest enough to admit that the right moment was one when she could justify writing as little as possible.

CHAPTER

ELEVEN

On a sunny Sunday morning, Audrey came into the kitchen at ten thirty, still in her pajamas, her auburn hair a bright mess. She squinted into the light coming through the window. "Ouch."

"Here." Frances took a cup from the cupboard, poured the coffee she had just brewed for herself, and handed it to her roommate. "You must have come in late. I didn't even hear you."

"Three thirty. I don't know why I bothered to go to bed."

"How was the movie?"

"Good. Jimmy Stewart's a dream. I don't know why he's so attractive, but he is. It was funny too. People were laughing and laughing."

"I'll have to go see it."

"You know who wasn't laughing, though," said Audrey significantly. "Your boss."

"What do you mean?"

Audrey took her cup of coffee over to the armchair and curled up in it like a cat. She was awake now; her eyes were bright and knowing.

"Hank took me to the Cocoanut Grove afterwards. And Mr. Merrill was there, with Miss Belinda Vail."

"I know. I ordered her corsage."

"Well, they were arguing about something. They were only a table away, so I tried to eavesdrop."

"Audrey."

"I'm shameless, I know. But it was the way she was sitting, too. Like this." She crossed her legs in the armchair and angled to the side, her body a forty-five-degree angle away from Frances. "You're him, and I'm her."

Frances sat down in the rocking chair, intrigued in spite of herself. "I wonder what that's about."

Audrey warmed her hands on the cup. "She was unhappy about something, that's for sure. The costumes for the film, from what I could tell."

"Really? The sketches are beautiful."

"She didn't think they were right for the character, I guess. I couldn't catch more without making it obvious I wasn't listening to Hank. But there's trouble in paradise, you mark my words. Totally predictable too."

"What do you mean?"

"Now that she's got the movie contract, she doesn't need to cozy up to him anymore. She got what she wanted."

Frances frowned. "If it were your boss, maybe. But Mr. Merrill is . . . well, it's hard to imagine she'd only be with him to get the role."

"True," conceded Audrey. "He's pretty handsome, as producers go." She regarded Frances with lively new interest. "Don't tell me you're harboring feelings for your boss."

"I'm too smart for that," said Frances glibly. "It's just that I didn't think this was a casting couch sort of situation. He doesn't seem like that kind of man."

"You, my friend," said Audrey, "have a much higher opinion of the male sex than I do." She took a sip. "Maybe he's tired of her and she's sensing that. It happens, even with women who look like her. Anyhow, you're a much better dancer than she is."

"Really?"

"You enjoy it a lot more, that's obvious. And you're much lighter on your feet."

"I'm just petty enough to be glad about that," said Frances.

"As you should be," said Audrey.

Belinda did not come to the office at all the next week. Curious as Frances was, there was little time to dwell on it; Mr. Merrill asked her to work later than usual on both Tuesday and Wednesday, and on Thursday she ate dinner at the commissary while he screened the dailies of the studio's latest musical. She returned to the office to take dictation, and it was nearly eight thirty before they finished. "Thank you for staying late again, Miss Healey," he said when she was done. "I just have a few things I need you to do tomorrow morning. I'm dropping by the soundstage early and won't be in until ten."

"Of course, Mr. Merrill."

"The *Bachelor's Dilemma* premiere, on Saturday. I'll need a table for twelve, after the show. At the Trocadero. Say ten thirty."

"I'll ask for the table in the back? It's the one you had last time."

"That's fine." He flipped the metal clasp of the wooden cigarette box up and down, absently, gazing out the window into the dark. Snap, silence; snap, silence. She shifted in her chair, recrossing her legs. Would he be there with Belinda?

"Shall I order a corsage for Miss Vail?" she asked delicately.

There was a pause. "No," he said. "She won't be there." She ventured a glance at his profile as he snapped the clasp up and down, but his face was inscrutable.

"Shall I arrange for Sherwin to pick you up afterwards?"

"No, it'll be a late night. I'll take a taxi." He turned to face her, still toying with the clasp. "And tomorrow after the meeting with Simon, I'll need to meet with Henrik about the score. One o'clock, if he can manage it, no later than one forty-five. Tell him to bring Fred Goates along." Snap, silence; snap, silence. "Leonard is coming at three, with Art Norris. Order some coffee in advance, please."

Frances scratched quickly on the steno pad on her knee. She was becoming accustomed to the rhythms of studio life, to the uptick in activity that happened during preproduction of a film, but this was an aggressive schedule even by those standards. It was a sign of the importance of the Miss Ridley film that he was driving himself so hard. Or—her mind wandered as she wrote briskly—perhaps the rift with Belinda meant that he was trying to distract himself with work. It's what a woman would do, she thought; perhaps men were the same.

As she made the last of the notes, she realized she was no longer hearing the snap-silence of the cigarette box. She glanced up from her pad.

Mr. Merrill was looking across the desk at her. More precisely, he was looking at her legs, which were crossed underneath the steno pad. And it was the kind of look a man gives a woman, not the kind an employer gives his secretary.

She had just enough time to register this when he raised his eyes to hers. For a moment they regarded each other, locked in mutual awareness. He had looked at her with desire; she had seen him do it; he knew she had seen it. Something seemed to hum in her ears. She could not speak, nor could she look away.

Then the phone in her office rang, and she started and dropped the pencil. She quickly retrieved it from the carpet and stood up, smoothing her skirt self-consciously. The phone seemed to have broken the spell; he reached for a folder on his desk and opened it.

"I'll just answer that," she said. "If there's nothing else, Mr. Merrill?"

"I believe we're done for now, Miss Healey." He glanced up, and his eyes were once again the neutral eyes of an employer. "Have a good evening."

Frances lay in bed that night, staring at the ceiling. She heard the front door open as Audrey came back from a date, her high heels clicking briefly before she slipped them off and carried them out of respect for her sleeping roommate. The gesture was appreciated but unnecessary. Frances wondered if she'd ever fall asleep.

Reaching for her glasses, she angled the bedside clock to read it in the light from the streetlamp. It was 11:42.

An hour earlier, she had tried to read—she was rereading *Pride and Prejudice* for the twentieth time, at least—but she had been unable to focus on the words. She kept remembering that moment in the office, the involuntary expression of desire in Mr. Merrill's eyes. It played itself over and over in her mind, like a scene in a movie, and it did absolutely nothing to relax her.

Enough, she thought. She punched the pillow savagely into a more comfortable shape and lay back down, willing sleep to come.

The next morning at the office, she busied herself watering the plants, making the calls he needed, and reorganizing the file cabinet. In spite of her difficult night, she felt not sleepy but tense and awake.

When he arrived at ten fifteen, he nodded at her in greeting. "I'll have some coffee, please, Miss Healey," he said, going into his office. When the commissary delivered it, she knocked on the door, which was ajar, and took it in. She was aware that her hand was shaking slightly.

She set it on his desk. "Will that be all for now, Mr. Merrill?"

"Yes, thank you," he said, not looking up from a letter he was reading. There was no charge in the air, no predatory or amorous electricity, nothing but the pleasantly businesslike tone of the last few months.

She went back to her desk, relieved. This was a job she wanted to keep. She wanted nothing to jeopardize that.

But at quiet moments that day—powdering her nose in the ladies' room, standing in line at the commissary—she remembered looking across the desk at him, both of them silent, a moment of startling honesty and intimacy. If the phone had not rung, who would have spoken first? Who would have been the first to look away? And each time she remembered it, she felt the reflexive, instinctive thrill of being desired by a desirable man. It discomfited her, that thrill. She would have thought she was immune to it, that her outings with Gene would have left no room for her to be affected by any other man.

If only her thoughts could be like a file cabinet or an office desk, tidy and predictable. There was a comfort in those things.

It felt too risky to read about Elizabeth and Darcy that evening. She took her secretary's handbook to bed, opened it, and let the directions on how to address a business envelope gradually send her into sleep.

CHAPTER

TWELVE

On Frances's next date with Gene, he took her to dinner at a new restaurant in town. "Would you like to stop by my apartment?" he asked as they were finishing their coffee. "I've got a new print I'd like to show you." She raised an amused eyebrow, and he grinned. "I really do. I'm too old-fashioned to seduce you. I'll make you a cocktail, though, if you want."

His apartment was a spacious one about a mile from hers. A huge eucalyptus tree, ragged and pungent, grew just outside the window. "That's quite a tree," she said, as Gene mixed the drinks.

"I've got a thing for trees. I'd live in the middle of a forest if I could."

"You should go east," she said. "To Pennsylvania. That's where you find real forests."

He handed her a glass. It was the classical hour on the radio, and the orchestra was playing a piece by Ravel, slow and languorous.

"To visit, maybe," he said. "But I'll settle here. No place like home."

She sat on the sofa and he sat down next to her, draping his arm across the back, his hand on her shoulder. She closed her eyes, enjoying the gentle tug of his fingers as he slowly twirled a lock of her hair.

"So how do you know the East?" he asked after a moment.

Frances opened her eyes. She leaned forward and traced the base of the glass with her finger. "I went to college there," she said.

"I didn't know you were a college girl."

She took a sip and nodded toward the wall opposite the window. "Which print did you want to show me? That one?"

Without waiting for the answer, she put the glass down on the end table, got up, and walked over to the picture in the frame. It was a copy of a portrait by Frans Hals, showing a seventeenth-century burgher tilting back his head and smiling, his face a mass of wrinkles and good humor.

"I like it," she said. "Where did you find it?"

She heard him get up and move beside her. He did not touch her, just stood a while in silence as she looked at the portrait.

"Frances," he said at last. "You have a habit of doing this."

"Doing what?"

"Avoiding talking about yourself, moving the conversation back to me." His hands were in his pockets, and his eyes were on her, intense under his thatch of blond hair. "And you already know all about me. You know that I grew up ten miles from here, that I fell out of a swing when I was eight and had to get stitches in my head. You know that I wanted to be a fireman when I was a kid and that I was sweet on my best friend's sister when I was sixteen. You know all of that, and you keep asking me more."

"I like getting to know people. I always have."

"Yes, I know," he said slowly. "But I think . . . I think maybe you ask the questions because you're afraid to answer them yourself."

Frances had to look away from his gaze. He reached out and took her hand, holding it fast.

"I'm not playing here, Frances," he said. "You're a girl I could see myself marrying someday. So I want to know you. Really know you. Not just the superficial things."

The radio was playing a commercial for Listerine mouthwash. The male announcer's voice was robust and overly animated, jarring in the silence.

"Gene," Frances said quietly. "I shouldn't be seeing you like this. I don't want to get married."

"Sure you do."

"No. I like having a job, working. I wouldn't be able to do that if I got married."

"You wouldn't have to work. I'd support you in style."

"But I like it. You don't understand."

He smiled indulgently. "You think that now," he said, "but give it five years. Will you still want to be living with a roommate, scurrying to the office each day? When you could have a house of your own, a family of your own?"

"Gene," she said, keeping her voice steady, "I don't know how else to say it. I have no intention of getting married. To anyone."

"But why not?" he asked. Then, after a long moment in which they regarded each other silently, he looked down at the hand he was holding.

"Never mind," he said, quietly and without bitterness. "I know you won't tell me."

The radio had begun playing a piece that she recognized as "The Swan" by Debussy, its graceful melody at odds with the tension in the room. She wanted to explain but did not know what to say. After a moment, he let go of her hand.

"I like you, Frances," he said. "I like you a lot. But there's probably no point in continuing to go out, is there?"

"I'm sorry, Gene," she said, and meant it. "I wish—"

What did she wish? That she did want marriage and a family, after all? That they could see each other lightly and casually, forever, never having to take a further step? That she could explain to him everything that had led her to this point, to this decision?

"I wish," she said finally, "they would play a different song. This one is all wrong for the conversation."

He was silent, looking at her steadily. She could read his

thoughts in his eyes. *Even now*, he was thinking, *she avoids talking about anything real.* She felt a sting of dissatisfaction at herself and her own transparency, at the fact that she was cutting off the attentions of a perfectly engaging man, the kind of man she once would have wanted to marry.

Then he grinned wryly, a glimmer of the old Gene. "What would be better? Beethoven's Fifth Symphony? The 'Ride of the Valkyries'?"

"Either one. I'm not picky." She felt tears in her eyes and blinked them away. He drew her to him, kissing the top of her head.

"Let's go," he said, squeezing her shoulder lightly. "Let's go dancing one more time, shall we? For old time's sake. Then I'll take you home."

He crossed to the radio and turned it off as she turned back to the print on the wall. The man in the doublet smiled at her, jolly but benevolent, like a favorite uncle or a fairy godfather.

"It's a nice print, Gene," she said.

"I've always had good taste, Frances," he said simply. She knew it was not a boast but a compliment.

He helped her on with the coat. They went to the Blossom Room and danced. And when he dropped her off and his car drove away, it took three chapters of the *Standard Handbook for Secretaries* before she could settle her mind enough to sleep.

Ever since reading *Daddy-Long-Legs* when she was eleven, Frances had wanted to go to a girls' college in the East. It looked enormously fun: gray stone dormitories cloaked in ivy, girls making fudge and learning Latin, snowy rambles in the countryside. "I'll get to know another part of the country," she told her father, who suggested a school closer to home. "It'll be good for me."

Mother Florence, surprisingly, proved an ally for Frances's cause. "A girls' college is safer than one with boys," Frances overheard her telling her father. "I don't approve of boys and girls living close together."

"Frances has never given us a moment's worry on that score," said her father. It was true; though Frances liked to date and had had two steady boyfriends, her parents had nothing to reproach her for. "She's sensible and wants to learn. She won't have her head turned by a boy."

"Still," said Mother Florence grimly, "one can't be too careful."

So Frances enrolled at Bryn Mawr and blossomed. She thrilled to the age and history of the college, to its long traditions, to the beauty of snowy days she'd only ever seen in pictures. Every class was enjoyable in some way; even calculus, which proved her Achilles' heel, was redeemed by the fascinating eccentricities of her professor. She made good friends and wrote for the college newspaper, at first articles about the latest happenings on campus, then a series of humorous pieces about the differences between California and Pennsylvania. She was even stopped in town one day by a resident who complimented her on her columns. Her father wrote letters once a week, while Mother Florence wrote far less often. Rita sent no letters at all ("I'm not much of a writer, lovey"), but she told Frances she'd be praying for her at nine o'clock every night, and if Frances was awake at midnight (as she shouldn't be), she could be sure Rita was thinking of her.

The first day of her junior year, Frances put on her new blue felt hat and gathered her books and looked at herself in the mirror. *Time for year three*, she thought, smiling at her reflection. She felt like an old hand at college life, but as she left her tidy dormitory room she felt a sudden premonition, a little shiver that something would happen that had never happened before. *A goose just walked over my grave*, she thought, remembering a phrase Mother Florence often used. Then she wondered how that expression ever came to be, and which goose had walked over whose grave, and she was so distracted as she walked to her new English class that she almost forgot she had ever had the premonition at all.

CHAPTER
THIRTEEN

Frances got to work ten minutes late Monday morning owing to sidewalk repair on a nearby street. Normally, she'd be mortified to be tardy, but Mr. Merrill was taking the morning off and would not be in until noon. It was unusual for him to do so; she wondered if the driving pace of the last few weeks, as well as the apparent drama with Belinda, had finally caught up with him.

After opening the blinds and uncovering the typewriter, she sat down at the desk, smoothing the skirt of her new dress, a bright red one with a white collar and cuffs. It was bolder than her usual outfits, but she had known it was a good purchase when Audrey gave a wolf whistle and said, "You should wear that color more often."

The door to the office opened and Jack, one of the mail boys, appeared in his green uniform. "Morning, Miss Healey," he said cheerfully. He, like many of the mail boys, was young and handsome; the job was seen as an entry into the studio for many hopeful actors.

"Good morning, Jack. What do you have today?"

He handed her a pile of envelopes with a flourish. "Here you are, milady."

"Anything interesting?" she teased him. It was a joke between them that he steamed open the letters and read them in the mail room.

"You bet. Two threats of blackmail, one ransom note."

"So the usual, then."

He grinned and nodded toward the open door to Mr. Merrill's office. "Good thing he's not around to hear this."

"Yes," she said absently, her attention commanded by a large envelope of cream-colored stationery.

"That one," Jack said. "Who knows who it's from. Somehow it made its way to the right place. At least, I think it's the right place."

It was addressed, in neat handwriting, to The Man in Charge of The Kitty Ridley Movie, VistaGlen Studios, Holly Wood, California. There was no return address.

"A San Francisco postmark," Frances said. She turned the envelope over, studying the back. "Intriguing."

"Maybe a love letter. Tell Miss Vail she's got competition." He touched his cap jauntily and left.

Frances had been told to open all mail not marked Personal or Confidential, so she slit the envelope and unfolded the paper. Her secretary's eye quickly noted the address and phone number at the top of the letter; then she saw a name that arrested her gaze:

Miss Kitty Ridley

Her heart began to pound. The letter was typed carefully, two mistakes corrected by hand.

To Whom It May Concern,

I am Miss Kitty Ridley, otherwise known as Madame de Cadenet de la Tour, the subject of the film you are apparently making. I hear that you are basing it on the book written by Myrtle Dobson. That book was written without my knowledge and without my approval. This movie is being made without my approval as well. I am extremely displeased to hear of it.

The book itself contained no end of lies about me and my life, and a movie based on it would do the same. I am hereby asking you to stop production of it. I know Hollywood is

probably a place of commerce and no sensitive feeling, but
common decency would demand that you follow the wishes of
an old woman.

This letter may be blunt, but I have lived too long to care
about that. As Shakespeare so eloquently wrote, "To thine own
self be true." At the age of ninety, I am nothing if not true to
myself. I have little time left to be anything else.

Sincerely,

Kitty Ridley

The signature was the shaky script of an elderly woman, but there was a flourish to the *K* and the final *y* that was brave, even flamboyant. It was the flourish of a woman who had signed countless autograph albums and fan letters and who had not forgotten how.

Frances looked up. Light poured in from the window facing the quadrangle, and she could hear a truck backing up outside. The clock said 8:24. She sat in the quiet office for a moment, one brief, calm moment before the storm; then she opened her address book, found Mr. Merrill's home number, and placed a call.

He answered the phone himself. "Lawrence Merrill."

"Mr. Merrill? It's Frances Healey. I'm calling from the office."

"I didn't forget an appointment, did I?"

"No. There's a letter that came for you. I thought you should know about it." She took a breath. "It's from Kitty Ridley."

"Who?"

"Kitty Ridley."

There was a pause. "I know you wouldn't joke about this," he said.

"I'm not joking. I have the letter right here. Shall I read it to you?"

"Yes."

She did.

Another pause. "Shit," he said.

Exactly, Frances thought.

"Shit," he said again. Then he added, belatedly, "Excuse me."

"It's fine," she told him. "I understand."

"Damn it," he said. "Goddamn it. Look, come here. Bring the letter. Get a taxi, and I'll pay you back."

"I will, Mr. Merrill."

"And right now."

"Yes. I'll leave now."

She had barely rung the bell when Mr. Merrill opened the door. He wore gray flannel slacks and a blue pullover, much more casual than the suits he wore to the office, but his face was drawn and tense.

"Thank you for coming," he said. "Would you pay the driver, Mrs. Daley?" The housekeeper, who was hovering in the background, took the money he offered and went out to the curb.

"This way," he said to Frances, indicating a room to the right of the entrance hall. As she moved toward it, a door opened and Sally appeared, holding a half-eaten piece of toast.

"Miss Healey," she said. "I thought that was you."

"Good morning, Sally. It's nice to see you again."

"Would you like some coffee?" Sally asked eagerly. "I think there's some in the kitchen."

"No," said Mr. Merrill brusquely. "Miss Healey is here on business."

Frances saw Sally's face change from hope to hurt, transparent as water. "All right then," she said, lifting her chin. She disappeared back through the door, banging it shut behind her.

Mr. Merrill ushered Frances into the living room. It was drenched in sunlight, with a yellow carpet and light walls and chintz curtains. French windows opened onto a well-tended back garden; she spied a line of rose trees.

"Have a seat," he said. She took the end of the nearest divan, opened up her pocketbook, and handed him the letter. Still standing, he read it. He examined the envelope, the stationery, and even lifted it to his nose as if that would offer some clue to its authenticity. She smiled involuntarily, having done exactly the same thing in the taxi.

"I'd like to think this is some imposter," he said. "That would be the easiest way out of this."

"But you think it's really her."

He nodded. "Honestly, I was afraid of this when we started the picture." He sat down on the chair facing her, his forearms on his knees, holding the letter in his large hands. "There's no record of her death, you know, just that crazy rumor about her being in a sheik's palace. We had the research department look into it, but they couldn't find anything definitive. Irving told me not to worry. He's not often wrong."

"But how could she come back to the States without being recognized?"

"She probably doesn't look anything like the photos anymore. And most people wouldn't know her married name. If she didn't want to be recognized, she didn't have to be."

"So what happens now?"

"I'll try to call her. She did include a number, thankfully." He got up and walked to the white phone on the table by the armchair.

As he placed the call, she looked around the room. It was the sort of room a decorator would put together, the mild abstract patterns of the upholstery making a perfect complement to the florals of the curtains. There was a handsome radio and a large oil painting of a ship at sea, and on the end table near her was a stack of three books. The top one, *The Last of the Mohicans*, was marked with a leather bookmark.

"Good morning," Mr. Merrill said into the phone. "May I speak to Miss Kitty Ridley, please?" A pause. "This is Lawrence Merrill, executive producer at VistaGlen Studios." Another pause. "Yes, I received her letter. Is she available for me to speak to her? I would very much like to address her concerns."

A longer pause. He looked at Frances as he listened. He looked at her for a long time, not shifting his gaze. She wondered if he had forgotten she could not also hear what was being said on the other end of the line.

"I understand," he said at last. "But I would like very much to speak to her. At her convenience, of course. I am certain that we can address her concerns. Let me give you my phone number at home," he said, "and at the studio." He gave them both quickly, as if the other party were trying to get off the line. "Thank you. I look forward to her call." He set the phone back on the receiver.

"Shit," he said, running a hand through his hair.

"Who was that?"

"Her housekeeper, Mrs. Martino. Miss Ridley is resting. There was no promise that she would call me back."

"So what do you do now?"

"Phone Irving," he said. "Notify Simon. And Grayson." He turned to her. "No one else can know about this right now, Miss Healey. That's imperative."

"I understand, Mr. Merrill."

"Most of all," he said, looking grim, "don't tell Miss Vail."

CHAPTER
FOURTEEN

The next few days were full of activity. Meetings were canceled, and Mr. Merrill had secret and tense conversations with Simon and Grayson and Irving Glennon, who was leaving for his daughter's wedding in New York but delayed the trip by a day. Frances could not help thinking it must be like working at the White House, a president's cabinet huddling to respond to a crisis.

It was really Miss Ridley, they agreed; the signature was an exact match, other than the shakiness that could be attributed to age, and the research department was able to produce a passenger list from a steamer nine years before, showing the passage of a Madame de la Tour to New York. A private detective in San Francisco was able to confirm that yes, there was an elderly woman by that name—"rather eccentric," said the neighbor, "used to live abroad, I think"—living at the address mentioned in the letter. "It's clearly her," said Mr. Merrill to Frances at the end of the third day. He looked haggard, drawn.

"Can I get you some coffee?" asked Frances.

"Coffee won't help. This is a nightmare."

"A cocktail, then?" she asked, and he smiled wearily. He was standing by her desk as if he wanted a break from his own office and the relentlessness of the conversations that were taking place there.

"This comes at a terrible time for the studio," he said. "And as if I needed another crisis, now I have to figure out how to get Sally up to the convent school."

"You have time to decide, don't you? It's only July."

"The sisters agreed to take her early, before the school year starts. She's going next week. It's too much, having her here."

"I see." Frances could not help thinking what a terrible idea it was. Sally alone in a convent for weeks with a group of women she did not know seemed like a recipe for misery.

"My sister Rosemary was going to take her, but she called last night. Her mother-in-law in Chicago has broken her hip, so Rosemary is going out there tomorrow. As she should, of course. But when it rains, it pours." He looked at Frances unhappily. "And we're breaking the news to Miss Vail today, telling her the picture is off."

She was shocked. "It's definitely off?"

"Irving thinks it's the only option. He's tried to phone Miss Ridley too, but the housekeeper gave him the same line. Said something about Miss Ridley wanting to go to the newspapers with her displeasure. That kind of publicity is toxic. It can ruin a film."

"I wonder why it didn't ruin the book. How did Myrtle Dobson get away with writing it?"

"If the steamship record is correct, she's only been in this country for the past nine years. The book was published a few years before that. If she was in France at the time, she probably didn't even know about it until it was too late to say anything."

"If only she had stayed in France."

"It would have made my life much easier," he said dryly, "but I've learned that the universe doesn't run according to my needs." He checked his watch. "What time did you tell Miss Vail to be here?"

"Four o'clock. And Mr. Kerr and Mr. Greene will be here too."

He nodded, started for his office, then turned back to her. "Thank you for all your help, Miss Healey," he said. "And your discretion. Let's hope we can find another picture for Miss Vail."

"I just wish there were a way to keep this project going."

"If wishes were horses," said Mr. Merrill, "beggars would ride. As my mother always used to say."

Belinda was smiling and confident as she arrived for the meeting. She greeted Simon and Grayson with warmth and Mr. Merrill with a cool nod, not a kiss. Mr. Merrill closed the door to his office, his face grim.

Frances tried not to eavesdrop, but it was impossible not to hear the muted voices, male ones, speaking gravely and slowly. Within minutes they were overpowered by a female voice. It was first urgent and alarmed, then it increased in pitch and volume, and then the buzzer on Frances's desk rang, and Mr. Merrill asked her to bring in a glass of water.

She opened the door to find Mr. Merrill leaning against the edge of his desk, Simon sitting near the window, and Grayson sprawled inelegantly and unhappily in the club chair. Belinda was standing, holding her pocketbook as if she had just risen from her seat. Mr. Merrill, catching sight of Frances, gestured toward Belinda, but the actress ignored the proffered glass.

"Ridiculous," she was saying. "It's ridiculous! Who gave her so much power?"

"It's because she is who she is," said Mr. Merrill. "Ninety years old. Living history."

"No one even knew she was living," said Belinda, "until now. You all thought she was dead, didn't you? So tell people she's an imposter." She was clutching her snakeskin handbag with fingers that were tipped in red but white at the knuckles.

"Have some water, Belinda," Mr. Merrill said. "And please, have a seat." She gave a dismissive shake of her head and remained standing.

"You see, Belinda," said Simon, "a film's success depends on the goodwill attached to it. Miss Ridley has already been vocal about her feelings. If she goes to the press, she could ruin this picture. Not to mention making things uncomfortable for the studio as a whole."

"So pay her," said Belinda. She gestured wildly with the handbag. "This is Hollywood, for goodness' sake. Everyone has a price."

"It's not always about money," said Mr. Merrill. "Sometimes a person cares about other things. Her legacy. Being heard."

"So listen to her," said Belinda. "Call her on the phone. Have a conversation. Make her see."

"We've tried," said Simon, "many times. She won't talk to us on the phone." He gave a sigh. "She's ninety years old; it's not her way."

"Then write to her," insisted Belinda. "Send a carrier pigeon. Or scratch it on rock, or whatever they did back in her day."

"She's ninety years old, Belinda," said Grayson in his dry voice. "Not a survivor of the Stone Age."

"Well, pardon me," said Belinda, her caustic tone at odds with the girlish beauty of her face. "I'm not as educated as you are, Grayson. You don't need to patronize me." He spread his hands, bowing his head in apology.

"We've come so far with this," said Belinda to all three of the men. Her voice was no longer brittle but pleading. "We've done so much work. You're going to throw it all away? Just like that?"

"A studio is a business," said Mr. Merrill. "Everyone in this room has had to make hard decisions based on profit and loss. It doesn't make them easy, I know."

"But to give up now," said Belinda. "After everything we've done."

"I know. These are not easy choices, Belinda."

"But I was expensive," she said. She lifted her chin and looked directly at Mr. Merrill. "You paid a lot of money to have me, Lawrence."

She was referring to the contract, Frances knew, yet the words and the tone made Grayson glance up swiftly, then look away uncomfortably. Frances realized that he, like she, could not help thinking of the other contexts in which a woman might say that to a man.

It suddenly occurred to her that perhaps it was no accident. Perhaps, she thought, studying the actress with growing wonder, Belinda had chosen her words to have precisely that effect.

Simon's discreet cough pulled her out of her speculation. Mr. Merrill was looking down at Belinda, his face inscrutable. There was the creak of the chair as Grayson shifted his weight.

"It would be folly," said Mr. Merrill at last, his voice quiet and perfectly controlled, "to make a film that has such potential to fail. Not just bad for the studio, Belinda. It would be damaging to your career."

"But I've wanted this part so much." Belinda's eyes filled with tears. "This is my chance to be more than some silly ingenue. To have a role that means something." Simon got up to pass her a handkerchief, and she wiped her eyes. "You know that, Lawrence. And you too," she said to the other men.

Some women were heartbreakingly lovely when they cried, and Belinda was one of them. She looked even younger and more vulnerable than usual, her face glistening with tears. Frances, still holding the forgotten glass, studied the three men. The purpose of the meeting had been to break the news to Belinda, to placate her, to offer the consolation prize of another role in another film. But all their plans, she realized as she saw the men exchange glances, were in question now that she had begun to weep.

Simon cleared his throat. "Perhaps, Lawrence," he said unhappily, "perhaps I could go to San Francisco and meet with Miss Ridley. Maybe she just needs a human face to go with the project."

"Oh, Simon!" Belinda looked up swiftly from her handkerchief. "Would you?"

"Or Grayson can go," said Simon. "Someone who can talk with the old lady, charm her."

"Charm her?" said Grayson. "Jesus Christ, don't send me. I'll make it worse."

"Me, then," said Simon. He exhaled. "God, this is the last thing I need." He checked his watch irrelevantly. "It'll put me behind on those edits, Lawrence. But I guess we can handle a week's delay."

"No," said Mr. Merrill. "No, I'm not sending you to San Francisco."

Four faces turned to him. He smiled grimly.

"I'll go myself."

There was a stunned pause, and then Belinda flew at him in a rush of blonde curls and emotion. "Oh, Lawrence!" She grabbed his arm. "Really?"

"I'm going to try." He looked down at her, his eyes wary. "You need to know, Belinda, that I may not succeed."

"Of course you will," she said joyfully. "You won't let me down." Her face was radiant. "You'll make this picture happen, I know you will."

"Better you than me," said Simon with audible relief. "Judith would never forgive me if I missed her birthday. But Lawrence, this will set you behind."

"I'll manage. I needed some way to get my daughter up north anyhow, to her new school. I'll do that on the way."

"Of course," Belinda said. "You can take Sally in person. It's all working out perfectly."

"Synchronicity," said Grayson. "It's a wonderful thing. Maybe fate isn't a bastard after all." He got up heavily from the chair and clapped Mr. Merrill on the back. "I'm glad, Lawrence. This isn't just any picture. I'd actually be sorry to see this one go."

"I would too," said Simon.

"I would too," said Belinda, beaming at each of the men in turn. "And now I won't have to."

After the others had left, Frances was feeding some carbon paper into the typewriter when Mr. Merrill paused by her desk. "Thanks for your help today, Miss Healey."

"You're welcome," she said. "I hope this works. I know it's an important film."

"Maybe this is a mistake. I've raised Belinda's hopes, maybe for nothing." He jiggled some change in his pocket, staring off into the distance.

"You'd probably feel worse if you didn't try."

"True." He sighed. "Well. San Francisco it is."

"Shall I book you and Sally some tickets on the train?"

"No, I'll take the car. Talk to Sherwin. I hope he won't mind being gone for five days, six at the most."

She scribbled notes on her pad. "When will you leave?"

"Monday. Tuesday at the latest."

"And what would you like me to work on while you're gone?"

He looked surprised, then apologetic. "I'm sorry, I guess I didn't say what I was thinking. You aren't staying here, Miss Healey. I'd like you to come along."

"Come along?"

"I'll need a secretary for my meetings with Miss Ridley. And honestly, you'd be a big help with Sally. She seems to like you. I'll pay you double for the time away. I know it's an inconvenience."

She thought of San Francisco, and the last time she had been there. Unconsciously, she pressed her index finger against the base of her thumb. She could refuse, surely; to travel up the length of the state with her employer and his daughter was far beyond the normal scope of her duties. But there was a look in his eyes as he waited for her to speak, an admission that he was asking for something that she was well within her rights to refuse.

"We're doing two things there, and two things only, Miss Healey. Depositing Sally at her school and meeting with Miss Ridley. We'll come back as quickly as possible." He gave a wry grin. "I'm not doing a good job selling this, am I? I should promise you a ride on a cable car or something."

She managed a smile as she thought of the city: foggy, hilly, crowded with people, some of whom she knew. But it was a big city, and the trip would be brief.

He stood, his hands in his pockets, waiting for her to speak. How odd that she was the one sitting behind a desk, and he was the one standing in front of it.

She cleared her throat. "I'll go, Mr. Merrill."

Relief washed over his face. "Thank you, Miss Healey," he said. "Thank you. That's the only good news I've gotten all day."

He returned to his office, visibly relaxed. She was so tense that she had to breathe deeply for a full half minute before she could return to her work.

PART
TWO

CHAPTER
FIFTEEN
Santa Barbara
1937

C yril Flike had once been the leading costume designer for VistaGlen Studios. Born in England, he'd had a successful career designing costumes for the London and Broadway stage before coming to Hollywood in the early twenties. Upon retiring, he had settled in Santa Barbara, in a spacious Spanish-style home with a tile roof. It was tucked in the canyon just above downtown, with a creek running through the property, and it had mature oaks and a rose garden and a courtyard that he'd had tiled to look like one he'd seen in Marrakech, with a square fountain in the center and curtains of jasmine over the walls.

He was a small, white-haired man who always wore a silk ascot. He was precise and had high expectations; even his dog, Sebastian, a greyhound who seemed oddly disproportionate beside his short master, was exceedingly well trained. No longer actively designing, Cyril would occasionally create a gown for a friend or for a charity event in town. Most of his days were spent reading from his extensive library of first editions (he was fluent in French, Spanish, and German) or walking the roads around the estate wearing a Panama hat, Sebastian at his side.

When he interviewed Frances, he was remote and unsmiling at first, his hands clasped on top of his ivory-topped walking stick. Finding him fascinating, she did not mind his cold manner. At a pause in the proceedings, when the housekeeper brought in tea, Frances commented on the tapestry on the opposite wall.

"That," he said. "Yes. An original." She sipped her tea and he sipped his. He watched her studying the tapestry. "Can you tell where it is from, Miss Healey?"

She put the cup down and walked closer to the tapestry, which showed stylized blonde people grouped around a stag in the forest.

"I would guess Flanders," she said. "Sixteenth century."

There was silence for a moment. Sebastian, curled by the armchair, yawned.

"You are exactly right," said Cyril.

She returned to the chair and took up her teacup. He looked at her with a visible thawing in his manner.

"Where are you from, Miss Healey?"

"Near San Francisco. South of the city."

"And where did you go to school?"

"Central Coast Secretarial Academy, in San Luis Obispo."

"You did not learn about tapestries at Central Coast Secretarial Academy."

"No," she admitted. "I studied for a time at Bryn Mawr."

"For a time?"

"I left partway through my third year."

"Did you?"

Her mouth was dry; she realized she wanted this job very much. "Yes."

His eyes were shrewd. "So tell me, Miss Healey," he said. "Did your leaving involve either dishonesty or theft?"

"No, Mr. Flike."

"That's all I need to know." He snapped for Sebastian and the dog sat up. Cyril reached down to rub his ear. "I like you, and I think you would suit me."

She smiled, relieved. "Thank you, Mr. Flike."

"One thing I ask of anyone in my employ," he said. "Discretion. There are those who would like to know more about me and my life. I have no interest in being known any more than I choose to reveal."

"I understand," she said. Then after a moment, she added, "Even as a child I was excellent at keeping secrets."

"A good secretary knows that 'secret' is part of her name." He stood up. "Come. I've a Hogarth print in the dining room that might interest you."

After three years in a law office, Frances found it fascinating to work for Cyril. She read and answered his letters, which came from all over the world; she arranged doctor's appointments and fielded periodic requests from Hollywood asking for his help on film projects, requests that he always denied. Once, over a two-week period, she juggled the numerous letters of a particularly tenacious starlet who wanted a gown for a banquet. "She will not take no for an answer," said Frances.

"She has no choice," said Cyril. "I will not design a gown simply to gratify a young woman's vanity."

The young woman in question was on the cover of *MovieFone* magazine: a stunner, with ebony hair and a face like a Roman coin.

"She would show off your creation very well," Frances ventured.

"No doubt," said Cyril. "But I am at a stage in my life where I can pick and choose what I do. And I choose not to."

"What excuse shall I give this time?"

"Exactly what I said before," said Cyril, calmly cutting into a breast of chicken. "The project does not interest me."

He glanced at Frances, saw the look on her face, and smiled.

"It pains you to be blunt, does it not?" he said. "But the honesty is mine, not yours."

F our months after she started, on a warm October day, Cyril announced that he was to have a visitor. "For how long?" she asked.

"Just for tomorrow," he said. "Morning until afternoon. I will be busy until she leaves. You may take the day off."

She could tell he wanted privacy, so she went downtown to have lunch and see a matinee. She returned to the house about four, and as she entered the courtyard she saw a waiting taxi and Cyril walking with an elegant, light-skinned young Black woman. She was a few inches taller than he was and was dressed in a periwinkle-blue suit, with a hat that was more stylish than anything Frances had seen outside a fashion magazine. They were arm in arm, and she held a small boy by the other hand. He had skin the color of her own and wore a coat and short pants and held what appeared to be a new celluloid duck in one hand.

Frances was prepared to make herself invisible, but Cyril turned to the woman. "Delia," he said, "this is my secretary, Frances Healey." The woman, who was stunningly beautiful, smiled warmly and said hello. There was something instantly familiar about her eyes. Frances wondered if she was a singer, or an actress, but could not place her.

"And this," said Cyril, indicating the boy, "is Baxter."

"Hello, Baxter," said Frances. "I like your duck."

Baxter regarded her with the suspicious look often seen in the faces of toddlers and held the duck more closely to his side.

"It's very nice to meet you," said Frances, then excused herself and went back to her room in the guest cottage, where she took off her hat, made herself a sandwich, and wondered.

After dinner she went to the kitchen to get Cyril a cup of tea. Mrs. Hoskins, the cook, looked up from the pot she was scouring.

"He wants tea, does he?" she asked. "Chamomile, to help him sleep. He always wants it after she comes to town." It was said not with censoriousness but with sympathy.

Frances was curious but said nothing. She didn't have to; Mrs. Hoskins was in a garrulous mood.

"She's his daughter, you see," she said as she filled the teakettle. "And that's his grandson."

So that was what she had seen in Delia's face: Cyril's features, one generation later.

"He met her mother in Paris. She died long ago." Mrs. Hoskins looked swiftly up from the kettle. "I only tell you this because I know you can keep a secret. This can't get out, Miss Healey. Imagine what the papers would say."

Frances could imagine. She could see it all clearly: the scandal, the vitriol that would rebound not just on Cyril but on Delia and her little son. "No," she said. "I won't tell anyone."

Curiously, Frances found that the visit from Delia seemed to make Cyril more talkative and eager for conversation. In the weeks that followed, he revealed more of his past than he had ever done before, sharing stories as they ate lunch or took walks together. She learned that as a child, he'd once seen Queen Victoria ("Short and squat, but utterly intimidating. She taught me you don't have to be tall to be commanding"). He talked about the cruel boys' school he'd been sent to as a child in England ("Only Dickens could have done it justice") and about his decades in Paris, where he had known Picasso and Matisse. At night in her room she thought about his stories, marveling at the breadth of experiences he'd had. She had wanted to work for someone fascinating, and she certainly was.

Then one February day, when the creek was rushing with water from the recent rains, he came upon her as she sat in the Moroccan courtyard. She was mending a stocking, enjoying the sunlight.

"I should pay you more," he said, sitting on the bench beside her, "so you wouldn't have to darn that."

She smiled. "I've no complaints. I find this calming, actually."

Birds fluttered in the oak above them. Sebastian raised his ears briefly at the sight of a squirrel, then relaxed again.

"You've been a tremendous secretary, my dear," said Cyril. "And I want to tell you this now, so you have plenty of time to plan."

She put down the stocking.

"I'm leaving Santa Barbara," he said. "Going to Paris. In April, if not before."

"For how long?"

He paused. "Forever. I'll be selling this house and most of its furnishings. I'm going with Delia. And Baxter."

"I see."

"She's my daughter, you know." He smiled gently. "I'm sure Mrs. Hoskins, bless her, has told you that."

She nodded.

"It's a sign of her trust in you. A trust that has been proven to be worthwhile. Under normal circumstances, I'd still need a secretary, and I'd offer to take you with me. But these are not normal circumstances." He tilted his head back, looking up into the oak. The skin of his face was thin; she could see the bluish veins at his temple. "You see, my dear, I am going to Paris to die."

She started, but he continued on, his voice calm.

"I have about a year, the doctors say. More if I'm lucky. And as much as I've loved this house, Paris was where life truly began for me. It's where it should end too. And I want to end it with the family I've not had the courage to claim here."

Tears filled her eyes. He reached out a thin, cold hand and patted her own.

"Don't be sorry for me," he said. "It's been a good life, all in all. And I still know many people in the industry. I'll write you a reference that will find you a place in the studios, if you'd like."

"Thank you, Mr. Flike."

He watched as she dabbed at her eyes and put away the handkerchief.

"If I may say something, Miss Healey," he said after a moment, "you are an excellent secretary, but I hope you will not be one forever. I hope at some point you will be in a place to continue what you once started." He snapped for Sebastian, who came and rested his head on Cyril's knee. He stroked the dog's sleek head.

"I think that ship has sailed," she said quietly.

He shrugged. "There's more than one ship on the ocean. Sometimes life gives you second chances. Sometimes they come as a cancer diagnosis, delivered by a doctor with a grave face. But you need to recognize them for what they are."

There was silence. They could hear the creek, full after the spring rains, below in the garden. Sebastian, peaceful, closed his eyes.

"A good sound, that," said Cyril, "after so many months of dryness." He, too, closed his eyes, as if the moment were one he wanted to remember. Then Frances did the same, and they sat together in silence.

CHAPTER

SIXTEEN

The first day of the trip, they didn't travel far. Mr. Merrill had a meeting that could not be postponed, and it was two o'clock before they left Hollywood. Sally sat up in the front of the car with Sherwin, while Frances, at Mr. Merrill's request, sat with him in the back so she could take dictation if needed. But much of the time he read a book that Frances had purchased at his request, *California in the Age of Gold*, to provide background for his talk with Miss Ridley.

Sally read *Sons and Lovers* steadily for the first half hour, then stared out the window. Later, she started a conversation with Sherwin, speaking without the accent, Frances noted. "What is Minnesota like?"

"Nice, Miss Merrill. All my family is there."

"You don't have family here?"

"No. Not yet."

"What do you mean, not yet?"

"My wife is having a baby."

"Oh. That's nice." She twirled a pigtail in one hand. "Do you want it to be a boy or a girl?"

"I don't mind, Miss Merrill." He glanced back in the rearview mirror, as if making sure the conversation was still acceptable to his employer.

"What does your wife want?"

"I think she wants a girl. She already has a name picked out."

"What name?"

"Valerie."

"That's pretty." Sally glanced back at her father, who was reading. "But I hope it's a boy," she said, raising her voice. "Girls are nothing but trouble."

Mr. Merrill ignored her. After a moment, Sally took out her own book and opened it, giving an ostentatious sigh.

Frances gazed out the window. They were in Santa Barbara County, with scrubby, rocky peaks to the right and the ocean to the left. The air, even in the closed car, smelled different than it did in Hollywood. She remembered the fragrance of Santa Barbara from her time with Cyril. It smelled not just of the ocean but of something else: of soil, perhaps, something elemental and soothing.

She closed her eyes, imagining Cyril in Paris. She saw him sitting at a sidewalk café under leafy trees with his daughter by his side and his grandson on his knee and Sebastian lying nearby, resting his head on his paws. Cyril was wearing his ascot and his Panama hat. He was thinner and pale, but he was smiling, as if he had waited his entire life to be where he was.

When Frances had booked the Santa Barbara hotel, there were only three rooms available, so she had planned all along to share with Sally. The arrangement came as a surprise to Mr. Merrill, who looked at her meaningfully at the check-in desk. "I should give you another day's salary just for that," he said in a low voice.

They settled in their rooms and met half an hour later, in the hotel restaurant. "Where is Sherwin?" asked Sally as she sat down.

"He went out to fill the car for tomorrow," said Mr. Merrill, "and he'll get his dinner on the way." He pulled out a chair for Frances.

"He's not going to eat with us?"

"No."

"Why not?"

"Sally," said Mr. Merrill, "decide what you want for dinner."

Silence settled on the table.

"What are oysters Rockefeller?" Sally asked after a moment.

"Something you wouldn't like," said Mr. Merrill.

"I might," said Sally. "You have no idea what I like and don't like."

She said it neutrally, in the English accent, but as the waiter poured water the words hung in the air. Frances spread her napkin carefully in her lap; it would be an awkward meal.

"You've hardly seen me the past two years," continued Sally distinctly. "For all you know, I might love oysters. I might love them so much I never want to eat anything else."

Frances glanced at her employer. He was looking at his daughter as if he could not decide whether to reprimand her for impudence or acknowledge the truth of what she had said. He could face hysterical actresses and temperamental directors, but a thirteen-year-old girl had him at a loss. She thought of something to fill the silence.

"I remember a quotation from Jonathan Swift," she said. "'It was a bold man that first ate an oyster.' I'm not sure I'd have the courage to be the first." No one responded, so she indicated the cup before her. "Or coffee. I wonder who first tried grinding coffee beans and making it a drink."

"Coffee is awful," said Sally. "It's so bitter."

"Or tea, then," said Frances. "Someone had to realize you could dry the leaves and brew them. It's kind of a strange thing to try, really."

"Maybe it happened on accident," said Mr. Merrill. "I heard that's how we got iced tea. At the World's Fair, when the heating lamp broke."

"Someone should write a book," said Frances, "about the history of various foods. I'm sure there are lots of good stories."

"I know how sandwiches were invented," said Sally after a moment. "The Earl of Sandwich invented them so he could eat while playing cards."

"And there's Coca-Cola," said Mr. Merrill. "Someone told me it started as a headache remedy."

Sally could not hide her surprise. "Really?"

"Really."

"It tastes too good to be medicine," said Sally. "It would almost be worth having a headache." The waiter came over to take her order. "I'll have a Coca-Cola," she said, "and the chicken cutlet with string beans. And what is your soup of the day?"

As the waiter answered, Mr. Merrill looked across the table at Frances. There was an expression in his eyes that she recognized as gratitude.

Frances went for a walk after dinner, passing shops and hotels and eventually reaching the beach. Because of the heeled oxfords she was wearing she did not go on the sand, choosing instead to walk along the wharf. She went slowly, picking her way along the rough boards. Gulls wheeled around her and pedestrians passed in both directions, clearly enjoying the balmy evening.

After a few minutes, she paused and leaned against the rail. Before her she could see the sun, a bright orange disk poised low over the horizon. There was a man a few feet away from her, in a hat and light coat, gazing in the same direction, partially blocking her view. She was just about to cross the wharf and admire the sunset from the other side when the man suddenly turned. "Miss Healey," he said.

"Oh, Mr. Merrill. I didn't realize it was you."

He indicated that she should move to his right, where she would have a better view. She did so, resting her hands lightly on the rail.

"It's a nice night," he said. "Is Sally asleep?"

"She was reading when I left. But she looked tired from the trip."

They both turned back to the sky. The sun had started slipping below the horizon, and they watched it in silence.

"It's strange," he said at last. "You can stare at the sun, but it's only when you look away that you really see how much it's moved." After a moment, he added, "I don't see Sally very often. I guess the changes always surprise me."

"How has she changed?"

"She's always been challenging. But there's something new. An . . . intensity, I suppose."

"I think that's typical of girls her age."

There was a pause as they both studied the sky. "What does a thirteen-year-old girl want, Miss Healey?"

"It depends on the thirteen-year-old."

"What did you want when you were thirteen? If you don't mind my asking."

She traced the rail with her finger. "I wanted to get along with my stepmother. My mother had died when I was two, and my father remarried when I was twelve."

She turned back to the horizon, watching the disk of the sun slip away. Light bathed the sky.

"What was she like?"

It was similar to the conversation with Gene at the beach, but this time Frances found herself answering. "My stepmother cared about appearances. I didn't. I was too . . . independent. Too selfish, she would say. We never quite got along."

"Do you get along with her now?"

"I don't have any contact with her now," she said quietly.

She could feel his eyes on her, but he did not ask anything else. It felt colder with the sun gone, and she turned away from the ocean, pulling her coat more tightly around her.

"It's getting chilly now, isn't it?" he said. "I'll walk you back to the hotel."

In the room, Sally was asleep, her hair spread out against the pillow. The curtains were open, and with the light of a nearby streetlamp Frances could clearly see her face. She looked peaceful and, in the unguarded expression of sleep, much younger than she did awake.

As Frances put down her handbag, she saw something on the table between the twin beds. It was a small picture frame, just the size to carry in the front pocket of the satchel. Frances picked it up carefully, turning it to the light.

It was a studio portrait of a blonde woman, her hair pinned up in soft waves. There was a patrician loveliness to her features. She was seated on a carved chair, and standing on a small stool, her arm around the woman's neck, was a tiny girl with a bob and with Sally's eyes. They were cheek to cheek, both smiling.

Frances felt an ache in her chest. She put the frame gently back on the bedside table, just as Sally had left it. Then she went to the bathroom and closed the door quietly before looking for the light switch. It took several moments of fumbling in the darkness before she found it.

CHAPTER

SEVENTEEN

T he next day, they drove to Monterey, which Mr. Merrill had selected as a stopping point. "It's not the most convenient place to stay," he had told Frances, "but Sally wants to see it. Some book she read, I think." Frances had been glad to hear that; it meant that Sally's wishes were not entirely irrelevant.

The road up the coast was rocky and beautiful, far more dramatic than the beaches near Hollywood. On an arm of land jutting into the ocean, a cypress tree stood notably alone. "I like that tree," said Sally. She looked over her shoulder at it as long as she could.

At the hotel the clerk greeted them politely. "I believe there is someone in your party by the name of Sherwin?"

"There is," said Mr. Merrill. He gestured to Sherwin, who approached the desk.

"We have a telephone message for him, sir." The clerk passed Sherwin a piece of paper. "This came in just an hour ago."

Sherwin thanked him and opened the paper. He looked stricken.

"Is everything all right?" asked Mr. Merrill.

"No, sir," said Sherwin. "It's my wife. She's—" He looked at Sally. "She's expecting, you know, and she's in the hospital. It says there were complications. They admitted her last night."

"Oh, Sherwin," said Frances. "I'm sorry to hear that."

"I'll call now, if I may," said Sherwin.

"Of course," said Mr. Merrill. They all watched silently as Sherwin went over to the booth, taking off his driver's cap as he picked up the phone. Even from a distance Frances could see how hard he was gripping the receiver.

Sally turned to her father, a look of urgency on her face. "What does he mean, complications?"

Mr. Merrill looked at Frances. Sally, following his eyes, did the same.

"Sometimes there are problems when women are expecting," Frances said. "With the baby."

"How do they know?"

Frances paused, uncertain what to say. "A woman might start to—bleed, say," she finally explained, "and they need to watch her."

"Does it mean that the baby is dying?"

"Sometimes it does, I believe," said Frances. "But sometimes not. Hopefully not," she added at the look of alarm in Sally's eyes.

They all watched Sherwin in silence. After a moment, he put down the receiver and came toward them.

"My mother-in-law," he said quietly. "Janice is in the hospital. She's all right, but they don't know about the baby yet. They want to keep her there and watch." He cleared his throat, passed his hand over his mouth and straightened. "I'll take the car out and fill it with gas again, sir, so we're ready for tomorrow."

"No," said Mr. Merrill. "You're going back home."

"No, Mr. Merrill," said Sherwin weakly.

"Yes. Your wife needs you." He gestured to the front desk. "Let's look at the train timetable."

"But there won't be anyone to drive you to San Francisco," said Sherwin.

"I can drive," said Mr. Merrill.

"I can too," said Frances.

"You see?" said Mr. Merrill, in the decisive voice she knew from the office. "It's all settled. I'll take you to the depot to catch the next train."

"Thank you, sir," said Sherwin. "My wife will be very glad to have me there." His face worked as if he were about to cry.

In the hotel room, Frances took off her hat, put her coat in the closet, and opened the window. She caught the muted sounds of traffic from the street below and the cry of a gull; the hotel was too far away to hear the ocean.

There was a knock at the door and she opened it. It was Sally. "I left my book in the car," she said.

"Your father should be back soon from the station," said Frances. "Why don't you wait here for him?"

Sally sat down on the bed. Her feet in their saddle shoes seemed larger and more ungainly than usual, her toes turning inward.

"What is your room like?" asked Frances.

"Like this one. Different wallpaper."

"Monterey seems like a nice town."

"The drive was pretty." Sally nibbled at a fingernail. "That tree all by itself. I liked that."

"I did too," said Frances. She glanced at the clock. "Would you like to take a walk, maybe? We could go to the beach." But Sally made no move to get up, so after a moment Frances sat down on the edge of the bed too. It felt good to sit. She had not realized how tired she was, a tiredness that went beyond the normal fatigue of travel. She beat back the thought that soon she would be in San Francisco.

"What did you like about the tree?" she asked.

"It seemed strong," said Sally. "It didn't need anyone else. It was alone, but it was all right." She dug into the carpet with her toe. "Or maybe," she said, "it wishes it had other trees around it. I wish I could tell Mrs. Wolf about it. She'd like it too."

"I think," said Frances after a moment, "that you have a wise soul, Sally."

Sally looked up. She blinked a few times rapidly. Then she straightened, looking at Frances with something approaching scorn.

"But it's only a tree, after all," she said derisively.

CHAPTER

EIGHTEEN

The Convent School of the Precious Blood had the look of an English manor house. Stately and somewhat forbidding, it sat on a large parcel of land in Hillsborough, in a neighborhood where beautiful old homes were shaded by oaks and the lack of sidewalks made it feel like being in the country.

A nun greeted them and brought them into a parlor with faded rugs and mullioned windows. A statue of St. Anne stood on a niche in the corner, and a large painting of a golden-haired Madonna hung over the fireplace.

"I'm Sister Mary Constance," said the nun. She was tall and quite pretty; the veil hiding her hair only served to highlight her classical features. Mr. Merrill introduced himself and Frances, and the nun smiled warmly. "And you must be Sarah," she said.

Sally, who was standing with her satchel clutched awkwardly to her side, nodded. "Sally."

"Sally. Welcome to the convent." Sister offered them tea, but Mr. Merrill declined, citing their need to continue on to San Francisco. The nun took them on a brief tour, showing them the first floor: the chapel, a wood-paneled library, a refectory with high windows.

"Men are not allowed in the dormitories, Mr. Merrill," said the nun, "but perhaps Miss Healey would like to come up and see Sally's room?"

Sally looked at Frances with pleading eyes. "Of course," said Frances.

They left Mr. Merrill in the parlor while Sister took them up a wide oak staircase and along a cool, dark corridor lined with doors alternating with framed art of religious subjects. A somewhat garish Sacred Heart of Jesus lithograph glowed right next to the door on the far end, which Sister opened to show a small room, sparse but clean. A crucifix hung over each of the twin beds, and a surprisingly large window gave a beautiful view of the front drive and the oaks.

"You will be sharing this room," said Sister, "when the school year begins. The other girls will arrive in a little over a month."

"There are no other students here at present?" asked Frances.

"Not yet," said Sister. "Your father arranged for you to come early, Sally. We are happy to have you."

Frances cast a glance at Sally. She was holding the satchel tightly as if she feared it would be taken away.

"What will I do each day?" asked Sally.

"You may help us catalog the books in the library; it's a big task. The chapel is always open for prayer. And you may walk around the school grounds, of course." Her eye fell on the bed. "It seems you don't have a pillow," she said. "Let me go get one. Explore the hall, if you'd like."

They listened to her footsteps down the echoing corridor. "I didn't know I'd be the only girl here," said Sally, looking almost frightened.

"I didn't either," said Frances. She cast about for some way to make it less terrifying. "Perhaps it will be nice. Like a peaceful vacation."

"But what will I do?"

"There's a library. I'm sure you can read."

"I don't think they have anything I'd want to read," said Sally. "Oh. That reminds me." She opened her satchel, took out *Sons and*

Lovers, and gave it to Frances reluctantly. "Will you keep this for me? I probably can't have it here."

Frances put the book in her own bag, then on an impulse took out her steno pad. She tore out the used pages and handed the pad to Sally. "Take this. You can use it to write a story, maybe, or a description of the convent. Or you can interview the nuns about their lives."

"I don't think they have lives."

"Well," said Frances, "you never know. But when I was thirteen, I always felt better when I had a notebook next to me."

Sally held the steno pad tightly. Her eyes were bright, and she blinked as if keeping back tears. She looked like what she was: a child about to be left alone with strangers, and Frances felt a fresh wave of compassion. She squeezed Sally's elbow, as Rita always used to do. "Write to me whenever you like," she said. "I promise I'll write back quickly."

A glimmer of hope came into Sally's eyes. "That makes two people I can write to," she said. "Mrs. Wolf, and you."

And your father, Frances thought. She opened her mouth to say so and then closed it again, keenly aware that she had no right to preach what she did not practice.

Mr. Merrill was quiet as they got into the car and drove out of the convent grounds. Sally stood on the top of the steps watching them go, an insubstantial figure in comparison to the nun beside her in the imposing black habit.

"I hope this wasn't a mistake," he said suddenly. "Leaving her here. But I can't bring her to meet Miss Ridley. That's going to call for delicacy, and you never know with Sally."

"Perhaps," Frances said. "I suppose everything is unknown at this point."

"Yes," he said with more force. "It certainly is." He glanced in the mirror as if trying to see the convent one last time. "At least the nuns seemed kind. Sally didn't speak in the accent, did you notice? That's a good sign."

Frances was silent.

"You don't seem to agree," he said after a pause.

She wasn't sure how honest to be, but the memory of Sally's eyes, bright with tears in the dormitory room, decided her. "Sally has spirit. It's inconvenient, yes. But it means she isn't defeated."

He said nothing for a long while. Just as she was beginning to worry about her candor he said, "For someone who is not a parent, you're very wise, Miss Healey. And I feel like a real heel, somehow."

She could not in good faith contradict him. And she had no chance to do so, because he was suddenly frowning at the street sign.

"I think we're going around in circles," he said as they drove past a paddock where a chestnut horse stood, swishing its tail. "I remember that horse. How do we get back to El Camino?"

"Go straight," she said. "Then take a left, then a right. Then you'll see it."

He turned to look at her, and she felt her color rise.

"I grew up not far from here." Her heart was beating fast. "A mile or so."

"I had no idea. So this is your home."

"In a manner of speaking. I haven't been back in five years."

He gave her one more sidelong glance but said nothing. "Take this left," she said, and he did.

CHAPTER

NINETEEN

I n her younger years, Frances had made many visits to Union Square in San Francisco, though she'd never before stayed at the imposing St. Francis Hotel. Her room on the sixth floor had an enviable view of the square, with its palm trees and flower beds and the column topped by a statue of a woman holding a trident and a laurel wreath. Couples and families were strolling around the paths, even though the day was foggy and cool. After a quick glance, she closed the curtains, watching the thick folds settle stiffly into place.

Only a few blocks beyond the square was North Beach, with its Italian groceries and restaurants and the twin white spires of the church of Saints Peter and Paul overlooking Washington Square. It was the neighborhood where she had stayed at the home of Rita's cousin Lucia, who kept a café that served very dark coffee and where a group of old men would come every day. In her memory she could still retrieve the cadence of their voices as they spoke in Italian. She'd picked up a few phrases, even, which had delighted them. "Francesca," they had called her. The name made her sound like another person, exotic and elegant, and in certain moments she could pretend to be so, could forget the reality and the wreckage she had left behind.

Frances drew the curtains more closely together, running her fingers over the gold flocking of the fabric. Tomorrow they would talk to Miss Ridley, and then the next day they would get back into the car and drive south again. It was July 21 now; with any luck they would be back in Hollywood on the twenty-fourth. As she did every July, she longed for the month to be over. She longed to be back in Hollywood, a place where most of the drama was manufactured, not real, a place where the sun shone freely and there was none of the fog that made even a summer's day feel raw.

As arranged, she met Mr. Merrill in the lobby at six. He was sitting in one of the leather armchairs, and it occurred to her that outside of Hollywood, he was effectively incognito. The people moving about the palatial lobby knew the movies he had produced, had regularly seen his name on the big screen, but would pass right by him without knowing who he was.

He saw her and stood up. "Ready for dinner? We could eat here or go out if you're feeling adventurous."

"I'd rather stay here."

At the hotel restaurant, the maître d' gave them a table for two near the window. "It's a lovely view of the square," he said, but Frances took the chair with her back to it.

"So," Mr. Merrill said after they had ordered, "tomorrow we close in on our quarry. The elusive Miss Ridley." He lit a cigarette; then, as if it had just occurred to him to do so, he offered her one.

"No, thank you," she said. "Do you know what you are going to say to Miss Ridley?"

"I've been mentally scripting it these last few days. It's all guesswork, of course. Who knows how the conversation will go."

"Would it help to practice? I could pretend to be her."

He grinned, then looked thoughtful. "Actually," he said as the waiter set down their drinks, "that's a not a bad idea. Let's try it."

The waiter left and Frances sat up straight, her shoulders deliberately back, doing her best to make her expression imperious. A flicker of amusement and respect crossed Mr. Merrill's face behind the screen of smoke. He put down the cigarette, folded his hands, and looked squarely at her. "Miss Ridley? It would be an honor for me to help tell the story of your life."

"You aren't telling the story of my life," Frances said with energy. "You are telling a bunch of lies."

He looked taken aback, and she dropped character. "Too much?"

He shrugged. "I have no idea. Maybe not." He took a sip of his drink, then assumed the expression she knew well: that of the producer, confident and sure he will prevail, who is nevertheless listening seriously to another's concerns. "Miss Ridley," he said earnestly, "it's a sign of the power of your name that we are making this film. Even decades later there is so much interest in you and your story."

"I know how old I am," said Frances frostily. "And I know how famous I am."

"Indeed. And you deserve the best people to tell your story. We've got Hollywood's brightest talent on this picture. The director will be Simon Kerr. You've seen *Drums of Revolution*?"

"I don't see movies. I rarely leave the house." It was heady, playing someone else; the character seemed to come without any effort.

"Well, all the people working on this project, from the director on down the line, are the very best at what they do."

"And the woman who will play me?"

"Belinda Vail. You've seen her, perhaps. *Heaven for the King*?"

"I've just told you I don't go to the pictures."

"Well, she's one of Hollywood's rising stars. Beautiful, a stunning girl."

"Many girls are beautiful. Why was she chosen for the role?"

"She wants to play a fascinating, complex part. All actresses do." He nodded deferentially. "As you know."

"So you give someone a part just because she wants it. Has she proven herself?"

"She's a good actress."

"Just good?"

"Fine. She's a fine actress, very much in demand at the moment."

"Fine and good," said Frances. "But not exceptional. Because if she were, you would have said so."

She was stopped by the expression on his face. His mask of executive persuasion had dropped; he was surprised. She could not tell if he was also angry.

"I'm sorry," she said, honestly contrite. "Maybe I got a little carried away."

He was still staring at her. After a moment, he reached for his drink.

"I think that's enough for now," he said quietly.

At eleven o'clock the next morning, they were in the car once again. This time they drove west, across the wide bustling axis of Van Ness, into Pacific Heights. The Victorian houses sitting shoulder to shoulder were all different colors, pastels mostly, their big bay windows looking out onto the street. One had to concede, thought Frances, trying to see the city as a tourist, that there was a unique charm to San Francisco.

They passed a large park that took up an entire city block. "That must be Alta Plaza," said Mr. Merrill, glancing at the map on Frances's lap. "Her house should be a block or two beyond it." The famously hilly streets sloped down north of the park; Frances caught a glimpse of the bay in the distance. It was quieter here, in the largely residential area, than it had been around Union Square.

Mr. Merrill parked on Jackson Street, and they found their destination, a light blue house with a gabled roof and bay windows and white gingerbread detailing. It sat snugly between two other houses, giving no clue as to the illustrious woman who lived inside. They stared at it in silence for a moment. "Well," said Mr. Merrill at last, "here we go."

There was a small flight of steps leading to the front door. They had to stand very close on the diminutive landing, almost flank to flank. Mr. Merrill pushed the buzzer.

There was the sound of footsteps, too vigorous for a woman in her nineties, and the door was pulled open by a woman in a blue housedress and apron, with graying curly hair and brown eyes.

"Good morning," said Mr. Merrill, removing his hat. "I'm Lawrence Merrill, of VistaGlen Studios. This is my secretary, Miss Healey. You are Mrs. Martino?"

"Oh, yes," said the woman. "The man from the pictures. I bet you want to see Miss Ridley."

"I know this is unexpected, but is she available?"

"No. She's in Napa."

"Pardon me?"

"In Napa Valley. Up north," said Mrs. Martino. "That's where she lives, mostly."

"Forgive me," said Mr. Merrill after a moment, "but the letter came from this address. When we spoke, you said . . ."

"Yes, I know," said Mrs. Martino. "I didn't know she was going up there again so quickly. But she left a letter in case you came." She moved out of the frame of the door for a moment, revealing a wall and an empty coatrack, then reappeared with a letter. "She's at the Ventimiglias."

"Where?"

"The Ventimiglias. The family she lives with up there."

"I see." Underneath his polite facade, Frances could tell he was both perplexed and irritated. "Is there a way to reach her?"

"She says so in the letter, I think." She gave a smile, as if to communicate her lack of control over her employer's whims. "I'm sorry."

"Of course." Lawrence nodded. "Thank you, Mrs. Martino."

She closed the door, and they silently descended the stairs.

On the sidewalk he held the letter so they could both read it. It was typed, as the first one had been.

Dear Mr. Merrill,

If you are reading this, you have come looking for me. I don't know why, as my wishes were very clear. But I do know something about the world of entertainment and the tenacity of the men who run it.

I've returned to the Napa Valley, which is where I live most of the time. I suppose it can function as a test. If you come looking for me, I will know how much you want to make this movie. It will not change my mind, but at least I will be able to tell you so in person. I live on the Ventimiglia farm outside St. Helena.

Sincerely,

Kitty Ridley

Frances glanced at Mr. Merrill. He looked up at the sky, swore under his breath, then read the letter again.

"So we have a choice," he said as he folded the paper. "We either admit defeat and go back to Hollywood, or we give it one more chance."

"She did tell us where to find her. I don't think she'd do that if there was no possibility of changing her mind."

"Perhaps." He handed her the letter, and she put it in her pocketbook. He took out a cigarette and lit it, then smoked for a moment, looking at the house across the street.

"We've come this far," he said at last. "Wasted this much time. If there's any little chance, we'd better take it."

"I agree."

"Do you know anything about Napa?"

"No, I've never been." She thought of pictures she had seen once in a book: golden hills with widely spaced oaks, and vineyards in neat, regular rows like decorative braid. "They make wine there; that's all I know."

He glanced at his watch. "Let's go back to the hotel. I'll call Irving and Simon, tell them we'll be a little longer. How long does it take to get to Napa?"

"I'm not sure. We'll have to take the ferry across the bay. No, wait," she said suddenly. "There's the bridge now."

He looked up, a flicker of interest tempering his mood. "Right. The Golden Gate. Have you seen it?"

"Not finished, no. I remember it being built."

"I guess we'll see it now, won't we? Our reward for going on this wild goose chase." He ground out the cigarette on the pavement. "Let's go back to the hotel. There's some work I can do long distance, and I'll have to." He smiled grimly. "An early dinner tonight, and then an early start tomorrow. Time to beard Miss Ridley in her den."

After another dinner in the hotel restaurant, Mr. Merrill went out for a walk. He invited Frances along, but she declined, choosing to go up to her room and read. But she found it hard to focus; her mind kept drifting and, as before, she found herself staring at the gold-flocked curtains. It was going to be a longer trip than she had expected, and she should let Audrey know. She slipped her shoes back on, combed her hair, and went down to the telephone booths in the lobby.

She half expected there to be no answer, but Audrey picked up the phone after one ring. "No date tonight?" Frances teased her. "I leave you for a few days, and the world turns upside down."

"I've got a cold," said Audrey. She sneezed. "I had to cancel with Fred."

"Colds don't usually stop you."

"He's not the fellow who gave it to me. It would have been awkward."

"I'm sorry you're all alone. I'd make you chicken soup if I were there. Or buy it, at least."

"I know. And thanks." There was a pause while Audrey blew her nose vigorously. "So how is your trip?"

Frances filled her in briefly, mindful of the cost of the call. "So I'll be gone a few days longer than I thought. Could you water the African violet in the kitchen window? It won't last until I get back."

"You trust me to keep it alive?"

"I don't have a choice, do I?"

"I'll try. If I can keep myself alive, that is." She sneezed loudly. "Oh, and you got a letter today."

"Who is it from?"

"Wait a second." There was a pause, then Audrey came back to the phone. "R. Iovetti. I probably said that wrong. Burlingame, California."

Frances felt her heart beat faster.

"Frances?"

"I'm still here." She wrapped the cord around her finger so tightly that it hurt. "Audrey? Will you read me the letter?"

"Okay." There was a rustle of paper. "Dear Frances: I am glad you sent your address. I hope you are happy in Hollywood. We are all good here. All except your father. He's in a bad way, Frances. I think you should call home or visit if you can. I know it is hard for you to come back, but I thought you should know. If you want to talk to me, your stepmother has Ladies' Club on Tuesdays at two and Garden Guild on Saturday at ten, so she will not be there if you call. I pray for you every night and God bless you. Sincerely yours, Rita Iovetti."

Frances stared out at the lobby, where a well-dressed woman was carrying a small lapdog under her arm.

"Frances?"

"I'm still here. Thank you."

"Sure," Audrey said gently. "Whatever it is, I hope things are okay."

"Me too. Bye, Audrey."

She replaced the phone and stood staring at the wall. The phone cubicle was paneled in dark wood, with a printed and framed sign of helpful local numbers, but she did not see it. She was remembering the last time she had seen her father, more than five years earlier, in the driveway of the family home. Mother Florence had not come outside, but he had waited as the taxi drove her off to the city. He looked lost, she remembered, standing irresolutely next to the rosebushes that Mother Florence had suggested he plant along the driveway, rosebushes that would catch the fabric of one's clothes if one parked too far to the left. He stood there and his face, normally gentle and benign, had an expression that was new to her. It was the expression of a man who had failed and who knew he had.

He had risked a lot to stand out there in the early dusk, where the nosy Mrs. Gould could see him. She was the sort of woman who would call, "Frances is going away, then? She just got home," and leave a wide, wondering space that had to be filled with an answer. He could have said a quick goodbye and gone back inside, avoiding that pause while the taxi driver stowed the bags, that long pause when the person staying behind can do nothing but stand there, conspicuous to the world. But he had not gone inside. He had stood there, in his green cardigan, as if keeping vigil. She had been the one invisible in the back seat of the taxi, blinking through tears, gripping her handbag with both hands.

Shaken, she swiftly left the phone cubicle. A man in an evening suit reflexively smiled as she walked past him; then his expression changed to alarm as he saw her face. The ladies' room was a few feet away, and she kept her head down as she hurried inside.

After washing and drying her face, she surveyed herself in the mirror. No powder anymore, no rouge; she looked as she felt, vulnerable and without armor. But she needed only to make it up to her room, and then she could be alone.

As she walked toward the elevator, she could hear music from a band playing in one of the ballrooms. People were dancing, laughing, enjoying themselves. *He's in a bad way*, Rita had said. What did that mean, exactly?

She stepped aside to let a woman, impressive in a mink coat, sail past on the arm of a distinguished-looking man. And behind the woman, a newspaper tucked under his arm, was Mr. Merrill. He smiled at her. "Miss Healey."

"Mr. Merrill," she managed to say.

He indicated Union Square with a tip of his head. "Amazing how much colder it is up here. I'm glad I brought my overcoat." Then he stopped, surveying her more closely. "Is something wrong?"

Her powder room efforts had clearly been in vain. She was ready to demur, to deny, but there was genuine concern in his eyes.

"I phoned my roommate," she found herself saying. "And there was a letter for me from home. It's my father. He's—not doing well." She rummaged in her bag to find a handkerchief, an action that was made more difficult by the tears that were beginning to fall. He put a hand on her arm.

"Here. Let's sit down."

He led her to an upholstered armchair. She sat in one and he sat in its fellow, handing her a handkerchief and waiting as she blotted her eyes.

In secretarial school, the head instructor, Mrs. Meese, had been adamant about the need to keep one's personal life separate from one's work. "Your employer does not need to know about anything unrelated to the office," she had told the class of young women. "You are there to support him, not the other way around. He is an employer, not a pal." She had said the word *pal*, Frances recalled, as if she were not used to using it; it sounded odd coming from the mouth of the severely dressed older woman.

But here, with the studio and her typewriter and Sherwin and every other reminder of Hollywood far away, the instruction was easy to ignore. Mr. Merrill was leaning forward in his chair, his eyes on her, curious and concerned, not neutral. It was not the look he had in Hollywood.

"Has your father been ill?" he asked.

"The letter didn't say. Only that he was in a bad way."

"You said you grew up in the area. Your family still lives here?"

"Yes. But I haven't seen them in years. Or spoken with them either." Her hands tightened around her handbag. "They have my address, but I don't write." To her own ears it sounded like a shameful admission. "It's . . . just some things that happened. Long ago."

"It's all right, Miss Healey," he said. "I won't pry." She thought about Sally, and the messy dynamics between father and daughter. Mr. Merrill, she realized, was unlikely to judge her for a lack of filial loyalty.

"But I don't know what it means," she said. "The letter was from Rita, the housekeeper. She said he was in a bad way, and I don't know what that means."

"We can go tomorrow and find out." He corrected himself. "You could go; I wouldn't intrude, of course."

Frances had a sudden image of Mrs. Meese's eyes widening in alarm. "But we have to go to Napa."

"We'll go after you see your father. It's not that far."

"It will make us late."

"A few hours, maybe. It's not like Miss Ridley is expecting us at a certain time."

"But you have so much work to do."

His eyes were direct, sympathetic. "Miss Healey? You must see that this is the least I can do for you."

She looked down, uncertain, kneading the strap of her pocketbook.

"It's your decision," he said. "But a delay of one day hardly matters anymore. And it won't change my opinion of you, no matter what you decide. I understand the complexity of the parent-child relationship." He gave a wry smile. "As you know."

She thought of her father standing in the driveway. His tie, normally so neat, had been askew. It was a tiny thing, but it had made him look even more vulnerable. Perhaps that was why she had deliberately suppressed the memory of it for years. But now she saw it again, the blue tie under his green cardigan, tilted to one side as if everything were out of whack, and she remembered that she had longed to straighten it but could not.

"I don't know," she said again.

"You're the only one who can decide," he said. "But for what it's worth, Miss Healey: I think this is the first information about yourself and your past that you have ever offered voluntarily."

She looked up at him, realizing he was right.

"And I think . . ."—his voice was quiet, gentle—"I think that might mean something."

CHAPTER
TWENTY

hey set out for Burlingame immediately after breakfast. It was a fine, bright day, and the city sparkled as if delighted to be out of the fog. On the drive Mr. Merrill brought up a few inconsequential subjects, and Frances responded, but she was preoccupied by thoughts of the impending reunion with her father.

As they drove down El Camino Real, lined with eucalyptus trees, they passed the street that had taken them to the convent.

"I wonder how Sally is doing," Mr. Merrill said. He, like Frances, glanced down the street as they motored by. "We won't be too far from there, will we?"

"Only a mile or so."

"I thought of stopping by the convent while you're with your family," he said, "but I'm afraid of upsetting the apple cart. I'll give her some time to settle in. We can see her on the drive back down instead."

There was silence. "Is that what you would do?" he asked when she did not respond.

"I don't know," she said. "I don't know what I would do." It was the truth; her mind was too focused on the upcoming visit to absorb anything else.

"I'm sorry," he said. "I shouldn't make my domestic dramas your own. But I trust your judgment, Miss Healey."

Even with all the tension flooding her body, even though she was dreading the next turn of the car, she registered the compliment. "Thank you," she said, then added, her heart pounding, "Take the next right."

He pulled across the street from the white Colonial with green trim, underneath trees that had grown taller in the last five years. There were still the rosebushes by the drive, with the cool, ice-white blooms that Frances had always disliked. There was no car in the driveway; there would not be, of course, with Mother Florence at her meeting. Frances clutched her handbag, almost regretting her decision to come.

"Miss Healey?" Mr. Merrill was looking at her intently. "Are you all right?"

Back in the office, she had excelled at keeping her face from showing her true feelings. Maintaining an expression of pleasant efficiency was an essential skill for a secretary, as important as typing or shorthand. But here, as she sat outside her childhood home, there was no face she could wear but her own.

"Are you all right?" he asked again.

Turn around and leave, she wanted to say, but she thought of Rita's letter and found her courage. "I think so."

He hesitated. "I was going to go for a walk, but I could stay. In case you need to leave sooner than you expected. I'll wait in the car."

"No," she found herself saying. "No, please come in with me. Will you?"

He looked surprised, and then his face cleared. He briefly touched her arm. "Of course," he said.

On the front porch Frances pressed the bell, its familiar ringtone audible even from the outside. After a few moments, she heard footsteps, and Rita opened the door. Her expression changed swiftly from shock to joy; then Frances was engulfed in as fierce a hug as she had ever known.

"Oh, lovey," said Rita, her voice breaking. "Thank goodness."

In the gilt-edged mirror, Frances could see her own face, white against the green pattern of Rita's housedress. She scanned the background but did not see her father.

Rita released her, tears in her eyes. "You came. I knew you would once you got my letter." Her gaze moved to Mr. Merrill, who took off his hat.

"Rita," said Frances, "this is—"

"Lawrence," said Mr. Merrill. "Lawrence Merrill. It's nice to meet you."

Rita nodded, then opened the door. "Come in, both of you."

"Where's Father?"

"He's here." Rita closed the door behind them. "He's—well, you'll see," she said, just as Frances heard a shuffling movement and her father, leaning on a cane, appeared around the corner from the living room.

His hair was grayer than before and sticking out on one side. His green cardigan was awkwardly buttoned, one button off. His face, though friendly and open, was blank of recognition.

"Hello," he said politely to Frances and Lawrence; then, turning to Rita, he asked, "Who is she?"

CHAPTER
TWENTY·ONE

I t was a joke, thought Frances at first, an uncharacteristically cruel nod to her five years away. But the sting was quickly replaced by the cold, terrible awareness that it was not a joke at all. She saw the cane, the slippers—her father never wore slippers in midday—the egg yolk stain on the front of his shirt, the pallor in his face.

"You know her, Mr. Healey," said Rita, her voice slower and more deliberate than usual. She opened her mouth to say more, but before she could, Frances saw her father's face change, saw the vacant look leave his eyes.

"Frances?" he asked.

"Yes, Father. It's me."

"I haven't seen you in a long time," said her father. "Have I?" he asked, turning to Rita, who shook her head.

"Well," he said, "let's come in the . . ." He turned toward the living room, then paused, as if searching for the word. "In the—"

"Living room, Mr. Healey," said Rita quietly.

"Yes. The living room." He started toward the sofa. "And you," he said, turning back to Mr. Merrill. "Do I know you?"

"No, Mr. Healey. My name is Lawrence Merrill."

"You live across the street, don't you?"

"No. I live in Hollywood."

"Ah. And you, Frances? Where do you live?"

"I live in Hollywood too."

"We got a letter from her, Mr. Healey," said Rita. "Remember?"

"A letter. Well, I am glad to see you, Frances." He eased himself into his favorite wing chair, and Frances moved to help him. His bicep felt thin under his sweater. "I missed you."

There was a glimmer of recognition in his eyes as he said it, which made Frances begin to cry as she sat down on the sofa. Mr. Merrill, holding his hat, sat down quietly on the other end.

"There, now," said Mr. Healey, seeing his daughter's tears. "You need a . . ." He frowned. "A . . . for you. That thing. Maybe I have one." He looked in his left pocket as if searching for a handkerchief, but not the right pocket. "Now where is it?"

A woman appeared from the dining room, a middle-aged blonde woman with a white nurse's uniform and a pleasant face. At the sight of her, Mr. Merrill rose politely to his feet.

"Visitors, Mr. Healey? How nice. Who are they?"

Rita started to answer, but the nurse raised a hand to stop her.

Frances's father frowned, looking at the guests. "It's my daughter," he said after a moment. "And . . . I haven't been introduced to this man yet."

The nurse looked at Frances as if assessing the accuracy of the information, and then she smiled. "I'm Nurse Brower," she said. "It's nice to meet you." She turned to Mr. Healey. "Let me help you change that shirt, Mr. Healey."

"I can't. I'm going to miss the doctor."

"He won't come until one o'clock. Remember? One o'clock. It's ten thirty now." She helped him out of the chair.

"I need to eat breakfast," he said as she led him away.

"You had breakfast. You had a soft-boiled egg, remember? And lunch will be in an hour or so." The door closed behind them.

Rita turned to Frances. "I know it's a shock, but he's better than he was, lovey."

"Rita. What happened?"

"A stroke. Happened at work, five weeks ago. He said his side felt numb and then he collapsed. He was in the hospital, and he's back now. The nurse comes every day."

"He—he didn't know me at first."

"It's like that now. He forgets things you've told him. This morning I mentioned the doctor's appointment, and he can't understand it's hours away. Thinks the doctor is coming at any minute. And he can't remember words sometimes; you heard him."

"Will he get better?"

"Probably, they say. It's different for each person, I guess, but the doctor is hopeful. And there are moments when it's the old him, like he used to be. His begonia garden—he remembers it. He was just complaining today about the weeds; he knows they don't belong there. So it's still him, under the forgetting."

"I had no idea, Rita. I had no idea."

"Of course not, lovey. But when you heard, you came." She smiled at Frances, sadly and fondly. "What are you doing up here, anyhow? You got here so quick."

"I'm—we're on our way to Napa. For work. It's for a film we're making." Before she could say more, she heard the unmistakable sound of heels on the front walk, coming up to the porch.

"Who could that be?" said Rita, rising from her chair. A moment later, the door opened and Mother Florence, in a blue suit with a gray fox fur stole and a hat with a veil, came into the entry hall, pausing to check her hair in the mirror.

"Rita," she called, not seeing Frances at first. "That list of volunteers for the harvest ball—have you seen it?"

Before Rita could answer, Mother Florence turned toward the living room and stopped short. Mr. Merrill once again rose to his feet, and Frances instinctively did the same. Mother Florence stared at her and Frances met her gaze.

"Well," said Mother Florence at last. "You came back, I see."

Frances attempted to smile. "How are you, Mother Florence?"

"Very well, thank you, Frances." Mother Florence's gaze slid to Mr. Merrill, who nodded courteously.

"Lawrence Merrill, Mrs. Healey. It's nice to meet you."

Mother Florence nodded once, then turned back to Frances, her eyes darting unmistakably to Frances's left hand as if looking for a ring. Her hair seemed blacker than before, and there were lines around her mouth and eyes that Frances did not remember. But there was the same cold formality and glacial restraint as always, though with a current of something else underneath, a palpable tension. Rita cleared her throat.

"There's coffee on the stove," she said to Mr. Merrill. "Maybe you'd like to come have some, Mr. . . . ."

"Yes," said Mr. Merrill, after first glancing at Frances. "Excuse me, please." He nodded to Frances and Mother Florence and followed Rita out of the room.

"So," said Mother Florence. "You're back. For the day? For good?"

"For the day. I'm on my way north."

"Alone?"

"With Mr. Merrill. I'm his secretary."

"His secretary," said Mother Florence. "I see." Her gaze flicked down Frances's body, and then she turned toward the mahogany desk. "I just came back to find the list I need for the meeting." She opened the drawer, found a paper, and took an envelope as well.

"You've seen your father?" she asked without turning.

"I had no idea. I'm—I'm sorry."

"I'm sure you are." The voice was still glacial, but there was a crack in it, a hint of something other than ice. She folded the paper, creasing it sharply. "He doesn't deserve this. He doesn't deserve any of it."

"I know."

"He gets by all right with the nurse, and with Rita here. But we can't leave him alone. I button his shirts for him every morning. He can't even button his own shirt." For a moment she paused, the paper halfway into the envelope. She seemed to sag, losing her normally perfect posture; then she mastered herself.

She turned around, and the two women looked at each other. Neither of them spoke.

"Well," said Mother Florence, at last. "Perhaps I'll see you again. If you care to come back sometime." She put the envelope in her pocketbook and snapped it shut. "Mrs. Burke is waiting for me in the car. Goodbye, Frances."

"Goodbye."

Her heels clicked as she moved to the front door; then she paused and turned back to her stepdaughter.

"Tell me this, Frances," she said suddenly. "Was it all worth it?"

Frances stared at her, unable to respond. And she was saved from having to do so by the sound of someone coming up the walk, a sound that made Mother Florence's face change, the intensity in her gaze becoming an expression of pleasant assurance. She opened the door and left, closing it swiftly behind her. "You were such a time, Florence," came a woman's voice, and Mother Florence said, "Oh yes, I'm afraid the list wasn't where I left it," and they went down the walkway, and Frances was alone.

She heard the car drive away, and birdsong from the maple outside. She heard the back door opening and closing; someone had gone into the garden. She heard Rita running water in the kitchen. And she could not stop hearing Mother Florence's question, which echoed in her mind like the clang of a cymbal.

When she went into the kitchen, Mr. Merrill was gone. "He went out to see the garden," said Rita. She offered Frances coffee and cake, and they sat in the breakfast nook, talking. It would have felt like old times except for the weight of the topic discussed and

Frances's awareness of her father, like a ghost of his former self, as he passed through the room in a clean shirt and properly buttoned cardigan. He remembered her this time, but he did not remember that they had already seen each other once that morning; he asked about her high school friends but could not recall that she was living in Hollywood. It was disconcerting, the dip in and out of memory. After a while, he moved slowly outside to the back garden, Frances opening the door for him. As he passed she realized that he smelled the same as ever, of Ivory soap and a hint of the aftershave he always wore.

"Can he shave himself?" she asked Rita, who shook her head.

"Your stepmother—she does it for him. Every morning. And I've never heard her complain either."

Twenty minutes later, Frances went out in the garden. It looked well-tended, the lawn newly cut; Rita had said the sixteen-year-old boy across the street came weekly to do it. The privet tree, which Frances had climbed and where she had incurred the ire of Mrs. Gould, was laden with the odd-smelling flowers it had each summer.

As she stood by a rosebush listening to the birds, she heard the sound of a trowel being set down on the concrete path and the murmur of a voice. She followed the sounds behind the garage, to her father's garden.

Her father was sitting on a stool on the concrete path, looking at the begonias. Next to him was Mr. Merrill. He was kneeling, using the trowel to loosen the soil, then pulling weeds and putting them into an aluminum bucket. His coat was off, as was his tie, both of which were folded neatly on the path. The sleeves of his shirt were rolled up to the elbows, and from behind she could see the back of his head, a slight thinning of the hair that she had never seen before, the breadth of his shoulders under the cotton shirt, the edge of an undershirt just visible as he leaned forward and stretched for a weed.

"That's a big one," her father said as Mr. Merrill moved back on his heels and dropped a large weed, bits of dirt still clinging to its roots, into the bucket.

"It is," said Mr. Merrill. "It's good to get that one out."

He worked and her father sat quietly, watching him. He seemed at peace, in a way he had not in the house. There was an ease between the two men, so palpable that Frances hated to speak and break the moment. Tears blurred her vision.

"Frances used to climb that tree, you know," said her father. "That privet."

"It looks like a good climbing tree."

Mr. Merrill pulled up another weed, knocking dirt off of its roots. He held it out to Frances's father, who nodded in satisfaction.

"Another big one," said her father. He took it in his left hand and Mr. Merrill moved the aluminum bucket a little closer, and her father dropped it in. It landed with a distinct thud, a small but satisfying sound.

As Mr. Merrill started the car half an hour later, Frances looked at his hands. There was dirt under the nails as he held the steering wheel. She had been silent as they walked to the car, silent as she waved to Rita on the front step, but now she spoke.

"Thank you," she said. "For helping my father in the garden."

"It was a little thing I could do. It seemed to distress him to see the weeds."

They drove on, the only sound the tread of tires.

"Are you all right?" he asked gently.

"No," she said. "No, I'm not." And she began to cry.

It was like the flipping of a switch; all of the feeling poured out of her in sobs, the kind she could not control. After a moment, she was aware that he was pulling the car to the side of the road. He parked and slid along the seat and put his arms around her and held her against his chest as she cried.

In any other context it would have felt odd; she would have been acutely aware of the strangeness of it. But the feelings of shock and pain were so strong they left no room for anything else.

CHAPTER
TWENTY-TWO

The drive back up to the city was quiet at first. Frances, spent by her crying and the emotion of seeing her father, was disinclined to talk. She leaned back and closed her eyes as Mr. Merrill started the car and turned back onto El Camino Real, only opening them after they had crossed the border into Millbrae.

As they drove on, Mr. Merrill spoke casually of trivial things: the weather, the eucalyptus trees along the road, the theater that was showing Paramount's latest picture. Gradually, Frances began to relax. She even laughed at his anecdote about an embarrassing misspelling on a marquee for a picture he had once produced.

"Are you hungry?" he asked at one point. "We could stop for lunch."

"No. I had some of Rita's cake."

They drove a mile or so before she spoke again. "Thank you, Mr. Merrill. For taking me there."

"You're welcome." He was silent, as if waiting to see if she wanted to talk about the visit, but she did not. Another city block passed before he spoke.

"I was thinking," he said, "that while we're out of the office, it's awkward for you to call me Mr. Merrill. Please call me Lawrence." There was a small pause as she, surprised, absorbed this. "If you care to."

"All right," she said. Then she added, frankly, "I can't promise that it will be easy."

"Understood."

"Then you should probably call me Frances."

"It's a nice name. We almost called Sally that."

"Really?"

"It was my mother's middle name. But my wife wanted to call her Sarah, which became Sally."

Frances watched as a blue coupe passed in front of them, a small boy looking out the center of the back seat window. He gazed at them, his chin resting on his hands. "Sally told me that she used to live with her grandparents in England."

"For a few years, until she was ten. Then she came back here, to school in La Jolla and then Tarrytown. She spent last summer in England."

"But not this summer?"

"No. They're getting older; it's harder to have a young girl about." He rolled down the window. "I often wish my mother were still alive. Sally never knew her."

"What was your mother like?"

"Kind, efficient. A pillar of the community. And good with her children. She would have known what to do with Sally."

"Where did she live?"

"Cooperstown, New York. A little colonial town near a lake, surrounded by forests. Very different from anything in California."

"The forests are what surprised me most," she said. "When I went East."

"When were you there?"

"For college. Bryn Mawr."

"That's a beautiful campus."

"It was." She shifted in her seat, opened her pocketbook unnecessarily, closed it again.

"You know," he said suddenly, "I thought of my mother when I was in the garden today. I thought about how she would have given Sally a trowel and told her to weed and not come back until the weeds were gone. That was her answer for most things. Something physical to get you outside of yourself."

"It's good advice," she said, then added, experimentally, "Lawrence."

He grinned. "See? That wasn't so hard."

"Actually, it was. I've been working up to it for the whole conversation."

He laughed. A few moments later, he began to whistle "Begin the Beguine," with perfect pitch. She looked out the window at the passing buildings, feeling closer to happy than she had at any time that day.

F rances was unprepared for the impact of the Golden Gate Bridge. Out of nowhere, there were suddenly rectangular towers, reddish orange against the blue sky. She made an audible exclamation of surprise, and Lawrence slowed the car to stare, apparently unaware he was doing so until a driver honked behind him.

Frances was glad she was not behind the wheel so she could tilt her head back and gaze freely. The towers under which they drove were astonishingly high. Her eyes followed the massive cables in their graceful upward arc, and she marveled at the weight they were supporting, all the cars and people. A gull settled on the rail, and she looked past it to the right, to Alcatraz off in the distance, plain and forbidding. There were boats on the bay, and there was the city itself, with buildings running down to the water. But to her left there was only the narrow mouth of the bay, framed by cliffs, and the vast ocean beyond.

She remembered learning in school about how explorers had sailed along the coast of California and passed right by the bay, its entrance concealed by fog. It looked like any other bit of coastline, yet what seemed like a wall was actually a gateway, the secret passage to an astonishing body of water stretching east and north and south. For a moment she felt the exultation and wonder of those men who had sailed through the Golden Gate, finding a place beyond their wildest imaginings, a vast panorama of coastline and islands and hills. How often in life, she wondered, did you have that feeling? How often did you find the beautiful, hidden thing that rendered you speechless?

Then the last of the towers were past, and they were winding through the brown hills of Marin County. She turned back for one more look at the brilliant orange bridge spanning the water.

Lawrence spoke first, and his voice was reverent. "That was an experience I'm going to remember."

They stopped to eat at a diner in Sausalito. In the booth there was a *Photoplay* magazine, left by a previous patron, with Belinda on the cover. She wore a white chiffon evening dress with a full skirt and an embroidered bodice, and she was leaning against a wall covered in deep crimson. Her head was tipped back against the wall, her mouth slightly open.

Lawrence was looking at the photo as the waitress set down the coffee. "Did you see her latest picture?" she asked brightly.

"I did," said Lawrence, his voice giving nothing away.

"She's my favorite movie star. I'd love to see her and Cary Grant in a picture together."

After she left, Lawrence lit a cigarette. "If she only knew who you are," said Frances quietly.

"It's nice for a change," he said. "Not being known." As he studied the cover, Frances studied his face. His eyes were not the eyes of a lover. There was distance in them, a sober assessment as he looked at the head tipped back suggestively, the partly opened mouth, the bedroom eyes.

"I saw this photo in the studio," he said. "It's carefully done. She can't play the ingenue forever, and she doesn't want to. But the public has to be brought into it gradually." He gestured to the dress. "White dress, innocent and virginal. That balances the pose and the expression on her face. It's all carefully controlled, for effect."

Frances thought of the art history class she'd taken her last year at college. Dr. Halliday, an elderly woman with astonishing energy, had called their attention to the smallest details in the paintings. There was the emotional impact of a picture, which came first, she explained; then there was the fascinating process of figuring out why it had affected you that way, how the artist's choices had created that instinctive response.

Belinda's arms were bare under the wide straps of her dress. Frances remembered the odalisque by Ingres, naked on her couch, looking invitingly over her shoulder. Dr. Halliday had spent half a class period on that shoulder. How far away that class seemed from this booth in a diner in Marin County.

"Belinda's going to be on tenterhooks," Lawrence said, "waiting to hear about our visit."

"Did you call to say we were going to Napa?"

"I sent a telegram last night. I didn't want to talk on the phone." He met her eyes. "All things come to an end."

"I'm sorry."

"Don't be. It's one of those things."

"I thought—" Frances hesitated. "I thought this was why you were working so hard to make this picture happen. For Miss Vail."

He smiled briefly. "A grand gesture of love?"

"In a way."

"No," he said. "I'm doing it for her, yes, but not for that reason." He picked up the salt cellar and turned it in his fingers, studying it as if it were something strange and absorbing.

"You told me once," he said, "that you don't like loose ends. You like things to be tidy. Getting her this picture is a way of tying up a few loose ends of my own. Ends that were there long before I knew Belinda."

She wanted to know more, but his face, looking down at the salt cellar, did not invite questions.

"I don't know Miss Vail very well," she said finally, "but I'm sure she's grateful."

He smiled briefly, more to himself than to her. "Belinda is tougher than she seems," he said, as if it were a logical response to Frances's comment. "The average fan would be surprised to know how hard her shell is. But for all that, she's vulnerable too."

He set down the salt cellar, lining it up carefully next to the pepper. Frances waited to see if he would say more, but then the waitress arrived with the soup and a basket of crackers, asking if they wanted more coffee, and the moment was gone.

CHAPTER TWENTY-THREE

The Plaza Hotel in downtown Napa sat on the corner opposite the county courthouse. It had none of the luxury of the St. Francis, but it was a handsome brick building with square towers and Palladian windows, and the inside was comfortable and tidy.

After changing into a fresh blouse and brushing her hair, Frances found Lawrence downstairs talking to the clerk, a pleasant middle-aged man with a bald head over which his remaining hair was combed with precision. The clerk was drawing a map on a piece of notepaper.

She walked toward the windows looking out onto the courthouse, waiting for Lawrence to finish. It was the same view as the one from her window on the floor above. The courthouse was an imposing building for such a small town, taking up nearly a whole city block. *JUSTICE*, it said in stone letters on the exterior wall.

That's what we all want, she thought. She pressed her fingernails to the base of her thumb, remembering her father. Mother Florence was right; he did not deserve that. He didn't deserve the stroke, the struggles to remember, the inability to weed the garden he loved.

Lawrence came up beside her. "I've got directions for tomorrow. It's up the valley a bit, eighteen miles. We can go early, hopefully wrap it up in a day."

"That would be good."

"I won't call them until morning, when we're about to leave. Otherwise, Miss Ridley might take a powder to Alaska or God knows where." He put the folded paper in his suit pocket. "It's dinnertime, isn't it? Let's find a place where we can get a bite."

After the bustle of San Francisco, Napa felt like a very small town indeed. The streets were golden in the early evening light as they passed the courthouse, walking in the direction of a church a block away, a traditional one with a tall, narrow steeple. "What a beautiful church," Frances said. "Like something out of a movie set."

"I was thinking the same thing. It would be right at home on the New England back lot."

They paused before crossing the street. "It's funny, isn't it?" she said. "Movies are supposed to reflect life. But when I see that church, all I can think is that it looks like the one in *Drums of Revolution*. As if the movies came first. As if they're more real than what's actually here."

She wasn't sure she was making any sense, but he nodded. "I know exactly what you mean."

As they crossed the street, she thought of Loretta DeWitt's comment about how the movies had taught her how to kiss. It was strange to think of all the ways that Hollywood had changed people's lives. The movies took something real and made it perfect, made it more exciting and glamorous. Perhaps reality would always disappoint, in comparison to the carefully managed version that was presented on film.

"I wonder," she said thoughtfully. "Everyone in the movies is so beautiful. You never see an ugly woman in a movie, or an ugly man."

"Well, there are character actors. But you're right, on the whole."

"Does it make us—those of us in the audience, I mean—does it make us dissatisfied with ordinary people? With ordinary life?"

They paused on the sidewalk to let an elderly couple pass by. Lawrence touched his hat politely.

"What you are saying, Frances," he said as they started walking again, "is something I've often thought myself. Movies have made the world larger. They've made us see our lives differently. And that comes at a price, perhaps."

Then he stopped, putting a hand on her arm. Just ahead, in front of the church, a hearse was pulling up to the curb. A handful of people had gathered on the steps, women in black hats and dresses, the men with black armbands. Lawrence took off his hat and held it as four men, neatly attired and somber, opened the hearse and removed a coffin.

The people on the steps watched in silence, punctuated only by sobs. A matronly woman held a handkerchief to her eyes while a young blond man of about twenty stood holding her arm, his face naked with grief. Another woman wept freely as the coffin was lifted by the pallbearers and carried slowly up the steps.

As the small group of mourners walked behind it, the young man turned toward Frances and she saw the tracks of tears on his face. He made no effort to wipe them away as he helped the older woman into the church. When all the mourners were inside, the sexton closed the heavy door slowly, not releasing it until the last possible minute, a small gesture of respect for their loss.

Lawrence replaced his hat. They continued walking but did not resume their conversation.

A block away they found a diner and sat side by side at the counter. A mirrored panel in front of them, behind the coffee machine and the rows of cups and a pie stand, gave back their reflections. She drew off her gloves and he lit a cigarette.

The burly waiter poured two coffees and Frances added cream, watching it swirl into the cup. She glanced up as she stirred, and in the mirror she could see herself and Lawrence to her left, his tall frame hunched on the stool.

A week ago, they had never sat like this. They had always been face-to-face, separated by the solid expanse of a desk. But the last few days, after sitting in the car for so many hours, it felt natural to be side by side. He moved the ashtray, and as he did so his elbow brushed her arm.

"Shall we take our luggage with us tomorrow, when we go see Miss Ridley?" she asked.

He took so long in responding that she didn't think he had heard her. At last he said, "Yes, probably," as if he were not really attending. He stubbed out the cigarette and reached for the coffee, turning the handle around so he could pick it up.

"It's strange, you know," he said. "The people crying in the street. I can't think of any other time it's acceptable to show your emotion in public. Only at a funeral."

"Or me, in the car today," she said without thinking. Then her cheeks burned at the memory of her emotion and of him holding her in his arms. He looked up and their eyes met in the mirror.

"But I know what you mean," she said quickly. "There is something different about death."

"I remember my wife's funeral. I cried and didn't even try to hide it. I hadn't done that since I was a boy. It was a relief, actually."

The waiter began making a fresh pot of coffee, blocking their view of the mirror. He had a broad back under his white shirt and black hair neatly trimmed above his collar.

"How old was Sally?" Frances asked.

"Almost three. She wasn't at the funeral. Someone's decision, my mother-in-law's, I think. I didn't fight it."

The waiter, still at the percolator, began whistling "Pennies from Heaven." In the mirror, Frances could see only Lawrence's left arm, the left side of his head.

"I'm not sure what it says about us as a species," he said. "Why it takes something as big as death for us to show what we really feel."

"People do it on happy occasions too. At weddings and things."

"That's different, though. In happy moments, you're already happy. You don't need the comfort of showing your feelings." He did not say any more, but she understood.

The waiter began rubbing down the counter, his back still to them, cleaning off ketchup spills and coffee stains. Again he blocked the mirror, and it was only because Frances could not see her employer that she was emboldened to ask, "How did she die?"

Lawrence took a sip of coffee, then put the cup down. It settled into the saucer with the gritty sound of cheap china. Then the waiter abruptly put down his rag and moved away to serve a customer, and she saw the two of them, side by side, just as Lawrence spoke.

"It was suicide," he said quietly. And his face in the mirror was tired and yet resigned, as if nothing anyone could say or do could hurt him.

CHAPTER
TWENTY·FOUR

Frances dreamed of her father that night. He was in the garden, as active and healthy as he had been before the stroke, whistling a tune. In that odd way of dreams it was clearly his garden, yet it was in the front of the house, not the back, and people strolling by could see him as he worked. They commented on the flowers, and her father thanked them. To Mrs. Gould he said, "Bring me over an empty pot, and I'll give you a begonia. Any one you like."

"But it will ruin your garden," the dream Frances told him.

"No, it won't," he said. "Begonias always come up again, after you take them out of the ground." And sure enough, when he dug up a red begonia and put it in the pot, a new one, large and full, appeared in the empty space in the flower bed.

Frances woke and lay blinking for a moment in the unfamiliar light of the hotel room. She reviewed the dream in her mind, replaying it like a movie. If she did not do that right after waking, her dreams always evaporated; she'd remember the vague contours of the story and the feeling it evoked, but the details would vanish before she could grasp them. Where did those dream memories go? Was there some part of the brain that stored them in a secret archive, a place hidden from all conscious thought?

It was five minutes until her alarm was due to go off, so she got up, washed her face and brushed her hair, applied her light makeup, then put on her stockings and slip and the red dress with the white collar. As she dressed, she recalled dinner the evening before, when Lawrence had told her of his wife's suicide.

It had been a shock. Frances had caught sight of her own face in the mirror, unguarded and horrified; the next moment, the waiter had come back, whistling, to refill their coffee. After he left, she'd been unable to say more than "I'm so sorry." Lawrence had nodded briefly, then the waiter had come with their meals, and they had eaten for a few moments in silence. When Lawrence spoke again, it was to comment on the route they would take the next morning to St. Helena, and to speculate on what Miss Ridley might be like, and she did not ask anything else about his wife, though she longed to know more.

It was his story to tell, she thought. Or not to tell, as he saw fit. But she hoped he knew how much she grieved for him. And she hoped he knew that she would gladly listen, if he ever wished to talk.

At nine o'clock, they were in the car heading north. The highway narrowed after a few miles, the tawny hills and trees drawing together as if trying to embrace the road. There were vineyards as well as orchards and an occasional farmhouse, often flanked by large oak trees. The palette was golden brown and olive green, set against the pristine blue of the sky.

Eventually, the road became the main street of St. Helena. There were old buildings with brick fronts and a huge Masonic temple and a firehouse. Beyond the business district, Lawrence turned the car west and they drove along a street that ascended, gradually, toward the hills.

They passed houses on small lots; then the land opened up and there were large stretches of vineyards and orchards on either side of the road. They passed a massive oak shading a small white house, but it was primarily agricultural land now.

At last, after turning left onto a dirt road, they came upon a low stone wall. Trees and shrubs grew behind it, creating a natural barrier from the road. Old wrought iron letters spelled out the name VENTIMIGLIA in an arch over the entrance.

Lawrence turned the car onto the driveway. There were lawns on both sides of the drive, and a line of oak trees made a perimeter separating the property from the vineyards and orchards beyond. To the left, in the corner of the property closest to the road, was a sprawling flower garden. Straight at the end of the driveway, beyond the lawn, was the house: a large yellow Victorian home, with a small square tower and a substantial porch.

The house was far enough from the oaks to receive a great deal of sun. There were roses in front of the porch, yellow blooms a few shades darker than the walls. The house itself had tall, narrow windows, and ornate brackets on the underside of the roof. It looked freshly painted, with plum-and-green trim.

Lawrence parked the car. A cat, white with black splotches, looked at them with mild curiosity from the porch, then meowed once and ran lightly away as they approached the steps and rang the bell.

A moment later, a woman opened the door. She was in her early thirties, and she wore a green housedress and a large apron on which she was wiping her hands. A small boy about two years old was standing beside her, holding onto her skirt with one hand. "May I help you?" she asked.

Lawrence took off his hat. "Good morning. I'm Lawrence Merrill, of VistaGlen Studios. This is my secretary, Miss Healey."

"Of course. My husband mentioned your call." She stepped back. "Please come in."

The hallway was large and light. There was an umbrella stand and a small table holding a pile of letters and a jump rope and a comic book. A staircase, wooden and impressive, wound upstairs. The rug in the hall was faded, worn by feet and sunlight.

"You're here to see Miss Ridley, I guess," said the woman.

"Yes," said Lawrence. "And to whom do I have the pleasure of speaking?"

"I'm sorry," said the woman. "I'm Celia Ventimiglia." It was an absurdly musical name, Frances thought, and it suited the woman, with her golden hair and green eyes and quietly pretty features. Celia gestured to the boy who was still holding onto her skirt. "This is Toby. He's a little shy." Upon hearing his name, the boy turned and ran off to the right, through the archway.

"Anyhow," she said, indicating the left side of the hallway, "that's Miss Ridley's part of the house. Go on in and wait there, please. I'll see if she's free to speak."

"I hope," said Lawrence cautiously, "we've come at a convenient time for her?"

"I'll see what she says," said Celia. "Please make yourself comfortable."

The room had high ceilings and a grandfather clock and an ornate fireplace. A dark walnut rocking chair with an embroidered cushion was pulled up next to a light blue chesterfield from the twenties. A phonograph and a stack of records sat on a small sideboard, near a lamp with a marble base. The walls were a light green against which the decorative white molding stood out like icing on a cake.

Frances paused in front of a glass-fronted cabinet opposite the fireplace. It contained a bird's nest, a cobalt-blue bottle, a peacock feather, a piece of what looked like Sèvres porcelain. On the wall nearby was a framed engraving of the castle at Neuschwanstein. The room, even with its many eclectic furnishings, felt light and airy.

Frances caught Lawrence's eye. He lifted an eyebrow, and she knew his thoughts as if he had spoken them aloud. *There was no way to plan for this*, his expression said. *We'll just have to take it as it comes.*

A wing chair was placed near the south-facing window. Frances moved closer so she could see the view. There was a large lilac bush, a strip of lawn, a line of oak trees, and, through the arms of the oaks, the vineyards; someone sitting in the chair would be able to see it all simply by turning her head. A small hassock sat in front of the chair, and upon the side table to the left was a leather-bound book and a water glass and a bell.

Then Frances heard a creak at the door and turned. Lawrence was instantly poised and alert, smoothing his tie. But the door stopped and stayed there, open only a few inches, for what seemed like the longest time. Lawrence finally stepped forward as if to offer help, but just as he did so the door swung all the way open and the slight figure of Kitty Ridley, leaning on a cane, appeared before them.

"Well," she said, her voice low and husky with age. "It seems you vultures have found me."

CHAPTER

TWENTY·FIVE

S he was tiny, almost shockingly so. Her hair, once famed for its golden brilliance, was entirely hidden in a turban made of green paisley. She wore a blue blouse with voluminous sleeves that made her seem all the more insubstantial. To Frances's surprise, she also wore slacks, dark ones that might have come right from the most stylish shops on Hollywood Boulevard. Her feet were in ox-fords, black ones with low heels, and she leaned on a cane topped by an ivory duck. Her face was no longer the smooth and dimpled one of the photos but deeply wrinkled, as if a sheet of paper had been crumpled and partially straightened. She wore a small bit of dark red lipstick, Audrey's favorite color, which sat jarringly on her face. There was little in her that resembled the coquette in the photos or the vibrant woman strolling through the Paris gardens.

But then Miss Ridley turned, and Frances saw the boot-black eyes, snapping and sparkling, from the book cover: the eyes of the young woman who had conquered gold miners, theater audiences, and the hearts of powerful men.

Lawrence spoke first. "Miss Ridley," he said, with a slight and apparently reflexive bow, "It's an honor to meet you. I apologize for descending on you like this."

"Descending. What an odd choice of words." She looked up at him. "But then you are much taller than I am, aren't you?"

"Please, let me introduce my secretary. Miss Frances Healey."

"It's a pleasure to meet you, Miss Ridley."

"Secretary." Miss Ridley turned to Frances, surveying her. "She's your secretary, is she."

It was a statement that sounded like a question. Out of nowhere, Frances recalled the moment in the office when she had caught Mr. Merrill looking at her legs. Maddeningly, she could feel herself blushing. From the slight change of expression on Miss Ridley's face, she knew the woman had registered her reaction.

"So." Miss Ridley waved her cane. "You followed me to Napa. I suspected you would." She turned toward the wing chair and Lawrence made a move to help her, but she motioned for him to stop. "Have a seat."

He perched on the very edge of the chesterfield, like a schoolboy. Frances took the rocking chair, doing her best to hold it still, while Miss Ridley settled herself slowly in the wing chair, then rested both hands on her cane.

"So you're here to convince me to allow this film. Even though I was quite clear in the letter that I loathe the idea."

"I understand your concerns, Miss Ridley," Lawrence said gravely. "I truly do. And I am sure we can work together to reach an agreement."

"'Work together.' I know what that means. It means you think you can charm an ancient lady, make me sign something that in my befuddled state I am no longer aware of." Her voice, even with the rasp of age, was impressive. "It means you will get your way at all costs. I know your type."

"Not at all, Miss Ridley." Lawrence was leaning forward deferentially, outwardly poised, but Frances could see perspiration at his temples. "We want you to be as excited about this picture as we are. We have the best people in Hollywood making it." He opened his mouth as if to say more, but she waved her hand to silence him.

"Enough. You'll only bore me if you go on." She leaned her head back against the high back of the chair and closed her eyes. She looked suddenly frail and insubstantial, her turban knocked slightly askew. A moment later, her eyes were open again, settling on Frances. "You're the secretary, you said?"

"Yes, Miss Ridley."

"You came to take notes on this meeting, I suppose. To write back to your people. 'Congratulations, we've convinced the old lady,' or 'Pack it up, gentlemen, the movie is off'?"

Lawrence leaned forward as if to demur, but Frances spoke first. There was something fascinating about Miss Ridley, about the frail body paired with the iron will; intuitively, Frances knew that honesty would be best.

"Not in so many words," she said quietly, "but it will be one of those two answers, Miss Ridley."

A glimmer of respect lit the woman's face. She regarded Frances for a long time as a breeze came through the open window, lifting the white lace curtain into the room. It rose and then fell gently, like an exhalation of breath.

Then Miss Ridley picked up the bell by her chair and rang it. "Where are you staying?" she asked Lawrence.

"The Plaza Hotel in Napa."

"For how long?"

Lawrence paused; Frances could see him considering the possible answers. "Our departure date is not yet fixed, Miss Ridley."

The old lady nodded as if satisfied. Celia opened the door.

"Celia," said Miss Ridley, "our visitors are returning now to Napa. But they will be back tomorrow." She turned to Lawrence. "Come at eleven. We will have tea. You too, Miss Secretary."

"Thank you, Miss Ridley," said Lawrence, politely concealing his disappointment at being dismissed.

"Until tomorrow." Miss Ridley's eyes were almost mischievous. "Have a nice day in Napa, Mr. and Miss." Frances could not tell if she had forgotten their names or had simply chosen not to use them.

‑☀‑

Celia walked them out on the porch, where Toby was sitting on a bench with a girl about twelve years old. She was reading him a book, which he was listening to with rapt attention. "I guess we'll see you here tomorrow," Celia said. "I hope you're not on a tight schedule."

"We are, somewhat," said Lawrence. Celia smiled in sympathy.

"Miss Ridley is not a person you can rush," she said. "It's best to accept that."

She was so friendly and matter-of-fact that Frances asked, "How long has Miss Ridley lived with you?"

"Almost eight years," said Celia. "She has the place in the city, too, but spends most of her time here."

"Is this . . ." Lawrence paused, as if uncertain how to proceed. "Is this your house?"

"Yes, my husband's grandfather built it." She would have said more, but a boy, about ten, appeared in the doorway with a half-eaten apple in his hand. "Mama," he said, "the water's boiling over."

Celia turned back. "I'm sorry, I'll have to run. I'll see you tomorrow."

As they drove out of the property, the same cat they'd seen on the porch was sitting in a patch of sun by the garden, its tail twitching. Once they drove under the archway back onto the dirt road, Lawrence spoke. "This won't be easy, will it?"

"It certainly won't."

"I'm glad you're here. This would be much harder alone."

She gazed at the road and thought of Miss Ridley, tiny and formidable, in her surprising clothes and turban. "I like her," she said. "She's difficult, but she's fascinating too. You don't know what she's going to say."

"Rather like Sally."

They were passing vineyards, rows upon rows of them. Beyond were orchards; Frances wished she knew what kind of trees they were.

"I wonder how Sally is doing with the nuns," Lawrence said suddenly.

Frances looked up at the sky, more yellow than blue with the increasing heat of the day. "I wonder too."

Back in Napa, they ate lunch, and then Lawrence dictated a few letters in the deserted parlor of the hotel. It was an odd venue for work, and it wasn't the only thing that felt different, for Frances was conscious of a slight change in their interactions. Perhaps it was the fact that they now called each other by their first names, but as she took dictation she felt oddly out of step, as if doing so was no longer as effortless as it had been in Hollywood.

Once they had finished, she went to her room and transcribed the letters neatly, wishing she had a typewriter. *July 24, 1938*, she wrote at the top of each one. You could not ignore the date when you wrote it by hand.

With grim focus she finished the letters, proofreading them twice. Then she powdered her nose and returned to the lounge, where Lawrence was smoking and looking out at the courthouse. He scanned the letters and signed them. "I'll check in with the studio while you mail these," he said. "I'm trying not to think of how expensive all these phone calls are."

Frances walked to the post office, then asked the clerk for directions to the library. She passed a drugstore and a shop selling gifts and housewares, pausing to admire the china bowls and figurines displayed in the window. The library was a two-story building made of gray stone with a tearoom on the first floor, and she had a cup of tea, looking out onto the street. Then she went up to the second floor, found a copy of *A Golden Life*, and took it to a table by the window to read.

It was astonishing to see the photo of the young Kitty Ridley, age twenty-two, on the cover. *I've actually met her,* Frances marveled. Kitty had blonde curls arranged half on her head and half over her shoulder, a high-collared dress and dainty earrings, and she was resting her chin on her hand, her elbow on a slender marble column. There was both charm and willfulness in her eyes, a willfulness that even the staid Victorian portrait could not hide.

It had been more than ten years since Frances had read the book. She settled into her chair and turned to the preface.

There is gold, wrote Myrtle Dobson, *and there is gold.*

There is the gold that James Marshall spied in the creek at Sutter's Mill in January of 1848. This is the gold that prompted the Rush, the frenzy, the movement of hopeful and brave men to the unknown land of California. They left it all: homes, birthplaces, families, professions. They left it behind, choosing dreams over reality, choosing unknown over known. Not for them, an ordinary life on the farms of Ohio or an office in New York. They gambled. And for a few—a very lucky few— the gamble was worth it.

And there is another kind of gold: the gold of a woman's silky hair, bouncing curls lit as if by the radiant sun, a flaming torch drawing the gaze of even the most hardened and cynical of men.

Oh, good Lord, thought Frances, raising amused eyes to the ceiling; she hadn't remembered the book being so saccharine.

This gold was found not in streams but in the glow of the footlights: the rough lanterns of a Sierra mining camp, then the footlights of the Bella Union theater in San Francisco, then the spotlights of theaters from Chicago to New York. This is the gold of Kitty Ridley, the Golden Girl, the Darling of the Sierras. And in its own way, this gold, too, attracted the hopeful. This gold, paired with sparkling black eyes and graceful feet and a natural, dazzling charm, proved to be a magnetic force all its own, inspiring men to leave home and stake it all, their entire lives and livelihoods, on the promise of her smile, her love.

But for most men—all but one, in fact—the gamble was utterly in vain.

Frances scanned the rest of the introduction, which had a few more paragraphs in a similar style. She gave her glasses a polish and turned to the first chapter.

She was the third child of Horace and Belle Ridley: the first girl, the only one of their brood to live past the age of five. Helen Isabella Ridley, called Kitty, born in New York City on July 29, 1847, was the culmination of all her parents' dreams.

Frances felt as if someone had doused her with cold water. For a moment she sat immobile, her heart pounding, staring at the page. Then she closed the book quickly, a movement so sudden that the man opposite her looked up from his reading.

July 29. How could she not have remembered? But when she had read the book as a teenager in the house on Chapin Lane, there was no meaning to that date. It was just a day on the calendar, nothing more.

Frances returned the book to the shelf and walked quickly downstairs and outside to the sidewalk, striving to regain equanimity. She took out a compact and scanned her face, something she almost never did in public. Her nose needed powdering, but she did not return to the library to freshen up. She snapped her pocketbook shut and walked swiftly back toward the hotel.

In five more days it would be July 29. For a moment she wished, with every fiber of her being, that she had never left Hollywood, that she was sitting calmly at her desk in the tidy office at the studio.

A horn honked, and she realized that she had stepped off the curb without looking. "Watch where you're going, lady!" called a man behind the wheel, more in concern than indignation, and she stepped back, shaken, raising her hand in thanks.

W hen they arrived at the Ventimiglias' the next morning, they were greeted at the front door by Celia, little Toby, and twelve-year-old Nancy, the girl who had been reading on the porch the day before. "You have another son, don't you?" asked Frances, remembering the older boy who had come out to warn of the boiling pot.

"Yes, Arthur is ten," said Celia. "He's around here somewhere." She showed them to a table on the side porch, set with a cotton table-cloth printed with baskets of fruit in primary colors. There was a silver tea set and a plate of biscotti, along with a tray of sandwiches. "Make yourselves comfortable. I'll just go see if Miss Ridley is ready."

It took twenty minutes, but at last the actress appeared, wearing the same turban and trousers but a blouse of bright orange. She responded to their greetings with cold formality. Celia helped her into the chair, poured the tea, and left. Nancy followed with visible reluctance, obviously wanting to stay and listen to the conversation.

Frances knew that Lawrence disliked tea, and she caught the tightening of his face as he took a polite sip. Miss Ridley did not make any move to drink or eat. She watched him avidly, her eyes narrowed, and as he put down the cup she said, "So. You find my life story irresistible."

"I do," said Lawrence. Folding his hands, he leaned toward her; his manner was grave, courteous, intent. "It's not just me, you understand, Miss Ridley. A studio is a team. Many people are captivated by your story. It's a sign of how much we admire you."

"Do you? How fascinating."

"The studio has invested tremendous resources into this project. More than we do for just any film, I assure you."

"That's what it comes down to, doesn't it? You'll lose a lot of money if you don't make the picture?"

"No," said Lawrence. He grimaced slightly. "That is, yes, but it's not my primary concern. Your story has captured the imagination of our entire creative team, Miss Ridley. Not just the screenwriter and director but the actors and actresses too. This is more than just a role to them."

"I saw the article in that magazine," said Miss Ridley. "You've chosen Theodore Grant to play my husband."

"Yes, we have."

"Bad choice. He's far too likable. My husband was a bastard through and through."

Frances almost choked on a bite of sandwich. Lawrence looked taken aback.

"Not literally, of course," Miss Ridley continued. "He was the legitimate son of one of the oldest families in France. But there wasn't a skirt passing by that he didn't try to get under. And you've hired Bonnie Benson to play me as a child." She waved a hand dismissively. "She's passable, but utterly lacking the charm I had. There's only one child who could convincingly play me, and that's Shirley Temple."

"She would be ideal, I agree," said Lawrence.

"She's a natural, just like I was. That Bonnie girl, you can see the wheels turning."

"I'm afraid Shirley is under contract to another studio," said Lawrence. "Believe me, we would have her if we could."

"And yet," said Miss Ridley, her eyes narrowing, "that girl you have hired to play me as an adult. Melinda?"

"Belinda. Belinda Vail."

"The article said she was under contract to another studio and you hired her away."

"We did, yes."

"If you could do it for her, why can't you do it for Shirley?"

"It's complicated, Miss Ridley," said Lawrence.

"Is it? I thought you could make anything happen, there in Holly Wood." She said the name as if it were two distinct words.

There was a pause. Lawrence looked at Frances, and she reached for her handbag.

"We've brought the screenplay, Miss Ridley," said Lawrence as Frances set it on the table. "We would like you to read it. We may even be able to change certain details to make them more palatable to you."

"I'm not reading all that," she said irritably.

"Can we perhaps summarize it for you?" asked Frances.

"No." Miss Ridley took hold of her teacup and lifted it to her red lips. Her hand trembled so violently that the tea almost slopped over the side. Lawrence opened his mouth as if to say something, then seemed to think better of it and was silent.

Miss Ridley lifted the cup a bit further, the tea coming dangerously close to spilling out, then she set the cup down without drinking. "It's too hot for tea," she said, as if one of them had insisted otherwise. Frances could see small wisps of white hair poking out from under the turban.

Silence fell. It was astonishing how quiet it was in Napa, thought Frances. You could hear the zip of an insect, the sound of a truck far off in the vineyard somewhere. You could practically hear your own thoughts. She saw Lawrence regarding Miss Ridley, and although the woman was thwarting them at every turn, cantankerous and difficult, she was surprised to see respect in his gaze. It was not feigned deference, the kind meant to disarm one's adversary, but genuine respect for the frail woman at the head of the table, the ninety-year-old actress who was the one thing standing between him and the movie on which so much was riding.

Miss Ridley broke the silence. "You've based it on the book, haven't you?"

"In large part, yes."

"I told you. That book is full of lies. Why would you make a movie about lies?" She turned to Frances. "Have you read the book?"

"Many years ago. When I was in high school."

"Did you like it?"

"At the time, yes."

"At the time?"

Frances paused; she could see Lawrence staring at her across the table. And to her right was Miss Ridley, like a tiny coiled spring, waiting for her answer.

"I reread part of it yesterday," Frances said. "And the writing of it was . . . rather overblown."

"Ridiculous, you mean."

"That too."

"She could have just written fiction, you know," said Miss Ridley. "She could have made up a story and called it a novel, and it would have been fine. But no. She had to write my story, or what she calls my story. And everyone takes it as truth."

"Perhaps—" started Frances.

"Perhaps what?"

"Perhaps we could work with you on the screenplay. Maybe you could tell us what is true and what isn't." She could see Lawrence shifting uneasily in his seat.

"And if I wanted to change the whole thing? Not keep any of your silly screenplay?"

"I think," said Lawrence from across the table, "you should read the whole thing first. Could we read it for you? Miss Healey and I, doing the parts?"

"No," said Miss Ridley. "I have no patience for amateur theatrics." She lifted her chin toward his cup. "You aren't drinking your tea."

Lawrence took a sip, glancing at Frances across the table.

"However," Miss Ridley continued, "you may leave the screenplay here. If I have time today, I will read it."

Lawrence set the cup down in the saucer. "I think, Miss Ridley," he said delicately, "that it might perhaps be more efficient if we were to read it to you? We have all day free."

"I told you," she said, steel in her tone, "I don't want amateur theatrics. I am fully capable of reading this if I am given time to do so."

"Of course," said Lawrence. "But I am—that is, we are—needed back in Hollywood soon."

"I thought you could stay as long as you needed."

"Well, yes," he said, "within reason."

"And I'm not being reasonable, wanting a day to read this? Perhaps you should take it back with you then."

She had boxed them in very neatly, Frances realized. Lawrence clearly knew it too, for he gave a tight, resigned smile.

"Not at all," he said. "Please, keep it here and read it."

Miss Ridley smiled, the smile of the victor. Then, as if suddenly weary, she closed her eyes. "I'd like to be alone now. You are free to go. Celia will call you tomorrow and let you know my progress." They had been dismissed.

T hey went back into the house through the front door, closing it quietly behind them. Celia appeared in the hall with Toby behind her, a stuffed rabbit in his hand.

She saw their faces and her expression became sympathetic. "No answer, then."

"Miss Ridley would like to read the screenplay," said Lawrence. "She'll get back to us tomorrow to let us know her progress."

"I see," said Celia. She looked as if she wanted to say something but then stopped herself.

"I'm afraid," she said finally, "this may not be a quick process."

"I'm getting that impression," said Lawrence grimly.

The sudden bang of a door in the back preceded the appearance of Arthur, who came bursting into the hall holding a baseball. He stopped short at the sight of Lawrence and Frances and stood awkwardly by, waiting for a pause in the conversation.

"Why don't you come for dinner tonight," said Celia suddenly. "Joe would like to meet you, I'm sure."

"Thank you," said Lawrence, "but we wouldn't want to impose. We're disrupting your life enough as it is."

Celia smiled, and Frances recognized it as the smile of a woman who routinely handles much greater disruptions. "It's no trouble. We'd be happy to have you."

"Then yes. Thank you very much."

"We eat at five thirty," said Celia. "Stay until then, if you'd like. It's a long way to Napa just to come back."

"I'm out of cigarettes," said Lawrence. "Perhaps I'll drive into St. Helena to get some." He turned to Frances. "Why don't you stay here, in case Miss Ridley decides she wants to talk about the script."

"I doubt she will," said Celia frankly, "but you're welcome to stay."

Arthur, with a child's instinctive ability to seize a pause in the conversation, broke in. "Mama, can I walk downtown to buy that comic book?"

"Now?"

"Yes."

"It's so hot today, Arthur."

"Please, Mama."

"If you are comfortable with it, Mrs. Ventimiglia," Lawrence said, "I could take him in the car. I'm going downtown anyhow."

Arthur's eyes lit up. "Can I, Mama?"

"That's very kind of you, Mr. Merrill. Yes, Arthur, you may."

"Can I see if Nancy wants to go too?"

"Yes. And what do you say to Mr. Merrill?"

Arthur, who had started for the staircase, turned around with a grin. "Thank you, sir. I can't wait to ride in your car."

"I'm afraid they may talk your ear off," said Celia as her son's footsteps pounded up the stairs.

"I don't mind," said Lawrence. "It'll make a nice change."

C elia poured Frances a glass of lemonade and Frances drank it on the porch, then strolled slowly around the grounds. She wandered across the front lawn to the flower garden, tucked in the southern corner of the property, four large beds bisected by paths. It needed care; some of the coneflowers had faded and wanted clipping, and the penstemon was leggy and unruly, but there were beautiful powder-blue delphiniums and marguerites with vibrant yellow centers. She reached out to rub a spear of lavender, and the tiny blossoms left a fragrant residue on her fingers.

She almost sat on the bench there, but it was entirely in the sun, so she crossed the lawn again and found another bench under the oaks to the north of the house. It was the Ventimiglias' side of the house, opposite the main hall from Miss Ridley's rooms. According to Celia, their lodger had not just the parlor but also a small bedroom and bathroom. "Her bedroom used to be upstairs, but a few years ago we moved it downstairs. It's much easier for her. She naps both morning and evening."

There was something about the warm afternoon sun that would make anyone feel languorous. Frances closed her eyes. The sounds around her—the rustle of a bird in the leaves, the far-off sound of tires on a road—were suddenly all the more noticeable. The air smelled of dry oak leaves and sunbaked dirt, with only the faintest whiff of the lavender from her fingers. The heat seemed to reach even into the shade under the oaks, but it was a dry sun, a dry heat. She thought of the humidity of Pennsylvania, which had surprised her so during her first year at college.

There had been a bench at college, one she had loved, under the trees. It was removed from the heart of campus, not overlooked by any of the buildings. It had been her favorite place to sit and read or write in her notebook: her favorite place simply to dream, looking up into the trees.

Frances opened her eyes. She stood up briskly and walked toward the back of the house.

Her steps took her past another large oak, beside which was a rough trestle table and benches underneath part of an old arbor. Directly behind the house was a service yard where red geraniums grew sprawling, and where an old pump handle spoke of the house's age. There were no trees here, and the sun beat down on the dusty ground, on the tricycle and wagon left by the side of the house, on the clotheslines in the sun. Celia was there with two baskets of laundry. She looked up as Frances approached.

"Would you like more lemonade? There's plenty in the kitchen."

"I'm fine, thank you. It was delicious." Watching Celia draw clothespins from the sagging pouch on the line, Frances was reminded of Rita. So many times Frances had helped her pin the laundry on the line at the side of the house by the gardenia bushes, a place not overlooked by any room but the kitchen, a place for sharing confidences. "May I help?" she asked.

"Sure." If Celia was surprised at the offer, she hid it well. "You can start on that basket there."

They worked silently. The sun was strong overhead, but handling the damp laundry took the edge off of the heat. Frances paused at one point, looking beyond the small fence to the vineyard, the barn, the orchards, and thought of the men working out there in the sun, as they did in all weather. Life on a farm was different from the glamour of Hollywood, different from her suburban childhood in Burlingame. And, she thought, lining up the shoulders of a blouse, vastly different from the life of a celebrated stage actress.

"How did Miss Ridley come to live with you?"

"It's not where you'd expect her to be, is it?" said Celia, shaking out a stiff pair of small overalls. "She settled in San Francisco first, after coming back from France, but then decided she wanted a quieter life. Her housekeeper in the city knows my mother-in-law, so that's how it came about. We made an arrangement to rent half the house to her."

"That must have been difficult. Giving up all that room."

"No, it was the answer to a prayer. We needed the income." Celia swatted away a fly. "The twenties were hard for the wine industry. We had a lot of debt."

Frances paused in her pinning of a cotton camisole, remembering the dry years of her childhood and adolescence. "Oh. I never thought about that."

"Well, you had no reason to. But when it's your livelihood, it hits you hard."

"What did you do?"

"We were one of the lucky farms. We got to keep some vines going for sacramental wine, for the Mass. That was never illegal. But we had to give a lot of our acreage over to prunes. Now, of course, we could put the vines back in. Maybe someday we will. Anyhow," she said, pinning a pillowcase to the line, "Miss Ridley's rent made all the difference. A lifesaver, actually."

"She's certainly a fascinating woman."

"She is. I like having her here."

"It's a lot more work for you, though."

"No more than it would be to have a grandmother living with us. Sometimes she tells stories of her life. She's been so many places, it's like I can travel through her. And there's the security from the rent. If we have a bad year, we know we'll still stay afloat."

"Does that happen often? A bad year?"

"Well, it's the nature of the business. The weather can change, and the market. You can only control so much."

Frances watched Celia push a lock of golden hair out of her eyes and draw a skirt out of the hamper. Ten feet away, Toby toddled after the cat, who was slinking off toward the geraniums. Behind them stretched the vines, rows and rows of them, the raw material for wine that would end up in restaurants in Napa and San Francisco and perhaps Hollywood. It all started on farms like this, run by women like the one standing beside her, pinning laundry in the sun.

"I think you're very strong, Celia," she said suddenly. "Stronger than I am."

Celia paused in her work and looked at her thoughtfully. "I'm not so different," she said. "I'm not sure any of us are in control. It's just that we—farmers, I mean—we can't ignore it. Maybe other people can."

Frances picked up a tablecloth and took her time shaking it, smoothing it with her hands. She knew it well, the feeling that your life was going as planned, organized and tidy: but she also knew how it felt to encounter the thing you had not predicted and could not control, a thing that was not the stock market or the weather, but which seemed inexorable all the same.

Halfway through Frances's sophomore year, she began a new column for the college newspaper, one in which she interviewed professors on campus about their lives before teaching. Not everyone was interested in participating; a few faculty members politely turned her down, as if fearing that answering personal questions would breach some invisible line, but most responded eagerly. Ada Halliday, the art professor, showed photographs of the grand tour she had made in 1887 and explained how it had launched her love of painting, and Frederick Chapman, the history chair, brewed overly strong tea for Frances in his office and eagerly produced the arrowheads he had collected as a child.

Frances continued the series her junior year. Her first interviewee was Donald McAvoy, the new English professor, just hired to take the place of the white-haired Dr. Hudson who had died of a heart attack during the summer. He was in his late twenties, by far the youngest professor in the department. He was tall and slender, but when he rolled up the sleeves of his shirt (it was a stiflingly hot September day, and he asked Frances's permission to remove his suit jacket), he had surprisingly muscular forearms, as if he moonlighted as a stevedore. His hair was reddish brown and his eyes reminded Frances vaguely of the portraits of Alexander Hamilton, whom she and her roommate had recently decided was the handsomest of the founding fathers. Professor McAvoy was from Maryland, and had the barest trace of an accent, audible only on certain words.

The interview, conducted in his office, went on for two hours before either of them realized the time. At the end, he praised her for her insightful questions. "I'm not normally so talkative," he said. "I hope I've not said anything that's unfit to print."

"Not at all," she said. "And even if you had, I wouldn't include it. I'm not out to embarrass anyone."

"Good," he said. As she packed her notebook in her satchel, he came out from behind his desk and leaned against it, watching her, his hands in his pockets. She was at eye level with his belt, which was new brown leather.

"I'm glad," he said, as she stood up, "that you're in my class. I suspect you're a formidable student of literature."

"I'm more a student of people, I think."

"Well, that's what literature is, isn't it? Novels in particular."

"That's true. Maybe that's why I prefer them to other kinds of writing."

"As do I," he said. He held her gaze for a moment. Frances once again noticed how warm the room was.

She extended her hand with a smile. "Thank you again, Professor McAvoy."

"I'll look forward to your article," he said. His hand was dry and solid. "It's been a pleasure, Miss Healey."

CHAPTER
TWENTY·SEVEN

L awrence returned with the children, who eagerly told their mother that he'd treated them to an ice cream soda at the drugstore. "They're nice kids," he told Frances. "They remind me of my sister and me, at that age."

Celia's husband Joe came in a few minutes after five. He appeared to be in his mid-thirties, with dark, wavy hair, a muscular build, and a heavy five-o'clock shadow. He also had the widest smile Frances had ever seen; like a car going instantly from zero to fifty, it illuminated every part of his face, making him look like a totally different person. He greeted Frances and Lawrence in the large room to the right of the hall, which was a reverse image of the parlor Miss Ridley used. A wing chair and a rocker and a small divan were all grouped near a radio, while an antique dining table took up the back half of the room. When Frances commented on the wallpaper, an appealing design of braided flowers and vines, Joe smiled. "That's been there forever. I helped hang it when I was a kid."

The dinner conversation flowed easily. Joe asked them about Hollywood—"We go to the pictures in Napa when we can. Especially Laurel and Hardy"—and offered them red wine, which was poured into tumblers as casually as if it were milk. Mother Florence, thought Frances, would never approve. Toby, sitting on cushions, was just tall enough to reach the table, and he alternated between staring at the newcomers and chewing on a heel of bread with great intentness. The older children listened wide-eyed to the adults' conversation, and Arthur came to life when Lawrence mentioned Jimmy Buttons and his series of pictures. He asked eager questions about the upcoming film, and to Frances's surprise Lawrence answered them, even though it was the kind of information that the studio normally kept under wraps. "Golly," said Arthur. "He's going to chase the jewel thieves through the sewers. I can't wait."

"It's top-secret information, remember," said Lawrence. His face was serious, but Frances could tell he was enjoying making the boy happy. "Keep it under your hat, young man."

"I will, sir," said Arthur gravely.

As they were having tapioca pudding and coffee, Celia excused herself and disappeared through the door into the kitchen. Twenty minutes later, she was still gone. "Will Celia be coming back?" said Lawrence. "I want to thank her before we leave."

"She's just getting Miss Ridley her dinner," said Joe. "She'll come back."

"Miss Ridley never eats dinner with you?"

"Almost never. She likes a little soup and some bread at night, not much."

"Whom does she interact with?" asked Frances. "I mean, socially."

Joe looked surprised by the question. "With us," he said. "Celia always talks with her as she's doing the mending. Celia does the mending, I mean, not Miss Ridley. The children visit with her too." Nancy, who was leaning against the arm of his chair and listening avidly to the conversation of the grown-ups, nodded.

"How does she spend her time?"

"She sleeps during the day and reads. When I play the accordion, she likes to listen. She always asks for more songs. And she walks around the yard, sometimes. We send Nancy or Arthur with her so she won't fall."

"She recites as we walk," said Nancy. "I know a lot of Shakespeare from her."

"Like what?" asked Frances.

"'The quality of mercy is not strained,'" said Nancy promptly. "'It droppeth as the gentle rain from heaven upon the place beneath.'"

"He was good, Shakespeare," said Joe. "When the rains come after summer, the first ones, it does feel like mercy." He gave his daughter's braid an affectionate tug. "Go help Mama with the dishes, Nance."

"Why do you think she doesn't want a film made of her life?" asked Lawrence as the girl disappeared through the door into the kitchen.

"Well, who would?" asked Joe reflexively. "A film is always going to get it wrong." Then he seemed to remember whom he was speaking to. "Sorry."

"That's all right," said Lawrence.

"That movie a few years ago, about the life of Louis Pasteur? That was good. But he's dead, you know. He doesn't have to see how wrong it is. It's not your fault. It's just you can't get a person's life into an hour and a half. Like trying to fit a . . ."—he looked around the room—"a rocking chair into a suitcase."

"Have you read the book about her?" asked Frances.

"No. I think Celia did, once. But she's a good tenant, Miss Ridley," he said, almost defensively, as if they had said the opposite. "Like having a grandmother in the house. She's kind, you know? Never a harsh word, even though—"

"Even though?" asked Lawrence.

"She's in pain a lot of the time. Celia's the one who cares for her, mostly. Some days are really hard. But you wouldn't know it."

"No," said Frances. "She hides it surprisingly well."

"Not so surprising." Joe lit a cigarette. "She's an actress, after all."

CHAPTER
TWENTY-EIGHT

Frances slept uncharacteristically late the next morning, and it was nearly nine when she descended the hotel stairs. As she did so she met Lawrence coming in from outside, holding a newspaper. "Good morning," he said.

"Good morning. Have you been up for a while?"

"Since seven." He folded his newspaper in half. "You look nice," he said. She was wearing wide-legged trousers in navy blue, and she realized that he'd never seen her in them before. Though slacks had been popular for years, they were hardly the kind of clothes a woman would wear to work.

"Thank you. I'm afraid I'm running out of clean clothes."

"I am too. We didn't expect a trip this long."

"I thought I'd ask if there's a laundry in town. Perhaps we can send some things over today, before we go see Miss Ridley."

"Good idea," he said. "But I spoke to Celia half an hour ago. She said Miss Ridley is having a bad morning, doesn't want to see us today."

"Oh, dear."

"She said she'd try to read her the script, get the kids to help. I asked if we should come and just hover, in case she changes her mind, but Celia said—delicately, of course—that it would probably hurt our cause more than help."

Frances remembered how Miss Ridley had called them vultures. "She's probably right about that."

"Probably. So," he said, changing his tone, "we have an unexpected day off."

She frowned, thinking. "If only I had a typewriter here. Maybe I could arrange with the front desk clerk to rent theirs? There must be some way to keep the day from going to waste."

"Your professional zeal is impressive, Frances," he said, "but no. I'll call the studio to check in, but if there are no fires to put out, today is going to be a real vacation."

A woman entered the hotel foyer, and Lawrence took Frances's elbow lightly, moving her closer to him to clear the path to the front desk.

"I realized," he said as he released her, "after a cup of coffee and a walk, that I could either treat this delay as an annoyance or a vacation. And the second option seems best. I haven't had a vacation in years. I'm overdue for one."

It wasn't easy for him to turn off the relentless professional drive; she could see that in his eyes. But she admired him for trying to find some good in the circumstances he could not control. She thought of the conversation with Celia at the clothesline.

"You'll still be paid for today, of course," he said. "Double, as I promised."

"Then I hope Miss Ridley takes her time."

He laughed. "Let's find some breakfast. I'll ask the clerk about the laundry. Then what would you like to do?"

She thought of the countryside, the golden hills, the oaks and the vines. "Just explore, I think. Drive around and see what we see. Maybe find a place with a view?"

After arranging for their laundry, they stopped at a grocer's to pick up a bottle of seltzer, some oranges, and a box of Ritz crackers. Near the register was a tray of homemade doughnuts.

Lawrence asked for four, and the young woman who was bagging their groceries added a fifth one free of charge. "My mother makes these. You'll love them."

They drove up north on the freeway, as if they were going to Miss Ridley's, but turned west after a few miles. They drove through vineyards and past farmhouses like the Ventimiglias'. The windows were down and Frances's hair was soon tousled, but she did not care; the whip of the breeze was wonderfully cooling.

"By the way," said Lawrence, "I asked Mrs. Daley about Sherwin. His wife is still in the hospital, but she's fine. And the baby will be too, they say, as long as she rests."

"I'm so glad," said Frances. She remembered Sherwin's face, his failed attempt at stoicism. "I know how worried he was. It was good of you sending him home like that."

"It was the least I could do," he said. "She needed him there." There was a sudden intensity in his voice that made her glance at him involuntarily, but his eyes, fixed on the road, gave nothing away.

They parked the car in the shade of a grove of trees and took a small dirt path up a golden hillside, carrying the grocery bag and a blanket from the trunk of the car. There was one patch where the ground, dry and full of little stones, was slippery, so Lawrence anchored his feet into the hillside and gripped her hand and pulled her up. She was not expecting him to be so strong. It was always surprising to her how much strength men had in their upper bodies, a power that they used casually, as if forgetting that women did not share it.

They were both warm by the time they found a flat space underneath a spreading oak. Frances lay out the blanket as Lawrence opened the seltzer. "We don't have any cups, do we?" she said.

Lawrence passed her the bottle. "Take as much as you like. I'll drink what you don't want."

"It's all right," she said, passing it back to him. "We can share."

It was pleasant to sit on the tartan blanket, to see the sun beating down on the long, dry grass and yet to be removed from its glare in the shade. The ground before them sloped down the way they had come, and beyond that were layers of round hills dotted with clusters of oaks and bays, a palette of gold and brown and olive green.

Lawrence took a swig of the seltzer, then offered her the bottle. She took a drink, conscious that she was putting her lips where his had just been. In spite of the heat, she felt alert, alive. Her senses were humming, like the insects off in the distance.

"Does it feel like a vacation yet?" she asked.

Lawrence was leaning back on his forearms, his legs outstretched, his stomach under the blue shirt making a tilted plane. "It does. I don't know the last time I've just sat in the shade like this."

"Hollywood feels far away, doesn't it?"

"Like another world." He suddenly lay down on his back, his hands laced behind his head, and closed his eyes. She shifted slightly on the blanket to be able to look at him more easily. With his eyes closed she could study the wide forehead, the light brown hair with a small piece of grass stuck in it, the mouth with the curve that somehow made it attractive.

"You get to thinking the studio is the whole world, don't you?" he said suddenly, opening his eyes. "Like nothing exists outside it."

It took her a moment to remember what they had been discussing. She nodded.

"It's a world we can control, I suppose, the studio," he added. "More than we can control the rest of things." He sat up easily, putting his arms around his knees. "Too hard to talk like that," he said as if in explanation. She opened the bag and offered him a doughnut, then took one herself. They ate for a moment in silence.

"What do you wish you could control?" she asked. "Besides Miss Ridley, of course."

"Actually, I wasn't even thinking of her." He brushed an ant off his hand. "It's Sally. Not that I want to control her, just the situation. She's not happy, and I don't know how to make her happy."

"It's a hard age."

"It's more than that. It was this change, about a year ago. She'd just come back from England for the summer and she started with the accent, trying to surprise people. Even before that she'd been difficult, but it was worse, last year."

"Have you considered having her closer to home?"

"She was, once. She went to a school in La Jolla, but she didn't like the girls there. So after the summer in England, she went to school in Tarrytown. She liked someone there: a housemother, I think."

"Mrs. Wolf."

"Yes, that was it. But it wasn't enough to make her toe the line. So here we are." He had finished the doughnut and held out the bag; she took another one, and he did too.

"I won't be hungry for dinner," she said. "But they're too good to resist."

They ate silently. When he was done, he brushed the sugar off his hands.

"I can't help wondering," he said, "how things would have been if my wife were still alive."

"Easier, I'm sure," said Frances, but the look in his eyes, a look both pained and sober, made her realize it was not so simple.

"You said your wife was English," she ventured. "How did you meet?"

She half expected him to change the subject, but he moved to a more comfortable position on the blanket as if settling in for a long story. "We met in New York," he said. "In 'twenty-two. Mavis was traveling with her sister and an aunt. I was a young filmmaker, just starting out in the studios there, and we met at a house party on the

Long Island Sound. She was this elegant blonde; I was dazzled the first moment I saw her. You're probably too young to remember those years after the war, Frances, but people were ready to play. And for all her elegance, Mavis was . . ."—he paused, staring out over the hills, choosing the right word—"she was magnetic. Daring, willing to try new things when her aunt wasn't around. Taking off her dress and jumping into a swimming pool in her chemise, that sort of thing. She had no insecurity, just this bred-in-the-bone confidence that bowled me over. And she liked me right away. The first evening we met, she told me she loved my accent." He smiled briefly. "I didn't even know I had an accent until she said that. She was intrigued by my connection with movies too. Not that she had any desire to act. It was just . . . different for her. Exotic, perhaps, like she was for me.

"So we got married. Her parents didn't approve, but the war had taken most of the young men in her own country, so they gave in eventually. We were married for about a year before she was expecting Sally."

"Were you still in New York?"

He shook his head and reached for a blade of dry grass, then broke it off and twirled it between his fingers. "We'd come to Hollywood. VistaGlen Studios began in New Jersey, then moved west. And she hated Hollywood."

"Why?"

"It was such a change from the world she grew up in. A huge house from the seventeenth century, a garden with a maze in it, Lady So-and-So, all of that. She had thought she wanted something daring and different, and I'd been proud to give that to her. But when we moved west, something shifted. It showed her the limits of that desire, maybe.

"And by then we'd been married long enough for me to see her ghosts. I guess you'd call them that. She could be witty, charming, full of energy, and then she'd go into a period where she could hardly get out of bed, where she could barely function. She told me that in those times it was like having a rain cloud always in her head.

"I didn't know how to help her. I introduced her to every Brit in Hollywood, thinking she was homesick. I hired a housekeeper from London, just to have a familiar accent, but it made no difference. And it wasn't like that all the time. She'd have those periods where she was full of life, the person at the party that everyone wanted to be near. Then the dark ones, where she just cried at home with the blinds down. And the worst part was that she knew the darkness would come again. She dreaded it.

"When she became pregnant, I was so nervous for her. Right after Sally came, Mavis went into one of those dark periods again. Then she pulled out of it, and for a while, everything was fine. She doted on Sally, hardly let the nanny hold her, took her for walks around the neighborhood in a huge English pram. But when Sally was two, it came back. Stronger, this time; I don't know why.

"The doctor suggested she go into an asylum." He grimaced. "I actually went to see it. It was a nice-looking place, nothing outwardly wrong, but something about it chilled me. The doctor I spoke with suggested deliberately giving her malaria, as a way to combat the moods. I didn't like him; it was like he thought he was a god, and there was no one there to check him. I couldn't do that to her. At least at home she was near Sally and me.

"But it was a busy time. The studio was expanding, and I spent hours there. The film I was producing had an actress who needed a lot of reassurance. She was only eighteen, and it was her first big role, so she was at the studio late, with me, quite often. And I spent more time there than I would have if Mavis had been in a better place." He paused, looking out toward the hills. "It was my refuge, you could say.

"Nothing happened with the girl. Casting couch has never been my style, Frances. But I'm always going to wonder if things would have been different if I had been home more, if I had kept Mavis from feeling abandoned." Once again he paused. "I failed twice," he added quietly. "Not knowing how to help her, and then turning away.

"The film had its premiere. Mavis didn't come. I'd invited her, of course, but she'd declined. She'd seemed almost happy that evening. But when I came home, I found her in our bed. Not asleep. She'd taken half a bottle of sleeping pills."

"I'm sorry," said Frances softly.

"She didn't leave a note," he said. "I looked for one, looked everywhere. But there was nothing." A muscle beat in his jaw. "If only there had been a note. If only there had been something. I've always believed it would have been easier to bear, to have some window into her mind."

He turned to Frances. She could see the pain in his eyes, the rawness of reliving the experience, but she could also sense that it was a relief to acknowledge it.

"I'm so sorry," she said again. They were such inadequate words for what she was feeling, but his mouth curved up briefly, fleetingly, as if he understood what she could not verbalize.

He turned to face the golden hillside. "I rarely speak about this, Frances. It was terrible, all of it, like a nightmare. Thank God for my sister. She was a rock. A great help with Sally. She was so small at the time, but she was old enough to know her mother was gone." A spasm passed over his face, and he closed his eyes.

Frances moved closer, almost touching him. They sat in silence under the soft shade of the oak. There was a slight rustling above them as a bird took flight from a branch.

"Sally doesn't know," he said at last, opening his eyes. "How she died. It's not recorded as a suicide. I wouldn't even have thought to hide it, but Irving told me I should, so her death is listed as sudden heart failure. He said to tell everyone it was a family trait. I later found out it did run in her family, ironically."

"Do her parents know the truth?"

"Yes. I think that's why they dislike me. But for reasons of their own, of course, they would prefer people think it was heart failure, so the lie persists. Only a few people know the truth." He took a drink of the seltzer, then put the bottle down, grinding it into the dirt so it would not fall.

"I always come back to the note," he said, "wishing she had left one. I don't know what drove her to do it, at the last. I have my guesses, but there are gaps in the story, like missing scenes. And she's the only one who could have filled them in, and she didn't."

"Will you ever tell Sally?"

He shook his head. "I don't know. I didn't even have to think about this when she was a child, but these last few years—I just don't know."

"And it's easier to send her away than to decide."

"I'm a coward, Frances."

"No, you aren't."

"That was a forceful no."

She grasped her right forearm with her left hand, rubbing the muscle with her thumb. "We all have hard things to deal with," she said. "It would be hypocritical of me to judge you for yours. We're all just stumbling along. Trying to figure it out."

There was compassion in his eyes, and a question. And for a brief moment, she thought of opening the door to the past and letting her own story tumble out. Perhaps if she spoke of it here on this hillside, the pain of it would spread far over the valley, dissipating like exhaust in the open air.

But she could not do it. She looked down at her forearm, realizing she had been holding it so hard it hurt.

As she took her hand away, Lawrence reached for it. He squeezed it gently, and she responded in kind before they let go. And they sat in silence, both looking off in the distance at the sun-drenched hillsides and the bright blue sky.

W hen they returned to the hotel later that evening, the clerk quickly rose to his feet. "A phone call came for you, Mr. Merrill," he said, reaching into the pigeonholes behind the desk and producing a folded slip of paper.

Lawrence read it. His face turned grim. Wordlessly, he handed Frances the message.

Sister Mary Constance called. Call the convent as soon as you can. It's urgent. "God bless."

"What time was the call?" he asked.

"About two," said the clerk. "We didn't know how to reach you. She was the one who added the 'God bless,'" he said unnecessarily.

"I'm calling now," Lawrence said to Frances, once again the decisive producer. "Wait here."

As she watched him placing the call in the phone cubicle, her mind ran with possibilities, picturing scenes like those in a movie. Sally, sneaking out of the window, climbing down the oak tree and running away; Sally stricken with appendicitis, lying palely in the hospital, the black figure of a nun keeping silent vigil.

After a few minutes, he replaced the phone on the hook and nodded to the clerk. His face, as he walked toward her, was reassuring: serious, but no longer worried.

"That was Sister Mary Constance. Sally's not eating, not sleeping. 'Languishing' was the word she used. I was told to pick her up and bring her back when the school year actually begins." He smiled briefly. "I don't know how she does it, that nun. She tells you to do something, and you don't even think of arguing. She'd make a terrific executive."

"When will you go?"

"Tomorrow. If I leave early, I can be back before dinner."

"Shall I come with you?"

"No. Stay and visit with Miss Ridley, as planned. I can drop you off there tomorrow morning."

There was no annoyance in his eyes, no weariness at the thought of a long and unexpected drive. All she saw was relief, pure and complete, that mirrored her own.

CHAPTER

TWENTY-NINE

C elia, the next morning, was full of sympathy. "I hope his daughter is all right."

"I think she will be." Frances watched from the porch as Lawrence's car turned off onto the road. "She's mostly lonely, I think."

"That's common, at her age," said Celia. She smiled wryly. "I don't know what lonely is anymore." As if on cue, Toby wailed and lifted his arms to his mother, who picked him up.

"Miss Ridley's feeling much better today," said Celia. "She spent most of yesterday in bed. But Nancy and Arthur did read the script aloud to her."

"Oh," said Frances. She cast her mind back over the screenplay, trying to recall if there was anything unsuitable for children. "I hope that was okay."

"It was fine," said Celia, reading her thoughts. "Nothing that they couldn't see. I was mending as they read, so I heard it too." She didn't say what she thought of the script, and Frances did not ask. Involuntarily, she recalled Grayson's comment: *It's pure unmitigated bullshit.*

"What did Miss Ridley think?" she asked.

"She didn't say."

"Is she awake?"

"Yes, she's in the parlor. Go on in."

iss Ridley was standing, looking out the window, her back to the door. She wore the turban and the slacks and a blouse, this time a white one. Draped over it all, in spite of the heat of the day, was a red paisley shawl with fringed edges reaching nearly to her knees. Her posture was surprisingly erect even as she leaned on the cane. For a fleeting moment, Frances could picture her on stage before a row of footlights as men with Victorian sideburns applauded and cheered from the darkness.

Then the actress turned. "Ah. You're here."

"Good morning, Miss Ridley."

"Where's your partner? The fellow?"

"He had to go pick up his daughter."

"Your daughter?"

"No, Miss Ridley. His."

"How old is this daughter?"

"Thirteen."

"Thirteen. Juliet's age, more or less." She pointed to the hassock with her cane. "Have a seat."

The seat was low, making Frances's knees uncomfortably high. She was grateful to be wearing her slacks.

"That's a better fit for Nancy," said Miss Ridley, settling herself into the wing chair. "But I want you close. It's taxing to speak too loudly."

They sat in silence. There was the sound of the front door opening and closing, then through the window Frances saw Arthur dart by across the lawn. A moment later, Nancy chased after him, both of them laughing.

"They're having fun," said Miss Ridley.

"They are. It's nice to see."

Silence fell again. Frances had no desire to take charge of the conversation. She sat quietly, comfortable with the pause, and after a moment Miss Ridley spoke.

"You know," she said, "when I was that boy's age, I had already made ten thousand dollars. In the camps, performing for the miners."

"What was that like?" asked Frances.

"Nothing like your silly screenplay," said Miss Ridley, her eyes narrowing. "It makes it sound like it was one big lark. Sometimes it was, but it was also exhausting. Traveling by wagon or mule up these dusty roads, trails more like, day and night. I had to learn how to sleep sitting up. And when the rains came, oh, the mud; you've never seen anything like it. The first year I performed, I was dancing down the platform one day after my last dance. I tripped going down the stairs and fell in the mud, my whole costume covered." She waved her hand to indicate her entire body. "I wanted to cry, but the miners thought it was part of the act. They laughed and applauded, so my mother told me I had to do it every night. She knew a moneymaker when she saw one, so if they wanted me to fall, I fell. I had to wash in the creek afterwards, after each performance, and that mountain water was icy cold. I was six years old, and I could never entirely get the mud out of my fingernails, and I used to cry about it. 'Stop crying,' said Mother. 'That mud becomes gold, you'll see.' She was right."

"Your mother," said Frances. "What was she like?"

"She's all wrong in your screenplay, just as she was in that ridiculous book. They make her seem like a Madonna, loving and giving. Drawn into that traveling life by necessity, just longing to go back to her tea and needlepoint. Not true. She was the shrewdest businesswoman I've ever met. Oh, I loved her, and she loved me, but we battled, the two of us. We battled.

"But it was good for me," she added. "When you are a performer, you need armor to survive. Especially as a child."

Frances was fascinated. "What was your armor?"

Miss Ridley smiled. "You ask good questions, Miss Healey. You should have written that fool screenplay. My armor was my smile. My armor was excelling at everything I did on stage. But it was also having a secret life, all my own. There were parts of me that my mother or the stage managers never knew about. Little things, you know, like the fact that I wrote curse words inside the wooden shoes I wore for my Dutch dance, or how I had a secret name, a rude one, for every adult I had to deal with. And how sometimes I became a cat and ran away." She reached for a glass of water on the table beside her and took a long drink.

"A cat?"

Miss Ridley put down the glass before answering. "Did you ever pretend you were something else? When you were a child?"

Frances nodded.

"Well, there was one time, at a mining camp in the mountains, when I was seven or eight. I'd had a tantrum and didn't want to perform one night, but my mother made me. I was standing there in my costume, so angry, and then I saw a squirrel streak through camp and scamper up a tree. They grow trees so big there, you know, in the mountains. I watched as he went up and up, and I wanted to be him. I thought about how he could hide in the branches and no one saw him, but he was so high he could see everything, not just the camp but the mountains and the moon and the stars, so close.

"So every time I was angry or upset, I imagined doing the same. But not as a squirrel. My name was Kitty, so I imagined myself as a cat, a tabby cat. I imagined myself running through the camp, finding the tallest tree I could and climbing to the top and being there all alone. I did this everywhere I went, after that day. Every new camp, every new place I went, when I arrived, I looked for the tallest tree. In my mind, I would climb it like a cat and sit there by myself, as close to the moon as possible. I even did that in cities, you know, look for the tallest thing I could see. A skyscraper, the Eiffel Tower, whatever it was."

She sat back, breathing audibly, as if sharing the memory had taxed her strength.

"I've never told that to anyone." Her eyes closed. "No," she said after a moment. "I told one other person." Her face tightened. "One other person." She fumbled in her sleeve, found a handkerchief and drew it out and pressed it to her nose.

"What's the tallest place here?" asked Frances.

"The tower in the roof. I used to go and sit up there. I can't get up those narrow stairs now." Miss Ridley looked at Frances, her gaze shrewd. "You have something to say."

Frances tucked her knees more closely to her chest. "I used to climb trees as a child. There was one in our backyard, a privet. I could see so much, even over fences. I felt so powerful. Like I was God, almost."

"Then you know why I did it."

Frances met Miss Ridley's eyes. The clock struck the half hour.

"I'm glad that fellow's not here today," said Miss Ridley. "I'd rather talk to you." She leaned forward, resting her right hand on her cane. "What are you doing in Hollywood? It doesn't seem the right place for someone like you."

"Do you often go to the movies?"

"I don't go anyplace now. Last movie I saw was a year ago." She added, a touch reluctantly, "When I first came back to the States, I went to the pictures often."

"What do you dislike about the movies?"

"Who said I disliked them? I just told you I went when I could. No, they're fine for what they are. Entertainment, when they don't pretend to be anything more than singing or dancing or comedy. But when they try to do more than that, that's when I dislike them."

"Like when they try to tell the story of your life."

Miss Ridley nodded. "I have no patience with people who only paddle on the surface of things. I want people who will dive into the water, hold their breath and look deep. That's why this movie is so maddening to me. The book is too. I didn't even know she'd written it, that Myrtle woman, until I came back to the States. I came under my married name, you see, de la Tour; I didn't want anyone to know it was me, Kitty Ridley, and no one did, because that fool woman hadn't even bothered to get my husband's name right. Maybe she did me a favor, that way. Still, that book was all tinsel, just a candy-floss story based on the rumors. And the screenplay, it's the same. They have a story in mind already, don't they? The actress who lights up the stage but is empty inside, only filled when she marries some handsome man. They want my life to fit that. But it doesn't. It doesn't."

She leaned back, resting her head against the wing chair, and grimaced slightly. Frances moved forward to offer her a glass of water, but Miss Ridley shook her head, not to be deterred.

"Shall I tell you," she said, "why I married my husband?"

"Yes."

"It's not like they have it in the screenplay. Oh, they got some parts right. I did meet him in New York, when he came backstage with a friend of his. He was handsome, no question, with a dark mustache and such fine features. I took his roses, but I was not interested.

"We saw each other several times after that. He was persistent, you see, actually followed me all the way across the country. He used to stare at me as if I were some rare and exotic bird. He liked being out in public with me on his arm. All men did.

"He proposed marriage in Golden Gate Park, in a carriage, and you know what I did? I laughed at him. It was too bad, really. No man likes to be laughed at, especially at such a moment. But he was so florid, so"—she fluttered her hand—"so effusive. He said I was his sun, and I accused him of stealing a line from Romeo. I refused him.

"Then four months later, there was a fire. That part was true. A fire in the theater, and it burned to the ground. I didn't need him to rescue me, and he didn't; I got myself out, and I got out two stage-hands as well, if you want to know the truth. No lives were lost, but much of my history went up in smoke.

"The screenplay says that's when I decided to marry him. Not at all. It happened a year and a half later. I took a boat to France, and he proposed in Paris, and I said yes. I didn't laugh at him that time."

"What had changed?" asked Frances.

Miss Ridley set her mouth in a stubborn line. "The book said it was the fire that changed my mind. That it made me realize—what did she write, that silly woman?—'the gossamer fragility of life.' Ridiculous. I had known about the fragility of life since I was five and my father died. No, it wasn't that. At all."

She stopped and leaned forward, so close that Frances could smell the fabric of her shawl. Miss Ridley's black eyes scanned her face and her hair; then she sat slowly back.

"You have nice eyes, if you can look beyond those glasses," she said unexpectedly. "Good cheekbones too. A pleasant face. But you're hardly beautiful."

"I know," said Frances, too intrigued by the turn of the conversation to be offended.

"You're lucky. Your face isn't your fortune. But mine was." She drew the shawl more tightly around her. "I could sing and dance and act, yes, but none of that would have mattered without beauty. And youth, of course. I could look sixteen when I was thirty-five. But shortly after the fire, something happened.

"I was in the new theater, in the new dressing room, one with stronger lights over the mirror. And I sat there to put on my makeup, as always, and I saw every line." She indicated her eyes and mouth. "Not as many as I have now, of course, but lines. I put on my makeup, saw it settle into the lines. It just made them look worse. And I wept.

"Things had started to change, you see, even before the fire. Sometimes I played to theaters that were not full, as they'd always been. There was a new actress in town, a sharp young thing; she played Viola and all the parts I used to play. Not Juliet, I still owned that one. But I went to see her, and I sat there in the theater and hated her for all the things she had that I was losing, youth and beauty. I heard the applause; I heard the praise. My star was slipping, just slightly. I was probably the only one to see it. But I've always been remarkably clear-eyed about myself."

She shrugged. "I had a choice, didn't I? Stay and watch myself fade, or go on my own terms. France is where they appreciated women who had lived a little, or so they said, anyhow. My French was good; I've always picked up languages easily. So I packed up and got on the boat.

"He followed me, found me in Paris. He'd told people back in the States that I was going to marry him. I didn't know this until much later, you know. Oh, I made waves at first, was in all the Paris papers, but I had a hard time gaining a foothold there; why, I never knew. And there he was, calling me the sun in his skies.

"Why not?" She shrugged again. "Marriage would be a role, wouldn't it? I'd have a new place to live, a new start. His family was scandalized. They were an old family, and they didn't marry Americans or actresses. It pulled me closer to him. His family wanted to keep us apart, Juliet and Romeo. Who can resist the lure of that?

"We were married a month before his true nature came out. A love affair with a woman in a neighboring village, the seduction of my own lady's maid. There wasn't a servant girl in the place he hadn't bedded. When I confronted him, he just shrugged; he was amused. I wasn't in America anymore, he said. He was one of those men who always needed something new, some shiny thing to chase and hunt. I had been it, for a while. But once he had me, the luster was gone. And there I was, in my forties, in France."

"What did you do?"

"I acted, of course. No one would ever know anything was

wrong. But in private, I raged. I cried. For a time I thought maybe a child would change his ways, but it was too late for me, that ship had sailed. Then one day I found him with the laundry maid, and two hours later, there he was in my bedroom, as if nothing had happened. I would not let him touch me. He never did again."

She put her head back against the wing chair and her chest rose and fell noticeably, as if her energy were depleted. Her eyes fluttered closed.

There was a quiet knock on the door, and Frances, spellbound, took a moment to respond. It was Nancy, holding a tray with a teapot, two cups, a plate of biscotti.

"I have the tea," she said shyly. She took the tray to the side table near Miss Ridley, carefully moving the water glass out of the way.

"Thank you, Nancy," said Miss Ridley without opening her eyes. The girl slipped out of the room, closing the door behind her. "Do you want tea?" she asked Frances.

"I don't need it now, Miss Ridley," said Frances, hearing the exhaustion in the woman's voice.

"I find I'd rather rest for a bit, Miss—"

"Healey. Frances Healey."

"I'll call you Frances. I once knew a stage manager named Healey. Had a laugh like a donkey." Frances grinned. Miss Ridley nodded toward the tea tray. "Take it with you. Share it with Celia. She could use a moment off her feet, that one."

Frances bent to pick up the silver tray by its narrow metal handles. "Is there anything I can do for you?"

"Yes." Miss Ridley opened her eyes. "You can come back in a few hours, after I've rested. I like talking to you."

Celia suggested they have tea on the porch, so they settled in after first moving a paper doll book and a pair of scissors off the table. On the lawn below them, Arthur was lifting Toby into the wagon. The small boy held onto the edges with a wider smile than Frances had ever seen from him, as if he knew the delights that awaited him.

"Ready?" said Arthur.

"Ready," said Nancy, who was leaning behind the wagon, her hands on the rim.

Arthur pulled the wagon forward at a run, with so much force that Toby's small body was jolted backward. He laughed, delighted, a sound like sunlight. The wagon rattled as they made a circuit of the yard, Nancy running behind, her braids bouncing. Toby squealed with joy as the wheels went over a large rock.

Celia watched him with the gaze of a mother looking at the child who worries her. "It's good to hear him laugh. He's so serious. And he doesn't talk yet, except to say Mama."

"Maybe he's too busy thinking," said Frances.

Celia laughed. "That's what Joe says. That he's thinking deep thoughts and when he does speak it'll be in whole paragraphs." She took a sip. "Maybe it's just being the youngest, with two chatty siblings. But he won't be the youngest for long."

It took Frances a moment to understand. "Oh," she said, involuntarily glancing at Celia's abdomen, which was hidden by the table. "Oh, congratulations."

"Thanks. A January baby. We haven't had one of those yet."

"You must be exhausted."

"Occasionally. At least I'm not sick anymore. There was a rough few weeks; Joe and the kids had to do all the cooking. But I've always wanted a large family. I like having a crew around me."

"How did you and Joe meet?" asked Frances.

"At a dance. I was a senior in high school; he was two years older. He'd already started working on the farm here. That smile, you know? The first time I saw it, I knew I wanted to see it every day. And every night," she added, with a surprising flash of impishness. "And here I am."

She held out the plate of biscotti to Frances, who took another.

"It sounds dull compared to your life, doesn't it?" said Celia frankly. "It must be so fascinating, working in a studio. Seeing movies being made."

Frances nodded, brushing a crumb off the table. "I like working there. It's never boring. But your life here—it seems like a good one."

"Oh, it is. Sure, I get tired, or the kids are fighting, or there's worry about the weather. But I can handle that. I think if the core of your life is good, then the edges don't matter so much."

They saw the wagon go rattling by, Arthur pushing and Nancy pulling. "They'll wake Miss Ridley if they go on that side of the house," said Celia. She got up and hurried down the steps, and Frances watched as Toby whisked by, still holding on with both hands, his golden head shining in the sun.

Joe, who had stopped by the house for lunch, offered to show Frances the vineyards, so he and Arthur led the way past the clotheslines and out the gate. Frances was glad she'd worn her sensible shoes and slacks, for the ground through the vines was pebbly and rough. It was fascinating to see the gnarled trunks, the big leaves, and the fruit, tiny reddish-purple globes glinting in the sun.

They walked up where the property sloped toward the hills, Joe pointing out where the grapes ended and the prune orchard began. Frances shared what Celia had said about the 1920s, and Joe nodded soberly.

"It was bad," he said. "And the thirties have been hard in their own way. Let's hope the forties are better, for all of us. Right, Arthur?" Arthur, who was twirling a piece of twine and whistling, nodded.

They paused near a truck parked at the end of the rows of vines.

From there the house looked tiny, like a doll's house. Beyond the trees Frances could spot the glint of the tower at the top.

"What's the view like, from the tower?" she asked.

"Nice," said Joe. "You can see farther than you'd think. You can go up there, if you want."

"Miss Ridley said she used to like it there."

"It was her favorite place, the first few years. But she's too frail to get up those stairs now. It's a shame."

Frances leaned back against the truck, looking out over the valley. It was tawny, like all California hillsides in summer. She followed the glint of a car far away on the road, watching until it turned and disappeared behind a grove of trees.

"Has she told you about her life?" Joe asked.

"A little. It's fascinating."

"You learn about the Gold Rush in school, but she really lived it."

Frances looked back across the valley. If you squinted you could almost imagine you were seeing pioneers off in the distance, heading west in their covered wagons, having already braved heat and snowstorms and the jagged Sierras. "It's astonishing," she said. "To think of those miners. Leaving everything behind, staking it all on California."

"It worked out, for some of them," said Joe. "I guess for some it was the right choice. But not for all." He crossed his arms on his chest and was silent, regarding the vines.

"I think they probably tried hard to make it work," he said unexpectedly. "If you sold everything, gambled it all on a life here—it would have to be worth it, wouldn't it? You'd do anything to make it worth it."

The words were not eloquent, but she knew what he meant. She knew it in her bones, in a place that was starting to ache.

CHAPTER

THIRTY

Bryn Mawr, Pennsylvania
October 1932

Frances strolled through her favorite grove of trees on a brisk afternoon. It was her third autumn in the East, but the splendor of it still thrilled her. The stone bench just off the path was a perfect spot to sit and admire the color, and she walked toward it slowly, hearing the rustle of a squirrel in the trees and the swish of leaves under her feet.

It was a day of alternating clouds and sun. Beams would shine through the branches, then vanish, then reappear with no warning. *It's like* The Scarlet Letter, she thought, recalling the hide-and-seek sunlight as Hester and Dimmesdale met in the woods and affirmed their love. At Burlingame High School, her teacher, the Bostonian Mrs. Kirkland, had told her students that they couldn't fully understand the scene until they'd actually seen a deciduous forest. "You have nothing like that out here," she'd said simply. The first time Frances saw the woods of Pennsylvania, she had understood. The trees, so dense and alike, offered no guideposts. It would be easy to get lost, consciously or not, in the forest.

She stopped short. There was a man on the bench: Donald McAvoy, in a tweed suit jacket, holding an open book but looking up at the sky.

Before she could say anything, he had seen her. "Hello," he said, rising, his face lighting up with surprise and genuine pleasure. "Admiring the fall color? I guess we had the same idea."

He moved aside, offering her the other end of the bench. She'd never talked to him outside of class or the interview in his office, but as she sat down there was the same instinctive ease she always felt in his presence.

"I was just rereading an old favorite," he said, indicating the book. "*Emma*. Jane Austen."

"I've never read it."

"You soon will," he said. "You'll be writing a composition on it too. Emma is one of the most lovable heroines in fiction."

"She can't be more lovable than Elizabeth Bennet," said Frances. "No one could."

He turned to her, his eyebrows raised in delight at the prospect of an intellectual argument. "Now that's a bold claim, Miss Healey. Can you back it up?"

"I can indeed," she said eagerly, and the next twenty minutes passed in an animated discussion of literary heroines and their flaws and virtues, as the sun appeared and disappeared, over and over, unnoticed by either of them.

"I'll grant you this," said Professor McAvoy, "when I first read *Pride and Prejudice*, I was half in love with Elizabeth Bennet myself. So perhaps you're right."

"When did you first read it?"

"Junior year in high school. And you?"

"Sophomore year. But the boys in my class didn't like the book."

"What insensitive louts."

She laughed and he did too. "They said it was dull, a book about girls looking for husbands. They liked stories where the stakes were higher."

"I'm sure you had a clever response."

"I don't know if it was clever, but I told them that in Austen's time women couldn't go to college or have a job. Everything hinged on who she married, so it was serious business. A matter of life and death, even."

His eyes lit up with respect. "I'd call that the perfect response."

"Thank you."

He said nothing for a moment, just looked at her. She felt her cheeks grow warm. Then he tilted his head to gaze at the trees before them. "It's true," he said. "What those boys failed to see is that the decision to marry—even now—affects everything, every part of life. This is just as true for men as it is for women. And if we men aren't able to grasp that, like you women do"—he turned to her—"well, then we're definitely the weaker sex."

There was a change in his voice, a new intensity that matched the expression in his eyes. For the first time in his presence, Frances could not think of what to say. She glanced down, brushing at a smudge of dirt on her stocking, trying to decide how to respond. When she raised her head, he looked up from her leg and met her gaze. He smiled.

"Enough of my pontificating," he said, rising abruptly. "I'll leave the autumn color to you. Hopefully there's some good daylight left."

"I'm sure there is." Just as she said that, the sunlight vanished. "I spoke too soon."

She was about to reference Hester and Dimmesdale when he indicated the sky. "It's like that scene in *The Scarlet Letter*, isn't it? With the light that comes and goes."

"That's just what I was going to say," she said with delight.

"Not for the first time," he said, "we're thinking along the same lines."

He shifted his book to the other hand and nodded his farewell. "It's been a pleasure, Miss Healey." His blue eyes held hers. "As always," he added.

As he walked back down the path, she watched until the trees hid him from view. She did not stay long after that, for the afternoon seemed much less colorful without him.

CHAPTER

THIRTY·ONE

hen Miss Ridley called Frances back in, it was nearly three o'clock. "I'd like to go for a walk outside. I know it's hot," she added before Frances could speak. "But I want fresh air."

"Where would you like to go?"

"Just the edge of the property there, the garden. Ask Celia for some pruning shears. We can cut flowers for the house."

They set out ten minutes later, Miss Ridley holding onto Frances's arm. It took a long while for them to navigate the stairs down from the porch. You could forget her frailty when she was sitting and talking about her life, Frances thought; the young, vibrant Kitty Ridley still shone through her eyes and the husky timbre of her voice. But guiding her down the steps, feeling her stiffness and trepidation at the idea of falling, you remembered her age.

Once they reached the flower garden beyond the house, Miss Ridley shrugged off Frances's arm and leaned on her cane. "There," she said. "Let's start with those." She nodded toward the apple-pink blossoms of the penstemon.

Frances snipped several stalks, then moved to the other flowers in the bed, slowly filling the long basket Celia had provided. After watching her in silence, Miss Ridley lowered herself down to the bench, resting her hands on the cane. "Shall I get you a glass of water from the house?" asked Frances.

"No. Just a moment off my feet, that's all." She seemed at once vulnerable and calm, the sun glinting off her turban.

"So, Frances," she said. "Are you married?"

"No."

"Ever been married?"

"No."

"Ever been engaged?"

Frances, who had been reaching for a marguerite, paused in midair and then snipped it carefully. "No."

She turned to Miss Ridley. The woman's gaze was fixed on her.

"Not exactly," said Frances.

"There is a story there."

Frances nodded and moved on to the lavender bush. Some of the spears were fading, the blossoms turning dry, but others were lush and purple.

"Careful," said Miss Ridley. "The bees like that one." As if hearing her, a fat yellow bee buzzed near Frances's hand, and she backed away.

"Leave it," said Miss Ridley. "Lavender is better on the bush, anyhow."

Frances breathed deeply, filling her lungs with the clean, sunwarmed scent. "It's so fragrant."

"Just like at the convent."

"Is there a convent near here?"

"No, I'm talking about the convent in Provence. Where I used to live."

Frances turned to her in surprise, and a few marguerites tipped out of her basket and fell to the ground.

"Yes," said Miss Ridley, "I left my husband and lived in a convent. Not as a nun; I'm not Catholic, for one. But if you had means and the inclination, as I did, you could pay to live there and have a quiet life. And that's the life I had. For eight years."

Frances picked up the fallen blooms. "What was it like there?"

"Silent, restful. Isolated. I talked to the sisters, occasionally to visitors."

"Who were your visitors?"

"My husband's family, at first, to convince me to come back. They didn't like me, but it was a scandal, you know, a wife living in a convent while her husband was alive." She smiled scornfully. "I have caused scandal by living too loud, by having lovers before I was married, by smoking in public. Then later I caused scandal by living a life of quiet seclusion. You can't please everyone, can you? Not if you are a woman, that is.

"But the lavender." A peaceful look came over her face. "The convent was gray stone, built in the fifteenth century. In a small valley, in Provence. And they grew lavender, and oh, at this time of year, July, it was glorious. A field of it. Purple, row after row, and the scent filled the air. The cleanest scent you can think of, isn't it? Like it washes away all that is ugly. And when I smell it now, I think of the convent, the stillness, washing away the ugliness of my marriage. The ugliness of the self-doubt I felt, and the way he acted once he found he could not bend me to his will. And the silence. It was a silent place, a place where no one saw me. No one was looking at me. I had nothing to pretend to be."

"That must have been a change."

"Oh, it was. I had spent a lifetime performing, you see. I was a Dutch girl, an Irish girl, singing whatever song the miners liked. Then when I was older, it was Shakespeare: Juliet, Portia, and there were other plays, some written just for me. But I was always someone else, even offstage. It was true, I was not entirely a ladylike woman. I did wear trousers; I did smoke cigars. I did take lovers, yes; not dozens, like that fool screenplay says, but a few. My husband was not the first man I'd been with, but the fifth." She raised an eyebrow. "That made him angry, the swine. As if he should be one to criticize. But when you are in the public eye, there are always stories about you, Frances. You become not yourself but the heroine of someone else's tale. The girl who wears jewelry fit for a queen and is squired by the world's most famous men and who bathes in champagne. They like that story. They keep telling it until it becomes more real than the truth. And if you wanted to be something different, you can't. They won't let you. The story has outrun you.

"And that's why I went to that convent in the valley. To leave it all behind. To be there alone, with no one to perform to, onstage or off."

"Did you find what you were looking for?"

"Oh, yes. It brought me peace. Time to think about my life, and to find the truest moments in it. It brought me to my knees, sometimes; I shed many tears. But when you see no one, when you live in silence with just the chants of the sisters and the sounds of the birds and the buzz of the bees, the howl of the wind, you are able to see. The clutter of the world falls away. And it's just you."

She sat on the bench, one veined hand grasping her cane. Her face was relaxed, and her voice was quieter than it had been before.

Frances stood in the sunlight, but she hardly felt its heat. She was struck by the change in the woman's demeanor, by her candor and vulnerability. She thought of Belinda, and her relentless pursuit of the Kitty Ridley role. "My chance to be more than some silly ingenue," she had said, as if she, too, were trapped in a story others had written for her.

You know what that feels like, said a voice inside.

"It's funny," said Miss Ridley. "According to that fool book, everyone thought I was in a harem. I was really in a convent. No one ever thought of that."

A bee buzzed past, and Frances waved it away. Miss Ridley nodded toward the light blue delphiniums. "Those are nice."

"I'll cut a few."

"I had a dress just that color once," said Miss Ridley, "when I was sixteen. It was silk. My first grown-up dress, made by Mrs. O'Leary, the woman who used to do costumes for the Bella Union theater. I felt like I could conquer the world in that dress. When you shifted in the light, the blue looked purple. I liked it very much."

She closed her eyes. Frances quietly snipped a few flowers, adding them to the basket, glancing from time to time at the tiny figure on the bench. Then Miss Ridley suddenly frowned and opened her eyes.

"When is he coming back? The movie man."

"Later this afternoon."

Miss Ridley nodded thoughtfully. Then she peered at Frances, her eyes narrowing. "You're supposed to be convincing me about that film, aren't you? Not letting me rattle on about my past."

"I suppose I am. I'm not doing a very good job of it, am I?"

"No, you aren't." She opened her mouth to say more, then seemed to change her mind. She sat up, with a shade of the imperious demeanor she'd had the first day.

"I don't understand it," she said. "Movie acting."

"Pardon?"

"They act in front of a camera, don't they? In front of a box. How can you possibly perform to a box?" Frances opened her mouth to speak, and Miss Ridley waved her hand impatiently. "I know, those French brothers made that movie of me, in Paris. That wasn't acting; it was just me out for a stroll. Those Hollywood actors—how do you tell a story that way? How can a camera tell you if you're any good?"

"There's a director," said Frances. "He stops the scene and has the actors do it again if it's not convincing."

"That's worse. How can you possibly act when it's chop, chop, chop like that? No time to let a whole scene unfold?"

Frances, who had been surprised on set to see how often filming was interrupted by the director's impatient "Cut!" could not help but agree.

"No, acting on stage is what's real," said Miss Ridley. "That's where you learn how to act." She pointed to the delphinium. "Get that one, on the far side."

Frances obliged. Miss Ridley got up with effort, leaning on the cane.

"You need an audience there, you see. You need to hear their reactions. What makes them laugh, what makes them cry, what makes them gasp. That's when you know that you're doing it right. Do you see?"

"I think so."

"It's a living thing, acting. They react to you; you take your cues from each other and respond. It's like being in bed with a man," she said surprisingly. "It can be horribly one-sided. Or it can be . . ."—she searched for the word, leaning heavily on her cane—"alive. Two people in tune with each other, listening and watching and reacting. Fully present." Her voice was triumphant. "There. Tell them to put that in their movie."

Her black eyes watched Frances, bright and defiant, as if waiting for shock. After a moment, her expression changed.

"You know exactly what I'm talking about, don't you," she said.

"I do," said Frances.

She was holding the delphinium in one hand, the pruning shears in the other. The flower suddenly became blurry, indistinct, and she blinked back the tears before they could fall.

A wrinkled hand reached for her own. It patted her lightly, twice, like a mother would do, with the soft jingling of bracelets like a wind chime.

"Well, then," said Miss Ridley. "Well, then." The words meant nothing, really, but somehow the soothing tone and gesture, made in the silence of the quiet garden, gave Frances the desire to open the book of her past. She tried to resist the impulse, but it seemed to take more energy to be silent than to speak. She put the delphinium in the basket and laid the shears carefully on the bench.

"It was in my last year of college," she said. It was not a story she had told before, and it came out haltingly, without the polish and confidence that comes from repetition. "He was a professor there. Young, and handsome, and intelligent, and I was drawn to him. He felt the same. We used to meet . . . in his office." She felt her cheeks burn, but Miss Ridley, standing beside her, was listening with no judgment on her wrinkled face. "I'd never done that before. But I loved it. We met there four different times."

"You remember every time."

Frances nodded.

"Did anyone find out?"

"Yes. Not while it was happening, but after."

"And you were 'not exactly' engaged to him?"

"No. I was engaged, but not—not to him."

"Where is he now?"

"Still teaching there, I think. I don't know."

"And you?"

"I didn't graduate. I went back to California and became a secretary."

"What did you want to be?"

"A journalist."

"I see," said Miss Ridley. Standing so close to her, Frances could see the sweat gathering around the edges of the turban, dampening the woman's temples. She felt a sudden qualm at keeping her out on such a hot day.

"Perhaps we should go back, Miss Ridley. It's so warm here."

The actress nodded but made no effort to leave. She stood there, her hands on her cane, the greenish veins prominent in the sun.

"I think, Frances," she said in her husky voice, "that you understand me. And I think I understand you."

Frances felt tears start again in her eyes.

"If you ever want to tell the rest of your story," said Miss Ridley, "it's safe with me. There's no better confidant than a recluse. Especially one in her nineties. Anything you share will go with me to my grave."

She nodded toward the basket. "We've done well here, I think. Look at those beauties." She looked up at Frances and smiled. "Let's go back inside."

You didn't mean it to happen, twenty-year-old Frances thought as she lay in bed and stared at the ceiling of her college dormitory room. If asked to explain how a sensible girl could embark on a love affair with her professor, her answer would be that it happened because you didn't intend it to happen. You didn't mean to be reading on the same bench a week later as Dr. McAvoy just happened to walk by, leading to another animated conversation, and you didn't mean to go back to his office to ask about an assignment and talk for so long you missed dinner. You didn't expect his look of frank admiration during a class discussion of *Great Expectations* when you said that Estella would have been far more sympathetic if Dickens were female, that a female author would have done more to tell her backstory. And you didn't expect that soon when he lectured to the whole class he would be looking only at you, to the point where you were both afraid it was noticeable and deeply flattered.

Your thoughts were aligned in ways you'd never experienced with any other man. Where they did not align, the challenge of your differences was heady, even exhilarating. For the first time you truly understood Jane Eyre and Rochester, sitting by the fire and talking for hours, intellectual equals.

But not just intellectual ones. For it was the semester of your art history class, taught by the gray-haired, diminutive Ada Halliday, a woman unembarrassed by the rippling flesh of the odalisques or the pink-tipped bosoms of Renoir's women. She talks about the artists' lines and coloring and the sensuality of the flesh in a way that makes you feel that there is more to this thing called the body than you had ever suspected. It was a lesson you never got from Mother Florence, with her tidy clothes and her waist nipped by a girdle. In art class you see pictures of women at home in their bodies, reclining naked in the sun, unashamed and content.

Your literature class follows the art history class, and you go from the paintings of nudes to the man who looks up and smiles as you walk in, so perhaps it's inevitable that on a rainy afternoon when you stop by his office to borrow a book, a day when the whole building seems deserted, he gives you the book and your hands touch and he is looking at you in just the same way you know you are looking at him, and then he pulls you to him and you are kissing each other as if you can't bear to stop. And soon pieces of your clothing and his are on the floor, and it occurs to you, in a sudden moment of ironic detachment, that a portrait of you at this moment would be called something like Study of a Nude in a Study. But the detachment does not last, for he says, "Your legs just go on forever, don't they?" and presses his lips to each ankle in turn, and you know exactly where the afternoon will go and you participate fully and rapturously, as if you lived in a world entirely without consequences.

CHAPTER
THIRTY·TWO

I t was after five when Lawrence and Sally arrived at the Ventimiglias' home. The car had barely stopped when Sally leapt out and ran to Frances and gave her a hug.

"You look tan, Frances." She righted her hat, looked up at the house. "This is so pretty."

"How are you, Sally?"

"I'm fine now. They were actually nice, the nuns. But it was too dark at night, too quiet, with all these creaks. I couldn't sleep, and I kept having headaches."

"Sally will go back," Lawrence said, closing the door of the car, "when the school year begins. But not before. Not until the other girls are there. We talked it over on the drive up."

"I won't mind if I'm not alone." She stepped back, looking up at the tower with delight. "Can you go up to that place on the roof?"

"Apparently so. I haven't been there yet."

Celia and Nancy appeared, Toby trailing behind. Lawrence introduced them and Sally was friendly, almost humble, obviously eager to please. She accepted Celia's offer of lemonade and followed her into the house, asking about the tower as they went.

Lawrence turned to Frances. He was more relaxed than she had ever seen him in the presence of his daughter.

"I thought she'd be defiant when I got there. Or sullen. But she wasn't. She was . . . surprisingly childlike. Happy to see me. I think it was being alone that put her on edge."

Frances remembered the echoing hallway, the somber religious lithographs. "I'm not surprised. That dormitory was awfully forbidding."

"You wouldn't have left her there, would you? If she were your daughter?"

"No."

He nodded once. "Well," he said quietly. "I'm learning." Crossing to the car, he opened the back door and took out Sally's satchel. "We had a good talk on the drive up. Surprising. I wasn't expecting it."

"About . . ."

"No," he said. "Not about Mavis. But about other things. It was the most time I've had alone with her in years. And that bridge is really something, even seeing it a second and third time."

"I'm sure Sally loved it."

"She did. She was practically speechless."

The door opened and Sally burst out, followed by Nancy. "We're going to see the vines," said Sally. "I've never seen grapes growing before."

Nancy had the proud, excited look of a girl eager to share her expertise with an older friend. "This way," she said to Sally, and they took off at a run, around the house, the sounds of their voices breaking the summer stillness.

"So much for being speechless," said Lawrence with a grin. As they went into the house, Frances realized Sally was no longer speaking with the English accent.

They did not see Miss Ridley that evening; she had gone to bed after the walk in the garden. "I hope the sun today wasn't too much for her," said Frances.

Celia shook her head. "It's not the sun," she said. "I'll check on her later."

They had dinner with the Ventimiglias. Lawrence was reluctant to impose yet again, but Celia waved it off. "Nancy would be angry with me if I took her new friend away so quickly," she said, watching the girls as they sat side by side on the sofa reading a magazine. "I hope you'll bring Sally here tomorrow, when you meet with Miss Ridley."

Back at the hotel, Lawrence booked another room for Sally. Frances offered to share hers, but Lawrence insisted. "I feel as though I'm trespassing on everyone's hospitality these days," he said. "You, the Ventimiglias."

"Will Sally be all right?" Frances thought of the fear the girl had shared about sleeping alone at the convent.

"I asked. She said she's fine as long as she knows I'm just a room away."

And in fact when they returned to the hotel, Sally, looking tired from the day's travel and activity, went upstairs right away. "I'll sleep better here," she said. She gave her father a brief hug around the waist, and Frances realized from Lawrence's quick expression of surprise that it was not a typical gesture.

After she had gone upstairs, the two of them sat in the lobby of the hotel, looking out at the courthouse. Its facade was almost ghostly in the moonlight.

"Did you get a chance to talk to Miss Ridley today?" he asked.

"I did." Frances found herself strangely reluctant to give the details. "We talked about her childhood. Why she married her husband, what he was like."

"Not as appealing as Theodore Grant, apparently."

"They didn't love each other. It's not like the screenplay. Not at all."

"Just when it comes to her husband? Or overall?"

"Overall, I'd say." Frances took a cigarette from the box on the end table, and Lawrence leaned in to light it for her. His large hands were close to her face. She could see, in the small flare of the match, the curve of his mouth and the look in his eyes. They had once been the impersonal eyes of an employer, but they were not anymore.

"It's all right if you don't want to tell me, Frances. I don't need to know the details."

"I couldn't explain them anyhow," said Frances. "I think she's the only one who can do them justice."

"Not Myrtle Dobson."

"Oh Lord, no."

"And not Grayson."

"No. Not Grayson. And I think he'd be the first to admit that."

Lawrence, who had lit his own cigarette, smoked thoughtfully for a moment. "Justice," he said, looking at the courthouse. "That's fitting, isn't it? Clearly no one has done justice to her story so far. Is there a chance we could, if we revise the script?"

"I don't know," said Frances, looking down at her cigarette. She tapped out the ash, slowly.

When she glanced back up, Lawrence was watching her. As their eyes met, he did not look away. A little flame leapt inside her, as if another match had been lit.

"I don't think I've ever seen you smoke before," he said.

"I don't very often. Just when—well, it's been an emotional day. Few days."

"Hasn't it, though," he said quietly. "It's like all of my Hollywood armor is falling away."

She realized it would be a mistake to keep looking into his eyes. She stubbed out the cigarette and rose from the chair, and he got up in turn.

"I think I'll say goodnight," she said.

"Thank you, Frances," he said. He did not say what he was thanking her for; she did not need to ask.

CHAPTER
THIRTY-THREE

The next morning, Sally was bright and cheerful, eager for what the day would bring. They took her to the diner for breakfast, sitting at the same counter where they had sat their first evening in Napa, and she stowed her cat satchel carefully under the stool. "I'm bringing a few things to show Nancy," she said. Frances wondered if the framed picture of her mother was one of them. It felt keenly painful to be sitting at the same place where Lawrence had shared the truth about Mavis while Sally happily stirred milk and sugar into her tea.

At the Ventimiglias', Celia greeted them at the door. "Miss Ridley's ready to see you," she told Frances and Lawrence. "And she'd like to meet Sally too."

The Miss Ridley of the garden—open, pensive, vulnerable—was gone, and the woman who greeted them was the same imperious one of the first day. She sat ramrod straight on the wing chair and did not smile at Lawrence when he came into the room. "You're back," she said.

"I am glad to see you again, Miss Ridley."

"I'm sure you are." She indicated Sally, standing in silent awe before her. "This is your daughter?"

"Yes. Miss Ridley. This is Sally." Sally smiled nervously.

"Thirteen, are you?"

"Yes, Miss Ridley."

"A little older than Nancy, then. She's a good girl, Nancy." Miss Ridley's black eyes were keen as she studied Sally. After a moment, she said, "Do you like acting?"

"Acting?"

"Pretending to be someone you're not."

Sally cast a glance at Frances, then at her father. "I think so, Miss Ridley. I can speak with an English accent."

"Let's hear it."

"What shall I say?"

"Tell me about your drive up here. With the accent."

Sally, suddenly looking far more comfortable, began to speak. "We drove over the Golden Gate Bridge. It was beautiful, so huge, with such high towers. You can see so much, and there is the ocean on one side and the bay on the other. I loved it."

Miss Ridley smiled. It was a genuine, admiring smile. "That was very well done."

"Thank you, Miss Ridley."

"I could do so many accents in my day. English, Scottish. Dutch. I could do southern, too, and a Boston accent. It's a gift, you see."

"Can I hear them?" asked Sally eagerly.

Frances saw Lawrence stiffen slightly, but Miss Ridley sat even straighter in the chair, put a concerned expression on her face, and said, "'Ach, and there's a terrible wind comin' over the heather. Best find McTavish, laddie. 'Tis a night for stayin' in with the fire blazin'.' That was a play I did in Chicago, a character called Catriona McBride. It was a dreadful play, melodramatic pap, but I still remember some of the lines."

"I've never been able to do a Scottish accent," said Sally.

"You could, with a little help. I'll teach you if you like. But now run off and find Nancy. I would like to talk to your father and Frances."

Sally smiled and left. Miss Ridley waited until the door had closed before speaking.

"I like your daughter," she said to Lawrence. She arranged the shawl, her bracelets jingling. "I like your secretary too. She and I had a good talk yesterday. Perhaps she told you."

"She told me you spoke, Miss Ridley. She did not tell me the details."

Miss Ridley turned to Frances. "I didn't ask you to keep it secret."

"I know." Frances thought of the garden in sunlight, the clean fragrance of the lavender, and the astonishing revelations of Miss Ridley, which had caused her own past to bubble to the surface like a spring. "I didn't think I could tell it like you did, Miss Ridley."

"If it's a matter of the accuracy of the story," said Lawrence, "we'd be willing to work with you on the script. We'd love to do that." It could have been a lie, delivered by an executive willing to say anything to achieve his purpose, but Frances knew he was absolutely sincere. "It's important to the studio—to me—that we are doing justice to your story."

"But perhaps," said Miss Ridley, "it's impossible for you to do justice to my story."

The clock ticked audibly in the silence.

"What if we told only a part of it," said Lawrence after a moment. "Focused on one section, went more deeply into it?"

"An episode in the life of Kitty Ridley," said Miss Ridley. "Her life, from age nineteen to twenty-one?"

"Something like that," said Lawrence cautiously. "Or a little bit later, perhaps."

"You are determined to tell the story of my marriage, aren't you?"

Lawrence opened his mouth, then shut it. "Yes," he said simply. "I will not pretend otherwise, Miss Ridley. A movie can have action and music and comedy. But above all, what the audiences want is a love story."

"But what if the great love story of my life was not with my husband?"

Lawrence looked at Frances, then back at Miss Ridley. "If you have stories still to be told," he said after a pause, "we may be able to use them."

"Use them," Miss Ridley repeated. "What a curious verb. As if the most intimate moments of my life were a broom, or a mop." The words were caustic, but her tone was not. She glanced at Frances, a twinkle in her eye.

"You know," she said to him, "I am turning ninety-one tomorrow."

"I didn't know," said Lawrence, with genuine surprise. "Happy birthday."

"I've never been much on celebrating it. My success always lay in hiding my age. But now"—she straightened, grimacing involuntarily—"this year, I feel the need to celebrate."

"Whatever we can do, Miss Ridley," said Lawrence.

"Come for dinner tomorrow, both of you. And your daughter. Perhaps I will have an answer for you then."

"We'll see you before then, I hope?" Lawrence's voice was cautious.

"Perhaps. But not now." She closed her eyes as if to sleep and kept them closed.

Frances and Lawrence went outside, down the porch and on to the lawn, instinctively seeking the shade of the oaks. Frances sat on the bench under the trees while Lawrence remained standing, his arms crossed. "I suppose we'll know tomorrow, then," she said.

He looked up at the lacework of the branches above him, filtering the sun. "What do you think her answer will be?"

"I don't know." She pressed her fingers into the base of her thumb. "When we first came here, I would have said no. But now—"

"There's a chance."

"I think so."

"She likes you, Frances. That's obvious."

"I like her too."

"Do you think," he said, "knowing more of her story than I do, do you think there's a way to tell it in a movie?"

Frances gazed up at the tower. Its windows glinted in the sun. She imagined a tabby cat, lithe and quick, scampering along the ground, then up the sides of the house, jumping noiselessly to windowsill and roof.

Before she could answer, Sally and Nancy came toward them at a run. "There you are," said Sally. "Mrs. Ventimiglia said I could sleep here tonight in Nancy's room. May I? Please?"

"That's very kind of her," said Lawrence.

"May I?"

"Yes, if you like."

"We won't talk all night, Mr. Merrill," said Nancy. "My mother made us promise."

"Also," said Sally, "Mrs. Ventimiglia says there's a river you can swim in."

"There is," said Nancy promptly. "In Yountville. My father takes us there on hot days."

"He can't take us there today," said Sally, "but maybe you can? You and Frances? Please?"

The girls stood side by side, the anticipation nearly vibrating off of them. Lawrence looked at them, considering the idea.

"If Miss Ridley won't see us for a few hours," he said, "then maybe we can." He turned to Frances. "Do you have a bathing suit?"

"I do."

"All right then. We're going swimming."

"You too?" asked Sally in delighted astonishment.

"Me too," said Lawrence.

CHAPTER
THIRTY-FOUR

C elia gave them directions and towels and packed a lunch: bologna sandwiches, sugar cookies, strawberries, bottles of soda to put in the river to stay cool. They offered to bring Arthur along, but he was helping his father with something in the vineyards. "Besides," said Celia, "it's good for Nancy to have something of her own."

They stopped at the hotel to get their bathing suits and Sally's bag for the evening, then headed north. They took the turn for Yountville, driving past a few cottages and farms; then Nancy pointed out a dirt road to the left. They parked the car, walked over bone-dry yellow grass and then up a small rise, where oaks and bays and hints of bright green indicated the presence of water. "It's here," said Nancy eagerly, and through the trees they could see the river, narrow at this point in its travels and looking more like a creek as it curved through the landscape. The air was palpably cooler than it had been by the car.

They scampered down a short but steep bank and found themselves in a little clearing. The river made a turn, and the water pooled in a small lake, almost like a swimming hole.

"It doesn't look very deep," said Sally.

"Wait till you go in," said Nancy. And sure enough, as Sally waded in the water went up to her waist, and she squealed in delight.

Lawrence turned to Frances. "Shall we join them?"

"I just need a place to change into my bathing suit."

"You could do it there," he said, indicating a clump of trees around the bend of the river. "I'll take a turn when you're done."

She picked her way along the bank, which was rocky and pebbly. The girls' shouts and splashes receded as she walked along. They were the only people there.

She found a group of trees overgrown with some sort of vine and undressed quickly. It was strange to take off her clothing outdoors. The air felt warm and her breasts looked so different in the dappled shade of the tree, light diced with dark over her pale skin. She thought of the art class in college, studying Manet's *Le Déjeuner sur l'herbe*, where a completely nude woman sat on a riverbank, easy in her own skin. Unconsciously, she relaxed. She did not hurry anymore, protected by the screen of the trees and its tent of ivy, the dry bay leaves at her feet releasing their spicy scent with each step.

When she had put on her suit and walked slowly over the stony riverbank, she found the girls floating on their backs. They hailed her boisterously. Lawrence, sitting with his feet bare, watched her as she came toward him, clothes rolled under her arm, shoes dangling from the other hand.

She put her things down on the bank and straightened. That look in his eyes: she had seen it before, one evening in his office. And here there was no desk between them, no steno pad, no phone to ring.

He stood up, tucking his own suit under his arm. "My turn," he said with a smile. As he passed her he held her shoulders lightly for a second, as if not wanting to knock her off-balance on the narrow strip of riverbed. The quick touch of his hands on her skin made warmth rise to her face.

They stayed for two hours, pausing to eat lunch. The girls alternated between swimming and splashing, walking slowly up the creek, tracking water bugs, and sitting side by side, their heads bent together, deep in conversation.

"This is unexpected," said Lawrence, watching the girls on the far side of the river. "Sally finding a friend."

"I'm glad. I think she's been hungry for one."

They were sitting on the bank, Lawrence in his swimsuit, his hair still gleaming wet from his recent dip in the water. His body was lean, but his shoulders were broader than she'd ever noticed; he wasn't as muscular as Gene, but when he'd thrown Sally playfully into the water, Frances had been surprised at the ease with which he did so. There were so many things you didn't learn about a person in an office, which you did learn on the road.

"They're a nice family," he said. "The Ventimiglias. Their children are lucky, to live in a home like that."

"I think so too."

Sitting with her arms wrapped around her bare legs, she thought of the moment she'd witnessed the night before. It was after dinner, and Joe was reaching up to close the curtains in the front room. Celia, coming up behind him, had laid a hand lightly on his lower back and stood on her tiptoes to say something in his ear. He had turned toward her, his hand still on the curtain pull, and looked down at her with his wide smile lit by desire, a smile not meant for anyone else to witness. Frances had turned away quickly, but not without a sudden pang of envy.

"Celia and Joe are lucky too," she said. "To have found each other, I mean."

"What about you?" he asked after a moment. "Is there a man in your life?"

It was a question that would have felt intrusive back at the studio but did not by the river. She leaned her head back against the rocky bank, found it uncomfortable, and sat up straight again. "No. I go out with fellows, but there's no one . . . special."

"Has there ever been?"

She paused. It was easier to talk to him when they were side by side, and yet she was as aware of his presence as if they had been face-to-face. "My last year of college." Her tone left the door open.

"What happened?"

On the far side of the river, a huge tree grew along the bank. Its root system was above ground, a tangled weave. It reminded Frances of a picture of the nervous system she'd once seen in an encyclopedia, a hidden thing brought out into the light.

"He was my professor," she said slowly. "I loved him, and I think he loved me too. It didn't last very long. But it was like something you read about in books, how we were practically able to finish each other's sentences. It was the kind of attraction that you can't—you don't—resist." She ventured a glance at him, but he, like Miss Ridley, was looking at her with openness and without judgment. How odd, after so many years of silence, to tell her story to two different people in two days. And she knew, as she watched the sunlight on the water, that she wanted to say more than she had told Miss Ridley, to go a page further in the story.

"He didn't tell me," she said slowly, "that he was engaged to someone else."

The girls, tired of their chat on the opposite riverbank, had slipped into the water with cries and shouts. Sally waved wildly at Frances, and she raised her hand in return.

"I apologize for my sex," he said quietly. "Men can be real cads."

There was more she could have said, and for a moment she almost did, but the girls were splashing toward them, so she simply said, "I won't disagree."

He brushed away a fly that had settled on his forearm. She looked at the muscle underneath the light brown hair. "Are you coming back in?" Sally called.

"In a while," said her father.

"Let's see how high we can make the water go," said Nancy, sending a shower of drops high into the air. Sally responded in kind, and the air rang with splashes and cries. It was a screen under which Frances could ask a question she'd been pondering for weeks.

"Lawrence, what happened with you and Belinda?"

He seemed to expect the question, or at least to recognize her right to ask it after what she herself had shared. He gazed at the water as if finding the right words.

"I think," he said carefully, "the best way to say it is that I was drawn to her until I wasn't. It wasn't just her beauty; it was the whole story. She may seem to have a charmed life, but there's more to it than that." He was silent for a moment; Frances could tell he was not sure how much to say.

"I've always felt the need," he said in a low voice, "to make it up to my wife. For not being what she needed, whatever that was. And I saw—I see—some of the same vulnerability in Belinda. She wants this part so much. I think that by getting it for her, I was making amends to my wife, in some way."

He turned to look directly at her. "You asked me, a few days ago, if it was a grand gesture of love for Belinda. It was at first. But a few weeks ago, I realized that . . . that it was best to end things with her. And I don't regret that. All the same, I want to do this for her. She's vulnerable in her own way, Frances. I'd like to have one woman in my life whom I haven't failed. So it's not a grand gesture of love. It's a gesture of expiation, I suppose."

"That does you credit," said Frances.

"Does it? I'm not sure anymore."

They both looked at the river. Sally was floating on her back like a contented Ophelia, her hair loose in the water, gazing serenely up at the lacework of the branches above her.

"This has been an astonishing place," he said simply. She knew he meant not just the river but Napa as a whole.

A bee buzzed by her ear and she involuntarily jerked away, brushing against Lawrence as she did so. "Sorry," she said, but he just smiled at her. Then to her wonder and surprise he reached up, and she felt a soft, gentle tugging of her hair. He drew his hand back, this time with a small bay leaf held between his fingers.

"Oh," she said, "I didn't know that was there."

"You've gone natural. It suits you."

"Maybe you should put it back then."

It was meant as a joke, but he took her at her word. She did not know where to look as he leaned in and carefully and deliberately tucked it back into her curls. So she closed her eyes, which only seemed to heighten everything else: the smell of the bay leaf, the sounds of the girls calling to each other on the river, and the gentle movement of his fingers in her hair, taking time to find exactly the right place.

CHAPTER
THIRTY-FIVE

W hen they took the girls back to the house, Celia invited them to stay for dinner. Lawrence politely demurred, citing the need to get back to Napa. As they drove toward town, Frances asked, "Was there some work you wanted to do tonight?"

"No. I just felt the need for a quieter evening."

"I can order you room service, once we're back."

"No, Frances," he said. "I can be quiet with you. Let's find a restaurant somewhere in town."

She felt her heart quicken and focused her gaze on the twilight landscape ahead.

"If you'd like to, of course," he added.

"I'd love to," she said. The bay leaf was in her pocket, where she had put it once they had left the river, and she traced its smoothness with her fingers.

N apa was not Hollywood or San Francisco; the dining options were limited, but the clerk directed them to what he called the nicest restaurant in town. It had a small dance floor, and midway through their meal a band set up and began to play. The musicians wore suits, not smart tuxedos as they would in Hollywood, but their playing could hold its own against the band at the Blossom Room.

Over dinner Frances and Lawrence talked about their childhoods—his in Cooperstown, hers in Burlingame. They spoke of their favorite books, of the places they had traveled and still wanted to see. They did not speak of Sally, or Miss Ridley, or Belinda. The conversation was easy, and yet underneath it there was a current of something else, something charged and alive. Once Frances glanced up from her plate to find Lawrence looking at her. He did not look away, nor did she, and it was only the arrival of the waiter that broke the moment.

They were finishing coffee when the singer arrived, to excited applause from the locals. She was in her thirties, unremarkable looking, with an ample figure; her curves seemed to be held in place by the satin dress she wore. She seemed out of place chatting with the band, as if a suburban housewife were playing dress-up.

But then the music began, and she moved to the microphone, confidently cradling it with her fingers. And she began to sing "This Year's Kisses," and her voice filled the room. It was a beautiful voice, clear and full of feeling.

"Would you like a better view?" Lawrence asked. He moved the chairs so that they were no longer opposite the table from each other but side by side, facing the band.

They sat without speaking and listened to the music. Out of the corner of her eye she could see his arm in the dark gray suit jacket resting on the table, his fingers turning a matchbook over and over. She stared at his hand in the semi-darkness, as couples around them went to the floor to dance, and as she did there was a warm feeling at the core of her, stronger than what she had felt with Gene or with the other men she had dated the last few years, a feeling both delicious and disconcerting. She could let herself feel it, or she could strenuously stamp it out, beat it down. In Hollywood, in the office, she would do the latter. But here—

He put down the matchbook and turned toward her. "Shall we dance?"

Don't ever dance with your employer, Mrs. Meese had admonished her class of secretarial hopefuls. *It only leads to trouble.*

Frances smiled. "I'd love to," she said.

They found their way to the crowded floor. As always when she danced, her spirits rose, and she felt light and happy as they drew apart and together. "You're a good dancer," he said after a while. "Really good."

"I love dancing. I always have."

"Do you dance often?"

"As often as I can." She liked the feel of her hand in his, his arm around her back.

"That singer," he said a few beats later. "She's excellent, isn't she?"

"Very good. As good as Helen Forrest."

"The sad thing is," said Lawrence, "she wouldn't have a prayer of making it in pictures. At the studio, they'd say she has the perfect face for radio. But she's phenomenal." There was a pause while he gave her a twirl. "It makes you think."

"And what do you think?"

"I think," he said slowly and unexpectedly, "that life isn't fair. And I don't know how to fix it."

The song drew to an end, with the trumpet holding the final note. The dancers applauded as the singer, smiling, bowed her head to acknowledge the praise. "That's a nice one, isn't it?" she said, and the applause grew louder in agreement.

"Now let's change it up and do a slow one," she said. There were whistles from some of the men in the audience. The singer grinned. "Yes, a real romantic one. Get your best girl, gents, and show her what you feel."

Frances stood still, paralyzed by indecision. The singer's words gave a significance to the dance that was unmistakable; she did not know whether to turn to Lawrence or start back to the table, making some bright comment about sitting this one out. She did not look at him, instead fixing her gaze on a tall, reed-thin saxophone player who was adjusting something on his instrument.

The band began to play the first few bars of what was clearly "Embraceable You." The saxophone player put his instrument to his lips. The singer looked at the band, fondly, her hand on the microphone, waiting to sing.

Frances felt a hand on her back. She turned, and Lawrence drew her slowly into his arms.

Dancing with him was different, this time. He was not smiling as he looked down at her. At first she thought of making a light remark, something humorous to neutralize the intimacy of the moment, but to do so felt false and wrong, so she said nothing.

The singer's voice, low and rich, filled the room. On the second verse, Lawrence brushed the back of her hand with his thumb, lightly; he did it once, which surprised her, then a second time, which did not. Instinctively she moved closer to him, and his arm, circling her back, tightened in response. After a while, it felt entirely natural to rest her cheek against his chest. The linen of his shirt was smooth against her face, and she could feel his heart beating.

She had been in his arms once before, in the car after seeing her father, but this was an entirely different experience, a different emotion. This time, there was no grief, just the warmth of his chest against hers, the scent of skin and linen and a hint of cigarette, and the feel of his chin now resting gently on her head, a feeling that she noticed with no surprise, only with the awareness that they fit together as neatly as nesting dolls. And in the background, there was the song, intimate and inviting, now drawing to an end.

The band played the last few chords, and there was a moment of silence before the dancers clapped their appreciation. It was only when the applause ended that Frances moved slowly out of the circle of his arms.

"And on that note," said the singer, "we'll take a break. Have another drink, ladies and gentlemen, and relax." She looked down at Frances and Lawrence and smiled knowingly. "Or go take a walk in the moonlight," she said with a wink.

They walked down the deserted streets of the small town, neither one of them speaking. Soon they were at the street overlooking the river, and they leaned side by side against the rail and looked out.

It wasn't a pretty river. It was prosaic and businesslike, the kind that seems built for cargo. There was a large brick warehouse across the street, looming in the moonlight, but it was the same river they had sat beside a few hours earlier, talking of the past. Frances recalled how his fingers had felt in her hair.

A tiny breeze stirred the air, and she shivered. "Are you cold?" asked Lawrence. He made as if to shrug off his suit coat.

"No," she said, even though she was, for to wear his coat was an intimacy she was suddenly too afraid to permit. He moved closer to her, and his sleeve brushed her arm as he leaned with his forearms on the rail.

A line had been crossed, irrevocably. She knew it, and she sensed that he did too. It had happened almost imperceptibly, in a string of little moments: his kindness to her father, the embrace in the car, the secrets shared on the golden Napa hillside, the afternoon by the river, and all those quiet hours driving side by side, miles slipping away behind them. She thought of the brilliant orange span arching over the bay. A once-insurmountable distance had been bridged quietly and nimbly, and here they were, on the other side, alone in the moonlight.

She could feel him looking at her. "You're pensive," he said. "Like you're thinking of something important."

"I am." She wondered if his thoughts were similar to hers but did not want to ask. The moonlight made a path across the water, wavering but bright.

"Frances," he said softly.

She was almost afraid to respond, for there was something in his tone she both wanted and feared. She lingered a moment, staring at the moonlight without seeing it, then turned to face him. His gaze held hers in the close, quiet darkness. Her nerves began to hum. *If I don't look away*, she thought, *he is going to kiss me*, and she did not look away.

There was a deliciously agonizing pause; then his eyes dropped to her mouth and he stepped toward her. As he did so she became aware that there was a car coming slowly along the road toward her, its headlights about to capture them in their glow. She stepped back and turned toward the sound.

It was a black sedan, a relatively new model. It paused and the driver rolled down his window. He was a man of about thirty, with the cap and coat of a professional driver. "Excuse me, sir," he said. "I'm trying to find the Plaza Hotel."

"The Plaza Hotel," said Lawrence, clearing his throat. "It's just one block behind you, facing the courthouse."

"Thank you, sir. Good night," said the driver, and he began to roll up his window. But just as he did so there was movement in the back seat, a light shape sliding to the driver's side of the car. The back window opened to reveal Belinda Vail, in a fur stole and a large hat, her lovely face wearing the expression of the actress making a perfectly timed entrance.

"Well, Lawrence," she said, "fancy meeting you here."

CHAPTER

THIRTY·SIX

Lawrence drew back. "Belinda. What on earth are you doing here?"

"I'm here to meet Miss Ridley. To save my role. You took so long, and you didn't answer my calls."

"I sent a telegram."

"A telegram." She rolled her eyes playfully. "It sounds like you need my help to convince her."

"No, Belinda. We're doing fine as we are."

"Are you? You've practically moved up here. The studio is wondering if you're ever coming back." She slanted a glance at Frances. "So I hopped on the train, then hired a car in San Francisco. Fred is my driver. He's been just wonderful." Fred, his hands on the wheel, was striving to look professional and uninterested in the conversation happening behind him. *What a story he'll have to tell*, Frances thought.

"Does Irving know you're here?"

"I told him I was going. He didn't try to stop me."

There was the sound of a car coming up behind them. Belinda opened the door, revealing her full figure in an expensive traveling suit of crimson. "Come in. We'll take you back to the hotel."

"I'll walk."

"Don't be ridiculous, Lawrence," she said lightly. "I won't try to seduce you on the way. But we might as well talk."

"Go ahead," said Frances quietly. "I'll walk back. I'd rather."

She saw in his eyes that the moment that had passed them by, the interrupted kiss, but she would not let herself think about it.

"I'll be right there. I promise," she said.

Belinda slid across the seat, and he got into the car behind her, folding his tall body into the back seat. He closed the door, and Frances turned back to the river so she would not see them drive away.

She lingered a while by the water and returned to the hotel twenty minutes later. It was bustling with energy. The clerk was wide-eyed, almost dazed, and an eager young bellhop was holding two suitcases and a hatbox. "Miss Vail will be in room 204," said the clerk, and the bellhop said, "Yes, sir," and bounded up the stairs like a young gazelle.

Fred was standing at the telephone booth, holding a room key. He recognized Frances as she came in and gave her a friendly, if awed, smile.

"Are you staying as well?" asked Frances.

"Yes, Miss Vail hired me for three days. My wife still can't believe it," he said. "I'm driving for Belinda Vail."

She managed a smile and headed for the stairs. As she passed the lounge, she heard voices. Belinda was sitting in a straight chair, Lawrence on the edge of the sofa. Her legs were crossed and she was leaning forward, her eyes wide and alert, listening intently. He was leaning forward too, speaking quietly, his hands clasped and his wrists resting on his knees. *JUSTICE*, said the courthouse behind them. Neither one of them saw Frances.

She turned and went silently up the stairs.

F rances had just put on her shoes the next morning when there was a discreet knock on her door. It was Lawrence, his hands in his pockets.

"Good morning," he said.

It was clear he wanted to speak to her privately, so she opened the door in silent invitation. He sat on the cane chair, and she took the edge of the bed opposite.

"Belinda's adamant," he said. "About meeting Miss Ridley. I hate to spring it on her. But she's come all this way . . ." His eyes asked for her understanding. She nodded.

"Perhaps it will help," she offered.

"Perhaps. But I think it's just muddying the waters."

"Which waters?"

He waited a moment before answering. "All of them."

He raised his eyes to her as she sat perched on the edge of the bed. Their knees were only a few inches apart. It would be so easy to reach out and take his hand.

She stood up quickly, briskly. "It's Miss Ridley's birthday today."

"That's right." He raised an eyebrow. "Belinda will be some birthday surprise."

"I saw something in the window of a gift shop the other day that I'd like to give her. If there is time for me to get it before we go."

"There's plenty of time. Belinda's not an early riser." Then he was silent, as if aware of what he had just revealed. "Yes," he said quietly. "You'll have time."

Silence fell. It seemed a lifetime ago that they had stood in the moonlight. Things that had been felt on the dance floor and by the river had no place in the light of morning. Their eyes met, and she looked quickly away.

He stood up to go, then paused with his hand on the doorknob. "July twenty-ninth," he said. "Why do I have the feeling this is going to be a day to remember?"

They set off for the Ventimiglias' just after ten. Fred had been waiting in the hotel lobby when Belinda came downstairs in an expensive kelly-green dress with a jabot and a matching hat with an upturned brim. "Thank you, Fred," she said, "but I'm going to drive with Mr. Merrill. Follow along in case I need you later."

Frances had intended to ride in the hired car, but before she could say anything, Lawrence turned to her. "Frances?" he said, indicating his own car. It was clear that he was avoiding a long drive alone with Belinda.

The actress took the front seat, sliding gracefully in as the two hotel maids, the bellhop, and a crowd of pedestrians stood on the sidewalk watching. Belinda waved to them with a smile as Frances took the back seat, the wrapped gift box on her lap. The car smelled of lily-of-the-valley perfume.

Not much was said on the drive up. Belinda checked her lipstick in a small mirror, and Lawrence kept his eyes on the road. But in the tilt of the actress's head, Frances saw the innate confidence of a beautiful woman. She would work her magic on Miss Ridley, as she had worked it on Fred, on the hotel clerk, on Irving. As she had once worked it on Lawrence.

And this was his chance, she thought, looking at his neck and the back of his head: this was his chance to put old demons to rest. He had failed one beautiful blonde woman, but he could be there for another. His eyes met hers in the rearview mirror. She could not read the expression in them.

Celia opened the door with Toby by her side, greeting them with a smile that turned to shock at the sight of Belinda. She stood frozen in the entrance hall.

"Celia," said Lawrence, "this is Miss Vail. She arrived in Napa last night. Unexpectedly."

"How lovely to meet you," said Belinda, reaching out her hand. It was awkward with the dish towel Celia was holding; she took a moment to respond.

"Miss Vail," she said, shaking her hand. "It's nice to meet you."

"You have a beautiful home," said Belinda, her wide blue eyes taking in the high ceiling of the entrance hall. She smiled down at Toby, who buried his face in his mother's skirt. "Hello, sweetheart. How old are you?"

Celia seemed to recover her poise. "He's two." She stepped back, opening the door all the way. "Please, come in."

As they moved into the hall, there was a clatter at the top of the stairs. "I heard the car," said Sally joyfully, descending almost at a run, but she came to a sudden halt at the sight of Belinda. Nancy, just behind, almost collided with her.

"Hello, Sally," said Belinda. "How nice to see you again."

"I didn't know you were coming, Miss Vail," said Sally. The unmistakable coldness in her voice made Celia look up at her quickly. Nancy, leaning over the banister, gaped at the movie star.

"And this is Nancy," said Lawrence. Belinda smiled at the girl.

"Hello, Nancy," said Belinda. "How pretty you are. Just like your mother."

Nancy beamed, then glanced at Sally. As if noting her friend's displeasure, she shifted her weight awkwardly and said nothing.

"Miss Vail surprised us by appearing last night," said Lawrence to his daughter. "She would like to meet Miss Ridley."

"She's resting," said Sally. "We were up late last night talking. She told us about her life."

"Come on in here," said Celia, indicating the dining room. "I'll make coffee. We can wait until she's ready for you."

Just then there was a noise behind the closed door to the parlor. It opened and Miss Ridley, this time wearing a yellow turban and a blue paisley shawl, appeared in the doorway.

"You're back again," she said to Frances, her lipsticked mouth breaking into a smile. "Good."

"Good morning, Miss Ridley. And happy birthday."

Belinda, with a swish of her chiffon dress, moved impulsively toward the old woman. She reached out as if intending to take her hand and then withdrew it in a gesture of humility. "Miss Ridley," she said. "What an honor to meet you. I can't tell you how astonished I feel."

Miss Ridley's hold tightened on her cane. "Who are you?"

"Belinda Vail. I'm going to play you in the film. If you are agreeable to it, of course."

"Are you." Miss Ridley turned her head toward Lawrence. It was a supremely eloquent turn, conveying disapproval as clearly as words would have done.

"Miss Vail arrived last night," he said quietly. "I was not expecting her."

"It's true," said Belinda with an apologetic smile. "I came all the way from Hollywood on my own, Miss Ridley. I couldn't pass up the chance to meet you. You're a living legend. Every actress aspires to the sort of life you had. I'm"—she pressed her hand to the jabot of her dress—"I feel so unworthy."

It was quite a picture, thought Frances: the beautiful woman with her porcelain skin and Cupid's bow lips and the full vigor of youth, leaning deferentially toward the elderly woman who was stooped over her cane, frail and small, with carmine lipstick on her wrinkled mouth. *Past and Present*, a photographer would caption it. In the pause that followed, Frances waited for a rebuff from Miss Ridley, a cold word paired with the imperious demeanor of the first day.

Surprisingly, Miss Ridley turned slowly back to the parlor. "Come in here, Miss Vail," she said. "Let's get better acquainted."

"Thank you. I'd love to."

"You come too, Mr. Merrill," said Miss Ridley. She turned to Frances. Their eyes met, briefly.

"If you don't mind, Frances," she said, "I think Celia needs some help in the kitchen."

Celia, standing at the kitchen table, was beating something in a mixing bowl. She was more flustered than Frances had ever seen her. "I don't even know what to think," she said. "Is Miss Vail staying for the birthday dinner?"

"She didn't say. I would assume so."

"She came in your car?"

"Yes. Oh," said Frances suddenly. "But she hired a car and had him follow. The driver is outside."

"He doesn't need to stay out there. Arthur?"

The boy, who was leaning over the bowl, looked up. "Invite Miss Vail's driver inside." He scampered off.

Celia pushed a strand of hair back behind her ear. "You didn't know she was coming?"

"No, truly. Neither did Lawrence. She just showed up in Napa last night."

"She's certainly beautiful." She mixed the batter vigorously. "It's strange seeing her in real life, not on a screen. It's like . . . make-believe is real." She looked out the window to the arbor near the outdoor table, where Sally and Nancy were hanging streamers. "I told the girls to decorate. We'll eat outside. I think Miss Ridley will be okay going a little distance from the house."

"Thank you again, for having Sally last night."

"It was no trouble. She and Nancy are thick as thieves." She smiled. "Sally got Miss Ridley talking about her life in the theater. She told some stories even I hadn't heard. And Joe brought down her trunk, and she showed the girls some old costume pieces. If you're not careful, Sally's going to want a life on the stage."

"She'd be good at that, I think. She's a good mimic."

"I'll say. She can even imitate Joe's way of speaking, those pauses he puts in his sentences."

"I hope he wasn't offended."

"No, he thought it was funny." Celia glanced at the clock. "I should take them some tea."

"I'll do it."

As Frances was filling the kettle at the deep sink, Celia spoke.

"Frances," she said. "I sense that Sally isn't fond of Miss Vail."

Frances waited until the kettle was full, then turned off the faucet. "That's true."

"You've met her?"

"Miss Vail? Yes. Several times."

"What do you think of her? Is she like she is in the movies?"

"Well," said Frances carefully. "She's an actress, after all." She realized it was exactly the answer Joe had given about Miss Ridley, a few nights before.

Frances paused at the parlor door, the silver tea tray in her hands. She knocked, and Lawrence opened the door. Behind him she caught a glimpse of Miss Ridley in the wing chair, resting her turbaned head against the back. "I have the tea," Frances said. "Is this a good time?"

"Yes," said Miss Ridley. "Bring it in."

Belinda was on the hassock, her hands clasped in her lap, leaning forward as she listened intently. Her face was rapt, her lips slightly parted. Frances put the tea tray carefully on the side table.

"You know," Miss Ridley was saying, "I always wanted to play Lady Macbeth. But the one time I proposed it, the theater manger would not let me. It wouldn't do for them to see me with blood on my hands. I wish I had insisted."

"I know exactly what you mean, Miss Ridley," said Belinda. Her voice seemed a register higher than it usually was. "Some men simply don't want an actress to try new things."

Frances moved the tray so it was in a more secure place on the table. "Thank you," said Miss Ridley. She gave Frances a quick, inscrutable glance.

Frances turned back to the door, and Lawrence hurried to hold it open for her. She sensed that he was trying to catch her eye, but she, feeling rattled and off-kilter, avoided his gaze.

She felt stifled, warmer than she had since arriving in Napa, even though the day was a shade cooler than the previous one had been. Leaving through the front door, she walked under the trees to the north side of the house and sat under the oaks on the hidden bench in the shade. In the distance, she could hear the voices of Sally and Nancy as they decorated the arbor for the party.

What time of day, she wondered, had Miss Ridley been born?

The vineyards, bright in the sun, seemed to shimmer in the heat. Rows upon rows, those vines, as regular and predictable as the tines of a comb. You could try so hard to keep your life tidy and organized, and then there would come a drought, or a death, or a love affair, just to remind you that you were not actually in control.

An insect buzzed past her left ear, and a bead of sweat trickled down her chest. She closed her eyes. It could make you feel sick, this heat, if you were not careful. She should go back to the house and get some water.

But she did not. She remained still, sitting alone in the quiet sanctuary of the oaks.

The nausea had been her first clue. She thought it was stomach flu, but there was no fever, and when she realized she had not had her monthly cycle for nearly seven weeks she stood in front of the mirror in the dormitory bathroom and stared aghast at her reflection, her face white against the walls. She could not be pregnant, she told herself. Don had said he was taking care of that, and his method, such as it was, was enormously messy, but she had trusted him. The thought of a baby promptly made her sick in the basin of the sink.

Her roommate, unaware of the cause of her ailment, bought her ginger drops. Frances lived on them for days, eating ginger drops and toast, using the bathroom three times as often as usual and praying to see a streak of red on the paper. There was nothing.

On a cold day, she told him. They were lying on a blanket on the old rug in his study, as they always did. From this spot on the floor she could see the underside of the desks and the armchair, all the bolts and tufts of upholstery, the small tumbleweeds of dust the housekeeper had missed. In previous weeks, she had found it exciting, this topsy-turvy view of the study that was his and hers alone.

As she told him she did not look directly at him, staring across his bare chest at the umbrella he kept furled in the corner. She felt his arm stiffen and his heart beat faster.

"I guess," she said nervously, "the method didn't work."

He sat up abruptly, dislodging her. She saw accusation on his face, which shifted into an almost embarrassed recognition of his own culpability. Then, for the first time ever, a shutter seemed to come down as he gazed at her.

"I didn't want this to happen," she said, her heart hammering. The look in his eyes was scaring her.

"Frances," he said. "I can't marry you."

She stared at him. He ran his hands through his tousled hair. "I feel terrible," he said. "But I can't."

"If you're worried about what my parents will say, we could elope, make it a surprise. They'll never have to know."

"No, Frances," he said heavily. "I'm engaged."

"Engaged?" She looked down at his hand as if to find a ring, but of course a man would not wear one. Shock was succeeded by horror. "You were engaged and you—did this?"

"I shouldn't have." His voice was agonized. "I should have told you. I'm sorry."

"But you can't marry someone else now. You can tell her about me, the baby."

"Frances," he said desperately. "I'm engaged to the daughter of Dr. Weatherall."

Dr. Weatherall was the head of the English department. His daughter Julia was a recent graduate, whom Frances had seen once at a college event: fine-boned, with a chilly prettiness.

"Since when?"

"Since last summer." He cleared his throat. "That's how I got this job, Frances." *And how I will keep it*, he did not need to say aloud.

His eyes were distant, wary, when just fifteen minutes before

they had been drowsy, and five minutes before that, dark with pleasure. She stared at him without speaking, and he reached for his shirt
and put it on.

"I'll give you money," he said helplessly. "I swear, whatever you
need. But—Frances, I've worked so hard for this job. It's what I've
always wanted." His fingers were trembling as he did the buttons. "I
couldn't jeopardize that. And I'd break Julia's heart. I can't do that to
her."

No, she thought, *you can break mine. You can send me back to
California and never have to think of me again.*

"Maybe you're wrong about this," he said. "I'm sure you are. Girls
can be late, right? A week from now it'll all be fine."

"No," she said. "I'm not wrong. I know I'm not."

"I'll give you money," he said again. "I'll give you as much as you
need. But I can't—I can't do more, Frances. Everything is tied up with
this engagement." She heard the echo of his words on the bench that
October day. "Everything."

There were things she could do, of course. She could go to Dr.
Weatherall, tell him what had happened. Wait a few months and
show her swelling figure to the college president and point the blame.
Write an editorial for the newspaper: *A Seducer in Our Midst.* But she
would not do any of them, for anything she did to reveal Don's con-
duct would reveal hers as well. He had much to lose, but she, the
woman who had lain with him on the floor of his office, willingly and
some would say wantonly, stood to lose even more.

She gathered her things and dressed quickly, not looking at him.
He did not lay a reassuring hand on her arm or detain her. He was
not the man she had thought, a paragon of intelligence and virtue,
but in one way she could give him credit. He was perceptive enough
to know that nothing he could say at this moment could possibly
offer her comfort.

CHAPTER THIRTY-EIGHT

With Belinda there, lunch was an odd, uncomfortable meal. Arthur gazed at her across the table with frank admiration, while Nancy, who might otherwise have done the same, took her cues from Sally and was silent, hardly looking at the star. Sally sat with queenly poise and was glacially cool to the actress while Joe watched their interactions with a puzzled look.

Belinda, upon meeting Joe, had been effusive with gratitude. "You are so kind to let me visit," she said. "I'm an intruder, I know."

"You're welcome, Miss Vail," said Joe, clearly taken aback by both her beauty and her unexpected presence in his home. And yet as lunch went on, Frances caught him looking at her with a slight drawing together of his brows, as if uncertain what to think. It was a relief; Frances realized she had not wanted to see Joe fall under the actress's spell. Celia was polite but quiet, which did not matter as Belinda did most of the talking.

"Such a fascinating woman, isn't she? It will be an honor to play her in the movie."

"If the movie is made," said Sally.

"Of course," said Belinda. "But your father has been working hard on that. This project is so important to the studio. And to me." Lawrence, reaching for his water glass, did not comment. "And her story is too good to keep hidden. The world deserves to see it."

"I think," said Celia quietly, "that Miss Ridley wants to be sure it really *is* her story."

"Grayson can change the screenplay to suit her. A little here, and there. He can do that in his sleep."

"The changes may not be so minor," said Lawrence. "We're learning that the screenplay—and the book—are fundamentally inaccurate."

"Well," said Belinda, "that may be. But Miss Ridley knows the value of entertainment. She was an actress herself, remember." She took a sip of lemonade; somehow she was able to do so without leaving a lipstick rim on the glass. "Often you have to exaggerate the truth to tell a good story. Surely she'll understand if you explain it like that, Lawrence. It's just a matter of how you phrase it."

"I believe," said Frances, "that every woman has the right to tell her own story."

She had not realized she was going to say it until she was mid-sentence. The words came out swiftly, with an energy that made Sally glance up from her plate.

There was silence around the table. Belinda stared at Frances across the plate of sliced tomatoes. Her fork was poised in the air, and she wore an expression Frances had never seen before. Then the actress laughed lightly, as if she had said something amusing.

"Are you saying Miss Ridley should play herself? Even the best makeup department can't make a woman in her nineties look like she's twenty."

"Belinda," said Lawrence.

"And I hardly think it would work for the love scenes."

"Belinda," said Lawrence again, more sharply. "Please."

There was an awkward silence. Celia unhappily turned her napkin in her hands while Sally looked mutinous. Belinda, glancing around the table, eventually settled on Joe. She smiled.

"You like the movies, Mr. Ventimiglia," she said, crossing her arms on the table and leaning in his direction.

"Yes, I do."

"You'd go see me in a movie about Miss Ridley, wouldn't you?"

Joe put his hands on the arms of his chair as if bracing himself for impact. He looked down the table at his wife.

"I think, Miss Vail," he said at last, "that you could make anybody believe anything." He stood up. "If you'll excuse me, I've got to get back to the vines." He touched his wife's shoulder briefly as he passed her chair.

A fter lunch Belinda was eager to continue her talk with Miss Ridley, but Celia reported that she had gone back to bed for a rest. "Of course," said Belinda. "But I'm not here very long, you know. I can't stay more than a day. Perhaps I didn't tell her that."

"You did," said Lawrence. "She always rests in the afternoon."

Belinda looked at the clock in the hall. "One thirty. What time is this party tonight?"

"We'll start at six."

She took out her compact, surveyed her face, tucked a curl behind her ear. "Perhaps I'll go back to the hotel, then. Relax for a bit." She turned to Lawrence. "Will you walk me out to the car?"

Frances watched them go through the hall and down the porch steps. It felt almost like Hollywood again, the two of them leaving together, and she went out the kitchen door to the service yard, where there was a pile of washing left by Celia. Automatically, she picked up a damp skirt and pinned it to the line. It was good to have something to do. She felt out of sorts, and glad to be alone.

Five minutes later, she heard the kitchen door open. "I thought I'd help you out, Celia," she called without looking back.

"It's me." Sally came down the steps, her hands thrust into the pockets of her red cotton dress. "I saw you come out here."

"Oh." Frances managed a smile. "Where's Nancy?"

"Making a card for Miss Ridley's birthday."

"That's nice. Are you making one too?"

"I already did." Sally picked up a clothespin and turned it in her fingers, a gesture that reminded Frances of Lawrence. "I like her. Do you?"

"Who, Miss Ridley? Yes, very much."

"She told us so many stories last night. It was wonderful."

"I wish I'd been here." It was an automatic comment, said without thinking, but it made Frances suddenly aware of what she had been doing instead: the dinner with Lawrence, the dance, the walk by the river. She felt again the current of desire between them, broken by the abrupt arrival of Belinda. Would it have been better if it had never happened?

Sally, who had picked up a dish towel, was eager to talk. "Do you know she showed me a trunk of her old costumes? They're gorgeous. I tried on the cap she wore as Juliet. I said a few lines, and she said I had a good feel for the rhythm of Shakespeare. She said it can be taught, but it's better if you have it naturally." She pinned the towel carefully to the line, then stepped back to look at it before picking up a shirt. "She's going to show me her photo album later. Do you know that when she played Juliet and Juliet kills herself, the audiences used to wail? Can you imagine anyone doing that nowadays? Everyone in the movies is so silent. She said people used to be so much louder, the miners and even people in the big theater in San Francisco."

She stood holding the shirt, a smile on her face as she stared toward the hills, with the faraway look of a girl absorbed in the past. Frances felt an ache in her chest. At times it was acutely painful to know what she did about Sally's mother, to be privy to the terrible knowledge that could destroy the girl's happiness. It wasn't the first time, Frances thought grimly, that she knew how it felt to carry a secret like an explosive device in her pocket.

"Do you know what Miss Ridley's real name is?" Sally asked. "It's not Catherine. It's Helen. She was only called Kitty because her mother said when she was a tiny baby she used to yawn like a cat. The name stuck."

"I didn't know that. That's sweet."

Sally shook out a tiny undershirt clearly belonging to Toby. She pinned it with one pin in the center, and the two ends drooped on either side. "When I was at the convent," she said, "there was a book there, of names and what they mean. I had nothing else to do, so I looked up almost every name I know. Mine means princess. Dad's name means shining one, which is funny, like King Midas or something. But the sisters told me that Lawrence was a saint who was roasted alive."

"Good heavens."

"I looked up Frances too. It means someone from France."

Frances smiled. "My mother loved Paris. That's probably why she named me that."

"What was she like?"

"I don't remember her. She died when I was very small."

"I don't really remember my mother either," Sally said. "Only a little. I have this memory, more like a feeling, of her putting a blanket around me and singing a song. It fits, because her name means songbird."

"Mavis means songbird?"

Sally looked up from the apron she was holding. "How did you know her name was Mavis?"

"Your father told me."

The girl's eyes were steady, thoughtful. Frances turned away, reaching back into the basket, which was now empty but for a housedress.

They heard an engine start, breaking the stillness, and then the sound of gravel on tires as a car pulled away. Belinda was on her way back to the hotel.

"I wish Miss Vail hadn't come," said Sally. "I looked up her name too. Belinda. It means serpent."

"Oh," said Frances. She dropped a clothespin and bent to pick it up.

"And it made me think of *Macbeth*. Where Lady Macbeth says, 'Look like the innocent flower, but be the serpent under it.'"

Frances felt gooseflesh on her arms, as if a breeze had just blown by, but the clothes were hanging limply, and the branches of the trees were still. *A goose walked over my grave*, she thought. She almost shared the expression with Sally, but the girl had turned and was gazing off into the distance again.

CHAPTER

THIRTY-NINE

W hen the laundry was done, Sally returned to the house and Frances went out beyond the fence, walking among the vines. She returned half an hour later to find Celia in the kitchen, icing the cake.

"Coconut," she said. "Miss Ridley doesn't eat much anymore, but this used to be her favorite." Toby, kneeling on a chair at the table, was rolling dough with a small rolling pin. "It's the extra from the cookies," said Celia. "He likes playing with it." She glanced at the clock on the wall. "Would you stay here and watch him? I'm in desperate need of a bath."

Frances looked at the small boy in his overalls, bent over the table. "Where are Sally and Nancy?"

"They walked across the road to borrow birthday candles. And Arthur's helping Joe. I'll be quick."

"I don't know anything about children," said Frances. "What do I do?"

Celia was visibly surprised at her ignorance. "Just make sure he doesn't do anything to hurt himself. That's all."

"All right."

"Thanks. As long as he has that dough, he'll be happy." She left quickly, hanging her apron on a nail by the door as she did so.

Her footsteps receded down the hall. In the silent kitchen, Frances closed her eyes, took a long breath, and opened them again.

The late afternoon sun slanting in illuminated everything in her line of vision: the sink; the bowl of lemons on the windowsill; the calendar from a local lawyer's office, which showed a romanticized drawing of Pompeii; the cake with its bright white icing; the tins for flour and sugar and tea, dented with years of use, lined up largest to smallest like children in a family photograph.

Across the kitchen, Toby was kneeling on his chair, his tiny bare toes like little pink shells. He was holding the rolling pin in his hands, moving it back and forth over the pile of dough. Frances watched him. His mouth was open as he concentrated on his task. It was so still in the kitchen that she could even hear his breathing. He seemed hardly aware of his mother's absence.

She was afraid to go near him and break his focus, so she watched as he rolled the small piece of dough as flat as he could on the surface of the table. Years ago, she used to help Rita with her baking, and she could still remember the feel of the handles of the old rolling pin, slightly loose but still holding fast. She recalled the way that long rolls of the pin flattened out the entire piece of dough and the way that small quick movements, applied to only one part of the dough, made it even. She remembered the small pieces Rita would let her eat, flavored with bits of lemon peel or more often with anise, which had always been her father's favorite flavor. For his birthday one year Frances had made him an entire batch of cookies, presenting them to him proudly with the announcement that he did not have to share. It was far more than any man could eat alone, she realized now, but her father had been delighted and had taken half of them to work "to have with my coffee." He'd never said that her gift was too much, or that most of them were overdone. He had given her a hug, smelling of his comforting aftershave.

Toby gave a sudden cry. The dough was sticking to the rolling pin, and he could not get it off. He scrabbled at it with his little fin-gernails. "Mama," he called, without looking up.

"Here," said Frances. She went over the flour tin, tipped a small bit into her hand, and took it to the table. She peeled the dough off of the pin and set it aside on the table, then spread a layer of flour over the rolling pin and another layer on the wooden board he was using. He watched her silently, his brown eyes following every moment.

"Now," she said. "Bunch the dough together. Like this." She pushed the scraps together, and he did the same with his small hands. There was a dimple at the base of each of his fingers.

"Now try rolling," she said, placing the rolling pin in front of him. He did, and when the dough did not stick, he looked up at her, his brown eyes wide with wonder, and he smiled. Then he returned again to his work, focused and determined.

The sun shone on the back of his neck, where the hair came down in a golden point. The blades of his shoulders were visible underneath the small shirt he wore beneath his overalls. She could once again hear him breathing with absorption and focus. A small boy, busy and content, in a home where he was loved.

Frances closed her eyes.

Celia came back downstairs, looking fresh and pretty in a white dress patterned with lilacs. "Thank you, Frances," she said. "I feel like a new woman. Oh, and Miss Ridley wants to see you."

"She's in the parlor?"

"No, in her room."

Frances had not yet been down the small back hall, which was carpeted and quiet. She knocked at the door. "Miss Ridley? It's Frances."

"Come in."

The shades on the tall windows were up, and the early evening sun flooded the room. Frances was so dazzled by the light that it took her a moment to register the single bed with the old-fashioned walnut headboard, the wardrobe with carved doors, and Miss Ridley, standing before a mirror-topped bureau, leaning on her cane.

Her turban was off, and she was almost entirely bald, with just a few tufts of white hair. Without the armor of her headwear she looked vulnerable, like a chick with pinfeathers or a newborn child.

She met Frances's gaze in the mirror. Before Frances could alter her expression, Miss Ridley smiled. "You don't need to pretend. You're shocked, aren't you?"

"A little."

"I am too, most days. That's why I wear it all the time." She nodded toward the turban on the dresser. "Help me, will you?"

The turban felt hollow, like an eggshell. Frances set it down carefully, so as not to cause any pain; the skin of Miss Ridley's scalp looked so shockingly tender. She gently tucked a wisp of white hair under the edge.

Miss Ridley was watching her in the mirror. "Thank you, Frances," she said when she finished. "Have a seat."

Frances sat down on the straight chair by the wardrobe. Miss Ridley moved away from the bureau, into the sunlight, closing her eyes as if savoring its warmth.

"The light here," she said, "in this valley. Pure gold. I'll never get over it."

"You look like a cat in a patch of sunlight," said Frances, and Miss Ridley smiled.

"We must live up to our names, mustn't we," she said. Then she grew serious. "It's good that I met her, Belinda Vail. She's certainly beautiful. Not as beautiful as I was, of course." She lifted her head, turning into the window as if it were a spotlight, as if she were on stage before an audience hanging on her every word. Then she turned back to Frances, a new urgency in her eyes.

"I told you I don't like movie acting," she said, "but it has one advantage over the stage. Movies last. Years from now, people will still be able to see Miss Vail, to see her act." She shifted her weight on the cane. "But nothing is left of my career. There are photos, and a few seconds of me walking in a park, but is anyone still alive who saw me play Juliet? Who saw me dance my Irish jig? A handful of people, maybe, and when they die, the memories go with them. No one will remember what I could do, what my voice sounded like. Oh, they'll always call me one of the greats, but it'll be hollow. The legacy of a stage actress always is, once she's gone."

Tiny dust motes danced in the sunlight as she paused for breath. Frances, struck by the fundamental truth of her words, watched her in silence.

"But you see," said Miss Ridley, "I had another legacy once. A child."

"You did?"

"When I was twenty-two years old."

"I had no idea."

"No one did. It was with my second lover. I couldn't marry him; he was married already. But I told everyone I was ill with asthma and went to New Mexico. And I had the child there, a girl. Blonde hair she had, little wisps of it, like mine. I couldn't keep her, of course, so she was adopted by a local family. But they let me name her, and I called her Portia." She gave a wry smile. "I didn't think they'd keep the name. I thought they'd call her Patsy or Jane or something more sensible.

"I left, went back to San Francisco, back on the stage. But it was different, you see. I was different. I thought of her often, wondering what she was doing and what she looked like. Once I saw a photo, when she was four years old. She looked so serious, but they all did, in those days. You could be joyful and you'd never know once you got into that portrait studio. And then when she was eight, I learned she had died of influenza. I took the train to New Mexico a year later, to see for myself. I had to. And there it was, a little grave. Portia Jane McKenzie."

"I'm sorry," Frances managed to say.

"Yes," said Miss Ridley. "So am I." Her voice was quiet. "But in the convent, all those years being alone—I realized that I had done the best I could do. I had given her to a loving family. They had a farm, a ranch, and she got to grow up riding horses. Those were some of my happiest moments, riding: you are never so free as you are on a horse. And when I went to her grave, there were fresh flowers there, daisies, like someone had just visited. And there was a card, written in ink. 'For Portia, with love from Mama.' I like to think the card was partly mine, in some way."

Tears streamed down Frances's face. "There is a handkerchief in the bureau," said Miss Ridley. The top drawer stuck, and Frances had to tug at it inelegantly, roughly, before it opened.

She stood, wiping her eyes. Miss Ridley was still standing in the golden shaft of sunlight, the dust motes gathering behind her head, looking at Frances as a grandmother would look at a beloved grandchild.

Frances opened her mouth to speak, but there was a sudden noise outside the window. It was Arthur and Nancy, toting a watermelon and bottles of Coca-Cola in the wagon, with Toby sitting behind, crowing with wordless joy.

"Come," Miss Ridley said gently. "No more talk of these sad things. I have a party to attend." She smiled at Frances. "And so do you."

CHAPTER

FORTY

The table outside had been set with a cloth printed with sprays of blue forget-me-nots. Celia was folding napkins, and Joe was hanging Japanese lanterns among the streamers running from the arbor to the arms of the oak. The sun was dropping behind the hills; it was still light, but the lanterns would be needed before long.

Miss Ridley sat down at the end of the table, with Frances's help. The wooden chair with arms, normally at the head of the dining room table, had been decorated with ribbons and moved outside for her.

"You're looking very smart, Miss Ridley," said Joe. "Is that a new shawl?" It took Frances a moment to realize it was an old joke between the two of them.

"It was new in the war, young man," she said. "The Civil War."

"It's pretty," said Frances. "With the purple flowers."

"That's what I forgot," said Celia. "Flowers. I wanted to cut some for the table."

"I'll get them," offered Frances quickly.

It was silent in the garden, for all the activity was behind the house. Frances was glad. She stood with the long basket in her hands and took a moment simply to be alone in the twilight, eyes closed, inhaling the scents of lavender and warm earth.

When she heard footsteps, she opened her eyes. Lawrence was coming toward her. He had taken off his suit jacket, and his sleeves were rolled up. He stopped near her on the path, by the bench.

"I've been looking for you," he said.

"I was helping Miss Ridley."

He put his hands in his pockets. There was a crease in his forehead, faint, but noticeable to her. She was glad the basket was between them. She held it like a shield.

"Shall I cut?" he asked. "You tell me what to take."

Frances surrendered the shears, and he grasped them easily in his large hands. They moved silently around the garden, as she searched for the best of the penstemon, marguerites, coneflowers, and delphinium. She held the stalks as he reached in and clipped them. The action kept bringing them close together; once his arm brushed her side. When their hands touched, she felt heat flare in her cheeks, as she recalled dancing with his arms around her, his chin resting on the crown of her head.

From the expression on his face, she knew his thoughts were parallel to hers. They regarded each other for a moment, just as they had by the river.

He put the shears down on the bench. He took the basket out of her hands and put it down too. Then his hands went into her hair, holding her head with an unmistakable intention. She looked at his mouth first, and then up at his eyes, and he bent his head and they kissed. And she was flooded with a pleasure that felt almost painful.

When he pulled away at last and gazed into her eyes, she felt tears starting in her own. He smiled gently, and then his mouth found hers again.

You could forget everything in a kiss like that. For several moments there was nothing else. She loved it and did not want it to end.

But he pulled away, finally, with a small exhalation. "Frances," he said softly. "Holy smoke."

She smiled at the expression. His hands were still in her hair.

"I don't know what to say," he said.

"Neither do I."

He held her head, gazing at her intently. She wanted to kiss him again, to lose herself in the wash of feeling, to be in the one place in that strange, unsettling day where the past was not scratching at the door. But there was the sound of a car turning off the road onto the driveway. Lawrence turned to look at it through the trees, and his face changed. "It's Belinda."

Frances stepped back and picked up the basket and shears. "I'll take these to Celia," she told him, her heart still pounding.

His eyes were locked on hers. She thought about how close they had just been, a moment before. She knew now what his lips felt like and how he liked to kiss, long and slow. The mere thought of it made her catch her breath, but the car was approaching, so she turned and hurried toward the house.

As she stepped onto the porch, she heard a car door opening. "Hello," said Belinda gaily. "Are we ready to celebrate?"

Frances shifted the basket on her arm, and a daisy tickled her wrist. Sally's quotation from *Macbeth* came to mind: *Look like the innocent flower, but be the serpent under it.*

By the time she had arranged the flowers and brought the vase out to the table, the only people not gathered around the arbor were Lawrence and Belinda. The children were scrubbed and wearing their Sunday clothes. Nancy's pigtails were braided so tightly Frances wondered how she could move her features. Joe had put on a suit, and even Toby wore a tiny tie.

Sally, in a light blue dress, was the most surprising. She wore a small cap on her head, a faded maroon velvet one edged with yellowed pearls. She kept reaching up to touch it, as if to verify its presence. "The

Juliet cap," she said reverently to Frances. "Miss Ridley said I could wear it today."

"It suits you," said Frances, and it did. Sally's hair was loose, no longer in pigtails; she looked older and more mature.

"Miss Vail's here, is she?" asked Celia, untying her apron. "I thought I heard a car."

As if on cue, Belinda appeared around the side of the house, holding Lawrence's arm.

"My," she said liltingly. "What a beautiful setting for a party!"

She wore a white satin evening gown with a V-neck, cut on a bias, its thin straps edged with rhinestones. In her hair was a white orchid and in her ears were diamonds. Her shoes were wispy heeled sandals, impractical for the yard, but she managed with the confidence of a woman used to navigating her way in uncomfortable clothes.

"This is so festive," she said. She smiled at Joe. "Hello again, Mr. Ventimiglia."

"Miss Vail," he said.

"Mrs. Ventimiglia. What a lovely table you've set up. And Miss Ridley, of course." She dropped Lawrence's arm and reached for the actress's hand. "The guest of honor. I'm so glad to be here with you."

There was silence under the arbor. It seemed not to bother Belinda, who surveyed the group with the ease of a woman for whom stunned tribute was to be expected.

"I'm so sorry to keep you waiting. It wasn't easy to leave the hotel. Word was out, and I had a lot of autographs to sign. I hate to disappoint people."

"Of course," said Celia. "Joe, why don't you pour drinks. Nancy, come help me in the kitchen."

"I'll come too," said Sally; the excitement seemed to have drained out of her with Belinda's entrance.

"Is your driver here?" Celia asked Belinda. "Maybe he'd like to join us."

"You can take him a plate of something on the porch," said Belinda. "I'm sure he doesn't expect to eat with us."

"Well," said Celia, with a glance at her husband, "I'll check with him anyhow."

Belinda, looking around for a place to sit, paused at the sight of the rough trestle benches. No wonder, thought Frances; a splinter would damage that dress irreparably. Miss Ridley indicated the dining room chair just to her left.

"Sit here, Miss Vail. Be careful with that lovely gown."

"Yes, it was made by such a clever designer. I've been looking for an occasion to wear it."

"There's nothing like having the right dress," said Miss Ridley.

"It makes such a difference, doesn't it?" Belinda sat down gracefully, complimenting Miss Ridley on her shawl.

Lawrence moved quietly to Frances's side. She did not have to look at him to feel the current still flowing between them.

"Our flowers look nice," he said, his voice low enough to be covered by the stream of Belinda's words.

"We did well there," she said. He put his hand on the small of her back, unobserved by the others, and she seemed to feel it in her lips.

CHAPTER
FORTY·ONE

W hen everyone was seated, they all toasted Miss Ridley, the children with Coca-Cola and the adults with red wine. The guest of honor smiled with genuine pleasure, seated at the head of the table like a benevolent queen. Dinner began with minestrone, followed by breaded chicken, meatballs, pasta, green beans, watermelon, and sliced tomatoes dusted with salt and pepper. As they ate, Miss Ridley told stories about acting with Edwin Booth and other luminaries, and about her childhood travels through the Sierras in all weather. She described the somber mood when Lincoln was assassinated. "He was the first president I can remember," she said. "To go in such a terrible way, and in a theater, no less. A great man."

As Celia served the coconut cake, Miss Ridley turned to Sally. "Have you been practicing the Scottish brogue, young lady?" she asked.

"Aye," said Sally, straightening in her chair. "'O my luve is like a red, red rose that's newly sprung in June. O my luve is like the melody that's sweetly played in tune.'" Celia applauded, and Lawrence smiled.

"Well done, Sally," he said.

"Very good," said Miss Ridley. "Almost as good as your English accent." She turned to Belinda. "You should hear her do that one, Miss Vail."

"I've heard her," said Belinda pleasantly. "In fact, the first time I met Sally I thought the accent was real." She glanced across the table at the girl. "I didn't know she was playing make-believe."

"You do accents too, Miss Vail," said Sally. She speared a piece of cake with her fork. "Maybe you can do the one you did in *Heaven for the King*? Then Miss Ridley can hear it."

Belinda's smile did not reach her eyes. "I don't perform on cue," she said.

It was such a ridiculous statement coming from a film actress that for a moment there was silence.

"I suppose," said Sally, "there's a time for acting and a time for being real." She said it with a thoughtful tone, but Frances caught the keen glance she darted at Belinda before turning her attention back to her plate.

O nce the cake had been eaten, Celia served coffee and cookies. The moon was out and the lanterns glowed colorfully in the dusk. The temperature was pleasant, with a tiny breeze occasionally stirring the oak leaves and the old vines in the arbor, and the air smelled of sun-warmed grass and a hint of coffee. A pleasant languor settled over the table, and Frances saw Toby's eyelids begin to droop as he rested his head against his sister. "If only there were lightning bugs," said Lawrence, leaning back in his chair, "it would be the perfect summer evening."

"I've never seen them," said Celia. "What are they like?"

"Little flashes in the darkness," said Lawrence. "Then gone, as quickly as you see them."

"They're lovely," said Sally. "They had them at my old school. Mrs. Wolf and I—she was the housemother—we used to sit on the bench and count them. But you never knew if you were counting the same one twice."

Belinda suddenly sat up and smiled brightly. "I have an idea!" she said. "I know what we can do to celebrate Miss Ridley's birthday."

"We're already celebrating it," said Sally. Belinda ignored her.

"We can each share a wish for Miss Ridley. One thing that we hope for her in the year to come."

Arthur frowned. "A wish?"

"Think of it as a gift. What would you give her if you could give her a gift?"

"We have a gift," said Celia quietly. "It's in the hall."

She nodded to Arthur, who stood up from the table, but Belinda waved at him to take a seat. "No, not real gifts. Those can come later. What would you give Miss Ridley if you could give her anything at all?"

It was not a bad idea, Frances thought, but somehow the easy mood of the table had gone. There was an awkward silence.

"Mr. Ventimiglia," said Belinda, smiling at him as if he were the leading man in a film, "you get to go first. What would you give Miss Ridley?"

Joe looked profoundly uncomfortable. "I'm not good at this," he said, turning his empty tumbler of wine in his hand. At last, he said, "Happiness. It's not very clever, Miss Ridley, but it's my wish for you."

"Thank you, Joe," said Miss Ridley.

"And Mrs. Ventimiglia?" Belinda asked. "What's your wish?"

"Good health," said Celia quietly. And Miss Ridley closed her eyes and smiled faintly and bowed her head.

Nancy, sitting next to her mother, said, "Fireflies. Because I'd like to see them too."

"Good choice, Nancy," said Miss Ridley.

Sally, up next, shook her head. "I'm not ready yet."

"Arthur, then," said Belinda. "What would you give Miss Ridley, Arthur?"

Arthur looked around for inspiration. He saw the roof and smiled.

"I'd build an elevator to the tower," he said. "So you can go up there again."

Frances had never seen so broad a smile on Miss Ridley's face. She pressed a hand to her mouth and indicated she was sending a kiss across the table.

"How nice," said Belinda. "Lawrence? Your turn."

There was a slight emphasis in her tone. Lawrence took a sip of coffee, putting the cup down before he spoke.

"I wish you peace," he said. "It's what I wish for all of us."

Belinda's smile wavered, almost imperceptibly. Miss Ridley gave him a nod of thanks.

"I know what I want to wish for," said Sally suddenly. All heads turned toward her.

"I wish that you could see someone you loved." She leaned forward, almost into her plate, her voice urgent. "Anyone you wanted to see, even someone who was dead. I wish they could come back into your life again, and you could be with them. Even just for a day. That's what I wish."

The intensity in her voice vibrated in the air. Frances met Lawrence's eyes across the table.

"That's lovely, Sally," said Miss Ridley softly.

"There's a nice wish," said Joe. "I'd like that too." Celia reached for his hand and held it.

In the silence that followed an insect fell onto the table with a thud, landing near the candle in its glass holder. Lawrence brushed it away. Then he looked at Frances, as Celia did, expectantly.

Frances opened her mouth to speak, but before she could, Belinda had risen to her feet, her white satin gown shimmering in the dusk. She stood like a goddess, commanding every eye at the table, but she spoke her words humbly, like a schoolgirl in front of an audience.

"We've shared our wishes with you, Miss Ridley," she said, "and I have one of my own. Today has been the most memorable day of my life. To meet you, a woman I've always known about and admired—

I'd never have dreamed this would happen. You've given me a price-less gift. And I want to give you something in return. My wish for you—my gift to you—is that I will portray you in a way that does credit to the tremendous legend that you are."

It was like tasting metal or hearing a wrong note in a song. The dissonance seemed to be sensed by every adult at the table. Frances saw Lawrence straighten in his chair, as she had seen him do so many times in meetings in the office, a grim look on his face she had not seen since Hollywood. But Belinda continued to stand, shining like an angel, her smile beatific. Somehow, thought Frances, she had managed to keep the orchid in her hair all evening, though on any other woman it would have fallen.

Toby broke the silence. "Mama," he said querulously, crawling into Celia's lap, and she, as if grateful for the interruption, stood up quickly.

"Bedtime for this fellow, I think," she said. "Nancy, Arthur, come with me. Help clear the dishes." Frances stood up too, but Celia waved her down. "No, please stay."

"I will put every bit of myself into this role," said Belinda, as if Celia had not spoken. "I took a risk, I know, coming up here without an invitation. But now that I've met you, now that I know you, I can put so much more into the film than I ever could before. It's all worked out so beautifully. As if it were meant to be."

She stood, slim and lovely, by the elderly woman's chair, waiting for her to speak. It was astonishing how much more frail and hunched Miss Ridley seemed in comparison.

But Miss Ridley was not looking at Belinda. She sat perfectly still and watched as Celia bore away the sleepy Toby, with Nancy and Arthur following, their arms full of dishes. Then her gaze swept the table, looking at Sally, at Lawrence, at Joe sitting ill at ease, and at Frances. It was strange, a trick of the light perhaps, but in that mo-ment, Frances saw her as she was in the portrait on the cover of the book: the confident woman, a half smile on her lips, her black eyes snapping with life.

"Have a seat, Miss Vail," said Miss Ridley. Belinda sat down eagerly.

"I thank you," said Miss Ridley. "I thank you all for your wishes. And I have an announcement to make."

It was so silent Frances could hear the clink of dishes far off in the kitchen. She heard the slight creak of the chair as Belinda leaned forward, the faint meow of the cat as he stalked through the dim light under the oak tree. But when Miss Ridley spoke, she was looking at Lawrence, not at Belinda.

"I have decided," she said, "what I decided before. The answer is no."

CHAPTER
FORTY·TWO

The silence was broken only by a thump and rustle as the cat leapt to the trunk of the tree and ran up into the branches. Frances turned to Lawrence, who met her eyes. In them she saw a flicker of relief.

"I am sorry," said Miss Ridley to Belinda. "You are a beautiful young woman with a bright future. But this is my life. I want people to know the truth. Or at least not to know a lie."

"But we could change the screenplay," said Belinda. "I know we could. Lawrence," she said, rising from her seat, "explain it to her. The screenplay isn't set in stone."

"We have discussed that, Mr. Merrill and I. The truth would not make a good movie."

"But it would. It would. The things you've done, the life you've had. You're such a rich character."

"Ah, but you see," said Miss Ridley, "I am not a character, am I. I am flesh and blood. For a while longer, at any rate." She nodded at Joe. "Take me back to the house, please, Joe."

He helped her up from the chair. Lawrence pulled it back to give her more room as Belinda and Sally and Frances watched in silence.

"Thank you," Miss Ridley said to Lawrence. She looked up at him, tilting back her head to do so. "I am sorry to disappoint you. I have come to like you, if that means anything." Her gaze moved to Frances, resting on her with fondness. "You too, Frances."

"I understand, Miss Ridley," said Lawrence simply. "I will respect your decision."

Miss Ridley turned to Belinda. "I've never seen any of your films, Miss Vail, but I can tell you are an excellent actress. There will be other roles. There always are, if you want them."

Belinda said nothing. Even in the darkness, Frances could tell how tightly she was grasping the back of the chair.

Miss Ridley stood for a moment, holding Joe's arm, leaning on her cane. She looked around at the oak tree, the Japanese lanterns, the arbor, the table with the remains of the meal. She nodded toward the vase of flowers.

"Frances," she said. "Bring those in for Celia, will you. And don't leave Napa without saying goodbye to me. Good night, then." She and Joe moved slowly back to the house while the others watched them in silence. At the top of the back door steps, Miss Ridley paused.

"Sally," she called through the darkness, "that Juliet cap is my gift to you."

Sally's face broke into a wide smile. "Thank you, Miss Ridley. I'll keep it forever."

There was the high-pitched creak of the screen door as Joe opened it, then the slap a moment later as it closed. The sound seemed to recall Belinda to life. She turned to Lawrence, urgency in her face and voice. "Go after her," she said. "Talk to her. Convince her."

"No, Belinda."

"You haven't tried. You haven't. You're just going to give up?"

"She doesn't want us making this film. You heard her."

"It doesn't matter. Do it anyhow." She gestured hysterically toward the house. "What's she going to do? Go to the papers? She likes a quiet life, she told me. She'd never go to the press."

"No, Belinda," said Lawrence. The steel of the executive was in his voice. "She's ninety-one years old. It's her life and her decision."

"Her decision?" she said furiously. "Who are you, Lawrence? I hardly know you anymore. How can you let yourself be whipped by that—that skeleton in a turban?" Sally gave a swift, startled gasp.

"This conversation is closed, Belinda," said Lawrence, but his tone had no effect on the actress.

"No, it isn't. It doesn't have to be. If you had any spine, you could make this movie anyhow. But you don't." A strap of her dress had slipped and she did not hike it up. "Well, maybe she'll die soon, and you can make the movie then. Unless you're still too big a coward."

Lawrence turned to his daughter. "Sally," he said, "go inside. Please."

"No," said Sally. She had risen from the bench, her eyes flashing fire at Belinda. "No. You can't say that."

"Oh, can't I?" Belinda's face was a picture of fury. "You don't know anything about it, Sally."

Sally grasped the table with both hands. "You don't know, do you? Because you only care about yourself. Not about him"—she gestured to Lawrence—"or Miss Ridley. Or anyone here. You act like you love them, but you don't. You're the most selfish person I've ever known."

Belinda's laugh was brief and harsh, utterly unlike the musical one of the films. "Oh, really? What are you, thirteen years old? Someday you'll know better. I'm no different from anyone else."

"Yes, you are. You're selfish and terrible."

"Open your eyes, Sally. You have a lot to learn."

"You think it's okay to be awful. You treated Miss Ridley like a queen, and now you want her to die. That's not right; that's not fair."

"Isn't that sweet," said Belinda. "You think the world is fair? That you survive by being kind? Try it, and see where it gets you." She hitched up the strap of her dress. "Life is a fight, Sally. It's not fair and it's not kind."

"If you really believe that," said Sally, "then I'm sorry for you. I'm *sorry* for you."

It was said with force and feeling, and with a kind of splendid contempt. Frances saw Belinda's hard expression change to surprise; then a flicker of raw, unfeigned emotion passed across her face. Sally had struck a nerve.

"That's enough," said Lawrence. "We're done here. Belinda, I'll walk you to the car."

But Belinda ignored him. She took a decisive step forward, lifting her head so she was looking squarely at Sally, like an archer aiming a bow.

"Sorry for me?" she said distinctly. "If anyone deserves pity, it's you. And you don't even know it."

With sudden clarity Frances knew what the actress was going to say next. Involuntarily, she started toward her, as if she could somehow keep the words from being said, but Belinda was already speaking, her eyes fixed on Sally.

"Your father never told you how your mother died, did he? But he told me." Her voice was clear as a bell, as if she were delivering the most critical lines in a film. "She killed herself. Took a pile of sleeping pills. She committed suicide. And that's the truth."

Even though Frances had expected the words, they still felt like a blow. For a moment she did not move, shocked by the violence of the revelation in the quiet summer night; then she turned to Lawrence. His face was stricken, and he was reaching for Sally as if his first instinct was to hold her, to keep her from crumpling at the shock of the discovery.

But Sally's expression was not one of shock. She did not step backward or flinch. She stood absolutely upright in her rumpled dress and incongruous cap, looked across the table at the beautiful figure in white, and said, in a voice full of both derision and pain, "I already knew that."

CHAPTER

FORTY-THREE

awrence froze. "What do you mean you already knew?"

"I found out last summer. At Grandmother's." Tears fell and Sally wiped them with the back of her hand. "Grandmother told me. About the pills, and how she killed herself. And that you didn't want me to know. She was angry at you one day and she told me."

"Jesus Christ," said Lawrence.

"Yes. I've known for a whole year." Sally threw the last two words at Belinda, who stood without moving, as if she had been turned to glittering stone.

"You never told me," said Lawrence.

"How could I? I knew you didn't want to talk about it. I told Mrs. Wolf, when I got to school." Sally fumbled in her pocket for a handkerchief and blew her nose vigorously. "She told me I could come talk to her when I felt sad about it. So I did. I talked to her a lot."

Her voice wavered, and Frances felt tears start to her eyes. And Lawrence, his own eyes bright, moved to Sally and folded her firmly in his arms. Frances could hear the girl's gasping sobs and see her shoulders heave, a year of emotion pouring out at last, and Lawrence's arms tightened in response.

"I'm so sorry," he said against his daughter's hair. "I'm so sorry." He held her like that, his shoulders shaking too, murmuring indistinguishable words.

Above them the lanterns glowed, and one went out. Belinda

turned to Frances but said nothing. The shoulder strap of her dress had fallen again.

Lawrence kissed the top of his daughter's head. "Come on," he said quietly. "Let's go talk." They walked off, his arm around her, out the gate and up toward the vineyard. Frances could hear their footsteps even after they had disappeared into the darkness.

Belinda hitched up her shoulder strap and roughly opened her evening bag. She took out a cigarette and lit it with a silver lighter. It glowed in the dark, a small point of light.

"Go ahead," she said at last. "Say it. I'm a bitch."

"I wasn't going to say that."

"No, because you're too nice, aren't you? Too nice to use a word like that."

Frances thought of Sally in her Juliet cap, facing the woman who was beauty incarnate, the woman who was now standing and smoking a cigarette as if she had not just delivered a blow meant to kill. "You didn't need to do that," she said with energy. "That was a terrible thing to do to a child."

"Oh, spare me the sermon, for God's sake. That girl can take care of herself."

"She's only thirteen. She's still a child."

"Stop saying that." Belinda's eyes flashed with anger. "Just stop. All I did was tell the truth. I did him a favor. Now he doesn't have to worry about telling her."

It was such stunningly terrible logic that Frances could not respond. Belinda exhaled a plume of smoke.

"The truth will set you free," said the actress. "That's what good people say, right?"

"It wasn't your truth to tell," said Frances. "It was Lawrence's."

"Lawrence," mimicked Belinda. "Gee, how cozy we are now. Is that what you'll call him, back at the studio? 'Lawrence, Mr. Glennon is here to see you'? That'll go over well." She flicked out some ash, which fell on the tablecloth. "What he did in Napa, out there for all to see. But he's hardly the first producer to fuck his secretary."

She turned to Frances. "You're not going to dignify that with a response, are you? Fine. Be self-righteous if you want. But don't judge me for what I've done."

Her hand was shaking as she lifted the cigarette to her lips. Frances remembered what Lawrence had said about Belinda by the river, what felt like a year ago: *She's vulnerable in her own way.* He was too perceptive to be entirely wrong.

"I wanted this part so much," Belinda said in a different tone. "So much. This kind of role comes along once every five years. Do you know how old I'll be when the next one comes around? Thirty, I'll be thirty. No, it has to be this one. I've given up too much to let it go. I've burned too many bridges."

There were tears coursing down her cheeks, not the pretty ones seen in her films. As she moved under the lantern to put the lighter back in her bag, Frances saw the dark tracks made by the mascara. The defiance and anger seemed to be draining out of her.

"Burned too many bridges?" Frances asked gently.

"You wouldn't know," said Belinda, "if you aren't from a small town like the one I grew up in. Plover, Nebraska. Three hundred people. Everyone knows everyone. Are you from a small town?"

"No."

"Hilda Olafson. That's my real name. You can see why I changed it. God, I wanted out of there. What was I going to do, marry the Eberhardt boy and take over his farm? Have ten kids in ten years? I asked for money and took a train west, telling my family I was just going to see the sights. I never went back.

"My father had cancer, but I didn't go back. I was in the middle of shooting a film. My first speaking role, two whole lines. But you know what would've happened if I'd gone? They'd have replaced me with someone else, some other blonde. I thought I'd have time once the movie was done. But then there was another movie, a bigger part. I wasn't about to give it up. Same story."

"And your father?"

"He died two years ago." She looked down at her cigarette. "My mother still hasn't forgiven me. Neither have my siblings. Neither has the Eberhardt boy, probably. So Plover, Nebraska, is one part of this country where Belinda Vail is totally unwelcome. A little dead zone in the middle of the cornfields. They say you can't go home again, and they're right."

Frances thought of her father, sitting on his stool, watching Lawrence weed. "I used to think that," she said. "But now—I'm not sure."

"Maybe you can go home," Belinda said. "But not me." She crossed her arms, standing in the unsubstantial dress, looking off in the distance.

"Do you know how I got that part?" she asked after a moment. "That two-line part, my first big break? Harvey Linton, the producer. He took me to Palm Springs for the weekend, to a hotel that Hilda Olafson could only dream of, and he got what he wanted and I got what I wanted. It all worked out, didn't it? Only he wasn't a good man to be with, not for your first time." She took another drag on the cigarette. "I thought I knew what to expect, but I was wrong. There are some things you don't learn about on a farm in Nebraska." She stubbed out the cigarette.

"And you know what's funny? That part, with the two lines? I was the little sister of Gary Cooper. The start of my career as the girl next door. I gave my virginity to play a string of virgins. Oh, it was fine at first. It's better than life on the farm. But it's not what I want anymore. I can do so much more, be so much more. That's why I wanted this part, why I wanted to play Kitty Ridley. She didn't care what people thought, she had dozens of lovers, she didn't give a damn, nothing could hurt her. That's the part I wanted."

She began to cry all over again.

"And Lawrence," she managed to say. "I shouldn't have let him go so easily. I thought it was safe, that I had the part, it didn't matter if he was cooling on me. But maybe he'd have fought more if we were still together." Her tears glittered in the dim light. "And I did like him, you know? He's not like other men in Hollywood. You could almost imagine bringing him home, almost imagine him sitting in the kitchen with Mama bringing him pie and coffee. But not anymore."

She rubbed her hand over her face, roughly; no actress ever cried like that in a film. It was the most human gesture Frances had ever seen her make. Then she grasped the chair, staring out across the table and the remains of the party.

"It's like this," she said to Frances in a low voice. "I gave up so much to be a star." Her face was tear-stained, but her jaw was set. "And it has to be worth it. It just has to be worth it."

CHAPTER
FORTY·FOUR

It was completely dark half an hour later when Frances returned to the house. She came through the kitchen, its light shining on a pile of dishes in the sink, and set the vase of flowers on the table. In the living room, Celia sat in the wing chair with Toby asleep on her lap, the floor lamp making a golden glow around them.

"There you are," said Celia. "I was wondering."

"I walked around for a bit. I just wanted to think."

"Miss Vail was here. She washed her face and left with her driver." She settled Toby more comfortably on her lap; he murmured and then quieted. "She seemed upset about the movie. I hear it's off."

"It is."

Celia looked at her steadily. "I'm sorry."

"It's fine," Frances said. "I'm actually glad."

Celia rested her chin on top of Toby's head. "I've got a pile of dishes to do," she said, "but all I want to do right now is sit here."

"I'll do the dishes," said Frances.

"No, don't," said Celia. "Miss Ridley wants to talk to you. She said she'd stay awake until you came in." She nodded toward the table. "Your gift for her is over there."

As Frances moved to pick up the small box, she paused over the sleeping boy. Celia was looking down at him with love and fondness even through her weariness. Frances reached out and gently ruffled his hair. It felt like feathers.

"He's so sweet," she wanted to say, but it was not what came out.

"You're a lucky woman, Celia," she said instead, emotion suddenly choking her.

M iss Ridley was sitting up in bed. She wore a surprisingly conservative nightgown of white cotton, with a high neck. Her turban was off, and with the wisps of hair she looked like a large child waiting to be tucked in. "Good. You're still here."

Frances pulled a small stool over to the bed and sat down. On the bedside table was an old-fashioned lamp with a glass shade. It was the only light in the room.

"And Miss Vail?"

"She's gone," said Frances. "Back to Napa. Then Hollywood, I guess."

"She's beautiful and ambitious. She'll do fine, that girl." Miss Ridley shifted slightly in bed, a fleeting expression of pain crossing her face. "But you—I am sorry for you, and Mr. Merrill."

"Don't be. I can't speak for Lawrence, but I suspect he feels the same way I do."

"And what do you feel?"

"Glad. That you made the decision that is right for you."

"I have few decisions left," said Miss Ridley. "I might as well make them right." She indicated the box. "For me?"

Frances held it out to her, but Miss Ridley shook her head. "You'll have to untie that ribbon." Frances did so, then gently opened the box. She took out the small lump of tissue paper and gave it to Miss Ridley, who unwrapped it.

It was a small china tabby cat, three inches high. It sat on its haunches, looking up, in exactly the attitude a cat has while deciding to climb a tree.

Miss Ridley's eyes were bright. "You remembered my story." She held the figure to the light, turning it to see it from every angle. There was a smile on her lips, which were devoid of their usual lipstick.

"Put it there, Frances," she said at last, indicating the bedside table. "Move it a bit, so I can see it from my bed."

Frances obliged, and Miss Ridley settled back against the pillows. Her hands, resting on the bedspread, were ropy with veins, mottled with spots. Those hands had done so much, Frances thought. They had held the reins of horses, lifted Juliet's dagger, been kissed by scores of men, and had—so briefly—held a baby, her baby, before it was given away.

Miss Ridley's voice broke into her reverie. "I told you," she said, "that there was one other person I told about being a cat. It was a boy. Danny O'Leary."

"O'Leary," said Frances. "You've mentioned that name before."

"His mother was the costume maker at the Bella Union theater. I spent two years at that theater, from fourteen to sixteen. It's where I first played Juliet."

"What was Danny like?"

"Tall and skinny. Black hair, curly. He walked with a limp—not quite a limp, but one foot dipped and dragged, as if he were on a rocking ship. He walked with his hands held up a little, like this. He was born that way. It made many people overlook him, you know.

"His mother was a widow, and she couldn't afford to keep him in school. He was a year older than I. He worked at the theater, doing sums and figures for the manager, and he had a rare mind, so quick; he never met a number that could defeat him. I used to think it was cruel of God, putting that brilliant mind in that poor body. But maybe it isn't. Maybe it's better that the gifts are spread out like that.

"But he was my first real friend, after all those years of moving from camp to camp. We used to sit on the edge of the stage at midday, the two of us, eating peanuts and throwing the shells. We made games with a piece of string, making it into shapes and having to guess what they were. He was so good at it. He could make that string look like the profile of the stage manager, or like a running horse. He understood me completely, Danny did. More than anyone has, before or since.

"And he was my first kiss too." She smiled. "I was sixteen, wearing the blue dress his mother had made. Oh, I felt so beautiful. And nothing has ever felt as right as that kiss. There were four kisses, in all, four different times. I remember every one.

"But my mother found out, and the manager found out, and that was the end of it. My star was rising, you see. I was sixteen, and men in their thirties wanted to meet me, men with arms full of roses, with diamond stickpins and millions. Danny was sent away to live with a cousin up in Fort Ross. It might as well have been Timbuktu in those days. They sent him off before I even knew he was leaving. My mother told me he was gone between acts of *Romeo and Juliet*. She was clever that way. It was the only performance I've ever given where my grief at the end was real.

"I had no choice but to forget him. I had to move on, to throw myself into the life I was living. I didn't think of him for decades, until I was in the convent. And then I found that I couldn't stop thinking of him. In that quiet space, I couldn't stop."

She looked at Frances fondly. "There's another handkerchief in the drawer."

Frances, not wanting to break the flow of the story, wiped her eyes with her hand. "Did you ever find out what happened to him?"

"No. Oh, I thought of trying to trace him, maybe thirty years ago, but I never did. But I'm comforted that I will know someday. It won't be in this world, but I'll know someday."

She reached out and took Frances's hand.

"Other men have given me pleasure," she said. "But those days in the theater—it was the one time in my life, the only time, that I have known love. With a crippled boy who left school at thirteen and had only one shabby suit of clothes. It doesn't make a good movie, but it made a good life. Those memories. I will always have them."

Frances could not hold back her tears. She wanted to speak, to share a story of her own, but Miss Ridley, suddenly exhausted, had leaned back against the pillows and closed her eyes. Her grip on Frances's hand slackened. After a moment her chest rose and fell in regular rhythm.

Frances stood up quietly, but before she could leave, she felt her hand squeezed gently. Miss Ridley was looking at her with eyes that seemed to read Frances's thoughts.

"I want to hear the rest of your story," she said in a voice that was barely audible. "Please tell me tomorrow. You'll be back tomorrow?"

"I'll make sure of it."

"Good." She held Frances's gaze for a moment, and a little bit of the old fire danced back into her eyes.

"Perhaps," she said, "there's someone else who would like to hear your story. In the meantime."

"Perhaps there is."

"Thank you for the cat. I like it very much."

Frances angled it slightly toward the bed. "Shall I turn off the light?"

"In a moment," said Miss Ridley. She lifted herself up with effort. "Frances, there's something I want to ask you. One more thing. Before I sleep."

"Yes?"

"Sit down a moment."

And Frances did.

The front of the property was hard to navigate in the darkness. There were no lanterns, as there had been in the arbor, but the moon was high, and Frances managed to make her way over the lawn and to the garden without stumbling.

She could not see her watch, but she knew it must be at least ten o'clock. When she had left Miss Ridley and walked to the living room, it was empty, Celia and Toby no longer sitting in the pool of light. She wondered briefly where Lawrence was. Perhaps he was still with Sally, up in the vineyard, talking. The memory of them walking away from Belinda, his arm around his daughter, gently and protectively, made something inside hurt just as much as it made her glad.

"Frances."

It was Lawrence. He got up from the bench where he had been sitting, a cigarette in his hand.

"Celia said you were talking to Miss Ridley."

"I was." She sat down on the bench, and he sat next to her. "Where's Sally?"

"Upstairs. I offered to take her back to the hotel, but she wanted to stay here again. I think that's a good sign."

He stamped out the cigarette and took her hand in his. His touch was unfamiliar enough to make her senses leap, but there was something stronger than desire in that moment.

"How is she?"

He tilted his head back, looking at the stars. "She's all right. No credit to me." Even in the semi-darkness she could see the set of his jaw. "To think she knew. All this time, she knew, and never said anything." There was a catch in his voice. "It kills me, Frances, to think of her suffering in silence like that. And that I told Belinda. I'll regret that until my dying day."

She put her other hand over his. There was a slight rustle in the flower beds, some nocturnal creature about its business.

"But it's out now, however terrible," he said. "And we had a good talk, Sally and I. She'll be okay, I know that. But I still feel like a failure as a father."

"You did the best you could."

"I suppose so," he said. "It's what parents need, I think, more than anything. Forgiveness."

He turned to her, studied her in the moonlight. His expression changed.

"None of this would have happened without you," he said. "If you hadn't been here, on this trip."

"Maybe."

"Not maybe. All of it—you, Miss Ridley, this place—it's all worked together to . . . to shake things loose, somehow, for Sally and me. And . . ."—he paused, looking down at her hand as he held it—"for me and you too."

She felt a wave of desire, but above it was a stronger, more urgent need. His gaze moved to her mouth, but she pulled back, and he looked at her searchingly, then with concern.

She let go of his hand. Her heart was pounding. "I want to tell you something," she said. "The rest of my story. The one I started telling you yesterday. I'll tell you if you want to hear."

"Of course."

And so, picking up where they had left off at the riverbed, she began to tell him. About the meetings in the office at the college, about the pregnancy, and about Don's betrayal. And about what had happened afterwards, in and around the house on Chapin Lane.

CHAPTER FORTY-FIVE

S he told her father and Mother Florence by letter, for she could not imagine doing so over the phone in the dormitory lounge. The letter was written hastily, four days after Don's dismissal of her. *I am expecting a child, the man is engaged, he knows but will not marry me.* She mailed it, and then waited.

In the days following she imagined the letter, like a tiny grenade, moving its way through the post office and onto trains and at last into a mail pouch carried to the curbside mailbox on Chapin Lane. It was a terrible secret to have, the awareness that something was on its way to her parents that would shatter their world.

Days later a telegram came, summoning her back home.

Making an excuse to the bursar, to the college president, and to her roommate, she packed and boarded the train. She had always enjoyed the trips across the country, and gradually her anxiety lessened as she let herself be lulled by the rhythm and regular sound of the wheels. The train seemed to be an in-between space, a place neither here nor there where she could temporarily suspend her worries about the future. She thought of the meetings in Don's office, the ecstatic pleasure of those evenings, wondering which one of them had been the decisive encounter. It was strange that something so momentous could happen quietly, without being detected by the people whom it would later affect so deeply. *I went to college to collect new experiences and knowledge,* she reflected with grim amusement, *and I certainly succeeded.*

At times, she wondered about the child. She could not have said why, but she kept thinking of it as a boy. Her hands rested on her abdomen as she watched the country scroll by outside the window. She had always liked the opportunity to observe and chat with people on trains, but this time her gaze stayed on the landscape, aware that for a brief, precious time she was in a quiet cocoon where she was safe and alone with her thoughts.

That peace was gone the moment she saw her father at the station. He looked not angry but haunted; there were shadows under his eyes, and she felt a wave of grief at what her actions had caused. He embraced her gingerly, as if he were not sure she was the same person who had left home months before. That, in itself, made her want to cry.

"I'm sorry," she said in the car on the way home. He looked anguished, and opened his mouth and then closed it as if he did not know what to say next. She was silent the rest of the way, blinking back tears.

W hen she walked through the front door, there was no sign of Mother Florence. It was Rita who came into the living room the moment she heard the door, who opened her arms and embraced her. "Welcome home, lovey." She smelled as she always had, of flour and fabric.

"You know?"

Rita nodded. She looked at Frances with concern, then squeezed her elbows. "Come in the kitchen."

Frances took a seat in the breakfast nook, and Rita sat beside her. Sunlight illuminated the bowl of daisies on the small table. "I'm sorry, Rita."

"Don't apologize to me," said Rita. "Girls have been getting pregnant since the dawn of time."

"Not me, though."

"No, that's true. But this isn't exactly an original sin, lovey."

Frances laughed shakily and Rita did too. It was a comfort to smile again.

"I've missed you, Rita." She stared at the yellow center of the closest flower. "What—what are they saying? About all this?"

"Your stepmother wasn't happy," she said simply. "Nor was your father."

"They are going to send me away, aren't they?" said Frances. "Some illness I have to recover from in Texas, or Europe. And I'll be back in nine months without the baby." Strange, how the thought of that made her feel cold inside.

"You can't keep it without having a husband," Rita said. "You sure you couldn't marry him?"

"He's engaged," said Frances. "I didn't know that when—well, I didn't know it."

"Just like a man," said Rita. She slapped at the table ferociously; Frances realized why when a fly, unscathed, buzzed triumphantly overhead and away.

"Damn flies," said Rita fiercely. "Always getting away with everything."

Mother Florence said nothing about the pregnancy when she came home, greeting Frances coolly with only a quick glance at her waistline. When Frances attempted, haltingly, to apologize, Mother Florence raised a penciled eyebrow and said, "Not now, Frances," before going upstairs.

Dinner an hour later was restrained and, for Frances at least, profoundly uncomfortable. Mother Florence talked calmly of trivial things, studiously ignoring any reference to the pregnancy. As much as Frances dreaded talking about it, it was far more taxing not to do so. It was almost a relief when, after the dinner plates had been removed, Mother Florence turned to Frances and said, "So. Here we are."

Frances glanced at her father, but he was looking at his wife.

"We will not go into recriminations," said Mother Florence. Her face was controlled, unemotional. "We will look ahead to the future."

"Where will I go?" asked Frances.

"Nowhere. If we send you away, everyone will know. You know the Taggarts, on Adeline Drive? Their daughter went to Albuquerque for eight months. For her asthma, they said. It fooled no one." She patted her lips with the napkin and folded it carefully. "No, your only option is to get married."

"But I can't. He's engaged to someone else."

Mother Florence looked at her as if she had said something obscene. "Don't talk about this any more than you have to, Frances, please. No, I'm thinking of someone else." She checked her silver watch. "My cousin's son, Ernest."

Frances looked at her father. He smiled, more like a grimace.

"He's a lawyer," he said, "recently moved to Menlo Park. Just starting out, but he's got a promising career."

The doorbell rang.

"And," said Mother Florence significantly, "he's here to meet you." She looked at Frances, who was sitting in shock. "Go fix your hair, Frances. Put on some lipstick too."

Ernest Rowe was tall, his dark hair carefully corralled with Brylcreem. He was not unattractive; there was a regularity to his features that was pleasing, and his manners were impeccable. He had good teeth, and he was extraordinarily polite, scrambling quickly to his feet whenever Frances or Mother Florence entered the room. *He is polished*, thought Frances. *His hair, his manners, his shoes: everything.*

After coffee, he proposed that he and Frances take a walk. "Yes, do," said Mother Florence, going to the window.

"I'm a little tired," said Frances. The conversation had been taxing, and her nausea was returning.

"The neighbors need to see you together," said Mother Florence pointedly.

Ernest helped her on with her coat. He opened the door for her. They walked along silently for half a block. Mr. Rhodes across the street was walking to his car and raised a hand in greeting, but Frances pretended she did not see him.

"So," said Ernest after a moment. "This is a nice city, and a nice neighborhood."

"Yes," she said.

"I'm hoping to buy here someday. For now, of course, it's the house in Menlo Park. It's small, but comfortable. The kitchen has a new icebox. And it's close to the office, which is helpful. There are other women with children on the street."

"That's nice," she said faintly.

They walked along, past a camellia laden with ruffled red blooms. He held out his arm as they crossed the street; she felt obliged to take it even though she did not want to. She held herself a little apart, so his arm would not touch her body.

"I've been too busy to go out much, these last few years," he said. "But I have always wanted to get married someday. I think this is the answer. For both of us."

She looked at the sky and was silent. A bank of clouds was scrolling up from the west.

"Especially for you, perhaps," he added pleasantly and pointedly. She felt a wave of nausea, and it took all her grit to hold it down.

There was no ignoring it. She could not keep the baby without marrying him. For a moment she wished she were Hester Prynne in Puritan New England, able to live alone in a cottage and raise her child in isolation, her only punishment to wear a scarlet letter for the rest of her life.

But it was 1933, not 1640. And the man walking beside her, polished, polite, and ambitious, was her only way out.

I n the week that followed, Ernest came to see her three more times. Every time, Mother Florence insisted that they take a walk or linger on the front porch where they were visible to the neighbors. Frances was forced to introduce him to the bridge club ladies who came over one evening when his visit just happened to coincide with theirs. He showed well, Frances thought with detachment. He was not one of them, but he was right on the edge, and the perfection of his manners, his studied amiability, was enough to propel him over the line into social acceptance.

"A charming young man," said Mrs. Reynolds after he had left. "I wish he could meet my daughter." She sighed. "It's her clubfoot, you know; it's so hard for her to meet men."

Mother Florence made a noise of sympathy. "She is a sweet girl, your daughter. But I do believe Ernest is rather besotted with Frances."

"I thought she wanted to finish college. She can't be thinking of marrying yet."

"Well," said Mother Florence, "sometimes love conquers all."

E rnest took her out the following evening. He had suggested dinner, but she, feeling the strain of making conversation across a table, countered with the movies; there she could gain the credit of an evening with him without having much to do or say.

They went to see a musical featuring Ruby Keeler, and for a while Frances was transported. She sat, her hands folded in her lap, watching Ruby dance with a series of handsome men in tails, her feet flying, her face rapt. What would it be like to spend your days whirling about in a beautiful dress without a care in the world? How glorious to live even temporarily in a world full of song, where you were guaranteed a happy ending.

Suddenly, she felt Ernest reach across her lap. Though her hands were folded, he took the nearest one, disentangling it roughly from the other, and pulled it so that it was splayed on his leg, halfway between the knee and the thigh. His own hand covered hers entirely. Her left hand, suddenly without a partner, sat cold in her lap.

The dancers continued, but she hardly saw them. She sat motionless, her nerves pulled like a string. It did not occur to her to move her hand away from under his. "This man is your savior," Mother Florence had told her after his first visit. But as the movie went on and he kept her hand pressed on his thigh, the thought flashed into her mind that perhaps she did not want to be delivered after all.

That evening he kissed her on the front porch under the light. It was unexpected, and she could not respond in kind. When he pulled away from her, he was all polish and correctness, smiling, saying, "Thank you, Frances," in a humble tone, as if she had bestowed on him a great gift. To be courtly, she thought, was his default position. It was his default position unless he was in a dark theater, when he took what was not being offered and kept it.

She could not fall asleep that night.

※

S he was finishing breakfast the next morning when Mother Florence received a phone call from a friend. Frances, one room away, could not help overhearing.

"Yes," said Mother Florence. "Isn't it exciting?" There was a pause. "Yes, quite soon. They will be married in Menlo Park." Another pause. "Well, yes, but you can't stop true love, can you? And you know, they first met many years ago. I'm not sure what she would have done with a college degree anyhow."

Frances put down her spoon and stared at Rita. Rita, standing at the sink holding a pot, stared back.

Mother Florence came into the kitchen, patting her hair. "Mrs. Anderson is so happy for you," she said. "She seems to want to be asked to the wedding. We will keep it small, of course."

"You've already planned the wedding," said Frances.

"Of course. I've booked the minister. It's a week from Saturday, at Ernest's house." At Frances's look, her face hardened. "You have no time to waste, Frances." She looked significantly at her stepdaughter's waistline under the cinch of the robe as she picked up the stamped letters sitting on the sideboard. "You know that."

"But he hasn't even asked me," said Frances. It was not what was bothering her; what was bothering her she could not say aloud.

Mother Florence slammed the letters down on the table. "You expect a Hollywood love scene, do you?" Her voice was no longer controlled; it was harsh, almost vicious. "Do you? If you wanted that, you should have kept your legs together."

The pot Rita was wiping fell with a clang. Frances stared at her stepmother. The mask was gone; her face was contorted in anger, pure and unfiltered.

"We are in Ernest's debt, you selfish girl. Without him you would never be able to hold up your head again. And neither would we." She left, slamming the door on her way out.

✦

Frances went to find her father. He was planting primroses, whistling, but as she approached he saw her and his face clouded over.

"Father," she said. "Mother Florence has scheduled the wedding. For Saturday."

"I know." He picked up a blue-violet flower and stood holding it, unhappily.

She pulled her cardigan more closely around her as she stood in the cool shade of the garage. She wanted him to know that she felt helpless, totally without agency, and that the thought of marrying Ernest made her feel ill in a way that the pregnancy never had. Just as she opened her mouth to say so, he spoke.

"Florence worked hard to make this marriage happen." His expression was pained, almost pleading, willing her to agree. "Not every girl has someone who would do this for her."

But I don't want it, she almost said, but a shutter had dropped over his face, and she saw that he did not know how to help her. He did not know how to defy the ancient tradition of condemnation for the girl who has a child but no husband. He liked peace, not conflict; he liked things to be orderly and neat. And in the way he brushed his face self-consciously, she saw that he wanted his family to be orderly and neat too.

He swiftly bent down to plant the flower, and she saw that her very presence was an embarrassment to him, a reproach. He could relax and enjoy her company again when she had done the one thing that would restore order to the family.

I have to marry Ernest to keep my baby, she thought as she walked slowly away. *And I have to marry him to keep my father.*

And a new thought came into her head, like a swift, disloyal arrow. She wondered if it was actually worth it.

The next day, Ernest took her out to dinner. "I'm sure it won't take you long to learn my favorite recipes," he said at the restaurant. "I'm not picky, but I do know what I like. And I live close enough to the office that I can come home every day for a hot lunch."

Driving home in the dark, they were stopped by a huge truck blocking the intersection. A policeman asked them to wait, and Ernest turned off the car; then he once again took her hand out of her lap and placed it on his leg, this time higher on the thigh than before, his hand over it, pressing it down, and she was relieved when the policeman waved their car forward through the intersection and her hand was free again. "Good fellows, those policemen," Ernest said benevolently.

An hour later, they were in the living room having coffee while he and Mother Florence talked about details of the wedding. Frances sat poised on the edge of the rocking chair and said nothing. "You are distracted, Frances," said Mother Florence. It was true; Frances found she could not focus on or absorb the conversation around her. She could not think of anything but the look on Ernest's face a half hour before, when he had helped her off with her coat in the entry hall.

He helped her with her coat every time they returned to the house, but this time she had seen something new. In the mirror, she had seen him give a quick, unguarded glance at her abdomen. It was a look that made her heart stop. There was none of the usual amiability on his face, no respectful courtesy. It was a look of contempt; it was almost, she realized with shock, a look of hatred. Then it had passed, and he was smiling again, but she had seen the expression, and she could not forget it.

In bed that night, she replayed the incident. To marry him would put her forever in his debt. If she felt any sort of love for him, or him for her, it might not matter. But in that moment, in the brief glance she had seen in the mirror, she had known that he would demand payment on that debt for the rest of her life. He would demand payment in the kitchen, in the living room, in the bedroom. And if she refused, she would find no ally.

Day after day, year after year. For the rest of her life, or his.

She put her hands on her abdomen. She thought of the child, a small speck of a life, curled up deep within her body. "I'm sorry," she said aloud as the tears fell. "I'm sorry."

CHAPTER
FORTY·SIX

"The next day," said Frances to Lawrence, "I told them that I would not marry Ernest. I refused to come down from my room when he came. Mother Florence raged. She told me I was destroying the family's reputation, my father's business, but I didn't give in. And in the end, they sent me away."

Lawrence had kept his eyes on her throughout the entire story. The compassion in his gaze had bolstered her through the halting unfamiliarity of telling it, through all the reliving of the memories she'd kept locked in silence.

"I went to San Francisco," she said. "Rita's cousin let me stay with her in North Beach, where we didn't know anyone. It might have been another country. The baby was born on July twenty-ninth. Five years ago today," she said, and he made a spontaneous expression of surprise.

"Frances. I had no idea."

"It was a boy. He had dark brown hair, lots of it. Hair with a part in it, almost like . . ."—she paused, letting herself remember—"almost like he'd been to the barber and had it combed. Like a little old man." Lawrence's arm went around her.

"He was so perfect," she said. "He had these tiny hands, these tiny fingernails." The tears fell freely as she opened the locked case of memories: diminutive curled fingers, the skin on them peeling, and the square fingernails, impossibly small, images that she had tried to forget for the pain of remembering. "The nurse at the hospital let me hold him. He opened his eyes, these dark eyes, and looked at me. It was like he knew me already. And then I fell asleep, and when I woke up he was gone. I asked to see him once more and they said I couldn't, that there was no point, that it would just be worse.

"I had known I would give him up. I made that choice when I wouldn't marry Ernest. But I wanted to say goodbye, at least. And I didn't. I never saw him again."

He handed her a handkerchief, keeping his arm around her as she blew her nose and wiped her eyes.

"They said he would be adopted by a family in San Francisco. That's all they would tell me."

"And your family?"

"They knew I'd had the baby and given him up. My father—he sent me a letter. He said he was sorry for what had happened, that I could come home when a few more months had passed. But I didn't. He had failed me when I needed him most, needed him to stand up to Mother Florence. It wasn't in his nature, I think. He couldn't do it. But I never went back."

"Where did you go?"

"San Luis Obispo. To secretarial school, and then I got a job at the law office there. It was a new start, in a new place. I wasn't unhappy. But then my best friend there, another young woman in the building, got married and had a baby. And it made everything real again. I needed to get away."

"That's when you went to work for Cyril?"

She nodded. "I think maybe he guessed it, what was in my past, but he never pried." The image of beautiful Delia rose before her eyes. Cyril had his own past. "And I was happy, working for him. If I couldn't finish college, I told myself at least I could choose the most interesting jobs I could find. I could go where I wanted, work where I wanted. I'd given up my child to be able to do things like that. And it had to be worth it." She thought of Belinda in her white gown, the mascara tracks down her face. The cat, who had come out of the flower beds, sat at Frances's feet and gave a loud meow.

"If you could have done anything, Frances," said Lawrence, "what would you have done?"

"Kept the baby without marrying Ernest. Raised him on my own, and still gone to work. It sounds ridiculous, doesn't it?"

"No," said Lawrence. "It doesn't. I think we—the world—have made it ridiculous. But it isn't."

She leaned against him, and he rested his head on her hair.

"In my time at the studio," he said, "more than a few actresses have had to go away. For 'health reasons,' they say. Sometimes they are able to see the child again; they give it to a friend to raise, or they call it a cousin, something like that. But they can never claim it as their own. It's cruel. But they have to do it to keep their careers."

"I could have married Ernest," said Frances, "and kept the baby, but I didn't. I chose my freedom instead."

"Would you do it differently now?"

"No," said Frances instantly. "No. If I had married him, he would have killed me. Slowly, little by little."

"My opinion means nothing," he said quietly, "but if it helps, I think you made the right choice."

"I know," she said. She remembered what Celia had said: if the core of a life is good, the edges don't matter. With Ernest, the core would never have been good. "I know that. But if I let myself think of the baby, it hurts. So I haven't let myself think of him. Not until now."

The cat meowed again and she reached for it. He arched into her caress, his fur soft against her fingers.

"I stayed in San Francisco for six weeks after he was born, and I almost never left the apartment. I was afraid that I'd see the baby on the street." She sat up and wiped her eyes. "And even now, when we were in San Francisco last week, I thought maybe I'd be walking on the street and see him and I'd recognize him instantly. And then I thought maybe I'd walk right by him and not know him. And I didn't know which one felt more painful."

He squeezed her hand.

"I don't even know how to explain," she said. "It can't be regret because I'd still make the same choice. But maybe it can be the right thing and still hurt. I haven't wanted to hurt. I've been avoiding it for a long time. But here . . . I couldn't escape it."

A slight breeze stirred her hair. The cat, tired of waiting for attention, got up and crept away.

"If only I knew, Lawrence. Who he was living with, that he was happy. That he had parents like Celia and Joe. But I won't ever know. They don't tell you. They took him and they wouldn't tell me anything. They just said to forget him."

Tears fell again at the memory of that small figure, wrapped in a blanket, in the circle of her arms. The hair, so sleek and damp from her body, coming to a little fringe in the back of his neck. The dark eyes on hers. The warmth of him, the weight of him.

"If only I knew," she said again.

The moon above them looked like a silver disc in the sky. It shone on the tower, with its tall windows. There were lights on upstairs in the bedrooms, and a light downstairs, in the front room.

"It's funny," Lawrence said. "Just yesterday I noticed that sampler in the hall of the hotel, by your room. 'Now we see through a glass, darkly, but then we will see face-to-face.' And I was thinking about Mavis. I always wanted to know why she did it, what pushed her to make that decision. But I've had to accept that I'll never know, until I die." His voice was quiet but steady. "I'm not especially religious, Frances, but I do believe we have a kind of knowledge after death that we don't have now. So for now, maybe it's about learning to live with the mystery. It isn't an easy thing to do, especially not for someone like me, or you, who likes things to be tidy. But some things won't be tidy. And life is one of those things."

"Maybe—" he began. He studied the night sky as if looking for the right words.

"Our movies," he said at last, "they have neat endings. 'The End,' in big letters. A clear villain, a clear hero. Maybe we've gotten people to expect that. But life isn't like that, most of the time."

"To my stepmother, it is," said Frances. "Ernest was the hero, and I was the villain. I was too selfish to fix what I'd broken. That's how she sees it."

"But you, Frances," said Lawrence. "How do you see it?"

She looked up at him. His expression was grave and intent.

"How would you tell your story?" he asked.

The square tower shone in the moonlight. Beyond it, stars were spread out across the dark blanket of the night, more stars than you ever saw in the Hollywood sky.

"I would say," she said slowly, "that I'm a girl who loved a man. I loved my child, and I also loved my freedom. I loved my father, even though I hurt him and he hurt me. And somewhere in the place where all those things meet—that's my story."

"It's not neat, is it?" she said after a moment. "You could never make a screenplay out of it."

"It's not neat," he said, smoothing back her hair. "But it's real."

She leaned into his hand, closing her eyes, waiting for the tears to come.

But they did not. She had no tears left, she realized. She felt spent, purged, and yet also, for the first time in a very long time, she felt a glimmering of peace. There was still pain at the thought of her lost child, but it was a pain she could share, had shared, with someone who understood. It was a pain she could share with Miss Ridley, too, who would also understand. Perhaps, she thought as his thumb stroked her cheek, perhaps everyone had some secret pain, a pain that they had to learn not to bury but to name, holding it up to the light.

She opened her eyes to find a smile in his gaze. His fingers moved in the hair just above her ear. "No bay leaf this time."

"No," she said.

His fingers kept moving, twining gently in her curls. The relaxed peace she felt spread throughout her body, followed by a swift wave of desire.

He was watching her. He would not make a move to kiss her, she knew, though he wanted to and she wanted him to; he would not be the one to end the moment, to change the holy space she had created with her past and her trust in him.

A light went off in the upstairs room. She glanced at her watch, but it was too dark to see.

"What time is it?"

"Late. Probably eleven."

She looked at the house and at the tower. Then she stood up.

"Come with me," she said, reaching for his hand. "There's something I still want to see."

They found Joe sitting in the wing chair, smoking a cigarette, the radio turned low. He greeted them with eyes that were tired but friendly.

"I'm the last one up," he said. "Everyone's in bed."

"Sorry," said Lawrence. "I hope you weren't staying awake for us."

"No, I wanted to do the dishes for Celia. Just finished." He held out the box. "Cigarette?"

"No, thank you," said Frances. "I was wondering—the tower. I haven't been up there yet."

"Sure. Go ahead."

"Will it wake anyone?"

"Shouldn't. Just don't have a party on the stairs." He stuck the cigarette in his mouth, stood up. "I'll give you a flashlight."

They had to scale two staircases and open a trapdoor to get there. It was cooler than the air outside had been, a square space, eight by ten, with faded antique wallpaper and a single old chair draped with a crocheted blanket. As Lawrence passed the chair, the blanket slid partly off to reveal a small leather pouch tucked underneath. He picked it up and weighed it in his hand with a smile of nostalgic recognition.

"Marbles," he said. "Probably Arthur's best ones. This is exactly where I would have hidden mine." He replaced the pouch, redraping the blanket carefully.

Frances looked out the window facing south. With the flashlight shining in the enclosed space, it was hard to see. From the outside the light would be visible, like the golden flare of a lighthouse in the darkness.

As if following her thoughts, Lawrence switched off the flashlight. Moonlight flooded the small space, and Frances, unafraid of the height, pressed her face to the window.

Across the expanse of shingled roof she could see the lawn below, and the gravel path. She could see the trees, dark shapes, some of them obscuring her view. She could see, if she craned her neck, the garden where they had just been sitting, and beyond that, the valley stretching before her.

Below her a family slumbered, Sally with them. Miss Ridley slept too, her birthday at an end, dreaming perhaps of a boy with a limp, or of a little blonde girl riding a horse in the desert. Somewhere beyond those hills, beyond the vines and farmland and bridge, was the city, and somewhere in that city there was a child who had just had his own birthday, a dark-haired boy who was living a life Frances would never share but—she felt the jagged pain make a new, unfamiliar shift into peace—which she could still bless. And she did so, sending a wordless prayer for her boy and his family across the quiet miles.

The tears began again, and Lawrence put an arm around her. She leaned into his shoulder. "I'm okay," she said. "I really am." And he pressed his lips to her hair, and they stood that way and looked over the quiet valley.

CHAPTER

FORTY·SEVEN

They did not speak much on the drive back to the hotel. The highway was empty, hardly any other cars around. At one point, Lawrence put his hand on Frances's knee and she rested her own on his; then he had to turn and took it away.

The hotel clerk was sitting down to a sandwich and pickle behind the front desk, a napkin tucked into his shirt. "Late dinner," he said apologetically. "It was a busy night. There were people all around the hotel. Miss Vail went back to Hollywood, but you probably already knew that."

"Yes," said Lawrence. "I did."

"What a day," said the clerk. "One to remember forever." He nodded with a smile. "Good night."

Lawrence walked her to her door. She fitted the key in the lock, glancing up at the verse on the sampler as she did so. She opened the door a few inches and stood in the hallway, her hand on the knob. In the quiet of the windowless hall, she could even hear the muted tick of the grandfather clock on the landing.

He looked down at her, still wearing his hat.

"I don't feel like saying goodnight," she said at last. "I'm not tired at all somehow."

"Neither am I."

There was privacy behind her door, a space to act on the feelings that had been growing for days. When she turned her head she could see the bed, the corner of its spread turned down invitingly by the hotel maid.

But there was also something she needed to tell him: this time not about the past but about the future.

"Come in for a while," she said.

Once inside she turned on the light and he put his hat on the bureau and smoothed his hair with one hand. She put her own hat next to his, their possessions side by side, as if they were a married couple, then turned to face him. He took her head in his hands, looking into her eyes for a long moment before their lips met.

The kisses were deep, more confident than the ones they had exchanged in the garden; already they had learned each other's rhythm. He pulled back at one moment and said her name, and she closed her eyes and then felt his mouth moving over her forehead and over her eyes, over her temple. When his mouth found hers again, the kisses became more passionate, and she could feel the desire in his body and the response in her own, and after a long while he took a step back, still keeping his arms around her.

"Frances," he said, "I want nothing more than to spend the night with you."

"I know," she said.

"But I think—" he broke off.

"I know," she said again.

He let go of her arms and took her hands in his.

"This would be the perfect place and time," he said quietly, "and yet it wouldn't. I don't want to take a step like that without promising you more." He paused. "And we go back tomorrow. Back to the studio."

It was a statement, yet he said it with an inflection on the last word that made it a question. She looked down at their clasped hands, holding them tight. She did not speak, knowing the silence would be her answer.

"It's funny," he said at last, "I've gained so much from this trip. But it cost me the best secretary I've ever had."

"It has to be this way, Lawrence."

"I know," he said. "I think I've known ever since we sat on that hillside together. But I don't want to lose you, Frances. I'll find you another job somewhere else in the studio. And we can keep seeing each other, seeing where this goes. I can't predict the future, and I don't want to. But I want you in my life. That much I know."

"I want that too," she said. "But—"

She stepped away and sat on the edge of the bed. He sat on the chair, moving it closer so he could reach out and take her hand. It was hard to be so close to him while saying what she had to say, to hold hands knowing she was going to let go.

"I've had an offer, Lawrence. From Miss Ridley." As she stared down at his hand, she thought of Miss Ridley's veined ones, hours before, in the dim light of her bedroom. "She told me something tonight. She's ill and doesn't have long to live. Celia knows, and Joe."

"I thought as much," he said quietly. "What Celia said at dinner."

"And she wants me to stay with her until the end. She wants me to help tell her story. Her life story, the real one. To get it on record, for history. She needs a secretary to help her. And she asked me if I would stay on."

Part of her expected the executive to come back into his eyes and voice, expected him to invoke her obligation to the studio. She felt instantly ashamed when his eyes were gentle.

"Have you accepted?"

"Not yet."

"Will you?"

"Yes."

He nodded, rubbing his chin with his hand.

"I'm glad," he said after a moment. "She deserves to have her story told. Her story, not Myrtle Dobson's version, or the studio's. And you're the person to do it. You make it safe for people to be themselves, Frances, and that's—that's gold. A rare and precious thing."

The words, and the look in his eyes, made her want to change her mind. To be seen and valued like that, by another person—for a moment her resolve wavered, but only for a moment. The fundamental rightness of what Miss Ridley offered had been clear from the first moment Frances heard it, as if a chord had sounded, resonating along her veins.

"I'll be closer to my father if I stay. I can get myself a car, go back and forth. I can help him and let him know I forgive him. And also . . ." She thought of looking out over the valley from the tower, with its possibility and perspective. "For the past few years I thought only one path was open to me. And now there's a different one. I need to take it and see where it leads."

He nodded, an unfamiliar brightness in his eyes.

"The executive in me wants you to come back to Hollywood," he said. "The lover in me"—he raised an eyebrow ironically as if uncomfortable with the moniker—"wants you to come back. But it's a precious thing, a child forgiving a parent. As I've just learned. And this opportunity . . . well, it's what you deserve, Frances. No less. But I hope you'll stay in touch. Maybe you can come back and visit the studio. Or I can come up when I visit Sally."

"Maybe. We can certainly write." She beat back her grief with humor. "If you can find a secretary who's half as good as I am at taking dictation."

He laughed, as she'd known he would. Then he grew serious. "No, Frances," he said slowly. "No. Letters to you—those are letters I'll write myself."

They looked at each other, a long beat. She fixed it in her memory:

his tall figure, slightly hunched, on the edge of the chair, his eyes fond and admiring and regretful, just as she knew hers were. And behind him the outline of the door through which he would soon leave. For now, hopefully not forever.

He stood up, and she did the same. He put his arms around her and rested his chin on her hair. They stood like that, listening to the silence of the small town at midnight.

"July twenty-ninth," he said. "What a day. I'll never forget it."

"Neither will I." His arms tightened.

"Will you remember it differently now?" he asked.

"I think so," she said. "It will still hurt, I know." She thought of the dark-haired baby, so tiny and warm in her arms, but she also thought of an elderly woman holding a china cat and smiling. She saw Lawrence and his daughter, walking off together into the vineyards, and she saw again the hillsides of Napa under the quiet moon. And she thought of the invitation to help tell Miss Ridley's life story, a story that had already opened new chapters in her own.

"It will still feel like an end," she said slowly. "But after today— like a beginning too."

EPILOGUE

San Francisco
February 1940

Frances left the Jackson Street house at eleven fifteen on a brisk Tuesday morning. She'd been working at the typewriter since eight, and though she was not as far in her work as she'd have liked, the sunlit day drew her outside.

There was nothing, she thought as she walked along, quite like a clear winter's day in San Francisco. The bright blue of the sky, the pastel colors of the houses: even though it was colder than it appeared from the window, it was wonderful to be out in the fresh air. The green lawns of Alta Plaza Park, up ahead, looked like a springtime sea.

Sometimes as she walked around the city, she saw it through Miss Ridley's eyes: the eyes of the young woman moving through a city of wooden sidewalks and mud and horse-drawn carriages and limitless possibility. Those months spent in Napa, hearing Miss Ridley's life story, had been precious. Hours would fly as Frances listened and took copious notes; then she would type them up, organize them and read them back to the elderly woman, who listened with closed eyes and said, "Yes, just like that," or "No, perhaps I need to make that clearer." Equally precious were the times they did not work but walked slowly around the Ventimiglias' yard, Miss Ridley leaning on Frances's arm. And the times Frances told the stories of her own past, sharing them as frankly as Miss Ridley did her own, stories received with compassion and understanding.

Frances started up the steep rise of the park. Others had also been drawn outside by the sun. She passed mothers with baby carriages, a white-haired man walking with what looked like his son, and a secretary with a brown paper bag, clearly searching for a spot to take lunch.

San Francisco felt increasingly like home to her. Miss Ridley had given instructions that Frances was to use the Pacific Heights house as her own, and until Miss Ridley's death in April of '39, Frances had divided her time between Napa and the city. When she was in San Francisco, she would frequently get in her black Ford and drive south. Sometimes she went to visit Sally at the convent, but more often she drove to her father's house, where she would help in any way she could.

Their time together, she reflected as she passed an old woman feeding pigeons on a bench, had been exactly what they both needed. At first, when she weeded his garden, he would sit beside her as he had with Lawrence. Gradually, as his strength returned, he was able to do the work himself. His memory had slowly returned, with only the occasional episode of forgetting, and eventually he was even able to return to the office a few days a week. Frances vividly recalled the joy of the day that he greeted her at the front door with recognition, a recognition that did not waver once during her entire visit. And she cherished the afternoon when they had been taking a walk and he had stopped and said, "I missed you all those years you were gone, Frances. I should have done so much more to help you." Though Mother Florence had never expressed a similar regret, she and Frances had drawn together in tacit recognition that they both cared deeply for her father. In one unguarded moment, she had even said that she was grateful Frances was there.

Frances paused at the top of the path to catch her breath. Just before her were the sunlit tennis courts, empty at midday on a Tuesday. A young woman passed by, her blonde curls peeking out from behind a wide-brimmed hat, and before seeing her face Frances had the fleeting thought that it was Belinda. But it was not, of course. Belinda was in Hollywood, the toast of the town after her role in *Great Expectations*. The film had been Irving's consolation prize for the loss of the Kitty Ridley role, and the critics had been unanimous in their praise. "As the heartless, wounded Estella, Miss Vail brings a flinty complexity that is utterly astonishing," wrote the reviewer in *Variety*. "Even more powerful is her character's transformation in the final scene, her face a haunting study of regret. There is more to Miss Belinda Vail than we ever knew."

Frances pulled her coat more closely around her and gazed to the north. She could see, far beyond the houses, a glimpse of the blue-gray bay. Beyond the bay was Napa Valley, the Ventimiglias' home, and Miss Ridley, buried as she had wished in the small local cemetery in a grave with a simple marker. Whenever Frances went to visit the family, she stopped at the grave. It was always lovingly tended, with flowers left each week by Celia, Joe, and the children.

Miss Ridley had directed that her story be published only after her death. "I don't want the attention," she had told Frances. "I just want the truth to be out. So publish it after I'm gone, and no one can hound me, or bother Celia and Joe." The book, when it came out, had been covered extensively in the press, and Frances had been contacted for interviews by many who were curious to know even more about Miss Ridley. She declined the interviews, telling them the book would speak for itself. "A secretary keeps secrets," Cyril had said. She smiled, thinking of him. More than once, she had wished he and Miss Ridley had known each other.

It was breezy at the top of the hill, so she started down the other side, toward the steep tiered steps that led down from the lawn to the street. Her week would be a busy one. After Miss Ridley's life story was published, she had been contacted by Alberto Benanti, an elderly North Beach resident and philanthropist, who wanted her to tell his story. There were notes to be typed before her next meeting with him, and some photographs and news clippings to organize.

But the work would have to wait, for at noon Lawrence would arrive.

They had not seen each other for more than a year, since saying goodbye in Napa. They had planned to meet at the convent the previous November to see Sally play Joan of Arc in the school production, but Lawrence had come down with the flu, so Frances had gone alone. He had telephoned Frances after the death of Miss Ridley, and a second time, upon hearing the news of Cyril's death in France the following month, but their contact had been almost entirely through letters. It had suited her to have it that way. She loved the slow and steady pace of their correspondence, and the chance it gave her to reflect on her experiences before sharing them with him. His own letters were handwritten, not typed, signed with the scrawl of a signature that she knew so well. As months passed his letters had grown more and more frequent, until finally he had phoned to say that he was coming north to see Sally, and to see her. "I'll be there at twelve o'clock on Tuesday," he said, "and if I get the flu again, damn it, I'm coming anyhow." It had thrilled her to hear his voice again. She had risen that morning with her heart full at the prospect of seeing him and had been singing as she brewed her coffee.

A third of the way down the hill, she paused on the broad path bisecting the stairs. Before her was an impressive view of houses, apartment buildings, and the Gothic roof of St. Dominic's Church. It was a city full of people, full of stories, as it always had been and always would be. Some stories were told publicly, like Miss Ridley's, and others were guarded quietly inside minds and hearts. *Where do you start telling your story? Are you comfortable with the parts you don't know? When there is no answer, can you rest with the mystery?* Those were the questions that guided her work with Mr. Benanti, as she gently helped him navigate seventy years of reminiscences.

Something bounced into her line of vision, breaking her reverie. It was a red rubber ball, which was followed by a young boy in a spruce blue suit and shorts. He dove to catch it, jostling her in the process. "I'm sorry, ma'am," he said penitently, but his face glowed with evident triumph at having saved the ball.

"That's all right," she said, smiling at him. "It would be hard to chase it down these steps."

"I lost a ball that way once." He had dark brown hair, neatly parted, and a few freckles dusted his face. "My mother tried to run after it, but she couldn't catch it either." He indicated a blonde woman coming slowly up the path, holding a tiny blonde girl by the hand.

"It's a nice park for playing ball," said Frances.

He nodded, bouncing the ball up and down. Then he turned, regarding her with dark eyes that were relaxed and comfortable, as if he already knew her. "I'm getting a bike for my birthday."

"How exciting." Frances watched him as he bounced the ball even higher this time, almost to his chin. "How old are you?"

"Six and a half. I'll be seven at the end of July."

"Six and a half," said Frances. "That's what I was going to guess." She almost asked what day he was born but decided not to. He stood gazing happily at the city before him, bouncing the ball and whistling.

His mother and sister were closer now, and he said, "I'm going ahead, Mama."

"All right, just watch for people around you," she responded, and he said a cheerful goodbye to Frances and continued on, bouncing the ball and chasing it down the path.

His mother smiled at Frances. "I hope he wasn't bothering you," she said. "He's always chatting with strangers. He just loves getting to know new people."

"Not at all," said Frances. "Have a good day."

She watched them go down the path, the boy running ahead, stopping and starting with natural grace. He managed to catch the ball deftly right before it bounced down the slope, and his mother called, "What a good catch, John!" and he beamed and held it aloft like a baseball player.

Frances watched them until they disappeared from view. It surprised her, that she felt so peaceful.

Then we will see face-to-face.

She glanced at her watch; it was eight minutes to noon. She did not want to miss Lawrence, so instead of continuing down the steps she turned and walked eagerly back up the hill, the shorter way home. At the top she paused to catch her breath, gazing at the glimpses of sparkling bay far beyond Jackson Street. Then she looked to her right. Somewhere among those tiny glittering cars, slowly working their way west, was surely one she knew well.

Anticipation made her pulse flutter, and she quickened her pace as she hurried down the hill. It wasn't long before she was running. She wondered briefly how she looked to the people she passed: like a secretary who had forgotten an appointment, perhaps, or a woman hurrying to catch a bus. But she knew the truth, and as she ran she could not keep from smiling.

The End

Author's Note

I've always loved movies from the Golden Age of Hollywood. They immerse me in another world, one where clothing and hairstyles and slang are different, but the essential human experience has not changed. It's a captivating blend of the familiar and the new: much like reading historical fiction, in fact.

It's also possible that my affinity for old movies comes from my family. My great-grandfather, William S. Adams, was a Hollywood movie cameraman in the 1920s, and the half-brother of James Stuart Blackton, founder of Vitagraph Studios. My great-grandfather's cinematography career took him on astonishing travels, given the time period; he brought back doll souvenirs to my grandmother from places as far away as China and Fiji. Tragically, he died in 1930 when my grandmother was eleven, of a fever he contracted while filming a movie in Borneo. My great-grandmother, Ruth Lillian Owen Adams, had a less glamorous but still important role working as a film cutter for Warner Brothers. I wish there had been a Frances in their lives, someone who recorded their stories of the early movie industry. I can only imagine the tales they could have told.

For anyone interested in learning more about the studio system of the 1930s, I recommend *The Genius of the System: Hollywood Filmmaking in the Studio Era* by Thomas Schatz. Also excellent are the impressively detailed *The Star Machine* by Jeanine Basinger and *Hollywood: The Oral History* by Jeanine Basinger and Sam Wasson. *Warner Bros.: Hollywood's Ultimate Backlot* by Steven Bingen was extremely helpful in my creation of VistaGlen Studios. The Media History Digital Library of the Wisconsin Center for Film and Theater

Research offers a treasure trove of movie fan magazines from the period, which are great fun to explore.

Kitty Ridley is a fictional creation, but she was inspired by a real person. Lotta Crabtree was a child performer during the Gold Rush who later became one of the most beloved and highly paid stage actresses of her time. For Kitty's early years, I borrowed some details of Lotta's childhood as described in *Troupers of the Gold Coast: The Rise of Lotta Crabtree* by Constance Rourke. Lotta's adult life is quite different from Kitty's, but it's fascinating in its own right, and the book *Lotta Crabtree: Gold Rush Fairy Star* by Lois V. Harris offers an accessible and well-illustrated overview of her entire story. Lotta's legacy lives on in San Francisco, at the meeting of Market, Kearny, and Geary streets, where you can find the fountain that she donated to the city in 1875.

Moving north, Lin Weber's book *Prohibition in the Napa Valley: Castles Under Siege* helped me understand the Ventimiglias' experiences as a winemaking family in the 1920s and 1930s. If you find yourself in Napa, it's worth a trip to the picturesque Goodman Library downtown. You may recognize it as the two-story stone library where Frances reads *A Golden Life*; these days, it houses the Napa County Historical Society and offers a very helpful exhibit on Napa Valley history.

Lastly, I want to acknowledge Valeria Belletti, secretary to Samuel Goldwyn, for documenting her experiences in the early days of movies. *Adventures of a Hollywood Secretary: Her Private Letters from Inside the Studios of the 1920s*, edited and annotated by Cari Beauchamp, gives an insider's view of the grit, diplomacy, and sense of humor found in the women who kept Hollywood afloat.

Acknowledgments

Huge thanks to all my friends, especially Tarn Wilson for giving wise advice in this year of change, Angela Dellaporta for being a sounding board at a critical time, and Celeste Beirne for reminding me to celebrate. When I wrote this book back in 2019-2020, I had the pleasure of interacting daily with my brilliant and inspiring English department colleagues, including Diane Ichikawa and Jordan Wells. Thanks to Mary Donovan-Kansora, my patron saint of creativity. Thank you to Amy for the fun and laughter and to Mom and Dad for always being such enthusiastic supporters of my writing, whatever form it takes. An extra treat for Toby, prince among dogs, for his quiet encouragement and canine antics.

Brooke Warner and Shannon Green of She Writes Press continue to inspire me with their vision, efficiency, and guidance. I'm grateful to Katherine Caruana for the editorial help, Julie Metz for the beautiful cover, and Caitlin Hamilton Summie and Rick Summie for their warmth and expertise at getting the word out. Thank you to Carolyn Kiernat for connecting me with Barrett Reiter, who kindly answered my layperson's questions about nineteenth-century architecture. I'm also grateful to Kelly O'Connor of the Napa County Historical Society for the research assistance.

I wish my grandmother, Ruth Adams Wolf, could have been here to read this Hollywood story, but I think her spirit lives on in Celia Ventimiglia. I'm grateful to Ken Wolf for documenting the Adams family story as only a historian can. To my great-aunt Carol Ann Marshall: thank you for introducing me to the wonders of Shakespearean performance and for being a cherished friend.

Huge thanks to Matthew and Luke, who patiently rode around the Napa Valley that hot weekend in 2019 while I periodically yelled, "Stop the car!" It means a lot to me that you are excited about this writing journey.

And thanks to Scott, for support that takes countless forms and never fails. I love you.

About the Author

GINNY KUBITZ MOYER is a California native with a love of local history. A graduate of Pomona College and Stanford University, she is the author of the novel *The Seeing Garden*, as well as several works of spiritual nonfiction. She lives in the San Francisco Bay Area with her husband, two sons, and one rescue dog. Learn more about her at ginnymoyer.org.

Looking for your next great read?

We can help!

Visit www.shewritespress.com/next-read
or scan the QR code below for a list
of our recommended titles.

She Writes Press is an award-winning
independent publishing company founded to
serve women writers everywhere.